INK MAGE

INK MAGE

VICTOR GISCHLER

Published by
47N○RTH

Text copyright © 2014 by Victor Gischler
Originally published as a Kindle Serial, October 2013
All rights reserved.

Published by 47North
P.O. Box 400818
Las Vegas, NV 89140

ISBN-10: 1477849300
ISBN-13: 9781477849309

Cover design by Sam Dawson
Illustrated by Chase Stone

Library of Congress Control Number: 2013948601

Printed in the United States of America

FOR JACKIE

CHAPTER ONE

The fortified watchtower overlooking the Eastern Sea was officially called Ferrigan's Tower for the engineer who'd built it, but to the miserable soldiers stationed there, the post was known as the Snow Devil's Asshole. The tower sat on a narrow peninsula of rock that jutted out to sea like an open palm, the rocks around it battered constantly by the tossing, foamy sea. When the wind howled, it drowned out the crashing waves.

And the wind always howled.

This night, small, stinging snowflakes rode the wind, coming in sideways. Tosh and the other four soldiers huddled around the fire pit atop the tower. They were "keeping watch," which meant that about once an hour they'd take turns grudgingly rising from the fire to walk to the parapet and glance at the empty sea.

It was a dull, cold, unhappy posting, generally reserved for soldiers who'd messed up in some way.

Tosh had gotten drunk on his night off and had vomited into the carriage of a minor nobleman. The next day, he found himself with his pack slung over his shoulder, marching with the rest of the replacement garrison to the Snow Devil's Asshole with the rest of the screw-ups.

"I'd fuck Berrig's wife." Tosh had to raise his voice to be heard over the wind. "I don't mind a big fat ass."

The others laughed, including Berrig.

Berrig said, "If you're daydreaming about my Luwilla, it just proves you've been up here too long in this frozen shithole."

They laughed again.

And that's how they passed the bleak months until they were relieved—telling soldiers' jokes, trying to keep warm, and keeping careful watch on a rocky stretch of desolate shoreline that hadn't needed watching in thirty years. When Tosh had first arrived, he'd taken some comfort in the salt smell of the sea, which he enjoyed. But that small enjoyment had waned quickly as the tedious weeks dragged on. He held tightly to one small ray of hope. In four days, his tour of the Snow Devil's Asshole would be up. The relief garrison would arrive and he could go *home*. And he could get a *woman*. Even one as fat as Luwilla would do.

Twenty men, three horses, one tower. All grinding time slowly and eventually into dust to be blown away by the howling wind. All twenty men thought the same thing every day: *Get the hell out of here and don't screw up again. Don't get sent back.*

But not yet. Four more days. And it was Tosh's turn to go glance at the ocean.

He heaved himself up and staggered away from the fire. The cold had settled into his bones. It was an easy thing to happen if you didn't move, didn't keep the blood circulating. He briefly stomped in a circle before finding his way to the parapet. The feeling came slowly back into his feet. He yawned and looked out to sea.

Nothing.

Well, not *entirely* nothing. He did note with mild surprise that a thick fog had descended. Visibility came to a sudden halt a quarter mile out to sea. After that it was all pea soup. These weather conditions were not unheard of at the Snow Devil's Asshole, but they were unusual. Above, the clouds moved away from the moon which beamed brightly down upon ...

Tosh blinked.

Something in the sudden moonlight, a shape in the mist. He squinted, leaned forward.

The prow of a ship coming through the mist.

Tosh opened his mouth to raise the alarm, hesitated, not sure if he saw what he thought he saw. He was wrong. It wasn't a ship.

It was two.

No, three—five—a dozen ...

He stopped counting. There were far too many. He froze, utter disbelief. At the same moment, another part of his brain reached back, groped for stories the old timers told at the tavern about Perranese raiders who'd hit the coast, loot and plunder and then flee back across the ocean. These ships had the same low, lean look and strange square sails he'd heard in the stories, with accordion folds so they could be raised and lowered like expensive window blinds. But this wasn't a raiding party.

It was an invasion.

Tosh drew a lungful of air, turned back toward his comrades and yelled, "Alarm! Alarm!"

They turned, gawked at Tosh. *What?*

"Ring the fucking bell!" Tosh screamed at them.

One ran for the bell and immediately began ringing it, the crisp, clear sound cutting through the noise of the wind. They'd hear it downstairs and saddle the horses. Berrig and the others joined Tosh at the parapet, bringing torches. They looked with bewilderment and terror at the approaching armada.

"Dumo, save us," breathed Berrig. He leaned out, looked over the side of the parapet.

Tosh wasn't very religious, but he'd gladly go to temple if Dumo appeared now and blasted the invaders with divine fire.

Berrig said, "Wait, is that—?"

Something flashed silver in the moonlight and buried itself into Berrig's left eye. Berrig screamed and twitched.

"Berrig!" Tosh moved toward the man.

A large metallic star with four, six-inch points. Tosh had never seen such a weapon. One of the six-inch blades had struck deep into Berrig's eye, reaching his brain. Berrig twitched once, opened his mouth as if attempting to say something, then collapsed dead at Tosh's feet.

Tosh grabbed a torch from one of the other soldiers. He leaned out with the torch, looked down along the side of the stone tower.

A Perranese warrior scaled the wall not ten feet below him. He wore a strange wide helm that flared out from his head and armor of overlapping black, metal discs like the scales of some dark sea creature. The warrior's head came up suddenly, locked eyes with Tosh.

Tosh screamed—rage, fear, anger—and hurled the torch at the warrior. It hit him square in the face with a sizzle, dislodged him. He tumbled silently back down to the rocks below. As the torch fell, it illuminated a dozen more Perranese warriors clinging to the tower wall, doggedly making their ascent.

Tosh turned to his comrades. "They're coming!"

The others drew broad-bladed short swords. They looked scared. "Get below, Tosh," one of them said.

Tosh offered a blank look in reply.

"You've got saddle duty. Go!"

Of course! Tosh ran to the trap door, flung it open and nearly fell down the ladder to the floor below. He took the twisting stone stairs three at a time until he hit the bottom floor, a combination of barracks, kitchen, stable. The place was in an uproar—men hastily putting on cheap leather armor, fetching crossbow bolts, making ready to be destroyed. A barely controlled feeling of panic pulsed through the place.

He felt somebody grab his shoulder. "Move your ass. The gray one is already saddled!" He was pushed roughly toward the section that had been blocked off for a stable.

The Captain. He had never liked the man, but suddenly felt sorry for the officer stuck with being in charge of this mess. The man had already turned to shout orders at the others.

Tosh ran for the horses. He was the last to arrive; the other two horses already had riders.

He briefly thanked military discipline, something he'd never done before. In this desolate outpost it would have been easy to let things slip. But they kept up the saddle rotation, drilled, maintained the watch. And Tosh was on saddle rotation. Dumb luck. He would ride away while the others died defending the tower. A stab of guilt vanished rapidly. He wasn't a hero and didn't have a death wish.

He mounted, looked at the other two riders. They nodded to each other.

The two soldiers at the thick wooden double doors waved at the riders. "As soon as we lift the bar and open these doors, you men ride like the Snow Devil himself is on your ass, you hear?"

They nodded again. Somehow it had become difficult to speak.

The soldiers lifted the bar and swung the doors open. Snow and bone-freezing wind hit them immediately.

The three riders shot out of the tower. Tosh found himself in the lead, dug his heels in, mentally willed the horse to fly. Flickering points of firelight streamed toward the narrow road from both sides. Torches! Warriors closing fast. The bastards must have landed ships farther up the coast to send troops to secure the tower before the armada arrived. Tosh wasn't a military strategist, just a grunt. But that's what he would have done.

No matter. He only had one thing to worry about now: ride fast!

He heard the hiss of an arrow followed by the thud of a body hitting the ground. They'd hit one of the riders behind him. More arrows cut through the air, one so close to his ear he felt the fletching tickle his lobe.

A scream. Tosh risked a look back over his shoulder. He was the only rider left. He hunkered down low and spurred the horse again, snow stinging his face.

He rounded the bend and headed toward the low mountain pass. Tosh looked back again. No sign of torches. He was going to make it. The *only* one to make it. Berrig and two others dead so far. How long would the others last? Or maybe the Perranese would surround the Tower, take the men inside prisoner. But the tales he'd heard about the Perranese didn't make them seem very merciful.

Never mind.

Tosh's adrenaline rush began to ebb. The cold seeped in. He realized that in leaving in such a rush he'd forgotten to don the heavy traveling furs. But Klaar was a small duchy. He'd be through the pass quickly and then ride down the other side maybe a dozen miles to the fur trapping village there. There was an outpost behind a palisade where he could change horses and get furs for the rest of the journey. Then another eighty miles of hard riding to the city.

To warn the Duke that war was upon the land.

CHAPTER TWO

High atop a castle wall, a giant stood next to a duchess. They watched the approaching army.

The giant was not technically a giant, not like the shaggy mountain giants that lived high in the mountains or the tree-climbing forest giants in the west. Rather, he was a giant among men, a fraction under seven feet tall, broad shoulders, rippling muscles. Powerful legs with thick thighs and calves. His name was Kork, short for some longer foreign name that nobody in Klaar used anymore. He had dark, olive skin and black coarse hair like all the desert people of Fyria in the far southwest, worn in rows of tight braids close to his scalp. What had brought him across Helva to the frozen reaches of Klaar was a story few knew and even fewer considered important. His beard was braided and forked, clamped at the ends in brass.

Kork had been born into the warriors' caste in Fyria, had held a sword before he could speak. His armor was traditional: bracers of metal bands affixed with thick leather, a fitted breastplate and a skirt of overlapping metal rectangles. In such climes as Klaar, he wore a heavy, fur-lined cloak which could be cast aside quickly should he need to leap into combat.

His sole reason for existence was to teach and protect the young woman standing next to him.

"That's more soldiers in one place at one time than I've ever seen before," Rina said coolly. "A pity for them it won't matter."

They'd come to the top of the wall to get a look at the enemy camp. Neat rows of round, crimson tents, banners flying in the wind. They completely covered the flat ground beyond the Long Bridge.

Kork grunted, a low guttural sound that could have meant he agreed, disagreed or didn't care.

Rina smiled. "Thanks for keeping up your end of the conversation, Kork."

Kork grunted again.

Just as the Fyrian was not technically a giant, Rina was not technically a duchess. Her father, Arlus Veraiin, was Duke of Klaar, and someday Rina would be duchess, but not yet. But in the private family wing of the castle, Arlus still referred to his daughter as "my little duchess," a habit left over from her childhood.

Rina Veraiin had just turned nineteen, a year from legal adulthood in Klaar and indeed most of Helva. She put the long, tightly rolled chuma stick into her mouth, inhaled, held it, then blew the gray smoke into the wind, watched it float away over the city wall.

"You smoke too much," Kork said.

She puffed again. Chuma was a habit she'd picked up recently. The low, broad-leafed plant grew in the river valleys of the lush flatlands. It was expensive to transport all the way to Klaar, but, really, what was the point of being the Duke's daughter if she could not enjoy expensive things?

"I had planned to shop in the town today," Rina said. "I suppose I'll just watch the war instead." She took another long, lazy draw on the chuma stick.

Kork grunted again. "You shop too much."

Rina grinned. "You think I do *everything* too much."

"Except practice."

She laughed and, without hesitating, unbuttoned her own heavy fur cloak at the throat and tossed it aside. She now wore only a wool blouse and a long wool "false skirt" that was really an overly blousy pair of pants. They resembled a skirt but allowed her to move and fight and ride a horse like a man. The cold hit her, exhilarating. Soon it would be numbing, but not yet. She drew the thin rapier from the scabbard at her waist.

Rina was lithe, athletic. Stomach flat and limbs toned from the exercise routine designed for her by Kork. She thought herself a bit too thin and boyish through the hips and occasionally thought it would be nice to have more curves, but she didn't dwell on this notion. It would be a lie to pretend she wasn't attractive. The sons of nobles had fallen over themselves to speak to her at court functions, especially the last couple of years. It had been tedious but also … interesting. The braids mingled into her long, glossy black hair were fastened with large sapphires and blue silk ribbons that perfectly complemented her eyes. Her startlingly white skin almost glowed.

She watched Kork draw his sword, readied herself.

In fact, Kork wore two swords. The huge hand-and-a-half sword on his back was a weapon he'd fallen in love with after coming to the northlands. It was nearly as long as Rina was tall and could be wielded one- or two-handed.

But the sword Kork drew was the thin, curved Fyrian scimitar, a more appropriate match for Rina's plain rapier with its simple knuckle guard and quillon. It was not a jewel-encrusted sword for fancy dress balls. It was a fighting weapon.

"So you think I need practice, do you?" Rina smirked. "The chances of you scoring even one hit are—Hey!"

Kork lunged. No salute, bow or warning.

Rina parried just in time, knocking the tip of the scimitar away and stepping inside Kork's reach for a counterthrust, but the big man spun, sweeping wide with the scimitar, deflecting the rapier. They backed away from one another, took stock for a split second.

Kork moved in fast, the scimitar a blur. Rina blocked every thrust and swipe. The metallic *clang* of their blades rang up and down the battlements. The guards along the wall turned to watch, soldiers and officers alike crowding around, some gawking wide-eyed, most grinning at the display. This was a show many of them had seen before.

Kork pressed and Rina fell back; their blades clashed. Rina had always been fast, and Kork had trained her to use that ability. Heavy battle axes and two-handed swords could deliver devastating blows but they weren't *fast*. Speed had always been Rina's gift.

The onlookers had formed a wide circle, and Rina allowed the huge Fyrian to chase her around as she deflected every thrust, all of her swordplay completely defensive. She'd sparred with Kork for years, knew his penchant for overwhelming skillful fencing with brute force, so she let him come on, drawing him in.

She was waiting for him to lunge, a big one he'd think would suddenly end the match. Two seconds later, he tried it, overreaching, trying to get the scimitar past her defenses. She dropped to the stone floor of the battlement, brought her foot around in a leg sweep. This was something they'd practiced only in the last few months, integrating weaponless hand fighting with fencing skills.

He jumped, easily avoiding the sweep, but his sword went wide as he spread his arms to balance himself. Rina was already leaping to her feet, thrusting the rapier. The tip *tinged* off Kork's breastplate.

Rina's point.

The gathering soldiers laughed and applauded.

She bowed, panting. "Thank you, thank you! For your further entertainment, the mighty Rina Veraiin will slay another giant after the lunch hour! Bring your friends to see the show."

Another small smattering of applause as the group of soldiers dissipated back to their posts.

"Still think I don't practice enough?"

Kork shrugged.

"Oh, now don't tell me you're *pouting*," Rina said.

"What is it you think you've accomplished?" Kork asked.

"Victory, obviously," Rina said.

Kork sighed, the sound of a bull ox snorting. "I have been … training you all wrong."

What? "Did I not just score that point? I think somebody is being a bad sport."

Kork scowled at her, and Rina knew she was close to stepping over a line.

She cleared her throat. "What do you mean?"

"I have been teaching you skills," Kork said, "instead of combat."

Rina blinked, confused. "What's the difference?"

Kork lifted his chin in the direction of the encamped army on the other side of the Long Bridge. "That."

Rina shook her head. "Wait, I don't understand why that should matter. I still *beat* you. I think you're sour because you lost."

She regretted saying it immediately. Kork had taught her everything. Her words were the words of a bratty, spoiled duke's daughter. And yet she couldn't make herself take them back.

Some stubbornness had seized her and refused to let go. It was a stubbornness that had infuriated her father on more than one occasion.

Kork wasn't fazed. He'd seen her this way many times. Up until about age eleven, the stubbornness was usually accompanied by the stomping of a little foot and a pouty lip.

"And if you'd touched the tip of your little sword against my breastplate on the battlefield? What would that mean?"

"It would mean—" She stopped. *What would it mean?*

Kork drew the enormous hand-and-a-half sword from the sheath on his back, held it out to her with one hand. With the other, he rapped a knuckle on his breastplate. A deep metallic ring. "You want to get through *this* armor, then you need a weapon with heft. Take it."

She took the hilt in both hands.

When Kork let go, the sword dropped, dragging her arms along with it. The tip hit the stone floor.

"You are soooo funny," she said. "You know I can't lift this ridiculous thing."

Kork sheathed his scimitar. "I'll even the odds for you." He drew a small knife from a hidden pocket sewn inside his cloak. It was what they called a gentleman's knife. The small four-inch blade folded into and out of a carved wooden handle. This one had a simple carving of a swan on a calm lake. It was a knife old men used to whittle while they sat around and gossiped about affairs of state and hunting and women.

Kork opened the blade, held it loosely in his right hand. "Come at me."

"Obviously, I can't—"

"This isn't a sporting duel," Kork snapped. "You do not get your choice of weapons. You do not get to rest and regroup between points. You get to live or die."

Rina didn't waste time with more talk. Kork expected her to drag out her protests as she would normally, trying to wriggle out of some unpleasant task or practice session. She had one chance to tag him and that was surprise.

She started her hips moving first then put her shoulders into it. It was the only way she could get the sword up for a proper swing. Her back was almost to him by the time the sword came around, but at least she had it up to speed for a strike.

One of Kork's gigantic hands was suddenly on her wrist, pulling her through the swing, using her own momentum against her. She started to go down and threw out her arms to catch herself, losing the sword. She cursed herself. *Amateur!*

Kork suddenly had one arm around her, pinning her arms at her side. With the other hand, Kork held the flat of the gentleman's blade against the soft, exposed flesh of her throat. Rina knew Kork would never hurt her—with the possible exception of some tutorial bruises with the wooden practice swords. But in that moment when she first felt the cold steel against her jugular, she also felt fear, the brief but palpable knowledge that she could be alive one moment and dead the next.

He held her that way, helpless.

Rina cleared her throat. "So. Do you yield?"

"Jibes will not save you on the field of battle."

"They're pretty good jibes."

He released her.

She stood away from him, one hand going instinctively to her throat. She half thought her fingertips would come away sticky with her own blood. They didn't. "Fortunate that I have no immediate plans to find myself on the field of battle, isn't it?"

"Plans are what people make when Fate is sneaking up behind them," Kork said. "Tomorrow we shall alter your training."

Rina sighed. "My dear lovely giant, you don't really think any army is getting over the Long Bridge, do you? This place is impregnable."

Another of Kork's grunts. Rina thought she detected grudging agreement.

The Long Bridge was named for the simple fact that it was a mile long, the only way over a deep and icy chasm to the fortress city of Klaar. The stone bridge was just wide enough for two wagons to pass each other and, as her father put it, could be defended by a cripple and an infant with slingshots.

The bridge ended at a large gate in the outer wall, behind which was the town of Klaar. In the center of town was the Duke's castle and keep. Theoretically, if the outer wall were breached, the citizenry could fall back to the keep.

No invading army had ever breached the outer wall. None had ever made it off the Long Bridge.

"How do you think they built it?" she asked, still looking at the bridge.

"Magic," Kork said.

She frowned at him. "An engineer from the University in Luxum designed it and supervised the construction. This is a matter of record."

Kork shrugged.

Rina said, "When I asked how they built it, I meant what sort of mathematical equations, the tools used, manpower. Those sorts of things."

"Magic."

"I keep forgetting you're a savage from distant lands," Rina said.

The hint of a smile tugged at the corner of his mouth.

Kork nodded at the army camped on the far side of the Long Bridge. "You've seen enough? We can go inside now, get warm?"

"I want to go down into the town," Rina said. She was restless, wanted to feel the tense energy of the commoners.

"I'd prefer you didn't, daughter."

She turned, saw the Duke with a gaggle of advisors behind him. "Father?"

Arlus Veraiin smiled at her. His presence was always reassuring. Still handsome at his age, with a perfectly trimmed white beard, hair thinning on top, but bright blue eyes just like hers.

"I need you dressed to receive guests," the Duke said. "Hurry along now, please."

"Guests? How could they have come through the Perranese army?" Rina asked.

The Duke said, "The guests *are* the Perranese army."

CHAPTER THREE

ee, this is why you don't sneak into the castle kitchens to steal a pastry, Alem thought as he walked the halls of the castle's residential wing, a wicker laundry basket under each arm.

Alem was a stable boy. No, *head* stable boy. He'd started as a shit-shoveler and had been raised to stable boy when he'd shown he could handle the horses. Now, five years later, he was head stable boy and would likely be stable master when old Nard retired or passed. The point was, Alem was definitely *not* a maid.

But that didn't matter to fat Bruny, who ran the household. She took one look at him skulking around the kitchen, pointed a finger at him and hollered, "You! Come with me now, boy." A fever had run through the castle maids, and half of them were down with sour stomachs and green complexions. There was a feeling of panic among the castle servants as beds went unmade and chamber pots were not emptied. Bruny had pressed into service any set of idle hands she could find, and since it was generally understood that indoor servants outranked outdoor servants, Alem had obeyed.

They'd even made him bathe! His pale skin was pink from a cold-water scrubbing, his feathery blond hair puffed and downy.

"You can't go among them nobles smelling of horse dung," Bruny had insisted.

Alem headed into the castle to gather dirty laundry and promptly got lost. *This place is enormous.* He slept on a straw pallet among the other stable boys and had come to think of his grandmother's three-room cottage as roomy and extravagant. But this... *Well, that's why they call it a castle, thicko.*

He finally found the right hallway. He'd been told that now was a good time to collect the dirty laundry from the bed chambers of the Duke and his family. They were out and about, up on the walls or down in the town, preparing for the Perranese. He opened the heavy wooden door to the first room, iron hinges creaking. He entered.

And froze.

A woman sat on a cushioned chair in front of a dressing table. She held a boot in her hand. The other boot was still on her other foot. The Duke's daughter. *You're not supposed to be here!*

"Uh..." Alem began to back out of the room. "I didn't know...I mean...I thought everyone was...I'll just..." *Faster, you idiot! Get out, get out!*

"Who are you?"

He froze again. "I'm—" He almost said Alem. *Thicko, she doesn't care about your name.* "Uh, the dirty laundry."

She looked him up and down, a quirky smile flickering across her face. "New maid?"

"Yes." *No! Stable boy. HEAD stable boy!*

She shrugged. "Bruny's become broad minded." She waved vaguely at the rest of the room. "Come on, then."

Alem left one of the baskets in the hall, entered her room with the other. He moved quickly around the huge canopy bed, desk, divan, picking up articles of clothing strewn over furniture or dropped on the floor. He never would have thought the nobility could be so messy. Alem supposed if he owned this much clothing he might get careless with it too.

He hurriedly scooped up breeches and skirts and thick woolen socks and blouses and ... something extremely thin and delicate.

Underwear.

Alem shoved it into the basket quickly. *Don't look at it!*

He glanced about. Nothing left. Good. He headed for the door. Fast.

"Wait."

The word hit him in the back like an arrow. He turned slowly, looked at her.

She crooked her finger at him in a *come here* gesture.

Alem went to where she sat at the dressing table. She lifted one foot, the one without the boot, pointing her toes at the ceiling. "Don't forget this." She took the tip of her sock between a thumb and forefinger and pulled it off. Her toes were small and pink. She dangled the sock a moment as if it were a fish she'd caught, and then let it drop into the basket.

She sat back, lifted the other boot and looked at Alem expectantly. "This one now."

Alem looked from the boot to her face and back again. *This one what?*

"I could barely get the other one off," she said. "They're new boots, not broken in. I think my feet have swollen."

And just what exactly did she expect Alem to do about that?

"I need you to help me get it off," she said.

Alem set the basket aside. He grabbed the heel, moved the other hand to take her by the calf, hesitated, his eyes flickering up to hers.

She nodded. "Go ahead."

He grabbed her leg, tugged on the boot. Tight. He was afraid to pull harder.

"Turn around," she told him. "You're not getting any leverage."

Alem turned, straddled her leg and grabbed the boot again. He pulled.

"That's better. I think it's coming." She put her other foot against Alem's backside, and his eyes shot wide, cheeks warming. He was glad he was facing away from her. She pushed. He pulled.

The boot popped off. Alem tumbled over the dirty laundry basket, went down in a heap.

The Duke's daughter trilled laughter, delicate fingers going up to her mouth.

Alem hastily got to his feet, scooping clothes back into the basket. His face flushed red, ears burning.

"How old are you?"

"Ma'am?"

"Your age?"

"Eighteen," Alem said. *Nineteen in a month.*

"Well, young man, when you're older and wiser—like me— you'll know never to walk away when a job is only half done." She lifted her foot, pointed her toes at him.

The confusion must have been pain on his face.

"You're here for the dirty laundry, aren't you?" She lifted an eyebrow and thrust her foot at him again. "Well?"

Her sock? That was it. She was insisting Alem remove her dirty sock.

He reached for the top of the sock, trying not to touch any of her bare leg. He felt moist behind the ears. *Why can't she just take off her own damn sock? Because she's spoiled nobility, that's why.* He peeled it slowly over her heel, up past the toes and off, not quite understanding why his heart beat a bit faster.

She lifted her foot within two inches of his face and wriggled her perfect pink toes.

Alem felt his head go light.

He glanced at her face. A smirk.

She's mocking me!

He shoved the sock into the basket, turned and stalked out the door, slamming it behind him, light and carefree laughter chasing him down the hallway.

CHAPTER FOUR

General Chen Maa'Kaa hunched over a table in the large command tent, glaring at the maps spread out before him. They had been drawn by the Emperor's spies, some painstakingly over a decade in preparation for the invasion, a few more recently to show updated activity, especially in and around Klaar.

Icy wind blew in from under the tent flap. He'd instantly hated this place upon arrival.

The largest and most thorough map detailed the entire continent of Helva from Klaar all the way to the Western Ocean nearly three thousand miles away. The map went north as far as the great Glacial Wastes and south to the Scattered Isles. How the Holy Perranese Emperor figured to take and hold such a vast territory wasn't General Chen's problem.

He slid the smaller map of Klaar over the Helva map and frowned at it. Chen understood the War Council's strategy even if he didn't agree with all of it. To the south of Klaar, there were literally dozens of better places to land an invasion force, places with more temperate climes, calmer seas, better port facilities and miles of open beach.

The coast of Klaar, however, was a different story. A majority of the coastline consisted of jagged rocks that would chew a ship to kindling. Chen ran a finger down the coast until he hit a dot on the map that marked a fishing village called Harran's Bay, which Chen suspected must be some kind of local joke as there was nothing resembling a proper bay there. But there was a break in the rocks and deep water and the only pier in the entire duchy that could accommodate large ships.

The people of Harran's Bay had, of course, fled the village and burned the pier. No matter. Such a thing had been foreseen. It's what Chen would have done if he'd been defending. Actions were already being taken to rebuild the pier. In the meantime, landing thousands of troops by longboat was tedious at best.

Chen heard the rattle of armor a split second before one of his officers entered the tent and snapped to attention. "General Chen."

"What is it, First Commander Skrii' Faa?" Chen said without looking up from the map.

"Ambassador Ra'Karro is … uh … displeased with the military escort he's been assigned."

Another man would have sighed and rolled his eyes, but Chen found such displays petty and indulgent. "Send the ambassador here."

The officer saluted and left.

So why Klaar? All of the advantages to the southern landing sites were also the drawbacks. Bigger populations, larger armies. Word would chase through the land like a tsunami wave, and troops would pour in to repel the invaders.

Klaar, by contrast, did not seem to be a region anyone gave a damn about. Chen's men had already intercepted two riders attempting to leave the duchy, and it was likely nobody else in Helva even knew the Perranese had arrived. And when they did eventually find out, it could be weeks from now, by which time Chen would already have a strong foothold. Furthermore, it was reported that the people of Klaar were fiercely independent and seemed to have little use for the king and the rest of the nobility of Helva. When the king heard Klaar was in peril he might not even care. Although Chen thought that too much to hope for.

Chen heard someone clear his throat and looked up to see Ambassador Ra'Karro standing there, nose in the air, aloof, fat jowls spilling over his high collar. He wore a sash of deep scarlet to indicate he represented the emperor.

"There is a concern about the military escort?" Chen asked.

"It would seem inadequate," the ambassador said. "I am going into a den of barbarians, after all. I'd like to come back out again. Four soldiers and a standard bearer offer little security."

The ambassador's security was of little concern to Chen. Still, the man was a representative of the emperor and deserved some measure of respect for that. He'd have to tell him something.

"They are dressed as ordinary soldiers, but they are men from the Elite Guard," Chen assured him. "Even the standard bearer."

The ambassador raised an eyebrow, a gesture that might indicate he was impressed or maybe simply didn't believe the general. Chen didn't care.

"Your escort is ready, ambassador, and you don't want to be late." A dismissal.

Ambassador Ra'Karro hesitated only a moment, then bowed slowly before leaving.

Chen turned his attention to the most recently updated map, the one of the City of Klaar and its environs and the long, narrow road leading up to the back gate.

~

Ungrateful sons of bitches.

It wasn't like Tosh had expected to be promoted to general, but he had ridden—very bravely—through a snowstorm to bring warning to Klaar. He figured *some* kind of reward had been in order. Instead, he'd gotten a slap on the back and a bowl of weak soup.

Then a burly sergeant had handed him a spear and told him to get onto the wall, saying something about needing every man at a time like this. Yeah, like Tosh and his spear would turn the tide of battle. When was the last time he'd even held a spear? Training, maybe.

A goblet of wine and a feather bed would have been better thanks.

He'd picked up some scuttlebutt from one of the other soldiers manning the wall. Apparently, this wasn't some typical Perranese raid but a full-scale invasion. *Yes, I know, idiot. I delivered that news myself.* Also, riders had been sent to alert the king. *Great, and if the riders get through, royal troops will arrive how many months from now?* And with all the soldiers and townsfolk and everyone from the lower valley pulled in behind the city walls, the wait for a whore at the Wounded Bird, the brothel near the city's back gates, could be at least three hours long.

Now *that* was devastating news indeed, Tosh thought. He had a lot of back pay coming and many dull hours to kill if the Perranese insisted on a prolonged siege.

"The Perranese are sending a delegation," the other soldier said.

Tosh reached back and rubbed his ass. He wasn't used to riding hard, and his time in the saddle had taken its toll. "I hadn't heard that rumor."

"No rumor."

The other soldier pointed to the Long Bridge. A haughty man in a scarlet sash marched toward them, flanked by soldiers on either side. Behind came the standard bearer, a banner with a dragon perched on a crescent moon, the sign of the Perranese Emperor.

Tosh squinted at the man in the sash. *An asshole if I ever saw one.*

CHAPTER FIVE

R ina ran. It wasn't ladylike to run.

But being late was worse.

The dress made running difficult. There was just so much of it, flowing and billowing and generally taking up a lot of space. That was from the waist down. From the waist up it was an entirely different story. The bodice was so *tight*. It pushed her breasts up in a way that made them seem impossibly ... full. Not that they were anything to sneeze at. They just weren't usually so *prominent*.

That's what all the best young ladies in Tul-Agnon and Merridan are wearing, she could hear her mother say.

This is Klaar, mother. I wore a wolf-skin cloak to the Trapper's Festival last year.

She skidded around the corner and entered the formal audience chamber, panting, a light sheen of sweat on her forehead and chest. She'd spent way too much time picking out a dress, and while she did think the forest green was ultimately the right choice, her father would not consider her detailed attention to fashion a good enough excuse to keep the Perranese delegation waiting.

Her father saw her, frowned. Her eyes scanned the large audience chamber. No Perranese. She blew out a sigh of relief.

"Cutting it a tad close, aren't we?" the Duke said.

Rina curtsied slowly, dipping low, making an elegant flourish with one hand.

"I'm not sure how you do it," her father said, "but you have the unique ability to curtsy sarcastically."

Her eyes flicked up to his, a smile playing across her face. She rose and said, "Exactly *why* am I needed here?"

"Oh, I'm sorry. The Perranese army at the gates and a prolonged winter siege are rather boring, aren't they?"

Gee, I wonder where I learned sarcasm.

"The fact is you will be duchess some day and need to learn these things," the Duke said. "Now come here."

She went, stood quietly, listening as her father conferred with his two chief advisors. Zarrik was general of Klaar's paltry army. Rina couldn't recall the man ever taking the field in a major battle, but he seemed competent enough in directing his men to run off the occasional bandit gang that sniffed around the border. He was running to fat, wore a spotless breastplate and a gleaming helm with a horsehair plume sprouting from the top and flowing down his back.

"The status of our forces, please, Zarrik," said the Duke.

"We were fortunate to have some minimal warning," Zarrik said. "It allowed us to pull in men from the outlying forts and outposts. In the confusion, it has been difficult to get an exact count." He looked sheepish at this admission. "But we have some thirteen hundred regular soldiers. And the militia has been called up from the peasantry, giving us another eight hundred."

"And the enemy?"

Zarrik frowned. "Six thousand, but that's not a final count either, my lord."

"Why not?"

"Troops are still coming up from the coast, I'm afraid." The general shrugged. "There's no way to guess how many."

The Duke sighed. "Then I apologize, Zarrik, but I'm forced to ask your assessment of our current situation based on imperfect information."

Zarrik puffed up his chest, stuck his chin out. "My lord, *nobody* is coming across the Long Bridge. That I can guarantee. The Perranese can send their army down the valley and around the mountains and take the Small Road up to the back gates if they like, but even at top speed that's a three-week trip. More like a month for an army that size. And the road is so narrow; we can drop rocks on them all day long as they try to come up at us. There's two ways into the city of Klaar, and both are death for any army."

"Thank you, Zarrik; that's what I wanted to hear."

Rina hid a smile behind her hand. Father had already known this information, of course, but letting Zarrik report it would puff up the man's confidence a bit. The Duke knew people, knew how to handle them. Maybe that's what her father wanted her to observe more than anything else. Yeah, it was important to know the numbers of troops and all that. But how to handle people, how to get them to do what you wanted and even get them to think that it was their idea—these were the important lessons for a future duchess.

The Duke's other advisor cleared his throat pointedly.

The Duke turned to him, offering a smile that didn't touch his eyes. "I haven't forgotten about you, Giffen. Please make your report."

Oh, yeah. Giffen. Rina *hated* Giffen. As the Duke's steward, it was Giffen's job to run the castle, manage the finances and basically keep tabs on all the facts and figures that made a duchy run. This was a tedious job, and in Rina's opinion, it took a tedious man to do it. He had an unpleasant, pushed-in face and thin strands of greasy hair spread flat across his head. No moustache, but a short, pointy beard. As a little girl, Rina would run around the castle, chasing after the servants' children, and Giffen would always sneer and accuse her of being "under foot."

Now Rina was older. Giffen was forced to treat her differently, but Rina could still detect the sneer behind his forced smile.

"In some ways we have been fortunate," Giffen said. "The winter grain shipment from the lowlands arrived just three days ago, so we are well stocked for a siege. Dried fish and potatoes are also in strong supply, and the city wells continue to produce enough fresh water for all even with the sudden population increase."

The Duke nodded, digested the information. "Then it seems unlikely they can take the city by force, and we've enough food and water to wait them out. I wish we had spies to tell us what their supply situation looked like, but no sense wishing for what we can't have."

The Duke looked at his advisors. "Anything else?"

"No, my lord." Giffen bowed slightly.

"We're as ready as we can be, my lord," General Zarrik said.

The Duke cleared his throat. "Then let's take our places and see what these damn Perranese have to say for themselves."

The Duke took the central throne on the slightly raised dais at the far end of the audience chamber, and Rina took the lower chair to his left. She glanced briefly at her mother in the chair to her father's right. Mother still looked sickly and gray. She dabbed at a light sheen of sweat across her forehead with a silk handkerchief. She'd had the same illness that had put many of the servants out of commission. She'd been a delicate and frail woman for as long as Rina could remember.

Rina's relationship with her mother had been strained the last few years as Rina grew older and more stubborn. Rina admitted it to herself. She'd been a handful. But when Mother tried to tell her with every breath how a lady should walk and talk and dress... well, Rina grew impatient with such things. It was like her mother wanted to make her into some lady of nobility to show off at fancy dress parties without ever considering what Rina might want.

Rina snapped her attention back to the business at hand as the gilded double doors swung inward, admitting the Perranese delegation. She craned her neck to look past the foreigners and into the wide hallway beyond. Ten soldiers stood at attention on each side. Ostensibly an honor guard to welcome the Perranese ambassador, but Rina guessed they were hand-picked men. Daddy wasn't taking any chances with strangers in his castle.

The great doors thudded closed again, echoing through the audience chamber. The Perranese standard bearer and military escort stopped just inside the door. The ambassador proceeded to the edge of the dais and bowed low.

He rose and said, "I am Ambassador Pilet Ra'Karro, emissary of the Most Holy and Divine Emperor of Perran. I bring you greetings... and a message of peace."

Rina's eyes shot to her father.

The Duke stood slowly. His bow to the ambassador was barely more than a nod.

"Peace?" The Duke's eyebrow rose, questioning. "Am I mistaken, or did I not spy an army on my front doorstep?"

The ambassador smiled, spread his hands. He teetered on the edge of simpering without tumbling over, a miracle of diplomacy.

"But, naturally, the Most Divine Emperor realizes how this must appear. Events progress as they must. The change of power is inevitable, but the Most Holy and Divine Emperor has blessed Klaar with the great distinction of being at the forefront of this shift in power. We wish only to gift the people of Helva with our divine rule."

Rina frowned. *Well, that's nerve.*

"The duchy of Klaar has neither the authority *nor the inclination* to acknowledge any such shift," her father said. "I cannot accept your … gift."

The ambassador shook his head slowly, dramatically. "That is a pity. We invite Klaar to willingly accept its place in the new order. However …" Here the ambassador smiled thinly. "… We understand that some force might be necessary to bring rebellious territories into line."

Rina's father returned the smile. "And so we come to it. Unless your generals are fools, they must know they can't come across the Long Bridge. Nobody wants a siege that could certainly drag on longer than a year if both sides are stubborn enough, and, my dear ambassador, I assure you the people of Klaar are as stubborn as they come. So what do you really want? Begin your negotiations."

The ambassador's thin smile didn't waver. "No negotiations. Simply an offer. Open the gates and let us take control peacefully. Many lives will be spared."

A long, tense moment as the Duke held the ambassador's stare. Rina studied her father's face. Could almost read his mind. Was he missing something? The Duke considered all of the potential subtleties before answering.

"I'm sorry to disappoint you," the Duke said. "We refuse your offer, obviously. To be blunt, I'm not sure what you hoped to accomplish by coming here today."

The ambassador nodded slightly, reaching into a billowy sleeve and coming out with a fan that he spread open with a flick of a wrist, the bright red material a sudden signal to the men behind him.

The soldiers and the standard bearer ran forward, drawing swords.

Rina stood, eyes shooting wide. She heard her mother gasp.

General Zarrik was first to react. "Guards!" He drew the short, broad sword at his waist.

The audience chamber doors flew open, and the twenty men on the other side rushed in amid the clamor of thudding boots and clanking armor and swords flashing from sheaths. They crashed into the handful of Perranese soldiers. Screams and death and the harsh ring of metal on metal.

"Treachery!" Rina's father flew down the dais, drawing his rapier and aiming a long sweeping stroke at the Perranese ambassador.

The ambassador flinched back, but not quickly enough, the tip of Duke's blade slicing neatly across his throat. Hot red blood spurted from the ambassador's jugular. His hands went to stanch the flow as he stumbled back, the blood seeping between his fingers, his red fan fluttering to the ground like a wounded sparrow.

Rina's gaze shifted from the dying ambassador to the clash of men in the audience chamber.

The Perranese soldiers whirled and danced among her father's men, swords striking, pulling back to block an attack, striking again. The movements were so fast, Rina almost couldn't follow them. The Klaarian soldiers fell. Others moved in to take their places, and they fell too, clutching at fatal, bloody wounds. The Perranese warriors were too good. Judging from the little combat Rina had seen, only Kork handled a sword better.

Where the hell is the big savage? The one time I actually need a fucking bodyguard—

Rina suddenly felt Zarrik's hand on her wrist, pulling her down the steps of the dais. "Lady Rina, hurry! We need to get you to safety before—"

Something metal flashed past her, and Zarrik grunted, twitched and let go of her.

The general fell dead at her feet. A ring of metal spikes had killed him, some sort of throwing weapon. One of the spikes had buried itself deep in the middle of his forehead. His eyes were open but lifeless, mouth twitching.

Oh, Dumo, help us. Her hand went automatically to the sword strapped to her waist, but it wasn't there. A young lady did not wear a sword with a dress on formal occasions.

Damn it!

The Perranese soldiers continued to slaughter the men of Klaar. In seconds, the battle would be over.

The Duke backed up the dais to stand next to his steward. "Giffen, take my wife and daughter and flee out the back hallway. I won't be able to hold them, but maybe I can buy you a few seconds to—"

The Duke's breath caught. He looked down, saw Giffen's hand holding the dagger he'd just jabbed into his side. The Duke's eyes came back up to Giffen's smiling face; he worked his mouth, trying to speak, but couldn't find breath.

Giffen withdrew the dagger, plunged it in again.

Rina watched in horror. "Daddy!"

The Duke dropped to his knees, the rapier tumbling from his hand to clatter on the stone steps. He turned his head to look at his daughter, his expression one of utter bewilderment.

Rina rushed to him, glancing at her mother who sat agape, nearly catatonic.

Rina scooped up her father's rapier and swung at Giffen in the same motion. The steward threw up an arm out of reflex and the blade tore a gash across the bottom of his forearm. He screamed and backed away.

Out of the corner of her eye, she saw the Perranese warriors approaching. She turned, sword in front of her. She was aware of all the bodies behind them. The Klaarian soldiers were dead to a man.

A young Perranese bounded up the steps, thrusting at Rina. His sword was long and curved, but only slightly heavier than her father's rapier.

Kork's teaching immediately took over.

His armor was made up of overlapping discs of some shining metal. Kork's enormous sword could probably bite through easily, but she'd need to find a weak spot for the rapier. The mesh under the arms might be fabric or dark, thin chainmail.

But the Perranese warrior's wide-brimmed helmet had no face guard.

She stepped past the thrust, parrying with the rapier. A flick of her wrist brought the blade around and over the warrior's sword hilt and at his face.

The Perranese warrior had been surprised twice in less than a second. First, by Rina's speed. Second, by the sword blade that buried itself deep into his left eye socket.

Rina almost lost the sword when the warrior screamed and turned away, but she held on and pulled it free of his skull, spinning to face the other warriors who came up more cautiously.

"Take her alive." Rina heard Giffen's voice behind her.

The remaining warriors stormed up the dais at her. She swung the sword, lunged, turned, swung again. She caught one on the hand, drawing blood, another on the thigh. Her blade bounced off of the chest armor of another, and finally she felt hands on her as they crowded around.

She kept thrashing as they pressed against her. There was no room to strike with the sword, but she swung backhanded and smashed the hilt into a warrior's nose, heard the cartilage *pop*; blood streamed from his nostrils.

"It's just one little brat," yelled Giffen.

Something sharp struck Rina on the back of the head. The world tilted and blurred and then went black.

CHAPTER SIX

S he heard the voices before she could open her eyes.

"Your men found the ropes at the secret spot near the back gate?" Giffen's voice.

"Yes." A light Perranese accent. "The men who came over the wall were in bad spirits. They had been hiding for two weeks, freezing their asses off." A small chuckle. "But that just made them fight harder, I think."

Rina still couldn't open her eyes. Her head was spinning, throbbing.

"Still, you must admit it was a good plan," Giffen said. "No one believes a threat to the back gate is possible. It was simple enough to position a score of men ahead of time, bringing them up by night. If they grew cold and lonely while waiting then they can be first in line at the brothels when you take the city."

"*If* we take the city," the Perranese voice said. "Taking the front gate from the inside was easy enough, but even now fighting continues in the streets. These people are sloppy fighters but stubborn. They are too stupid to know they are beaten."

"You have my full confidence," Giffen said. "I'm sure your men will soon subdue the remaining—Ah, she's awake. Good."

Rina blinked three times, her vision snapping back into focus. Her face pressed against the cold stone floor. Her head felt heavy like a bag of rocks knocking together. She shifted her line of sight enough to see Giffen and one of the Perranese foreigners looming over her. He had some kind of plume in his broad helmet; an officer maybe.

Giffen grinned down at her. "Get up, brat."

Rina propped herself up on one elbow, head throbbing in protest. That was as far as she could get. The headache behind her eyes was nearly blinding.

Giffen snapped his fingers impatiently. "Get her up."

She felt rough hands grab her under the arms and drag her to her feet. Her head flopped, chin bouncing against her chest. She forced herself to look, lifting her head. She was still in the audience chamber. How long had she been out? There were at least twenty Perranese warriors in the chamber now. What had happened?

She glanced sideways at the steps of the dais. Her father still lay dead, sprawled where he'd been murdered by the traitor Giffen.

A sob welled up in her chest suddenly, wracked her entire body. *Father...*

Giffen lifted her chin with a finger. "I know you grieve. But believe me, it can get worse. It can always get much worse."

She wanted to curse him, but couldn't summon the words. Her vision blurred with tears.

"Bring her!"

But Giffen hadn't meant Rina. The Perranese warriors parted as two soldiers dragged another woman through the crowd.

Mother!

They threw her to the ground, where she knelt, her hands over her head, trembling.

"First, we show that we're serious," Giffen said.

He signaled one of the Perranese soldiers standing over Rina's mother.

The warrior grabbed a fistful of the woman's hair, jerked her head up and in one smooth motion slit her throat with a long, curved dagger.

Rina screamed, a long, anguished animal howl. She struggled fiercely against those holding her, murderous rage blinding her to everything but sinking her nails into Giffen's face.

An instant later, she went limp, crying helplessly. *Oh, Mother, how did this happen? I'm so sorry. So sorry.* Mother and Father dead. Duchy seized by invaders. In an eye blink, everything had been taken away.

Giffen bent to look her in the eye. "Now, I think I have your attention, yes?"

Rina spat, the warm wad of saliva hitting the side of his nose.

He straightened, frowned and sighed, wiping the spittle away with a pinky finger. "A brat and a fool to the very end, I see."

Giffen swung suddenly, backhanding her across the face, the slap of skin on skin echoing through the audience chamber.

Sparks went off in Rina's eyes, her cheek hot and stinging.

She forced herself to suck in a mouthful of air, let it out slowly, trying to clear her head. When she met Giffen's gaze again, there were no more tears. Only cold fury. Somehow she would survive this. She would live to hold Giffen's heart in her hand. She would hack it out of his chest herself, with a dull rusty hatchet.

"The Perranese are putting me in charge of Klaar," Giffen said. "We know how stubborn our citizens can be, and they'll take it better if one of their own rules over them instead of a foreigner. I even have a little story prepared, how on his deathbed your father asked me to take charge of the duchy, to act as a buffer between his beloved people and the savage invaders from across the sea." Giffen shrugged. "As a loyal subject of Klaar, what else could I do but respect your father's dying wish?"

"They'll see through you in ten seconds," Rina said. "They'll rip you to shreds as a traitor and hang your corpse from the city walls for the buzzards."

"I don't think so," Giffen said. "But as an aid to my little fiction, I want your father's signet ring. I'd like to show it to the people as I deliver my tearful speech, telling them how the Duke's final thoughts were of their well-being, and how we should persevere even under Perranese rule. We've searched your family's living quarters. You wouldn't happen to know where that ring is, would you?"

"Go fuck yourself." In fact, she didn't know. Not a clue. But she wouldn't tell Giffen even if she did.

"I want you to imagine that a dank cell in the bowels of the castle dungeon can seem like paradise compared to...other things," Giffen told her. "We might even manage to toss you a crust of bread once a day."

She said nothing, glared her defiance.

"Think about where that signet ring is hidden," Giffen suggested. "It won't change my plan one bit if I don't have it, but, unlike when I was a mere steward, I expect to *get* what I want and we might as well start with *you*. So I'll ask you the same question again in an hour, and you'll have another opportunity to demonstrate your obedience. In the meantime, it's my understanding that these men," he gestured to the score of Perranese warriors, "have been without female companionship for a number of weeks."

Rina went cold.

The chamber echoed with the fall of Giffen's boots. He passed through the big double doors and they *thunked* closed behind him.

Silence stretched, and Rina was aware only of the panicked heartbeat thumping in her ears.

Then the hands holding her frantically pawed at her clothes, a sleeve ripped. Rina screamed. The other men crowded, reaching in, all trying to get at her all at once. She heard more cloth ripping. She struggled, tried to kick, hands on her legs, pushing her dress up. One of the men produced a dagger, sliced the laces of her tight bodice, and it popped loose. Her breasts shifted under the thin fabric of her shift. One of the men had a handful of her hair. She could not remember a time when she wasn't screaming.

They lowered her to the stone floor, and one of the warriors knelt in front of her, pried her knees apart. She kicked at him, but others moved in to grab her ankles.

She tried to thrash, squirm, anything. Her arms and legs were held fast. This was it, the end. She had a desperate thought that maybe she could grab a dagger from one of the other warriors' belts and plunge it into her own heart, but they held her too tightly.

Rina looked at the man kneeling before her, pleading with her eyes, hoping he could feel some sort of mercy.

A blur of movement, the glint of metal.

The head popped off of the warrior who'd been kneeling in front of her, tumbling through the air and raining blood. Rina blinked, unsure of what she'd seen.

Another metallic blur, and the hand holding her ankle separated at the wrist. Impossibly, the men crowding her seemed not to notice. They pushed in, hands grabbing at her breasts through the thin, silken shift. The point of a thick blade, thrust through the open mouth of a warrior holding her arm. His eyes shot wide as blood fountained out of his mouth and down his chin.

Now the Perranese warriors realized something was amiss. They released Rina, backed away, drawing their swords.

Kork whirled among them, swinging his sword in two-handed fashion, severed limbs flying in arcs of blood. They tried to rally and rush him, but he ducked beneath their sword swings, dodged their thrusts, batted aside their blades.

Kork's hand flicked toward Rina. Something landed in her lap.

She fumbled for it, head swimming. A glass vial wrapped in leather. She uncorked it, the *ting* of steel on steel echoing in the audience chamber. She brought it to her mouth, the pungent tangy odor hitting her a split second before she tilted it back and drained the vial. It's warmth raced through her body, reaching every part of her at once.

Her head cleared, pain fading.

A healing elixir. They were fabulously expensive. *Never mind that now!*

Kork spun among the Perranese warriors, the brute force of his huge blade hacking easily through the armor. Everywhere Kork struck, another invader stumbled back, spraying blood and screaming.

Rina shrugged off the bodice and scooped up one of the fallen Perranese swords. The would-be rapists had unwittingly done her a favor. Wearing only the silken, sleeveless shift, she was able to move more fluidly. The foreign sword was single edged, made more for slicing and hacking than thrusting. She instantly recalled Kork's lessons with such weapons and waded without hesitation into the combat.

They didn't even notice Rina at first, all of them crowding around Kork, trying to bring down the big man.

Rina swung the sword, an upward, backhanded cut. The blade slid under the back of a warrior's broad helmet, laying open the base of his skull. Blood and brains spilled out hotly onto the floor as the warrior fell.

She turned to another, stabbed at the weak area of the armor under his arm. She pulled the sword out fast, felt a hot spray of blood across her face.

They'd noticed Rina now, and two of the warriors broke off their assault on Kork to come at her. She knocked one's sword aside as he stepped in for a thrust, but flicked her wrist for a quick strike at the other, the blade dragging down the warrior's bracer until it caught the fleshy part between his thumb and forefinger. He flinched back, hissing pain.

Instead of following up with a kill strike, she turned back to the other one, who was moving to chop down at her with a two-handed swing. She blocked, ducked around and tried to slice low at his belly, but he got his blade back in time to parry her.

Now both came at her at once. They were well trained, she realized, and not underestimating her as had the warrior she'd killed earlier.

Think, idiot. What would Kork tell you?

He'd say to remember your strengths.

She wasn't strong, but she was fast.

Rina launched at the two warriors, her blade a blur between the two of them, metal *clanging* and *tinging*—thrust, block, stab. They were forced to stay on defense. Rina roared, high-pitched and ragged, not in grief as before, but in pure rage. She kept pressing forward, the muscles in her sword arm beginning to burn hot. How much longer could she keep this up?

You know what Kork would say. "You think your muscles hurt? Try a blade in the belly."

One of the warriors slipped in a puddle of his comrade's blood. He righted himself instantly, but his defense wavered. Only for an instant, but it was enough.

Rina thrust the sword into the warrior's throat. He fell back, gurgling blood, his eyes beaming disbelief. It looked painful.

Good.

But you don't have time to gloat, stupid girl.

She turned to the other one, swinging wildly now, desperate to end the fight. Her heart thundered against her chest. She panted, lungs burning. Kork had pushed her often in practice sessions, emphasizing the importance of good conditioning. But it was never the real thing—the smell of blood and sweat, the screams of the dying, the thrill of blood lust through her entire body while simultaneously feeling she could collapse any second.

Her foe took advantage of her sloppy swings, knocked her sword aside and stepped in, aiming a thrust at her midsection. If her reflexes had been any slower at all, he would have finished her there, slicing open her belly, but she sidestepped just in time. The thrust cut a long slice in her shift, and she gasped as she felt the sword tip draw a shallow four-inch line across her side.

But Kork's training held. Even as part of her brain registered the wound, another more decisive part took in the enemy's posture. He'd had to give up some defense to make his attack. Rina brought her own sword down hard, and only the warrior's bracer kept him from losing his hand at the wrist. The bloody wound was enough to force him to drop the sword.

Panic blazed suddenly in his eyes as Rina pressed her attack. He tried to go for a dagger on his belt, but Rina swung, once, twice, three, four times, some of the blows glancing off armor but others biting through into flesh. He went down, babbling his foreign tongue. Rina imagined he was begging for mercy.

You've come to the wrong shop for mercy.

With two hands, she jabbed the sword down into his open mouth, felt it punch through the back of his head and helm and strike the stone floor.

She yanked the sword out immediately, held it in front of her as she spun a complete circle. Where was her next enemy? From which direction would the next attack come?

She saw only Kork, pulling his great sword from the torso of a Perranese warrior.

And the bodies.

Oh, Dumo, so many bodies. More than a score she could see now. Most lay still, but others twitched. None rose to trouble her. The hall was thick with the copper stench of death and loosened bowels.

Rina looked down at herself, a sweaty, blood-spattered mess. Her hands, completely slick and red, did not seem like her own. She blinked stupidly.

Kork was suddenly next to her, dragging her by the wrist. "Come."

Rina tore her gaze from her hands, blinked at Kork. "What?"

"There is no time," Kork said. "The castle is overrun. They may already be looking for you. I don't know. Now hurry."

And suddenly Kork was pulling her through the castle hallways. She followed numbly, her heart going leaden, knowing hopelessly that the nightmare continued, and she couldn't wake up.

CHAPTER SEVEN

Rina wasn't paying attention to where Kork was taking her. She didn't care. If Kork had let her, she would have simply crawled into a corner and gone to sleep, and if she never woke up again, that would be just fine.

It wasn't until she'd tripped down her fourth flight of stairs that Rina grew curious. In Castle Klaar, *down* wasn't synonymous with *out*. At least not in this case. They'd already passed the storage rooms and were heading to the dungeons. Kork paused at the doorway to the little room reserved for the jailer, cocked his head and listened for a long moment.

Kork nodded, satisfied. "He's not in there. Probably died out on one of the walls, defending the city."

Yes, Rina remembered. All able bodied men reported for duty at such times. How many butchers and blacksmiths and stable hands had thought themselves safe behind Klaar's walls only to die at the end of a Perranese sword?

She thought fleetingly of the boy who'd helped her with her boot. She'd thought him cute and had teased him on a whim. Oh, Dumo, had that really only happened a few hours ago? It seemed like a lifetime. And now he was dead like the rest, whoever he was. The world in which she could tease boys on a whim was gone forever.

Kork took a torch from the hallway bracket and handed it to Rina. "Hold this."

He opened the door, and they entered the jailer's room. It was squalid. A chair and a narrow bunk.

Kork heaved the bunk aside, knelt and brushed dust off the floor until he found a perfectly round stone about the size of a grapefruit. He used the hilt of his sword to push down hard, and with a quiet scraping sound, the stone lowered into the floor. More sounds, clunks and scraping, and a panel of stones behind the bunk swung inward. The secret doorway was barely four feet high. Kork ducked his head and entered.

A moment later he reappeared and gestured to Rina. "Come on."

She followed him into the secret passage. He pulled a lever and the doorway closed behind them. In the flickering torchlight, she saw a man-made passage, angling gently downward. He gestured her to follow.

"Kork?"

"Yes?"

"Where... Where were you?" She heard the tremble in her voice, steadied herself.

"Giffen," Kork said. "He found me, told me your father wanted me to inspect the defenses. I'm sorry, Rina. Sorry I wasn't there. Sorry I failed you."

"No." She sniffed. "But if you'd been another minute..." She gulped breath, trying to hold back a sob.

"Don't talk now," he said. "We need to hurry."

She trudged after him for what seemed like hours. The tunnel leveled off and soon turned into a natural cavern. The floor grew slick, a sudden stench hitting her. Rina realized with revulsion that the castle's sewage system must feed into these tunnels.

She tried not to think about it, putting one foot in front of the other, but it became ankle deep. She gagged, turned her head and retched.

"Come," Kork said. "We're nearly out."

She convulsed and vomited again, giving up some meal she didn't even remember eating, consumed by a different person, living another life. She stumbled, shivering and light-headed, through the filth, felt Kork lift her by the elbow.

A hundred more steps and then Kork tossed the torch into the watery sewage at their feet and it sputtered out. Before Rina could ask why he'd plunged them into darkness, she saw the light at the end. They'd come to the tunnel's exit.

They marched toward the blur of light and thirty seconds later found themselves outside, ankle-deep in the snow. The cold seeped into her wet, thin slippers immediately. She shivered, the icy wind piercing her thin shift. As if it had been waiting for them, a steady snowfall began. The sky was a dark gray, almost like night.

She fell to her knees. The snow was bitterly cold but clean. She grabbed a handful of it, rubbed it on her lips, rubbed more on her tongue to remove the acid taste of vomit. She tried to stand, couldn't, looked up blankly at her bodyguard.

Kork lifted her again, took off his blood-splattered cloak and draped it around her.

The tunnel had come out in a ravine below Klaar. She turned to look back. Pillars of smoke rose here and there from the city.

"Some still fight, I think," Kork said.

"Can they win?" Rina asked. "Can they take the city back?"

"No."

She began to cry. "Kork, they … Mother … Father …"

He took her shoulders in his enormous hands. "Look at me."

Rina looked up at him, his face hazy through her hot tears.

"You are still alive," Kork said. "Many are dead, but not *you*. I live for one thing. To see to your safety. That is my honor oath to your father, an oath that endures even after his death. But I need help."

"Where can we get help out here?" Rina asked. "It's … impossible."

"There is the old mage."

"The … what?"

Rina shivered almost uncontrollably now, teeth chattering. She was tired and bloody. She tried to recall some faint memory, something about an old court mage, but her brain wouldn't work. She was exhausted. "What are you talking about? What mage? Where?"

Kork turned, pointed to the rocky, snow-capped mountain that loomed over them, rising into dark clouds. "There."

CHAPTER EIGHT

Alem dug himself deeper into the hay of the stable loft, the screams of the dying loud and clear in the street just outside. Below him, the horses snorted and fidgeted. They were well trained and not easily spooked, but none had heard such fierce fighting in the streets of Klaar since ... well, it had *never* been heard.

Somehow the enemy had come across the Long Bridge. The gates had been opened.

A grizzled veteran had shoved a dull infantryman's axe into Alem's hands along with a wooden shield and pointed Alem toward the battle. If an officer hadn't urgently demanded a horse, Alem would now lie at the bottom of a pile of bodies. He'd sprinted through the chaos, back to the stable and had frantically saddled a sturdy gelding. He'd returned to find the officer and his entire platoon slain, the buildings along the cobblestone street in flames.

So Alem had done the only thing he could think of. He had run back to the stable and hidden. And there was no point feeling like a coward. He was no warrior, and anyway, the city was hopelessly and obviously lost.

Now he held his breath under the hay as the stable door creaked open. But instead of Perranese soldiers, it was a man of

Klaar who entered, an ordinary soldier in chainmail and a simple bowl helm. A bland man of medium height, a broad, lazy face, brown hair curling from under the rim of the helm.

Alem allowed himself the fleeting hope that by some miracle the Klaar military had rallied and turned back the invaders. The thought that this soldier had come to tell those in hiding that it was safe to come out now turned laughable as Alem watched the soldier toss aside his armor and livery.

The soldier was a deserter, and Alem suddenly felt an irrational pang of disgust. *Okay, yeah, I'm hiding under a pile of hay, but this guy is supposed to be a professional.*

Alem leaned out over the edge of the loft. "What are you doing?"

The soldier yelped and flinched, turned abruptly. "You startled the shit out of me. Who the hell are you?"

"Shouldn't you be fighting the battle?" Alem said.

"Battle?" The soldier snorted. "That's no battle, kid. That's a fucking slaughter, and running out there and taking a spear in the gut won't change anything. So if it's all the same to you, I resign."

Alem bristled at the word *kid*. And he was pretty sure you couldn't just resign from the army whenever you felt like it.

On the other hand, the man didn't want to die, and Alem could understand that.

"What's your name?" Alem asked.

"Tosh."

"How bad is it?"

"Bad," Tosh said. "I think somebody must have opened the gates from the inside. They came pouring across the Long Bridge and there was no stopping them. I threw my spear, but I didn't even see where it landed." He shrugged. "Next I knew they were all over the walls."

"How many did you kill?"

"How many did I—?" Tosh shook his head, rolled his eyes. "Look, kid, I didn't kill anyone. A bunch of us pressed through a mob of those foreigners trying to get off the wall and retreat back to the keep. I took a swipe at one of the bastards, but he deflected me. Half the time I didn't know if the man behind me was one of ours or one of theirs. Next I know, half my guys are dead and we're just *running*, okay? That's when I had the thought maybe I could come here and grab a horse, maybe ride for it. But there's no way I'd make it to one of the gates."

Alem frowned. If Tosh was a typical example of the Klaarian army it was no wonder the city was lost.

Tosh correctly interpreted the look on Alem's face. "Whatever glorious nonsense you've heard about war, just forget it. It's all screaming and confusion and trying not to shit yourself."

Alem considered his brief sprint through the chaos when the officer had sent him for a horse. That was in the early part of the battle, before things had gone from bad to worse. Alem imagined himself in Tosh's position, with death coming at him from every direction. *Okay, so maybe I shouldn't judge the man.*

Still, it would have been nice to think his countrymen had put up *some* kind of fight.

And that's when Alem started to feel it in his gut. What had been simple fear before was now a cold feeling of dread as he realized the battle and the slaughter in the streets of Klaar was only the beginning. For the survivors there would be... what? Alem didn't know, and surprisingly the unknown future like a blank slate in front of him was terrifying. Would the conquerors enslave the survivors? Torture them? Or maybe a stable boy was too unimportant to even be noticed. Maybe he'd wake up in the morning, muck out the stalls, feed and water the horses as usual, the new masters no different from the old.

But he wouldn't know until it was happening to him, and by then it would be too late.

In a stab of panic, he seized on Tosh's scheme to steal a horse and ride out fast. His grandmother lived down in the valley. He could hide there. Most of the lowland villages had evacuated to the imagined safety of the city walls, but Alem knew his grandmother wouldn't budge. She was stubborn and would die on her own land, and anyway she was too old to make the climb up the mountain road. Or at least that's what she would claim. Maybe he could get lucky, ride past all the Perranese warriors before they could…

The door to the stable slowly creaked open again.

Alem quickly retreated back into the hay, gestured for Tosh to get out of sight, but the deserter was already in motion, frantically trying to find a good hiding place.

Tosh backed against the wall where reins and harness hung, grabbed a horse blanket off a peg and tossed it over himself. He squatted next to a barrel.

Four Perranese warriors strode into the stable. Alem watched them through an opening in the hay. Even their most casual movements seemed precise and catlike. With swords and spears, they would make a lethal fighting force. Klaar had never really had a chance once the gates had been thrown wide.

One of the Perranese pointed at the horses, gibbered in his foreign tongue to the others who nodded along. Alem's heart sank. Of course; they'd just come across the ocean, and horses would be in short supply. They'd take these for their own use and with them Alem's idea to ride out of town.

The warrior in charge motioned to the other three, barking orders in his quick, clipped language. They went to the stalls and picked out three horses, all large stallions, and led them out of the stable.

That meant the gelding Alem had selected for the officer was still in the end stall. Still saddled.

When the other three left, the remaining Perranese turned away from Alem, reached under his scale mail skirt. A second later, Alem heard the stream of urine splashing against the stable wall.

Okay, he'll finish pissing, and when he leaves I'll hop on the gelding and make a run for it.

The warrior finished, turned back to the stable door. Paused.

He looked down at Tosh's discarded chainmail on the ground. Alem's stomach lurched. *Oh … no.*

The warrior gripped the hilt of his sword, turning his head slowly to scan the stable. His demeanor had changed, like a wire now pulled tight. Alem held his breath. Silence fell heavily over the stable, broken by one of the horses snorting. The warrior slowly drew his sword from the sheath.

The hiss of metal made Tosh flinch beneath the horse blanket. Not much, just the barest hint of movement, but it was enough. The warrior lifted the sword over his head, walked deliberately toward Tosh's hiding spot.

If Alem had been given ample time to plan his next move, it would never have occurred to him to rise from his hiding place under the hay and leap from the loft at the Perranese warrior below.

But that's exactly what he did.

CHAPTER NINE

Rina could no longer feel her feet. Limbs cold and heavy. She knew she was still moving forward by the sound of snow crunch. Only Kork kept her from dropping where she stood, lying down in the snow, and falling asleep forever. She was dead on her feet, and it was almost a blessing. Little energy was left to think of the horror that was only a few hours old. Her fingers ached holding Kork's cloak closed in front of her. She would never be warm again.

And if she did sprawl in the snow to surrender to sleep, a dim awareness told her Kork would simply heave her over his shoulder and keep climbing the mountain. A shred of pride in her wouldn't allow that. The man had done so much for her already. He shouldn't have to carry her too.

But when she slowed, began to drift, she'd feel Kork's large hand take her by the elbow, pull her along until she was able to tap into some hidden well of strength.

The snow fell harder.

They climbed higher.

She looked back. Klaar was far below them. Smoke still rose in parts of the city, but it didn't seem as bad. Maybe the fighting was over. Not that it mattered. Klaar belonged to the Perranese now.

Rina couldn't feel anything about that. She was too numb.

"Come." Kork had her by the elbow again.

Rina realized she'd stopped hiking, had been staring unblinking at the city below. She allowed herself to be led, trudging with a rhythm like a dirge through the snow which was now knee deep. The numbness in her feet circled around to pain again, reaching up into her hips. She'd heard of trappers being caught out in blizzards, losing toes or even a foot to frostbite. *I don't care. Take my feet, my legs. Take it all.*

She turned her head to look at a low marker of gray bricks about the height of her waist. One of the top bricks displayed the seal of the Duchy of Klaar. A path marker. Of course. Kork wouldn't lead them randomly up the mountain. He'd known the way all along, but she hadn't seen the path so thickly covered with snow.

There was another marker at the foot of a well-worn set of stone steps leading steeply up the rocky slope. It was very nearly invisible beneath the snow, but Rina knew what to look for now. They started up the stairs, and within minutes the muscles in her legs burned. She refused to complain, biting her lower lip to keep from groaning until she tasted her own blood.

Up. Endlessly.

She looked down again at Klaar but couldn't see it. It was lost amid the thick snow flying sideways on the bitter wind.

The stairs ended at last at the opening of a cave. Rina turned to Kork, her expression unmistakable. *Really? In there?*

"The cave of the old mage," Kork said. "He was banished by your father's father. I don't know why. But the Duke told me if all other hopes should fail to bring you here. He told me this only this morning. I wonder if he had a premonition that maybe the Perranese threat was more than suspected. He was right, I'm sorry to say. So I have brought you as instructed."

Rina gazed into the dark cavern as if mesmerized. Her father had told Kork to bring her here? "What else did he say?"

Kork grunted.

"Kork."

"He said nothing more. But he seemed… conflicted. I think he was reluctant to send you to this mage."

They stood a moment in the mouth of the cave. The wind howled behind them.

Kork put a hand against the cave wall to steady himself. He slid down into a sitting position, his other hand held tight against his side. Rina looked at him. The big man was covered in blood, and for the first time it occurred to Rina some of it might be his.

"You're hurt."

Kork lifted his chin, indicating the depths of the cavern. "In there. Go."

"Alone?"

"I will guard the entrance." He drew the large sword from the scabbard on his back, set it next to him. "My wound is minor. I only need rest. You must go on."

She hesitated, then nodded.

She advanced into the cave. The sound of the wind dwindled behind her. She rounded a long gradual bend, and it grew darker then lighter again, firelight glowing ahead. The cavern opened into a wide chamber.

A shrunken old man sat perfectly still on a threadbare rug. He did not move, look up or open his eyes at Rina's approach.

The room was lit by a low, brass brazier, the flames casting misshapen shadows on the chamber walls. When the heat of it reached her, Rina almost wept. She stood, letting the warmth seep into her, not caring for the moment about the old man. Hot needles pricked her feet as they thawed. Now she did weep very softly, fat tears rolling down her cheeks and over her lips.

Rina knelt in front of the old man, wiped away the tears with trembling fingers. She leaned closer, looking at him. She wasn't even sure he was alive. His head was down, chin almost touching his bony chest, eyes closed. He wore a tattered and faded woolen robe of muted red. Bald. Completely clean shaven and wrinkled. He sat cross-legged, gnarled and spotted hands on his knees.

Rina cleared her throat.

Nothing.

"I'm Rina Veraiin." Her voice was barely above a whisper. "I...my father..." Would names even mean anything to him? How long had he been here?

A long pause, then the old man spoke without lifting his head. "You are Little Belly's daughter?" His voice was like heavy stones grinding together.

Rina searched her memory. They'd called her father Little Belly as a child because he had a little round belly. Relations would rub it and tickle him. Rina had thought the story silly at the time. She had to master herself to keep from sobbing. Her father would never tell her another story again.

"Yes," Rina said. "Dead now."

He lifted his head. Opened his eyes. One was completely clouded over, the other a clear, rich brown. Shadows played across his face, making him seem strange and sinister. "Something's happened."

"Yes."

"Tell me."

"The Perranese," Rina said. "They came across the Long Bridge. Somebody opened the gates." She stopped talking. Couldn't bear to recount all of it. The pain was still too close.

He nodded. "I'm surprised you are here. Little Belly must have turned out different from his father."

She didn't know what to say to that. She'd never known her grandfather.

"What do you want of me?"

"I don't know," Rina said. "I was brought here."

"I see," the old man said. "You are duchess then."

Am I? Yes, she supposed she was. With Father and Mother dead, Rina was now Duchess of Klaar. It was meaningless. Klaar might as well have been the moon. It wasn't hers. Not anymore.

"So, Duchess, how may I serve you?"

"I don't know," Rina repeated. "I ... need help."

"I have already decided to help you," he said. "I am dying. I am killing myself with every word I utter to you. I have the wasting disease in my belly and in my lungs. You understand this sort of sickness, yes?"

Rina nodded. An uncle on her mother's side had died that way.

"It takes all my energy and focus to keep the sickness at bay," he said. "So in deciding to help you I am welcoming death. Even this simple conversation is enough to divert my energies. Do you understand this?"

Her eyes widened.

"Yes, I see that you do," he said. "So let's make it worth it, shall we? Let's try to focus with clarity on the best way I can help you. For it will be my dying act. Do you wish to live?"

She blinked at the question. "Do I wish to live?"

"You've brought yourself here in a blizzard. Not easy. In your despair it would have been simpler to throw yourself off a cliff. This would end your grief, yes? But you didn't do that. I infer you prefer to live."

"Yes," she said. "I want to live." A strange and simple admission but effective. In spite of everything, she did want to live, to go on even though it all seemed so hopeless.

"That's a start, then," the old man said. "We've established you want to live. Now what shall you live *for*?"

What?

He sighed, impatient. "Something must drive you, girl. Find something. Foreign savages have killed your family and taken your land. Do you want revenge? Do you want to take back what is yours? Tell me. I am neither a priest nor a philosopher. I won't judge you."

She hadn't thought about it. Would she take revenge on those who had robbed her of everything if given the chance? She saw her father's face, surprised at Giffen's betrayal. Would she seize any opportunity to slide cold steel into Giffen's belly? "Yes."

"Now we have direction," he said. "And what do you have to accomplish your task? Do you have an army with which to recapture Klaar? Generals to do your bidding?"

The old man acted like he wanted to plant an idea in her head one second then disabuse her of it the next. But of course he was right. "I have nothing. Just myself."

"That's more than you think." He stood slowly, joints popping and creaking as if he'd been sitting there for centuries.

He gestured, and Rina followed the gesture with her eyes. Strange syllables fell out of the old man's mouth, tickling her ears and then vanishing. The old man flicked a pinch of some fine powder into the air. Halfway across the chamber, a small fire sprang to life beneath a large brass tub.

"The water will heat soon," he said. "You must bathe."

"But…" She looked down at her clothes, back at the old man.

"Don't be silly. Modesty is a peasant's virtue, Duchess. Besides, I am old and harmless." She thought she saw a smile tug at the corners of his mouth.

"Why a bath?"

"Because I'm going to give you a gift," he said. "And we must prepare you to receive it."

CHAPTER TEN

The Perranese warrior had just enough time to turn his head, his eyes popping wide as Alem slammed into him. They went down hard, and the warrior's chin caught the edge of the barrel near Tosh's hiding place.

With Alem's weight on his back, the warrior's head was forced back sharply. There was a sickening snap, and the two of them went down in a heap.

Tosh sprang from his hiding place, tossing the horse blanket aside, a short dagger in one hand, ready to fight, but the Perranese warrior lay lifeless, eyes wide open, mouth agape. Tosh nudged the body with the toe of his boot. "Damn, kid, you've killed him."

Alem sat up next to the dead warrior. He rubbed his side, winced. Flying through the air and slamming into a fully armored man had bruised a few ribs. What had he been thinking?

"Guess I owe you one," Tosh said. "But his pals could come back any moment, and finding us here with their dead captain won't go well for us."

Alem lurched to his feet, grunted, one hand holding his ribs. It hurt like blazes, but he prodded his side with tentative fingers and didn't think anything was broken. "Pick one of the mares in back and saddle it," Alem told Tosh. "I'll be right back."

"Kid, I told you already. There's no way we can ride out past them."

Alem ignored him and limped across the room to the stable master's tiny room. It wasn't much. A cot. A stool. A small iron stove for cooking and warmth. Alem crawled under the cot, pried up the floorboard where old Nard the stable master kept the little strongbox. Alem wasn't sure how many coins might be in it. Probably not many. When visiting nobles lodged their horses in the stable, they would often flip the stable master a coin to pay for extra oats, replace a lost horse blanket.

Nard's going to be pissed when he finds his money missing.

No, Alem realized. He wouldn't. Nard was dead. He was old but in good health and they would have shoved a sword into his hand and sent him to the wall. He would be dead like so many others.

Alem bashed the strongbox against the iron stove until he sprang the cheap lock. He spilled the coins out onto the cot and counted them. Fourteen copper coins, but the real score was the two silver pieces. From his belt he took his small leather purse, which contained only a single copper, one he'd been hoarding for months. He added the coins from the strongbox and retied the purse tightly to his belt.

It struck him that he was making a life decision. This would be a pivotal point in his very small, very predictable existence. First, he'd need to live through the next twenty minutes. The clang of crossing swords no longer reached him from the street, but people were fighting and dying beyond the walls of the stable.

He remembered the Perranese captain. He'd broken his neck. *They're dying in here too.*

So in the unlikely event he lived to the end of the day, it would be only the beginning. Where would he go? How would he live?

He had no answers. If he wanted to live, he'd have to leave behind everything he'd ever known.

He grabbed Nard's spare riding cloak from the peg near the door. It was ugly and patched but thick and warm. It smelled like Nard's pipe tobacco.

Alem walked out of Nard's room and froze. Another Perranese warrior, his back to Alem, stood in full armor, holding a sword. Alem's stomach lurched. He wouldn't even make it out of the stable. He'd spent his life here. Now he would die here.

The man in the armor turned. Tosh's face grinned at him from under the broad helm. "I got an idea."

CHAPTER ELEVEN

Rina stepped out of the tub. As soon as she hit the cold air, her skin broke out in gooseflesh. She stood dripping on the cold stone floor of the chamber. The mage had his back to her, pulling a leather-bound book off a low shelf along with a collection of arcane implements Rina didn't recognize.

She began to shiver. "I'm wet."

He glanced at her with his good eye. "You can't use a towel. Your skin must be perfectly clean, and I won't risk lint or stray threads. Stand near the fire, but not too close. You can't sweat either."

She stood just close enough to the brazier to feel the warmth, beads of water tickling as they rolled down her skin. At first she'd felt self-conscious standing naked in front of the old man, but he was obviously uninterested. The mage bent over one of his old books, squinting at the magical writing.

Her skin warmed, and she took a step back from the fire. She watched him pull a chair up next to a small table. He laid out various small objects she didn't recognize, plus a small vase of clear glass, dark liquid within. He lined up other materials like he was preparing to cook some obscure recipe.

He is a mage, after all. That's what they do, I guess; potions and so on. And it struck her suddenly that this old man could be up to anything. She didn't even know his name.

She turned to dry her other side. She couldn't see him now, and that somehow unnerved her. The chamber was dark, the brazier having burned low.

She cleared her throat. "What are you doing?"

He made a low noise in his throat, dislodging a wad of phlegm. "What do you know of magic?"

Rina considered a moment. There were stories, of course. Tales of magic splitting oceans in two, dark wizards bringing down the stars to destroy a city, seductive sorceresses twisting kings into knots with charms dripping from honeyed tongues. But they were only stories, and which sprang from some grain of truth and which were utter fancy she couldn't say.

"Nothing," Rina said. "I don't know anything about magic."

The old man snorted. "Then how shall I explain? Where to start?"

"The fire to warm the bath," she said quickly. "You lit it from across the room. That was magic, yes?"

"Yes, okay. We'll start there. What did you see?"

"You held out your hand," Rina said. "And the fire sprang to life."

A low chuckle. "I'm a mage, not one of the gods. What did you see? Details, please. The demons are ever in the details."

She closed her eyes, replayed the scene in her mind. "You released some kind of powder."

"And?"

"Words," Rina said. "They sounded clear but then sped by quickly. I can't remember any of them."

"It takes discipline to hold those words in your mind, Duchess. It can get crowded between your ears. A journeyman wizard can hold four or five spells. More than that and the brain gets mud-dled, starts hearing voices that aren't real. A master might hold eight or ten. They say the Blue Wizard of The Lakes held more than a dozen, all chattering and running around in his brain. More than one mage has lost his mind trying to cram in too many. Those spells want *out*. It takes a strong mind to keep them *in*."

Rina's back grew hot, and she stepped away from the fire. "How many can your mind hold?"

The old man made a noncommittal noise. A pause. "Not enough. Never enough to make a difference." He coughed and something rattled in his chest. "Never mind. It doesn't matter now. I'm an old man in a cave. I'll give you the last of my magic, Duchess. Come. You're dry now."

She turned and saw him sitting hunched and gray in the chair. He looked bad, skin sallow and slick, dark circles under his eyes. He was deteriorating rapidly. The shock must have shown on Rina's face.

"I told you I was keeping the sickness at bay," he said. "Now that I'm no longer fighting it, it's come rushing in, making up for lost time. I—" He coughed again, stronger this time, racking his whole body.

"Never mind." He gestured her forward. "Come closer. Within arm's reach."

As she approached, she glanced at the little table next to his chair. He'd laid out the spell book alongside a line of thin, metal instruments. Some looked pointy, and a flutter of nerves twisted Rina's stomach.

"Damn you, what is *that?*"Anger flared in his good eye. He rubbed a finger along the shallow gash in her side, and Rina winced. "This wound is fresh."

"During the escape," she said.

"Your skin needs to be completely clean and blemish free." The irritation was plain in his voice.

"I didn't get myself slashed just to annoy you, okay?" It wasn't a deep wound, but it *hurt*.

"Shut up, girl. I'm thinking."

She opened her mouth to shoot something back at him, closed it again. Maybe she was learning.

"Yes, yes, that might work to our advantage after all." He chuckled dryly, which turned into another fit of racking coughs.

He composed himself, stood. "Wait here." He went to the shelf and returned with a fat jar the size of a teacup, seated himself again.

"Turn around."

She turned.

A second later she felt his hand slather something on the wound, like goose grease. Immediately, a warmth spread out from the wound, the hot sting of the sword-gash fading.

"A healing balm," the mage told her.

She thought about the little vial Kork had tossed her during the rescue. "Is it the same as the healing elixirs, the kind you drink?"

"Most of the same ingredients, yes. But elixirs work fast. The balm works slowly, more appropriate for what I have in mind. I'm getting a little inventive. This will either work out very well for you or ruin the entire process. We'll see, I suppose. Now kneel."

"Kneel?"

"I need to work on your back and shoulders, and be damned if I'm going to stand for the whole thing. I'm too old, and this will take some time. Kneel."

She knelt. The rough, stone floor dug into her knees, but she kept still, heard him flipping pages in the book behind her. "You still haven't told me what you're going to do."

"I'm going to give you a tattoo."

She frowned. "You mean like sailors have?" She'd seen them before, fanciful illustrations of mermaids and sea dragons.

"Yes," the old man said. "And no."

Yeah, that's informative.

"The principle is the same," he said. "But crassly decorating yourself is not the goal."

"I … I don't know if I want a tattoo," Rina said.

The old mage sighed extravagantly. "You arrived here, orphaned, with nothing but the rags on your back. Foreigners have overrun your land, and where you go from here is anyone's guess. I have doomed myself merely discussing this with you. What say we throw caution to the wind and get a tattoo today, Duchess, or do you have better offers?"

"I'm sorry," she said. "How is it done?"

"Needles," he said. "To insert the ink under the skin. Although we'll be using quite a bit more than ink, I can assure you."

Needles? "Will it—" She swallowed. "Will it hurt?"

A pause too long for comfort. "Yes. Very much."

CHAPTER TWELVE

At a distance, the disguise worked. A Perranese warrior on one horse, leading a captive on another.

Up close was a different story.

Tosh didn't have the narrow eyes or the saffron skin of the Perranese, but he tried to sit straight and haughty in the saddle. Perranese foot patrols who spotted them down side streets merely saluted from a distance and kept going. Alem rode with his wrists together in front of him, rope wrapped around loosely to give the appearance they were bound. When Perranese soldiers looked like they might come too close, Tosh would veer off down another path. In this way, they zigzagged toward the city gate, often turning in the opposite direction and having to circle around again.

Snow fell. It was cold.

Alem leaned forward in his saddle to speak low to Tosh ahead of him. "This is taking forever."

Tosh frowned back at him. "If you have a better idea, I'm all ears."

Alem did not have a better idea.

The plan, as Alem understood it, was to use the disguise to make it to one of the city gates and then do ... something.

Thinking about it now, in the battle-torn streets of Klaar, Alem realized it was a completely and utterly *terrible* plan. He supposed they'd figured to sneak through the gate in some way, but Alem couldn't imagine how. Occasionally, he'd spot a citizen of Klaar darting furtively among the rubble, but most of the city's population was in hiding. Most members of the army or militia were dead. Three times, they came across a scattering of bodies where the men of Klaar had turned to make a stand only to be cut down by the swarming invaders.

They reined in the horses under the tattered awning at the entrance of a burned-out shop, the shadows offering some slight concealment and cover from the snow. Alem almost didn't recognize that he was at the wide square just inside the city's front gate. On any normal day, the square would be filled with carts and stands, peddlers hawking wares, the healthy bustle of commerce.

Now the stands and carts had been cleared away so the Perranese army could use the square as a staging area. A steady line of troops trudged in through the open front gate. Many pulled carts piled with enough goods and supplies to suggest a long stay. Perranese troops also led occasional groups of captured Klaarians. Alem didn't recognize any of them. Maybe they'd been gathered from the low-lying villages.

Alem felt a stab of concern for his grandmother. He hoped the Perranese would leave an obviously harmless old woman alone, but he couldn't quite convince himself. The invaders didn't quite seem evil, but they did go about their business with a ruthless efficiency. If they'd been ordered to clear the villages, Alem doubted they would make exceptions.

"Are we just going to sit here until they notice us?" Alem whispered.

"We're waiting," Tosh said.

"For what?"

"I don't know, okay?" Tosh said. "Just be ready to ride like the blazes if I give the signal. *Can* you ride?"

"I can ride. Don't worry about me." Alem had spent all his life around horses. When on a hunt, invariably some fat noble's ass would get saddle sore, and Alem would be picked to ride the horse back to the stable. He always took the long way back, riding the forest and mountain trails of Klaar. Yes, he could ride. He could ride like the bloody wind.

They waited.

Ten minutes became twenty and then half an hour. The square appeared to be controlled by a bull of a Perranese sergeant, head bald except for a glossy black topknot that swung like a whip whenever he turned his head to shout at another group of men. If the men marched through the front gate too slowly, he shouted at them. Too fast, and he shouted at them. If he needed them to halt so a troop column could march past, he shouted at them. Nobody in the Perranese army seemed to be doing anything exactly to his satisfaction.

So when a cart piled high with furs (no doubt confiscated from the outlying trapper villages) lost a wheel, and the cart tipped directly in front of the city gate, the sergeant shouted with redoubled ire at the culprits. He stormed toward the cart, gesticulating and yelling. Alem didn't need to speak the language to understand that blocking the flow of traffic into and out of the city gate was the single thing most likely to inflame the sergeant's fury.

At the sergeant's angry gestures, the Perranese guards who'd been holding spears and standing at attention on either side of the gate bolted from their posts to assist in righting the cart. All of their backs were to Alem and Tosh.

"Now!" Tosh spurred his mount forward.

"What?"

Alem hesitated only a split second, digging his heels into the gelding's side, the horse leaping after Tosh.

In a flash, Alem saw what Tosh was doing. The broken-down cart might be the only distraction they were going to get, and the guards had left the gate. There was a gap just big enough beside the damaged cart for a single horse and rider to fit through.

The gelding was a better horse than the fat mare Tosh had selected, and Alem passed them within a second. The thundering hooves on the square's cobblestones drew the attention of the Perranese, who turned as one to gawk. Alem passed stunned expressions in a blur as he shot through the narrow gap and beyond.

The crowd on the other side scattered as the horse erupted from the gate.

Alem neared the Long Bridge and saw that Perranese organizational skills had worked in his favor. All of the incoming traffic had been moved to the left side of the bridge to allow clear passage for the outgoing. He leaned low, spurring the horse onward as fast as it would go. The horse pounded past the line of soldiers and incoming carts; heads turned as it passed, nobody quite understanding what was happening or lifting a finger to stop him.

He sped past the end of the bridge, heart threatening to thump out of his chest. He hadn't felt a spear or an arrow in his back. Not yet.

The Perranese camp was a hundred yards ahead. Many of the invaders had moved into the city, but there were still many tents and soldiers ahead of him. If they could catch the camp by surprise, ride past them suddenly like they had at the gate, they might just have a chance. Horses were in short supply, so it was unlikely the Perranese could give chase.

Alem allowed himself to hope.

But the guards at the edge of the camp exploded into activity at his approach, pointing at him and running to intercept. Evidently the Perranese were not keen on letting an unidentified horseman streak through their midst at full speed. If they'd drawn swords to kill him, Alem would be dead, but the soldiers ran at him empty-handed.

He veered from a trio of sprinting soldiers coming fast from his left, but that allowed the one approaching from his right to make a grab at him. It looked like they wanted to capture him alive, and Alem felt a hand on his calf, yanking at him.

Alem's foot came up out of reflex, flattened the warrior's nose. Alem felt the cartilage snap under his heel, and the warrior went down in a spray of blood. He jerked the reins and battered another warrior aside with the horse as he turned for the clearest path through the camp.

The first arrow passed within an inch of his face.

They weren't trying to take him alive anymore.

He was in the middle of the tent rows now, dodging along the narrow pathways, between cooking fires and startled warriors.

Alem rounded a large tent, desperately looking for open ground, and ran into a dozen warriors with swords drawn. The gelding reared, a hoof flailing and crushing the skull of a lead warrior, helm flying off with a metallic *clang*. More arrows flew past him.

I'm going to die!

Alem pulled the reins hard, and the gelding turned sharply into one of the open tents. Perranese warriors scattered camp chairs as they leapt for spears. The gelding bucked in a panic, back hooves flying out to crush another soldier with a sick crunch as both armor and bones beneath were crushed.

He spurred the horse out of the tent, knocking aside more warriors, flinching back from a sword swing that came within a hair's width of his nose.

Alem galloped around another tent, and the horse balked at a low wooden fence in the way. A hasty corral had been erected to pen in a dozen goats. He wheeled the horse to return the way he'd come.

Two dozen Perranese spread out in front of him. They'd wised up, choosing to advance slowly with long pikes, attempting to pin him against the goat corral. Alem turned the horse again, kicked it forward as hard as he could, leaning low. How many times had he practiced jumping fences?

Zero times. I have never jumped anything. You are going to break your neck, idiot.

He came to the fence.

The gelding jumped.

Horse and rider came down hard amid the panicked and bleating goats. Alem came out of the saddle and back down again hard, jarring his tailbone all the way up to his skull. He flung himself forward to grab the horse's neck and almost lost his grip when the gelding jumped the fence on the other side of the corral.

He came down hard again, a foot coming out of one stirrup. Only grabbing a fistful of the horse's mane kept him from bouncing out of the saddle. He righted himself and rode fast. He was beyond the camp now, galloping down the forest road to the lowlands.

Alem glanced back. No pursuit. He laughed in giddy relief. He exhaled raggedly, felt almost dizzy. *I'm not going to die.* He saw an arrow stuck in the material of his cloak under the arm. Another near miss. He started laughing again.

It was only then he realized Tosh wasn't with him.

CHAPTER THIRTEEN

A t first, the pinpricks felt like hot fly bites down the soft white skin over her spine and along her shoulders.

The first time Rina flinched, the mage had admonished her harshly. She hadn't moved again.

Her knees hurt on the rough stone. Her muscles ached. The mage worked the needle behind her, sewing his strange magic into her flesh. A slow fire built under her skin, along her backbone, growing warm and uncomfortable. His rough hands worked steadily. He paused to cough, making a sick noise in his throat, then went back to work.

Rina already regretted her decision. Each jab with the needle felt hotter and deeper, the fire down the center of her back growing more intense.

"I'm going to talk to you." The mage's voice had grown rough and weak in the past hour. "This will take your mind off the discomfort, perhaps, but it's also information you need to know. Don't answer back or move. Save your questions for later."

Rina clenched her teeth. *Discomfort*, he'd called it.

"People think magic involves calling forth something from nothing." He coughed. "It's not. Remember the pinch of brimstone."

She pictured it, the mage flicking a pinch of the powder when he lit the fire for the bath water.

"You must have an essence of the thing you wish to control or create," he said. "It is one of the fundamentals of magic."

Rina felt his hands lift from her back. "You can ... talk a moment now ... if you like. But keep still." He sounded out of breath.

"I thought the words of the spell created the magic," she said.

"That's the mage talking to the universe, telling it what to do." He coughed. Cleared his throat. "Instructions."

She wasn't exactly sure what he meant.

The old man must have correctly interpreted her silence. "The tattoo relieves you of the responsibility of speaking the language of the universe. The words will be written into your flesh with ink and the other materials, the essence of the magic you will soon control."

His next fit of coughing was so violent she almost turned to help him.

He gasped for breath, mastered himself. "I am running out of time. If you have a final question, ask now."

Her mind raced. "But how can I ... how does it ...?"

"Quiet yourself. Think."

She drew in a breath, let it out slowly. "You said magic wasn't getting something for nothing. That it didn't work that way."

"Ah, very good, Duchess." He sounded pleased. "I will work while I answer. Be still."

She felt his dry, gnarled hands on her back again.

"There is always a price," he said. "You won't need to study a book of conjuring, won't have to memorize complex spells. But the universe demands payment. Always."

The magical heat along Rina's back burned fiercely.

"When you use your powers, Duchess, you pay that price from some store within you," he said. "You tap into ... well, wizards have been arguing for centuries about what to call it. Your willpower. Some say you are spending your soul, although that always seemed melodramatic to me." A cough. "Let's call it your spirit, eh? Every time you use this magic, you tap into your spirit. The more spirit you have the better. But you can use it up. You can kill yourself spending all your spirit. Ink mages did it all the time during the Empire Wars, burned themselves out. Oh, you will be tested, Duchess. When you're in the frenzy of battle and the spirit has you in its grip, then you'll know. Will you control it, or will it control you? I hope you have the will to turn it off. To step away."

He withdrew his hands as he was racked with a fit of coughing, but Rina's concern for the old man's health faded into the background of her thoughts. She was afraid, terrified of the terrible gift he was giving her. How could this be what Father had wanted for her?

The old man sucked in a ragged breath. "Listen to me. There's not much time now. This tattoo I'm inking is just the start. It is the key. There are others like me, others who know the secrets of the ink mage. They may have different stencils, can give you different powers. Seek them out."

He coughed again, and this time moaned in pain afterward. When he spoke again, his voice sounded like dry sticks dragged over gravel.

"So much ... to tell you." He kept working the needle into her flesh. "I may have done something special for you here." He prodded the healed wound on her side with bony fingers. "The healing balm might have fused with the ink magic. It is ... an experiment. Time will tell if it works. I won't be around to see it. A pity. I do take pride in my craft. I should like to have known."

Rina sensed him shifting behind her, his hands now on her shoulder. "I can go you one extra, I think. Yes, there is time. There *must* be time."

The needle hot across her shoulder. She sensed urgency in his hands.

"Your sword arm," he said. "This is for strength. I'm mixing bull's blood with the ink. Ogre's blood would be better, but one must make do." He uttered more unintelligible syllables, which danced briefly in her ears and then vanished. Her shoulder flared hot.

She heard his chair creak behind her. "It ... is finished."

Rina's body hummed with raw power, slow at first but expanding rapidly to fill up every part of her.

"You feel it ... don't you?" He coughed again, his voice now barely a whisper. "The power. You've tapped into the spirit."

Rina felt calm. The fire down her spine, the pain of her knees on the hard cave floor, the ache in her muscles—it was all still there, but merely as facts. She was apart from it. It was as if she was aware—and in control—of every part of herself.

"The spirit," the old man repeated. "You can run without fatigue. Cold will not touch you, nor heat, nor fear. But you spend spirit every second. How deep your well might be isn't for me to say. Beware, Duchess, for you are still human. You must eat and sleep and refill what you drain from the well."

Rina banished the cold. Her muscles no longer ached because she told them not to. She forbade her knees to feel pain.

"There is a wizard named Talbun who lives on the edge of the Nomad Lands," the mage told her. "Talbun knows the secret of the tattoos. Few wizards do. Talbun owes me a favor and might be persuaded to help you."

And Rina knew already she would go to the Nomad Lands and find the wizard Talbun and add to her power. In her mind, she pictured the map of Helva in her father's study. The Nomad Lands were west and south. She saw the map perfectly, every detail, even the purple ring where her father had set a goblet of wine on the map's corner.

She would gather power, and she would return. She would kill Giffen herself. There was no passion in this thought. It was simply a fact. With complete clarity she knew how she would swing the sword, where it would catch Giffen in the neck, how it would look when his decapitated head flew through the air.

Rina would reclaim Klaar, however long it took. Whatever might stand in her way.

The first step was Talbun. The journey would be long. She remembered that she did not know the old man's name.

"Mage, tell me your name." Her voice was calm and strong.

She heard a sound behind her, a hiss of breath like a rapier slowly sliding back into its scabbard.

"Mage, your name. So I can tell Talbun who sent me."

Nothing.

She turned.

The old man sat limp in the chair, dead.

CHAPTER FOURTEEN

Tosh had fallen off his horse.

That's what he realized as he sprawled on the cobblestones, shaking the bells out of his ears. The foreign helmet had kept him from completely bashing his brains out. He propped himself up on one elbow in time to see his mare trotting away. It took him a moment to remember how he'd ended up like this.

Oh, yeah. That stable boy. Alem. He'd sped past him and through the front gate. That had caused an uproar, and a Perranese soldier had stepped right in front of Tosh. The mare he'd been riding had reared and tossed him off. Tosh had landed hard, but he checked himself now and seemed not to have suffered serious injury.

He had to get up and move. The Perranese warriors were still gawking out the gate at a rapidly escaping Alem, and the big, angry sergeant was berating the guard who'd let him pass. But soon they'd turn their attention to the dumbass who'd fallen off his horse. Tosh scrambled to his feet, trying not to hurry or look out of place, turning his face from the crowd. In the corner of his vision, he could see a warrior grabbing his mare by the reins.

So much for reclaiming his mount. He couldn't let any of them see his face.

He walked toward an alley which led away from the square. He expected one of the warriors to call after him, or to feel an arrow hit his back, but he kept going and rounded the corner without incident. Tosh blew out a sigh of relief. Even in this cold weather he felt beads of sweat rolling down his back. He was safe, but only for the moment.

Okay. Time for a new plan.

He retreated from the main gate by a different route, using the same strategy as before, letting the Perranese armor disguise him from a distance and turning aside when he spied somebody who might get close enough to see his face clearly. It was more difficult on foot.

Tosh wondered at what point the disguise would do more harm than good. It would just be his luck to be knifed in the back by one of his overly patriotic fellow citizens. But for the time being, the Perranese ruled the streets, and he would keep the armor.

He still needed someplace to go.

He headed east, walking steadily for thirty minutes until he hit a shabby neighborhood of inexpensive homes built up against the city's outer wall. Known simply as East Side, it wasn't Klaar's worst neighborhood, but it was close. The place was crowded with the city's working poor, an occasional beggar or pickpocket thrown into the mix to keep things colorful. It wasn't a knife-in-the-back sort of neighborhood like Backgate, but it was still not the kind of place to walk through late at night, unarmed, with a fat coin purse jingling from your belt.

Backgate. Huh. That gave Tosh an idea.

The narrow lane along the city wall curved all the way south to Backgate. It was a longer walk than cutting across the city center but probably safer. The neighborhood was quiet, and he hadn't heard the distant sounds of battle in a while. The Perranese must have swept away the last of the resistance. He wondered how many of his fellow soldiers now lay dead, some he'd known for years. How many innocent civilians had been caught in the violence and killed? It would take a while for Klaar to put itself back together again, and with the Perranese as their new masters, the city would likely never be the same again.

He kept walking, twice ducking into shadows when Perranese patrols passed at the double march. He heard them coming a fair distance off, armor and weapons rattling. He wondered if that was the purpose, a way to signal to the people of East Side that there were armed enemies in the streets, so stay indoors or get killed.

The shabby homes of East Side eventually gave way to the sheer dilapidation of Backgate. Abandoned buildings with doors kicked in, some charred husks gutted by fire. Except the buildings weren't all really abandoned. The dregs of the city haunted Backgate—beggars, the insane, cutthroats, confidence tricksters, fugitives. Backgate wasn't a large neighborhood, and Klaar considered it an acceptable solution to set aside this one barrel for all its rotten apples.

There were two reasonably safe places in Backgate, and on another night, Tosh might be here to visit the first, the Wounded Bird, which was Klaar's most popular brothel. The proprietors of the whorehouse sent a clear signal to the denizens of Backgate that any illegal activity in and around the immediate area of the Wounded Bird that might frighten off paying customers would result in the garroting of those who perpetrated said illegal activity.

Tosh passed the Wounded Bird with a longing sigh. He was on his way to the other safe place in Backgate which was, of course, the gate itself.

He pressed himself flat against the rock wall of a half-caved-in building and peeked around the corner at the guardhouse adjacent to the gate. Tosh remembered it as being a cushy posting a few years ago, partly because of the gate's proximity to the Wounded Bird, but also because duty at the back gate had been fairly easy. A squad of soldiers led by a sergeant, they had each taken turns walking the guard post over the gate while the others tossed dice and smoked pipes in the guardhouse. In the year Tosh had been posted there, they'd opened the back gate exactly once for a wandering fur trapper who'd trudged up the Small Road with a bad case of frostbite.

Unlike the front gate, the back gate admitted no commerce, no traders or wagons going to market, no visiting royalty, nothing, and Tosh had mused more than once that a lack of all such activity might be the reason the Backgate neighborhood was an utter ruin, completely deserted except for criminals and prostitutes.

Tosh wasn't optimistic. He clung to some shred of hope that in the confusion of battle, maybe the Perranese hadn't gotten to the back gate yet. No such luck. A half-dozen soldiers in the livery of Klaar lay dead in the street before the guardhouse. Smoke rose from the guardhouse's chimney. The new tenants had taken over. Tosh looked up. Two Perranese guards passed each other on the parapet walkway atop the gate wall. The gate itself was shut tight and barred.

So the back gate was guarded. Tosh didn't really have much hope it would be otherwise. But there were far fewer Perranese troops here than at the front gate, so maybe he could cobble together some kind of plan. Possibly he could get over the wall under cover of night, but that would put him in the middle of the frozen, inhospitable wilderness. He'd need travel furs, food, a fire-starting kit. It would take preparation. So okay. He'd prepare.

He wished he could get his hands on a map to plan his route once he was over the wall. Once things calmed down a bit, maybe he could get on the roof of one of the structures built up against the other wall. From there he could reach the top and climb over. Not all the dilapidated buildings looked safe enough to climb on, but a few seemed okay if he were careful enough to—

Tosh pulled back, watched a Perranese warrior emerge from the guardhouse, stretch and yawn and take in some fresh air. Tosh had done the same thing himself many times. With a bunch of sweaty men smoking and belching and farting in the small guardhouse ... well, even on the coldest days he had found the need to go outside for a breather.

A beggar in rags shambled past, paused at the Perranese warrior with an open palm. The beggar was either very brave or simply had nothing to lose. *There's always more to lose*, Tosh thought. But the warrior didn't run the beggar through with his sword. He did what almost everyone does when a beggar approaches with his hand out. The warrior shook his head, gestured the beggar away dismissively before turning back to the warmth of the guardhouse.

The beggar resumed his shamble.

Seemed like the Perranese were already in occupy mode. Leastways, they weren't hacking down random citizens. Tosh decided it was time to abandon the armor and blend in with the rest of the Klaarian people. As long as he wasn't wearing the military livery, he'd probably be okay.

He looked about. The street was clear.

Tosh dashed across the street to a narrow alley. He rounded the corner where there was a small open space between a building and the city wall. He sniffed and wrinkled his nose, the acrid smell of urine almost making him gag. He eyed the muddy slash in the ground along the city wall with mild revulsion. Evidently, the guardhouse soldiers had relocated their piss trench since Tosh had been stationed here.

He tried to ignore the stench, rapidly unbuckling the foreign armor, fingers fumbling with the unfamiliar straps.

Footfalls in the mud, the clank of armor. Somebody approaching.

Tosh considered the Perranese sword hanging at his side but immediately discarded the idea. He'd never trained with the weapon, and anyway, he had a better blade for close-quarter fighting. He pulled the ten-inch dagger, held his breath and waited.

A second later, a Perranese warrior rounded the corner, scale mail skirt parted in front, breeches open, his pecker in his hand. Tosh was already thrusting the dagger, and the warrior's eyes shot wide, his other hand coming up fast to catch Tosh's wrist.

He's quick! Even with one hand full of his own genitalia, the warrior had almost negated Tosh's advantage of surprise.

Tosh twisted, brought his knee up hard into the man's exposed groin. The warrior grunted, the air going out of him, but didn't release Tosh's wrist.

They grappled, and Tosh felt the heel of his boot skid along the mud, both of them going down in a heap. Tosh tried to roll on top and bring the dagger to bear, but they kept rolling.

Into the piss trench.

Tosh ended up on top, pushed the warrior's head down into the urine-soaked mud. The warrior's other hand came out of the mud and latched onto Tosh's throat. Tosh grabbed the pinky finger of the hand choking him, bent it back. At this point, most men would let go. The Perranese didn't. The finger snapped. Tosh had to break the next finger too before the man released his hold.

The warrior's helmet had shifted back on his head. Tosh leaned forward, smashed his forehead into the warrior's nose, flattening it and splattering mud, blood and urine. That took the rest of the fight out of him, and the warrior released Tosh's wrist.

Tosh plunged the dagger into his neck where there was no armor. Blood gushed. He pulled the dagger out, stabbed again; the warrior's body quivered under him. Another stab. Again.

The warrior went stiff then eased into death, lying quiet and half-submerged in the mud.

Tosh rolled off him, climbed the bank of the shallow trench and kneeled there panting, covered in filth and blood.

He looked up into the pale face of a little girl.

Tosh blinked. She blinked back.

She was maybe eight years old, face smudged, fine blonde hair blowing in the icy wind. She looked at him blankly with huge blue eyes. Her clothes were far too thin for the cold, and she clutched a tattered rag doll to her chest.

Tosh looked from his bloody dagger, back to the little girl. "Uh ... hey. It's okay. That was a bad man. He—"

She turned and ran without a word.

That's just fucking fantastic.

He looked down at himself. He was a disgusting mess. He finished unstrapping the Perranese armor. He tossed it through the open window of an abandoned building.

He glanced back at the dead warrior in the piss trench.

Hell and damnation.

Eventually, another warrior would come for a piss, and when they saw their fallen comrade they'd put Backgate into an uproar looking for the murderer. The last thing Tosh needed was troops swarming the neighborhood while he was trying to arrange his escape from the city.

He stepped back into the piss trench, sinking past his ankles into the mud. He reached under the dead warrior's armpits, up to his own shoulders in filth. He dragged the warrior out of the trench and over to the window where he'd stashed the armor. Tosh would need a bath and a change of clothes immediately. Smelling himself almost made him retch.

He heaved the corpse into the window, but it stuck at the waist, legs dangling limply. Tosh shoved. *Get in there, you dead bastard.*

Tosh was shoving for all he was worth when the two men came around the corner. One was as wide as a hay barn, muscles bulging under his clothes, a wide bald head like a melon and a flat nose. His thighs were as thick as brandy casks.

The other man was bigger.

Both held cudgels in tight fists.

The little girl stood in front of them and pointed an accusing finger at Tosh. "There he is!"

CHAPTER FIFTEEN

Rina felt the old mage's wrist for a pulse, confirmed his demise. She noted it coolly, realized in some objective way that she might have a more emotional response to it later.

It was time to leave.

She walked to the tub where she'd bathed earlier, felt like she was floating. The power hummed along her limbs, pulsed deep within her. Rina welcomed the hot fire down her spine. It felt like strength. It was hers to direct and control.

She looked down at her discarded clothes next to the tub, soiled and ripped. They wouldn't do, but she needed something to wear. The cold couldn't touch her, but she couldn't go back among people in the raw. Drawing that kind of attention would be ... counterproductive.

Kork's cloak was blood splattered but still in relatively good shape. It was a quality garment made of fine, heavy cloth. She picked it up, draped it loosely over one shoulder.

The cave now seemed like something from a dream, an illusion, as if she could wave her hand and it would all swirl away like smoke. The world turned around her like something unsubstantial, unimportant, like Rina herself was the only thing solid, real, the sum total of everything that existed. And yet at the same time, the cave was more vivid. She saw every pebble on the floor, every crack in the wall, a drop of water from the ceiling falling, landing.

Rina found herself at the mouth of the cave with only a vague memory of getting there. She looked down at Kork. The snowfall came gently now, puffy flakes drifting by on a light breeze. The valley spread out below her like a white wonderland, the city of Klaar distant and deceptively peaceful.

Kork still slouched against the cave wall. He would never rise again. His skin had gone gray, and a pool of blood spread from where he sat, a frosting of snow where the blood puddle had reached the mouth of the cave. The hand holding his side was completely red. His wounds had been far worse than Rina had realized earlier. He'd never said a word.

He looked up at her with eyes as old as the world. "You saw him?"

"Yes." She'd spoken softly, but it had sounded loud in her mind, like her voice would fill up the sky if she wanted it to.

Kork nodded, a sigh leaking out of him, long and final.

With his other hand he reached for his sword, dragged it toward him with stiff fingers. He couldn't make his hand close around the hilt. "Take … take it."

She bent, took the sword, lifted it one-handed. It seemed to weigh no more than her rapier now.

He watched her with the sword, nodded again, approving. "R-Rina …"

She watched the light go out of his eyes. One moment Kork was there, and then he wasn't. Just like that the final connection to her old life had been stripped away.

Grief rushed in so quickly that it almost broke through to touch her. But she'd tapped into the spirit. Felt the power of it pulsing through her. Rina told grief to wait until later. If she allowed it in now, she'd collapse beneath the weight of it.

She looked one last time at Kork. She wanted to remember his face, to remember this moment, so she could add it to her list of grievances against Giffen, a personal litany of hatred.

Rina left the cave, flakes falling silently around her, and began her descent, bare feet crunching in the snow.

The howls drew her attention. *Wolves?* No, these were more like guttural wails than howls. Up this high in the mountains it could only be snow devils. The creatures were the reason most trappers didn't venture to this altitude.

She lifted her sword, counting calmly as she watched them come through the mist from below, three of them coming up the stairs, loping apelike, running half hunched over, using their arms, snarling and snapping.

Two more coming down the steep slope to her left. A full hunter pack.

She dropped Kork's cloak so it wouldn't tangle her up, spread her arms, held her sword high in one of the basic stances Kork had taught her to receive an attack from multiple foes.

She wondered idly what their blood would look like on the clean, white snow.

CHAPTER SIXTEEN

"Tell us again how you killed him in the piss trench," the little girl said.

"No," said one of the prostitutes, the big redhead. "Tell us again about falling off the horse at the front gate. I like a good laugh."

All the whores gathered around laughed at that. They seemed eager to laugh, needed it.

This room in the brothel looked like any other tavern he'd ever patronized: rough wooden tables, a long bar along one wall and a big roaring fireplace. Another place where the establishment could separate clients from their coin while they waited for their turn with one of the women.

Tosh tilted the flagon back, drained the beer, wiped the foam from his mouth with the back of his hand and belched. "Ladies, ladies, never fear. I will give a full account again for any latecomers. Only too happy to share my adventures with such gracious hosts." He shrugged, smiled sheepishly. "But it is thirsty work."

Another cold flagon appeared instantly on the table in front of him.

Tosh drank deeply, wondering if he were going to wake up and find out this was all a dream. The little girl was the daughter of one of the whores—which one again? The faces and names were beginning to blur, but he thought the little girl was the daughter of the skinny blonde with the enormous blue eyes. They fed him, let him wash and change out of his muddy, urine-soaked clothes. But it was more than simple hospitality.

The women of the Wounded Bird were treating Tosh like he was some kind of hero.

One might not think of whores as patriotic, but they were every bit as much citizens of Klaar as was Tosh, and they'd watched furtively through the cracks in shuttered windows as the Perranese troops had swept through Backgate. Many of the fallen were regular customers of the girls of the Wounded Bird, men they had known and serviced for years. Helpless women save for the two enormous bruisers with cudgels Tosh had met earlier. They were a pair of brothers and served as the brothel's bouncers. He'd forgotten their names as well.

He drank half the beer in a gulp.

So the Perranese were not loved at the Wounded Bird. In the minds of the prostitutes, Tosh's desperate act of self-defense against a lone Perranese warrior who'd merely wanted to relieve himself was nothing less than a defense of the honor of Backgate itself. Or at least that's how it seemed to Tosh, the way the women were fussing over him. It may simply have been that the brothel was empty of patrons, many of whom now lay dead in the streets. And now here was Tosh, a soldier of Klaar, fighting for their pride.

Sort of.

He decided to retell the bit about falling off the horse. That seemed to be a crowd-pleaser, and he launched into it with the enthusiasm of a carnival jester. He exaggerated his clumsiness this time, the terror of the incident almost forgotten after four flagons of beer. When he told about crawling along the ground after the horse had thrown him, he pantomimed covering his head with his arms, his ass sticking high in the air as he scooted along. The women clapped and laughed.

Another mug of beer appeared.

During a lull in the laughter, a lean, hawkish brunette with a shawl wrapped around herself leaned in and asked, "Did you happen to pass the guard station on Temple Street?"

The others turned to her, and she lowered her head, embarrassed. "My … my brother is posted there."

Then he's dead. "I'm sorry. I didn't pass Temple Street."

That started them all talking at once.

"Did you see Tailor's Row? My uncle—"

"My sister lives in East Side—"

"Was Boar's Head hit hard? I have friends who—"

"My aunt is a maid in one of the manor houses on High Point—"

"My father—"

"My cousin—"

"My priest—"

"Okay, that's enough," said the blonde whom Tosh had identified as the little girl's mother. "Let the poor man be."

Tosh was grateful. Reality had come crashing back down on him, the earlier whimsy obliterated. He felt suddenly exhausted. He sipped the last of the beer slowly. "I'm sorry, ladies. I guess I don't really know too much."

"I just wonder if they'll shut us down." The brunette pulled the shawl tighter around her. "They'll get around to us sooner or later."

"They won't," the blonde said. "Armies need brothels. Even foreign savages."

"Don't know if I like the idea of that," spoke up a chubby one with frizzy hair. "Men folk from strange lands might have odd … needs. All perverted like."

"What's it matter which sweaty bastard is riding you?" said the red head. "Long as he pays up."

That set off everyone talking at once again, speculating about living under Perranese rule and giving detailed accounts of just exactly what some men expected for their money, which made Tosh squirm in his seat. He felt a hand on his shoulder and looked up into the face of the blonde.

"You must be tired."

"Yes."

"Darshia will show you to a room," she said. "You can rest. You've earned it."

The red-haired woman led him away from the others, down a dim hallway. *Darshia, the redhead's name is Darshia.*

She opened a door and gestured him inside.

The room was small but clean, a double bed with a small nightstand and a whale oil lamp next to it. He pulled off his boots, thought about removing the rest of his clothes, decided he didn't have the energy and fell face first onto the bed. It was soft. Fresh sheets. He heard the door click shut, raised himself on one elbow and turned to look.

Darshia was still there.

Tosh raised an eyebrow. "Uh …"

She reached behind her back, untied her dress. "You didn't think the Wounded Bird's hospitality was limited to food and drink, did you?"

"I … uh …"

She let the dress fall. Naked. Darshia's skin was impossibly white, like fresh snowfall, nipples bright as raspberries. She pulled her coppery hair loose and it fell in waves past her shoulders. The red patch between her legs had been cropped into a narrow strip.

The less-exhausted parts of Tosh's anatomy immediately rose to the occasion.

Darshia climbed onto the bed, straddled him. His hands immediately went to her plush backside. She leaned toward the small table next to the bed, and one of her pendulous breasts brushed Tosh's face. He went dizzy. She blew out the lamp.

In the total darkness, he felt fingers tugging at his belt.

"Just relax," Darshia whispered. "Let me do all the work."

~

Some hours later, Tosh felt soft hands shake him roughly by the shoulders.

"Wake up! Hurry!" Darshia's voice, a frantic whisper.

Tosh tangled naked in the sheets. It took him a moment to remember where he was. Ah, yes, lovely, lovely Darshia and her talented hands and amazing mouth and soft, creamy—

"Get up! Now!"

"A moment, my love," Tosh mumbled. "I can be ready for you in a moment, I promise." The woman was hungry for more? Well, who was Tosh to refuse a lady?

"Not *that*, idiot. Wake up."

It dawned on Tosh that something untoward was afoot.

He sat up in bed, rubbed his eyes. "What's going on?"

She shoved his clothes into his hands. "The Perranese are here."

He stood abruptly, attempted to put on his pants.

"No time." She grabbed his arm, dragged him to a small closet and opened the door.

"Don't you think they'll look in the closet?"

She ignored him, knelt and pried up the floorboards inside the closet. There was a ladder underneath, leading down into darkness. "Get in."

"Where does that—"

"Get in!"

He got in.

He heard Darshia replacing the floorboards overhead as he descended into darkness, fumbling to keep hold of his clothes and boots. Ten seconds later, the ladder ran out, his foot dangling in midair. The floor might have been two inches below or fifty feet.

Tosh was still trying to decide what to do next when strong hands grabbed him roughly from behind, another hairy paw clamping down over his mouth.

CHAPTER SEVENTEEN

Rina watched the snow devils, appraising them deliberately even as they bore down on her, snarling, from the steep slope to the side and up the stone steps in front of her. She understood how fast they were moving, closing quickly, a deadly and efficient hunter pack.

But she watched them in slow motion—the tufts of hair curving out and up from their foreheads like horns which earned them the devil name. The flat, apelike faces, curved tusks, long arms and gangly legs propelling them through the snow. Their high-pitched wails echoed through the valley.

The lead snow devil, the bull, leapt for her.

She was already spinning, cutting it in half across the chest, blood spraying in a fine mist. Rina came around again to catch the second one at the neck, its head popping off in a fountain of gore.

The third understood in some animal way that this prey was not as easy as it had first seemed and hesitated, thought about retreating even as the point of Kork's sword entered its chest and came out the back in a wet, bloody splatter. To Rina, the Fyrian's sword felt like an extension of her own body—natural, easy. It was her sword now.

She withdrew it from the snow devil's body just in time to wheel on the two coming down the slope.

Rina laughed. In the last few hours, events had given her many reasons to cry, but she set aside those thoughts until later and delighted at the ease with which she had dispatched the snow devils.

A sword through the throat. She withdrew it in a spray of blood, swung at a hairy paw reaching for her, severed it, brought the blade around to behead the beast.

The skirmish ended before it had begun, the snow devils in a bloody semicircle around her, a scattering of limbs, intestines, blood. The spirit still hummed along her limbs. Rina held the sword over her head, ready for the next wave of foes.

None came.

She lowered the weapon slowly. She backtracked a few paces to where she'd dropped the cloak, retrieved it, wrapped it around her shoulders. She didn't feel the cold but understood it would bite her eventually when she released the hold on the spirit within her. There would be fatigue, an eventual price to pay. But not yet.

First she needed to make it down the mountain, find shelter in one of the valleys below Klaar.

Rina hiked effortlessly. An hour took her down the stone steps. Another hour took her within the shadow of the city, and then into the forest beyond. If she had her bearings right, there was a lake to the south and an inhabited area ahead of her. She soon found herself trudging into a small village. The snow was coming heavily again, filling in her tracks a few yards after she'd made them. A large barn to her right drew her attention. Shelter.

She entered, closed the door behind her. She noted warmth. Two cows, three goats, five pigs.

There was a pile of dry hay at the far end of the barn. Rina burrowed into it, wrapped the cloak around her as she curled into a tight ball, and released her hold on the spirit.

The world crashed down upon her.

Physically at first. Her shoulders screamed hot agony, knees and ankles burning. Even in the shelter of the barn, the cold was bitter. She shivered violently, teeth chattering. Every muscle protested.

But the physical hurt was nothing compared to the wave of emotion that slammed her square in the chest. She put her arms over her face, sobs racking her body. She cried endlessly for her mother and father. For Kork. Everyone Rina loved—who had loved her—was dead. Her world lay in ruin.

She cried, pain and heartache blurring into an ongoing, gray misery until utter exhaustion at last pulled her into a bottomless black well of sleep.

CHAPTER EIGHTEEN

Alem had immediately turned off the road, spurring the gelding through the forest. He didn't want to meet Perranese troops coming from the other direction. But to shoot the gap down to the lower valley, there was no option but the road. He sat astride the horse a moment in the trees about fifty yards from the road's edge, tilted his head, listened.

Stillness. Calm. Quiet.

The horse clop-crunched through the snow and out onto the road. All clear.

He walked the horse down slowly, and two hours later the lower valley spread wide in front of him, the village of Crossroads already in sight. It was one of Klaar's larger villages, with about forty small but well-kept dwellings and a tavern and attached stable that attended to travelers and their horses. The tallest building in the center of the village was both the town hall and the Temple of Dumo.

The village was named for the self-evident fact that it clustered around a major crossroads in Klaar. If Alem kept riding west, the road would take him into the wide world of Helva. The road curving north went to fur-trapping territory and ended eventually at Ferrigan's Tower. The road south went through the scattered lowland villages and curved distantly around the mountains, turning into the Small Road which led up to Klaar's back gate.

Alem rode through the village and took the road south. He looked and listened but detected no sign of life. Most of the villagers would have evacuated to the city, and any who stayed behind would have been frightened off by the Perranese army marching down the northern road.

He followed the track south out of the village for a half mile then turned off onto a small path; it was almost unnoticeable under fresh snow, but Alem had walked it many times. He followed it into the forest, walking the gelding slowly. An hour later the snow-crusted pines thinned into a clearing, a small, frozen lake icy blue in front of him. Since the body of water was called Lake Hammish, the village perched on its shore was also called Hammish.

For the first time ever, it occurred to Alem that the Klaarian method of naming things tended toward the direct and obvious. He made a note to be more observant in the future.

Hammish was much smaller than Crossroads: nine cabins spread along the shoreline, a score of small wooden boats pulled up on the dark sand. Eight of the nine cabins housed fishing families, who earned a living off the big tiger gars that lurked in the lake's depths.

Alem reined in the horse and dismounted in front of the ninth cabin.

His grandmother Breen had repaired fishing nets, tackle and lures for decades. She was very old, and her sight was failing, but her fingers were still as nimble as when she was a girl. Some even came up from the river country to purchase her handiwork.

Alem paused before knocking, looked at the other cabins. Smoke rose from the chimneys of three. Hammish was tucked away. They might not have even gotten the word to flee to the city. Not that Breen would leave anyway.

He looked at the lake. It was very deep, but not far across, and he could see the large hunting lodge of a minor noble whose name Alem couldn't remember. He'd never been over there.

He knocked.

The door creaked open. "Alem!"

Breen threw her bony arms around her grandson. They hugged.

"You got here just in time," Breen said. "I was on my way to Agatha's."

"Agatha?" Alem remembered the wife of the elder fisherman was named Agatha.

"A stranger in town," Breen said. "Agatha is in a tizzy about it. She's so easily spooked." She waved a dismissive, wrinkled hand as if that explained Agatha.

"Is it the Perranese?" If a scout had found the little village, others could follow. At the very least, they would take Alem's horse. At worst ...

Breen cackled. "Oh, dear me, no. Nothing so dramatic." She closed the door behind her, turned and walked toward a cabin down the shoreline. "She's just found some girl in her barn. Strangers disturb the goats."

The three of them stood together, peeking inside through a crack in the barn door. It was a communal building and all of the village's animals were inside. Agatha was a squat, weathered, sturdy woman with vacant eyes and a frowning, worried expression. As she was the wife of the elder fisherman, the barn fell within her jurisdiction.

The bleating of the goats inside was constant and annoying.

Alem turned to Agatha. "So ... there's a girl in there?"

"That's right," Agatha said.

"You don't know her?"

"Never laid eyes on her before," Agatha said. "Went in to milk them cows, and there she was in the hay, sleeping."

"Sleeping, you say."

"Yes."

"Sinister."

Agatha blinked.

"So." Alem was trying to understand this. "You went in, saw this girl, and then ... then went to tell Breen."

"Well ..." Agatha shrugged, gestured to the barn. "I mean ... well ..."

Alem glanced at Breen standing behind her, and the old woman shrugged.

"Would you like me to take a look?" Alem asked.

Agatha sighed relief. "Dumo bless you, lad."

Alem entered the barn.

He found he was holding his breath as he tiptoed back to the haystack. Ridiculous. And yet, this wasn't the sort of village anyone came to by accident. It was off the beaten path. Agatha's reaction was comical but understandable too. Strangers popping up out of nowhere just *didn't* happen in Hammish. And, frankly, Alem would not be surprised to find out that Agatha had never been out of the village in her life. A stranger unannounced might actually be a shock to the system.

Alem suddenly felt mature and worldly, coming from the big city of Klaar. Not bad for a stable boy.

Head stable boy.

He peeked around the corner into the hay-filled stall. A lump under a cloak, half covered with hay. If she were indeed sleeping, then she slept the slumber of the dead because the racket from the goats was about to drive Alem crazy.

He approached slowly, trying to get a look at her.

She stirred, and Alem froze.

The girl in the hay pushed herself up to her knees, her back toward him. Her cloak fell away. The red-inked tattoos across her shoulder and down her spine startled him. There was a large circle with an intricate design between her shoulder blades, a twin line of fine runes down either side of her spine. More red lines leading up into her hairline and across the width of her shoulders. She was beautiful, strange, exotic, and Alem felt his heart beat a little faster.

He tried to focus on the circular design, but it resisted his observation, seemed to shift and move beneath her skin. He gasped.

She turned at the sound, brushing hay and strands of black hair out of her face. Their eyes met. He recognized her and gasped again.

Impossible.

CHAPTER NINETEEN

Tosh gave up struggling almost immediately. More than one pair of big hands had grabbed him, enormous, hairy, powerful arms lifting him and spiriting him along the pitch-black passage.

Trolls. That fucking whore tossed me into a fucking troll pit.

But they weren't trolls. They rounded a corner, and the dim light from a single candle showed Tosh he was in the iron grasp of the two "cudgel brothers," as he'd come to think of them; indeed, from the angle at which they carried him he could see one of the cudgels stuck into a wide leather belt.

The candle was on a small table with a jug of wine, a wheel of cheese and a plate of thick, dark sausages. They set him upright next to the table. Tosh could see chairs now and a small stove. The "smaller" brother—a foot taller than Tosh—whispered, "Keep it down, eh?" before removing his hand from Tosh's mouth.

"This here's our hidey hole," the bigger brother said.

In the candlelight, the brothers looked strange and unreal, like they'd been mashed together out of clay, their ears and lips thick, bald heads large and round.

"I'm Tosh."

"We know," said the bigger one.

Tosh frowned. He'd hoped they would tell him *their* names. "Sorry, gents, but I forgot how you're called."

"I'm Lubin," the smaller brother said.

The bigger brother thumped his chest with a massive fist. "Bune."

"Glad to make your acquaintance again." Tosh took in his surroundings. He was in a natural cavern augmented with stone work and buttressed with thick, wooden beams. Part of the ceiling overhead was natural stone, and part was thick wood. It had the look of a place long used. "So what is this place and why am I here?"

Lubin sat down on one of the chairs, grabbed the jug of wine. "A cave." He drank, smacked his lips and handed the jug to his brother.

"Perranese," Bune said then drank deeply.

Ah. Clear as mud.

They handed the jug to Tosh.

He shrugged. *Why not?* Tosh drank and almost spit it out. *This for damn sure isn't the good stuff.* He braced himself and took another, smaller swig to show he was a good sport. He handed the jug back to Lubin.

Tosh cleared his throat, belched fire. "Okay, fair enough that maybe I don't want to meet any Perranese troops right at this particular moment, but why are *you* down here?"

"Better to be safe," Lubin said. "The new bosses won't hurt the whores."

"Men like whores," put in Bune.

Ah. The intellectual one.

"But it is different for armed men. We are here only to protect the women, but these foreigners might not understand. Better to be safe for now and wait."

Lubin took another swig from the jug, then handed it to Bune, who drank and then held it out for Tosh again.

Yeah, why not? It's not as if I've got anything else to do.

He drank, winced; a mellow warmth spread through his body. The stuff wasn't half bad on a second go.

The high-pitched ring of a small bell startled him. Tosh glanced up, saw a little brass bell in the corner where the wooden part of the ceiling met the natural stone. A length of thin, brown twine led up through a hole in the wood. Somebody above yanked on the twine again, and the bell rang.

"What's that?"

"That's Mother," Lubin said.

∼

"Come in," she said.

Tosh entered the third-floor room and closed the door behind him.

It was a nice room, and in that sense it didn't seem to fit in with the rest of the Wounded Bird. It was more like a nobleperson's study: padded leather-covered chairs, a large polished desk, oil lamps hanging overhead providing good light, not smoky. He looked down and saw he was standing on a thick carpet with an intricate pattern, exotic, probably hauled all the way from Fyria or some other far-off land.

As if you know how the nobles live, idiot. Just pay attention to the lady.

She wore a blue silk dress of a modest, modern cut and could have passed for merchant class or minor nobility, but Tosh already knew who she was. She ran the Wounded Bird, although whether she was the owner or merely running the place for somebody else, Tosh didn't know. She tended toward the plump and had rosy cheeks, cool blue eyes, black hair streaked with white. A handsome woman, probably quite fetching in her younger days.

"You're Tosh?"

"Yes."

She looked him over, eyes shrewd, and Tosh suddenly felt strangely exposed.

"They call me Mother."

"No name?"

"I have a name," she said, "but it wouldn't mean anything to anyone. But everyone in Backgate knows who Mother is."

"Thanks for taking me in," Tosh said.

"Don't," Mother said. "It wasn't my idea."

Uh-oh.

She tilted her head, considering. "Not that I *necessarily* disapprove."

Tosh shifted his feet, rubbed the back of his neck. "Well ... thanks anyway."

"Sorry for your rude awakening," Mother said. "But we had to get you down into the cave. I can offer you better hospitality now."

Mother gestured to a chair near the desk. Tosh sat.

She turned to a silver tray behind her on which was a crystal decanter and matching crystal wine glasses. She filled one, handed it to Tosh.

He sipped. Better than the brew he'd been swilling downstairs although it didn't spread that warm feeling through his limbs as quickly. "Thank you."

"I have a brothel to run," Mother said. "Part of that is keeping my girls happy, and it lifted their spirits to take you in and treat you nicely. I imagine you represented every father, brother and granddad killed by the invaders."

Tosh didn't know what to say to that, so he sipped more wine.

Mother paced slowly as she spoke. "A sour little officer from the Perranese army came to tell me what I'd already guessed. We've been asked—*ordered,* actually—to open for business. Their general isn't a fool. He knows what it takes to keep soldiers in line, and discipline can only take you so far."

"What did you tell him?"

She smiled tightly. "Why, that we were only too eager to oblige, of course. We reopen in two days."

Two days. Damn.

"My immediate concern is what to do with you," Mother said.

"Me?"

"You."

Tosh cleared his throat. "Maybe you need another man about the place. Another bouncer?"

"There are times when an extra pair of hands might be useful," admitted Mother. "But to be frank, Lubin and Bune are generally all the muscle I need. More than enough, actually."

Tosh again didn't know what to say. He emptied the wine glass. Mother did not offer to refill it.

"The Perranese are rounding up the remains of the Klaar military and putting them into labor gangs to clean up the battle damage," Mother told him. "So it could be worse. No executions. Prisoners are given a warm place to sleep and three meals a day."

Ah, so Tosh was getting the old heave-ho from the Wounded Bird. This was Mother's way of breaking it to him gently, but Tosh didn't relish the idea of becoming a war slave. He frowned, reconsidering his earlier idea of gathering supplies and climbing over the city wall.

"You're not warming to that idea as an option, are you?"

Tosh shook his head. "No, ma'am."

Mother sighed. "Can't say that I blame you."

She rubbed her eyes, tired, sagged against the desk. It was odd to Tosh to see even this small dent in her poise. She'd probably been through a lot in the past day or two.

Yeah, well, so have I, lady. The desperate ride from Ferrigan's Tower, the harrowing battle, the botched escape. It hadn't been Tosh's idea of a laugh, not a moment of it.

"We don't tolerate idle hands at the Wounded Bird." She cleared her throat, straightened herself, lifted her chin and cast an appraising eye on Tosh. "Can you cook?"

CHAPTER TWENTY

Alem watched Rina Veraiin from the doorway as she sat at his grandmother's small, wooden table sluggishly spooning soup into her mouth. Both spoon and bowl were simple, wooden. The soup was thin, but at least it was hot. *She's a long way from the castle and fine things. I wonder how she ended up in Hammish.*

He'd tried to pepper her with questions back in the barn, but Breen had intervened, immediately recognizing that the young lady was in no condition to be pestered. His grandmother had put her in the chair by the fire while she warmed the soup and sent word through the village for spare clothing.

She still had the fine cloak draped around her shoulders but underneath wore a ragged wool sweater provided by Agatha. Her husband had grown too fat for it five winters back, she'd explained. The pants were too long and had to be rolled up and were so patched they could have been part of a carnival jester's costume. Nobody in the village was fool enough to give up their boots in the middle of winter, not even for a duchess, but they'd managed to scrounge a pair of canvas summer shoes. They'd be soaked through after ten steps in the deep snow but were better than nothing.

There were still a few stray bits of hay in her mussed hair, and with the ragged clothing, she looked like ... like ...

She's beautiful. All you have to do is look a little more closely and you can see the duchess there. Ragged hand-me-down clothes can't hide that.

Alem closed his eyes, shook his head. *What are you daydreaming about, thicko?*

Rina picked up the bowl, drained the last of the soup, wiped her mouth on her sleeve.

She looked around as if seeing the interior of his grandmother's cabin for the first time, and blinked at Alem. "What village is this?"

Alem took that as an invitation to enter the room, nodded a half-bow to her. "Hammish, milady."

She nodded slowly, like she was trying to make the word have meaning.

"I had a sword."

Alem gestured to the enormous blade where it leaned against the wall near the fireplace. It was a fine weapon, worth more than the whole village, Alem guessed.

She stood, moved toward the front door. "Yes, Hammish. I remember now."

Alem followed tentatively. "Uh ..."

She ignored him and was out the front door a second later, Alem trailing after her.

Rina walked toward the shore, shoes sinking in the snow, a slender hand coming up to shield her eyes from the setting sun which spread red-orange light across the frozen lake. "Is that Hammish's place?"

Alem followed her gaze to the hunting lodge across the lake. "Hammish's place?"

"Baron Edmund Hammish," Rina said. "The lake is named after his family. And the village."

Alem blushed pink. He'd been born in Hammish and hadn't known, hadn't even thought to wonder who the village was named after. He suddenly felt about as worldly as a turnip.

"Can you see if there's smoke rising from the chimney or not?" she asked.

He squinted. It was too far. "No."

"I have to go there."

"It will be dark soon," Alem told her. "You can't go across the ice. Even the fishermen won't risk thin ice in the dark."

"I'll have to go around." Rina glanced at the gelding still tied up in front of the cabin. "Who owns that horse?"

I do. No, that wasn't true. Alem had begun to think of it as his. The Perranese would have confiscated it anyway, and having a horse would have been very useful to begin his new life away from Klaar. He should have known better.

"It's your horse," Alem said. "From the castle stable."

Her gaze snapped back to him. "You were there? You got out?"

Alem nodded.

"Tell me."

"We made a run for it with a couple of horses. Another man and I. He was a soldier. I don't know what happened to him."

Her face grew hard, like she was bracing herself. "And the city?"

Alem shook his head. "So many dead. I ... I don't know ..."

Rina touched his arm lightly, and he held his breath.

"I'm glad you made it out," she said. "I need the horse."

She let her hand drop, went to the gelding to check the saddle and harness.

Alem followed, stopped himself. It was all slipping away, plans crumbling with the appearance of Rina Veraiin. He'd planned to ride the horse south and west. Not only was it transportation, but a horse was a valuable possession. But it wasn't his. He had no right to claim it.

"You shouldn't go alone." He grabbed at straws. "A woman." And now he was being insulting. He couldn't stop himself. She'd take the horse and leave and then what would Alem do? Where would he go?

She frowned. "I can take care of myself."

"I'm sorry," he said quickly. "I just meant the trails. It's easy to get lost in the dark, especially on the east side of the lake in the thick forest. I know the way. I just want to help." This was true. It had been a few years, but he knew the trails around the lake.

She looked away, sighed. "You can ride behind me."

Even with Alem directing her, they lost the trail in the forest, and the thick snow made it even more difficult. Alem found the trail again quickly, to Rina's surprise—in the opposite direction she'd thought—and Alem hoped he was proving his worth.

Even before they'd packed their meager provisions into the horse's saddlebags—smoked fish and a water skin provided by Breen—the sun had set, and in the dense forest, with moonlight unable to penetrate, the complete darkness convinced Alem it had been foolish to set out at night.

But Rina was determined, driven. She was damaged in some way, but it had hardened her. He wondered if it had something to do with the tattoos. He couldn't get the vision of her out of his mind.

And what was with that giant sword? She couldn't possibly wield it, and there was no graceful way for her to carry it. Even if they'd had a scabbard, she couldn't strap the thing to her waist or her back without the tip dragging along the ground. They'd finally rigged leather straps to secure the sword under one of the saddlebags, the hilt sticking out toward the front.

The forest thinned ahead of them, opening into a broad meadow with the lake on their left. The snow glowed white in the moonlight. They were close to Baron Hammish's hunting lodge.

"If we just follow the shore around now, it should be no problem," Alem said.

Alem held her from behind just above the hips. His heartbeat had only just returned to normal, and it was more than the fact she was nobility.

Stop it. You're going to make a fool out of yourself.

No. He wouldn't. Rina Veraiin was a duchess. Alem was nobody.

He might as well fall in love with a marble statue of a goddess. It was no more real than that. Alem laughed.

"What's funny?" Rina asked.

Oops.

The hunting lodge loomed into view and saved him. He pointed. "There."

She looked at the warm glow in the windows, visible even from this distance. "Damn. I was hoping nobody would be there."

CHAPTER TWENTY-ONE

Rina was cold. *Very* cold.

She knew how easy it would be to tap into the spirit, push the cold away, but she'd already experienced the price she'd pay. And anyway, the Hammish hunting lodge was only a hundred yards away now, and she'd soon be inside and warm. She was hungry too. The old woman's small bowl of soup seemed years in the past.

The lodge wasn't empty as Rina had predicted. It wasn't the season for hunting and sport fishing, and she thought it likely the servants had fled. Was it better or worse that the lodge was inhabited? She was hoping for shelter, supplies, something she could sell for money. Taking Klaar back from the Perranese wasn't going to happen overnight, and in the meantime, she needed to provide for herself.

On the other hand, she could use allies too.

Or maybe the Perranese had gotten there first.

It didn't matter. They'd arrived.

They climbed the wooden steps of the wide covered porch and stood before the wooden double doors of the lodge. Rina turned to ask ...

What was his name? Rina hadn't thought to ask.

Never mind. She was going to ask him to take the horse to the stable behind the lodge, but on second thought they might need to leave quickly.

Rina raised a knuckle to knock, hesitated. Might as well retain the element of surprise as long as possible.

She turned to the boy, put a finger to her lips. He nodded his understanding. She grabbed the iron ring on the front of the door, pushed inward. The big hinges squeaked only a little, and they stepped into a small foyer, quickly shutting the door behind them.

Oh, Dumo, it's so warm.

Rina glanced at the cloak pegs on the wall, saw the single cloak hanging there; it was of a quality material of deep blue, with a collar of white snow-devil fur. She felt the hem. Slightly damp. Someone had come in from the cold. Recently.

She rounded the corner. It had been four years since she'd last visited the lodge, during a carefree summer that seemed like a fuzzy memory, but her recollection of the lodge's great hall had held up over time. The huge stone fireplace was twice as tall as she was. At fifteen she'd just been able to stand up inside it. She was two inches taller now. The modest fire in the hearth now provided some of the room's illumination.

Various candles provided the rest. The big grizzly-skin carpet was as large as she remembered it, but seemed a bit more threadbare. Leather-covered furniture of a rustic style but of fine quality was placed around the hall in such a way as to encourage conversation and merriment. Antlers from trophy bucks took up most of the wall space save one section reserved for weapons—various spears and hunting bows and a few other blades. Good. She'd claim one of the swords for herself. The only way Rina could wield the sword Kork had bequeathed her was if she tapped into the spirit, and that might not always be the best option.

But at the moment, the most inviting thing in the hall was the fire. She moved toward it—

A flash of steel glinted in candlelight, and Rina flinched back only just in time, the tip of a thin sword blade sweeping within an inch of her face. The boy yelled a warning behind her.

The man had been hiding behind one of the enormous, rough-hewn wooden pillars that supported the great hall's arched roof. He advanced, swinging the sword, and Rina had to dodge again.

"Sneak up on me, will you, you bastards?" he shouted. "You'll get your money when you get it, bloodsuckers. I'll skewer you like a shank of mutton!"

He was tall, good-looking in a sloppy kind of way; rich brown hair, mussed, hung down past his ears. Brown eyes, tan, fine, angular features. An expensive silk shirt, unlaced halfway down his chest. Brandy sloshed over the rim of a silver goblet in one of his hands as he advanced, swinging his blade wildly with the other.

"Brasley, stop!" Rina shouted. "It's me."

He froze, arm cocked and ready for a backhanded swing. "Rina?"

Rina nodded. "The Hammishes were a bit more hospitable last time I visited."

Brasley Hammish lowered his sword, blowing out a huge sigh of relief, his shoulders slumping. "I thought they'd found me. Glad it's you." His eyes shifted to the young man standing timidly in the entranceway. "And your ... friend?"

"He showed me the way here from the village across the lake," Rina said. "Our horse is outside."

"Ah, that's good." Brasley tossed his sword onto a nearby divan, turning his attention back to the brandy. "The servants were all gone when I arrived. Blast if I know where they've got to." He made a dismissive gesture. "Take Rina's horse around back to the stable and see to mine as well. As a matter of fact, all the animals probably need watering and feeding. See to it, will you, lad?"

Rina's eyes shifted to the village boy. He'd gone red, jaw tight.

"Go ahead," she said.

He nodded curtly, then turned and left, closing the door a little too hard behind him.

Now why does that seem familiar? That boy slamming the door...

Rina went to the wall where the hunting weapons were displayed. She took down a bow and quiver, slung them across her back. "I'm taking some of your weapons, Brasley."

He shrugged, went to a sideboard and refilled his goblet from a small silver pitcher. "Not *my* weapons. This is Uncle Edmund's place. He said I could visit whenever I pleased. So by all means help yourself. Can't have a woman wandering unarmed through the snow in the middle of the night... which raises the question: *Why* are you wandering unarmed through the snow in the middle of the night?"

"For the same reason your servants ran off, I would imagine." Rina picked a rapier and scabbard off the wall, belted them around her waist. It was a little larger than the one she was used to, but she'd adjust easily enough.

"Hmmmm. I'm not sure I see the connection." Brasley grinned. "Are you sure it wasn't to give me the chance to steal another kiss?"

Rina snorted. "I was *fifteen*. I've hardly seen you since. And anyway, that was before I found out what a drunken, loudmouthed—" She paused, her expression becoming serious. "Wait, you really don't know, do you?"

"I know that if you've come to seduce me, you've dressed all wrong for it."

She looked down at herself. She looked like a beggar. An unfashionable beggar. "Show me your cousin Miliscint's room. I need to borrow some of her clothes. And then we need to talk."

"Talk about what?"

"Brasley, when's the last time you were in Klaar?"

~

Alem was still scowling as he led the gelding into the stable.

Who are you calling lad, *you jackass?* What had Rina called him? Brasley. The man was only a year or two older than Alem at most.

What did you expect? They're nobles. You're nobody.

He spotted Brasley's horse immediately, a big black stallion, loosely tied to a post. Brasley hadn't even bothered to put the horse in a stall or remove the saddle. *Of course not. He expects servants to do it.*

Servants like me.

Klaar had fallen, and what was different? He was still a stable boy.

Head stable boy. Alem laughed. At himself.

Okay, thicko, what are you going to do about it?

He still held the gelding's reins, mulled his options. He could feed the horse a quick handful of oats, hop into the saddle, and be miles away by the time the nobles in the lodge finished sipping wine and eating pheasant or whatever they did while the servants worked their fingers to the bone. It wasn't his horse, and yet...

What shall I choose to be? Servant or thief?

He glanced about the stable. There were three other horses in the stalls. So he wouldn't be depriving Rina of anything, not really. And that's how he convinced himself it was okay. Alem wasn't a bad person. He wouldn't strand her, but she wouldn't care which horse she rode. Nor would it matter to someone like her if a village boy ran off into the night.

Alem wouldn't be hurting anyone. It was decided: he'd take the gelding and go.

He remembered the sword strapped under the saddlebag.

The blade was remarkable. It would fetch a hefty price if he could get as far as a town, find somebody to sell it to. For somebody like Alem, it would be a fortune. If he were frugal he could live for a year. Or he could set himself up in some business, open his own stable. That was an appealing idea. He knew horses, knew how to run a stable, but he'd be working for himself. He wouldn't be a servant anymore. It was almost too tempting to resist.

No. That was going too far.

Rina wouldn't care about the horse. The sword was different. It would mean something if he took it, and Rina would hold it against him, and even though he'd never see her again, he didn't like the idea of her out there somewhere hating the nameless stable boy who'd stolen from her.

So, the horse, yes. The sword, no.

Alem packed the saddlebag with oats, fed a handful to the gelding.

He went quickly to the stable door, opened it a crack and peeked through. If they were still occupied, he could lead the horse back to the path and—

Two lines of torches beyond the lodge, coming along the same tree line from which Alem and Rina had emerged earlier. They marched in straight lines, the torches evenly spaced. Army.

One guess which army.

Alem muttered an oath so vile, his grandmother Breen would have washed his mouth out with soap.

CHAPTER TWENTY-TWO

"I assumed you were hiding out here because of what happened in the city," Rina said.

Brasley chuckled, refilled his brandy again. He was putting it away fast.

"I *am* hiding out," he said. "There seems to be a misunderstanding with a few of Klaar's more prominent gambling dens. They suffer under the misapprehension I'm unable to pay—which is of course ridiculous."

"Of course."

He lifted the silver pitcher. "Pour you one? It's quite good."

"Maybe later."

He shrugged, topped off his own goblet. "I told them I had to send for my funds, but they're uncouth and impatient."

Rina grinned. A braggart and spoiled brat but always amusing. She couldn't quite bring herself to dislike the handsome devil. Then her grin faded. "The gambling lords of Klaar might have bigger worries than *you* right now, Brasley."

"No matter. They aren't here, are they?" Brasley moved toward her, trailed a finger down her arm. "It's just us. And a warm fire." He toasted her with the goblet. "And some good brandy."

She didn't flinch from his touch, but she did stare daggers straight into his eyes. "You're drunk."

"I suppose. But not *too* drunk... if you understand me." His hand slipped around her waist to the small of her back, drew her close to him.

Rina went rigid, lifted her chin as Mother had taught her. Mother always said a girl needed to know how to look aloof, regal. How to freeze underlings with a stare. How to make heads of state give pause. It started with narrowing the eyes, lifting the chin.

"Let go of me, Brasley."

He laughed. "I don't think you really want me to."

She put as much steel into her voice as she could muster. "I am Duchess Rina Veraiin of Klaar. You *will* show me the appropriate respect."

"Duchess? Getting ahead of ourselves, aren't we?" He pulled her closer, leaned in for a kiss.

Looks like we'll have to do this the old-fashioned way.

Rina punched him in the stomach, didn't hold back.

He bent, stumbled back, grunting, and dropped the goblet, which clanged on the floor, contents spilling. He teetered a moment then went to one knee, hunched over and vomited, half digested brandy splashing acidly in front of him.

"W-well..." He panted. "T-there goes a lot of good brandy w-wasted."

Rina bent to talk into his ear through clenched teeth. "Mother and Father are dead. I *am* Duchess of Klaar. And you owe me your fealty."

A glimmer of understanding in his eyes. Her words had penetrated his booze-addled brain. "Dead?"

"The city is overrun with Perranese invaders," Rina said.

"That's... impossible."

"While you've been wallowing in drink and hiding in your uncle's lodge, the world has changed under your nose," Rina told him. "I came here for weapons and valuables. I'll leave the brandy for you."

"Valuables?" Brasley still rubbed his gut where he'd taken the punch. "I don't understand."

"I'm fleeing Klaar," Rina said. "I need to fund my journey. I have places to go."

A cruel grin spread across her face, no mirth touching her eyes. The look of a dune cat about to sink its fangs into a desert antelope. "But I plan on coming back."

Brasley was still trying to digest what she'd said. "The Perranese ... but ... they haven't ... in years ..."

"They have now," Rina said. "And I plan to be gone before sunrise. Before—"

The windows around her filled with the orange glow of flickering torchlight.

Rina's eyes grew wide. "Oh, no."

"What is it?" Brasley lurched to his feet.

She paused, listened, heard the muffled scuffling of boots outside on the front porch.

"Brasley," she whispered.

"Yes?"

"Pick up your weapon."

Captain Tchi Go'Frin approached the lodge, waved a dozen men around back and the other dozen toward the large front double doors. The men made only nominal efforts to maneuver quietly. They weren't expecting trouble.

The information Tchi had been given was that the lodge would be empty. Maybe a few servants, perhaps even a lord or two who'd fled the city. Certainly nothing to give two dozen men any trouble, and anyway, the rest of the column—eighty men— was a half hour behind him with the supply wagons and confiscated livestock.

Tchi's mission was simple: scour the countryside for provisions to bring within the city walls. They would need everything they could get to last the harsh winter in this frigid, forsaken place, and it might be months before the Empire sent supply ships.

He'd been told, with some urgency, to keep his eye out especially for horses. Scuttlebutt through the ranks indicated this had been a particularly weak area of the advanced scouting information provided by Perranese spies. Klaar had no cavalry and few horses, and none had been brought across the sea by the Perranese.

A gentle interrogation of the noodle-spined Klaarian nobility had convinced more than a few of them to mark on a map the various country estates and holiday homes where horses might be found. This lodge was the hunting retreat of—Tchi checked the map—a noble named Hammish. He planned to secure the horses, spend the night in comfort and then move on in the morning.

But the sight of dim candlelight in the windows suggested there might be sword work to do first. Nobles would be captured, servants slain as a matter of course—unless they happened to be pretty young women.

The soldiers standing on either side of the double door looked back at Tchi, waiting for his signal. They crouched, weapons in hand, ready to rush inside the lodge. Tchi raised his hand. When he lowered it, they would go, and at the sound of the commotion, the others would enter through the back. Both squads together would clear the lodge in a matter of seconds, and then—

The front doors flew open, and two figures rushed out, cloaks flapping in the wind. Steel glinted in torchlight, the *ting* of blade on blade reaching him across the wind. In two seconds, three of his men tumbled down the front steps clutching bloody wounds.

Tchi drew his own sword, ran toward the fray even as he watched another of his men fall.

"To the front!" He screamed. "Fighting in the front of the lodge. To me!"

A man and a woman. His men crowded in to get at them, but the porch was too small. The man seemed mostly to be on the defensive.

The woman was something else.

Her swordplay was a blur, a thin blade moving with precision as she spun from one opponent to the other, stabbing, slicing, searching out exposed skin, weak points in the armor.

Another of Tchi's men screamed death, clutching at his throat, stumbling away as blood sprayed through his fingers.

Tchi had reached the bottom of the steps, sword held high to attack. Then a moment of distraction, a noisy galloping behind—

Something slammed into his back, sent him skidding through the snow, the world a tumble of moonlight, torchlight, snow, bells ringing in his ears. He tried to get up, couldn't. He'd had the wind knocked out of him.

Tchi turned his head. Three horses. That's what had happened. One of the horses had slammed into him. A third man stood tall in the saddle, beckoning to the other two. They leapt onto the other horses, and a second later all three were riding away fast to the south.

Strong hands lifted him. "Captain!"

Tchi sucked air, felt along his ribs and back. Nothing broken. "Check the stable for more horses," he ordered. "Hurry!"

～

Alem kept looking back for any sign of pursuit. So far they were safe.

He glanced sideways at Rina. The woman he'd glimpsed on the porch of the hunting lodge, the spinning demon delivering cold death with her steel, was gone. In her place was a tired girl, sagging in the saddle, shoulders slumped.

Alem trotted along beside her, grabbed the reins of her horse, stopped in an open, moonlit clearing.

Brasley slowed to a halt next to them. "Are you crazy? They could be coming after us any minute."

Alem scowled at him but turned back to Rina. "Are you okay?"

She turned her head, eyes focusing on him with effort. "I'm … fine."

"While I'm all in favor of running away from the foreigners trying to kill us with swords," Brasley said, "just exactly where are we *going*?"

Alem ignored him, still looking at Rina. He pitched his voice low. "Are you sure?"

"I said I'm fine." She closed her eyes, rubbed them.

"What you did back there—I've never seen—"

"Forget it." She said quickly, strength returning to her voice. She turned to Brasley. "I'm heading for the Nomad Lands, if you must know."

"What? That's weeks away! Look, I have friends around the mountain in Colson Wells," Brasley said. "We can hide there until—"

"The time for hiding is past," Rina said. "At this very moment, I am Duchess of approximately nothing. I'm going to change that. And to do it I must journey to the Nomad Lands. I could use some help, but come or stay as you wish."

She turned the horse, left at a trot.

"You're mad!" Brasley called after her. "The three of us? That's not much of an army!"

"It's a start," she said without turning.

Brasley looked at Alem, the expression plain on his face. *Is she out of her mind?*

Alem smiled crookedly and shrugged as if to say, *Well, that's a duchess for you. What can you do?*

He spurred the gelding to gallop after Rina, didn't bother looking back to see if Brasley followed.

Hoped, in fact, he wouldn't.

CHAPTER TWENTY-THREE

Giffen spread his hands grandly as he addressed the people in the courtyard below. He stood on the balcony of the Duke's personal office where the Duke himself had addressed holiday crowds so many times, cheering Klaarians who'd packed the courtyard, crowds spilling into the street beyond.

The huddled group of a hundred citizens below was paltry by comparison. The Perranese had rounded them up specifically to hear Giffen's words. They were obedient if not exactly enthusiastic. They would be enough, Giffen thought. Word of his speech would spread through the taverns and markets, often enhanced by Giffen's own agents, and by the end of the week would be hailed as a speech of hope and Klaarian perseverance by one of Helva's most gifted orators.

"And when the Duke himself—*with his dying breath*—asked me to watch over his people ... well ... how could I refuse?" He paused, pretended to wipe away a tear. "With all of the diplomatic skills I possess, I have managed to convince the Perranese that the Klaarian people *must* be ruled by a Klaarian. We can hold our heads up and know that our way of life *will* continue. I am here for you! Thank you, my people. And Dumo bless you!"

Giffen's shills in the crowd led a ragged cheer as Giffen waved and backed into the office behind him. He shut the doors and wiped the sweat from the top of his head with a handkerchief.

General Chen sat at the Duke's desk, a bored expression on his face. "Let us hope your address had the desired effect."

"If you want a docile populace, then leave everything to me, General Chen." Giffen's eyes shifted to the officer standing at attention over Chen's shoulder. "And who is this? Does he have something to report?"

Chen made an offhand gesture. "Tell Giffen what you told me, Captain Tchi."

"Two nights ago, a woman single-handedly killed a dozen of my men." The captain leaned past Chen to take a small framed portrait from the Duke's desk. He turned it around to show Giffen. "It was this woman. I'm sure of it."

Giffen blinked at the painting. He remembered when Rina Veraiin had sat for the portrait last year. One of Klaar's better artists had captured her likeness well.

Giffen shook his head. "It can't be."

"She's still missing, yes?" Chen asked.

"My men scour the city for her even now," Giffen said.

"She is no longer in the city," Tchi said. "I sent two riders after her. One returned to report in which direction she fled. The other continues to pursue and keep track of her. He will leave signs for the trackers. We have much experience with this. I can find her again, but I need men to take her."

"Bah!" Giffen backhanded the air, a gesture of annoyance. "She's no warrior. There is some mistake."

Tchi stood rigid, chin up, but didn't dispute Giffen's words.

"What about the slain men in the great hall?" Chen asked. "She left a slaughter in her wake when she escaped."

"I told you. That was her dark-skinned savage. The bodyguard is more than capable of such bloodshed." Giffen's attention shifted back to Tchi. "There were others with her?"

"Two men."

"You see?" Giffen said. "One was obviously that Fyrian giant of hers. He killed your men. It would have been easy for him."

"There was no giant," Tchi said. "I know what I saw."

Giffen opened his mouth to argue, but shut it again when Chen waved him to silence.

The general sighed, massaged his temples. "It doesn't matter. She must be dealt with. If she returns to the city, she will undermine Giffen's ruse. If she flees to her kin in the west, she could alert them to our presence before we consolidate our defenses. How many horses do we have?"

"Seventy-four," Tchi said.

Chen *tsked*. "So few? Very well. Take twenty horses. You and your tracker and eighteen of the elite guard will pursue our errant duchess. Kill any who see you. Kill those who ride with her. Move swiftly."

Tchi bowed. "Yes, general."

Chen said, "And I know it is best for you to travel light. Bringing back just her head should suffice."

CHAPTER TWENTY-FOUR

Tosh wiped the sweat from his brow, tossed another log into the iron stove and kicked the door closed. It had taken him three weeks working in the kitchen to learn how to maintain the coals at the exact level he needed. He moved fast, slapped down the skillet, dumped in the diced potatoes, garlic, salt. Another deep pan next to it. Sausages.

He paused to drink water. It was hot work. He wore only boots, apron and breeches. He'd lost eleven pounds in three weeks. For years he'd marched and drilled with the army yet always maintained a soft layer around his middle. It took laboring in the kitchen of the Wounded Bird to finally burn it off.

"Smells good, don't it?" Bune's voice came from behind him. The big man tried to squeeze past Tosh, a meaty hand reaching for one of the sizzling sausages.

Tosh smacked the back of Bune's hand with a spatula, cracking a knuckle with a metallic clang.

Bune jerked his hand back, eyes shooting wide. "Oi!"

"That's for paying customers," Tosh said.

Tosh elbowed the big man out of the way, sort of like trying to elbow a mountain, but Bune stepped back and allowed Tosh to get at the huge cooking pot hanging in the kitchen hearth.

He removed the lid, sniffed at the lamb stew inside. By the time the late evening crowd rolled in, it would go perfect with fresh-baked bread.

"Dumo knows where Mama found lamb what with all the shortages," Tosh said. "You've got to hand it to her."

Bune grunted.

"Is there a reason you're in my kitchen, you enormous lump?"

"Table two wants food."

"I cook," Tosh said. "The girls come in and fetch the food."

Bune shrugged. "Tenni said."

"Tenni said, huh?" Tosh had learned the blonde with the little girl was named Tenni. "They must be pretty busy out there."

"No empty seats."

"Right." He took his shirt from the peg on the wall, slipped it over his head. He'd been told that hairy, sweaty, shirtless men were not an aid to the appetite.

He filled a plate with sausage, fried potatoes, a chunk of dark bread, and took it out front.

Tosh scanned the crowd, spotted table two. *Ah. Him again.*

He set the plate in front of the grinning Perranese warrior. "Welcome back, Corporal."

The corporal grinned wider, gap-toothed, nodding his thanks. "The potatoes … they are the best. In my land, we have only rice and steamed fish and seaweed. Very healthy but tastes like … like ass." He greedily scooped a spoonful of potatoes into his mouth.

"Only ass we serve here is upstairs." Tosh winked.

The corporal paused in mid-chew. It took him a moment to get the joke. "Oh! Very good! Very funny!"

"You've been in here every day," Tosh said.

The corporal pointed at Tosh with his spoon. "You master potato chef. Master!"

Tosh smiled. He never gave officers much credit, but he had to admit whoever the Perranese general was, the man was a genius. Opening the Wounded Bird allowed the Perranese warriors to blow off steam in the usual way. But it was more than that. It also gave the people of Klaar a chance to get used to the foreigners. Tosh looked around the common room, saw locals sitting at tables next to Perranese. The scene was being repeated at taverns throughout the city. How long before both sat at the same table together? How long before all this actually seemed *normal*?

Thankfully Lord Giffen had been put in charge of Klaar. Tosh would hate to think what life in the city would be like directly under the iron thumb of the invading general.

The day passed quickly. Tosh worked hard, cleaning his kitchen between meal prep. If he ever returned to the army, maybe he'd put in for cooking duty.

Eventually the Wounded Bird grew quiet and empty, only a few straggling customers in the upstairs rooms getting their final kicks with the ladies. Tosh scrubbed the last pot, set it in the rack to dry. The final thing he did before calling it a night was to consult his supply list. They were dangerously low on salt and bacon and flour. He decided to take the list up to Mama's office. The woman was a miracle worker, seemed to have some direct connection with the black market. And never failed to come up with the needed supplies.

Tosh folded the list and headed upstairs.

He passed the second floor, paused when he heard the scream.

Tosh had learned early in the going that one heard a variety of screams inside the Wounded Bird, and few of them called for the bouncers. Passion and enthusiasm were often the culprits.

Another scream, panicked, afraid. The smack of flesh on flesh followed by the thud of overturned furniture.

That's not passion.

Tosh ran down the hall. More screams. He stopped in front of Tenni's room, banged on the door with a fist. "Tenni!"

The sounds coming from Tenni's room were more masculine now, ragged harsh grunts, the sound of pain. Shuffling feet, movement, a struggle. Tosh threw his shoulder against the door, rattling the lock.

"Bune!" *Just when you actually need one of the big bastards…*

Tosh threw his shoulder against the door again, heard something crack. The third time did the trick, wood splintering as the door flew inward. Tosh rushed into the room, fists up, ready for anything.

Tenni was covered in bright blood.

Not her blood.

She stood over a naked Perranese warrior, flailing awkwardly at him with his own sword, holding it tightly and clumsily in her slender hands. The warrior was slick with his own blood, back against the bed as he writhed on the floor, one arm up uselessly fending off Tenni's frantic blows. He was covered with a dozen random slashes already.

"Get away from me! Get away!" Tenni screamed, slashing at the man again, a length of flesh coming away from his forearm, blood splattering. "I'll kill you!"

Tosh grabbed her from behind. "Tenni!"

She screamed again, struggled violently, but Tosh held on.

When she saw it was Tosh she dropped the sword with a clatter, and Tosh let her go. She backed against the wall, shaking her head. "H-he hurt me. Just k-kept hurting me and w-wouldn't s-stop. He was s-so drunk and c-cruel…"

"It's okay," Tosh said. "It's okay now."

She started crying, slid down the wall into a sitting position, putting her face in her bloody hands, shoulders bobbing as she sobbed.

Tosh drew his dagger, approached the bloody, writhing figure on the floor. The warrior had been hacked all over, a number of the cuts messy and shallow. Tosh saw at least two wounds that were more lethal, bleeding freely. The warrior twitched, more blood foaming from his mouth as he silently opened and closed it, maybe trying to say something.

Tosh tried not to slip in the blood as he got closer with the dagger. A quick stab in the throat would finish him.

Tosh looked into the warrior's eyes. It was the corporal he'd served potatoes to earlier that morning.

Oh, no. You bastard. You stupid fucking asshole bastard.

Tosh stabbed him in the throat.

Tosh sat hunched over his mug. The Wounded Bird's common room was deserted and dark save for the light of a single candle. He felt exhausted, but couldn't sleep. He'd become fond of the foul brew Lubin and Bune had introduced him to that first morning in the cave. Not quite wine, not quite brandy, it went down harsh but warmed the body quickly. He took another sip.

Lubin and Bune had shown up to dispose of the body. Tenni's room had been cleaned. No evidence remained of what had happened. It would be daylight soon.

When you're the cook at the Wounded Bird, you're not just the cook. He hoped there would not be many nights like this one.

He heard something, looked up.

Tenni sat across the table from him.

She'd cleaned up. Pretty. Thin face, high cheekbones. Golden hair pulled back into a ponytail. He face looked blank, maybe a little haunted around the eyes.

Tosh asked, "You okay?"

She nodded.

"Good."

"I guess I made a real mess up there," she said.

Tosh shrugged. "A man can take a lot of abuse before he goes down. It can get ugly. A sword can kill with a single blow, but you have to know how to use one. It takes training."

"You were in the army," she said. "You've had training."

"Yes."

Tenni pulled the Perranese sword out from under the table. It had been cleaned up and had found its way back into its scabbard. It was a long single-edged weapon with a slight curve.

She placed it on the table between them. "Teach me."

CHAPTER TWENTY-FIVE

Tapping into the spirit didn't give Rina superpowers—the exception being the bull tattoo, which gave her the strength—but it did let her exploit her senses to the fullest. Hearing, for example. It was no keener than before, but tapping into the spirit allowed Rina to more closely examine what she was hearing, categorize it, separate one sound from another.

She sat with her back against a giant fir tree, cross-legged, eyes closed, the long, two-handed sword across her knees. She listened.

The crunch of footsteps, still distant, a hundred yards away at least. Five men, heavy steps implying armor and weapons although they were doing a good job of keeping their metal from clanking. Other sounds … the wind, birds, a babbling brook a half mile away. No snowfall to dull the sounds on the wind. It was still cold, but since they'd come out of the mountains and kept south, there had been no new snow. Just what was already on the ground in patches here and there.

Rina formed a mental picture: the five men spread out among the trees, coming through the forest slowly, weapons drawn. They suspected she was close. Not sure how close. Not sure where the camp was.

It was two hundred yards ahead in a small clearing at the bottom of a shallow dell. Brasley stayed to watch the horses. They'd left the campfire lit. The smell would lead them on.

Part of her brain monitored the sounds of the forest. Another part mused that she did *not* enjoy camping. She missed her room and her bed and hot meals in the castle. She missed everything.

When Rina had remembered the sapphires braided into her hair, they'd veered toward Kern, the closest city of any size where they could sell the fine gems. The proceeds had not only allowed them to properly outfit for the journey, but it had also funded two gloriously warm and comfortable nights in a reasonably clean inn.

And clothes. She wore a pair of black leather pants, good travel boots and a simple but clean white shirt. She'd had Kork's cloak cleaned and hemmed for her shorter stature. It was still her warmest garment.

Sleeping on the ground was *not* warm. Every night she wrapped herself tightly in her bedroll *and* the cloak and slept as close to the fire as she dared without risking catching herself on—

She tilted her head, refocused her attention on a new sound. Footsteps, but quicker and lighter than the others, a rustling of cloth. A child or a woman, Rina thought. Not armored.

Out here?

Rina pressed herself flat against the tree, twisted, peeked around the wide trunk.

A second later, the girl came running through the undergrowth, long, garishly colored purple and yellow skirt scooped up in one arm to let her legs run. A heavy wool shirt that almost concealed a full figure. She was striking. Pale glowing skin and deep red hair, full and wind-blown. Rina thought her older at first, but she looked scared and young. Maybe sixteen.

The girl paused, looked back anxiously.

She's afraid. And she's stumbled right into the middle of what's about to happen. Rina gripped her sword hilt firmly, readied herself.

The girl was about to turn and continue running when an armored warrior erupted from the foliage behind her. She screamed, tried to dart away, but the Perranese warrior latched onto her wrist. The girl screamed again, tried to twist free.

Rina had already leapt to her feet, sword in hand, sprinting toward the two of them.

As always when she tapped into the spirit, the world unfolded before her in slow motion. Dashing toward her from the left were two more armored warriors. She understood that normally these men would be assaulting her at blinding speed, swords prone to strike, grim and lethal professionals.

The first one lunged at her middle. She slapped the blade past her, stepped in to strike backhanded on the return swing at the neck of the second one. The blade bit deeply, an arc of blood trailing on the follow-through. The warrior's head flopped on his ruined neck. He hit the ground hard, writhing and quivering, some parts of his body still not accepting death.

Rina brought the follow-through around in a complete circle to swipe at the one now behind her. Swords clanged in the cold air. She pressed the attack. He defended well three times before she found her way past his guard. The armor over his chest might as well have been parchment, the thick blade pierced his chest so easily. He grunted, wilted, slid off the blade and hit the ground with a thud.

Rina glanced quickly at the girl, who still struggled in the grasp of her attacker. The warrior backhanded her, spinning her head around.

But Rina couldn't go to her. Two more warriors ran at her, swords raised.

She dropped under a wide sword swing and kicked out, the heel of her boot connecting with a warrior's knee. The knee was well armored, but Rina drew on the bull strength flowing within her. There was a *crunch crack* as the armor caved in, the kneecap shattering.

The warrior screamed, tilted and went down.

No time to finish him.

She rolled away as a sword struck the ground where she'd been a split second before. She lay on the ground and thrust her sword back and over her head, the point piercing the warrior's ankle.

He screamed, staggered back, sword held up defensively to hold her off.

She'd already scrambled to her feet, absently stabbing the one with the crushed knee through the throat.

The one with the wounded ankle looked side to side, hoping for a way out. He knew he couldn't run, not with the ankle.

He was still thinking about it when Rina moved in quickly, batting his sword aside, slicing hard and two-handed at his belly. Guts and blood spilled from the rent in the armor. He went down, shock and panic on his face, his hands trying to stuff his steaming guts back inside the rip in his belly even as death took him.

Rina realized she was too late to save the girl.

She ran toward her, but the warrior had already drawn and raised his dagger to finish her.

There was a metal *tunk* as the crossbow bolt pierced the warrior's armor.

The warrior went stiff, fell over backward, but kept his grip on the girl's wrist, pulling her on top of him. She screamed again.

Alem was there in an instant, setting aside the crossbow. He pried the warrior's dead fingers from the girl's wrist, grabbed her shoulder and turned her over.

"Are you okay?"

She blinked, looked up into his eyes, the expression on her face as if she were waking from a dream. "Who ... Who are you?"

CHAPTER TWENTY-SIX

T he girl glanced over her shoulder at Rina, Alem and Brasley who followed her along the narrow, winding trail on foot, leading the horses. "This way," she said. "Almost there."

She'd told them her name was Maurizan and that her people would welcome them.

"Her people?" Rina whispered to Brasley who walked beside her.

"Her clothes make her look gypsy," he whispered back. "But I've never seen a red-haired gypsy. A pretty little thing, isn't she?"

Rina frowned, sped her pace to walk ahead of him.

Brasley had stayed back in camp with the horses, and they'd gone to fetch him after the ambush. The camp wouldn't be safe. The rest of the Perranese would come eventually although they didn't know how many or how far behind they were. It had been cat-and-mouse since leaving Kern.

Maurizan had told them her people were camped somewhere safe and hidden.

They hiked another half hour, down into a lush gorge, a vine-covered wall of natural rock rising up on one side of them. Maurizan stopped abruptly, sweeping aside a curtain of low-hanging vines to reveal an opening in the stone wall, a narrow passage with bright sunlight beyond.

"I would have ridden right past this," Brasley said.

"You have to know what you're looking for," Maurizan said. "It's unlikely anyone would find it by accident."

"No, but we left a trail," Alem said, glancing behind them. "Especially the horses."

She put a hand on his arm, smiled warmly at him. "It will be taken care of." She looked up into one of the trees.

They followed her gaze. Several men with bows slung across their backs squatted on thick branches high up in the canopy. They wore garish clothes similar to Maurizan's but had dark complexions and black hair. Their expressions were frowning and dour.

"They will obscure the trail after we enter. Come." She brushed aside the vines and entered without looking to see if the others followed.

Rina looked at Alem who shrugged. They followed Maurizan.

The passage was just wide enough for people and horses to walk single file. It opened into a high arch almost immediately on the other side, and a green valley spread out before them, a shallow river running through it and a camp of maybe a hundred brightly painted wagons on either side. There were numerous cook fires, lines of drying laundry like bright pennants strung between the wagons, children and adults going about various activities, all dressed in the same style of billowing bright clothing.

"They're gypsies, all right," Brasley whispered at Rina's elbow. "Keep your hand on your coin purse."

A trio of men broke off from the main camp and were coming up the trail fast to meet them.

"Why doesn't that seem like a welcoming committee?" Rina said.

The men stopped within ten feet, hands resting on long daggers tucked into wide leather belts.

The man in the middle stepped forward. He wore a bright red shirt with a tight yellow flower pattern. A thin, dark moustache traced his upper lip. A gold hoop in one earlobe. Black hair, glossy in the sunlight. "What is this, Maurizan?"

"These are friends," she said.

Rina thought the girl sounded tentative. *This was a mistake. We should have gone our own way.* She tensed. It was an effort to keep her hand off the rapier hanging from her waist.

"We don't bring strangers to our camp. You *know* this."

Maurizan glanced back at Alem, looked apologetic then turned to the man in front of her again. "Don't embarrass me, Gino. They saved my life. And I think Mother will want to talk to them."

"Your mother's position does not mean you can break our rules," Gino said.

"Well, it's done now, isn't it? Take me to Mother."

The one called Gino looked furious. He pointed at Rina, Alem and Brasley. "You stay here. Wait. You understand?"

"We understand," Rina said.

Gino turned and led Maurizan back toward the camp. The other two gypsies paused halfway down the trail to keep watch on the strangers.

Alem, Brasley and Rina gathered in a small circle, each still holding the reins of their horses.

"I don't like this," Brasley said.

"Exactly what *have* you liked since we've left Klaar," Alem asked.

"You might be used to sleeping with the horses, stable boy, but I could do with a bit of comfort. I don't see why we ever left Kern."

"Gentlemen, enough. We've already been through this," Rina said.

Brasley had wanted to present himself and Rina to the Baron of Kern, loudly declaring their noble status and asking for sanctuary. Under other circumstances it would have been a perfectly reasonable course of action. Kern was one of Klaar's closest neighbors to the south. Rina's father had met with the man numerous times. The Baron had even sent a few lesser sons of marrying age to Klaar to sniff around Rina. Thankfully nothing had come of it. The Baron would want to know the Perranese had invaded. In fact, Rina did feel a pang of obligation to raise the alarm.

But not yet.

Presenting herself to the Baron of Kern would set off a diplomatic chain reaction that would trap her in a dress as she met with the ranks of nobility, all eager to talk and talk and not *do* anything. Rina would likely be passed up the political chain of command all the way to the King of Helva, who would express sympathy that foreign invaders had seized Klaar and then maybe do something about it. Or maybe not.

And in the meantime, weeks would be wasted, and Rina had other plans.

No argument Brasley would make could dissuade Rina from seeking out the wizard Talbun who dwelt somewhere on the border of the Nomad Lands. How she would convince the man, a complete stranger, to help her was a problem she decided to think about later.

So Rina had doggedly stuck to her plan, Brasley complaining loudly and often every step of the way. She'd told him a dozen times that he could take off on his own anytime he liked. He'd usually answer with something like, "Oh, please, you'd both be dead in an hour without my supervision." Rina suspected it was really the fact he was broke and had nowhere else to go that kept him riding along.

Alem had been the exact opposite sort of traveling companion, relentlessly upbeat and helpful. Not once had she ever suggested to Alem he'd be better off going his own way. The long miles would be unpleasant without him, and she felt a bit guilty and selfish about it. Would she really drag the poor boy all the way to the Nomad Lands?

Yeah, I will. Brasley is charming company and amusing when he's not bellyaching, but I can count on Alem. When Brasley drinks too much brandy and falls off his horse, Alem will still be there to pull guard duty, tend the horses, and a dozen other things without so much as a word of complaint.

But it was more than that, wasn't it? It wasn't just that Alem was useful. Alem was … Alem was …

"I say we turn around and ride out of here fast," Brasley said. "Back the way we came before these gypsies can saddle up and give chase."

"That won't work," Alem said sharply. "The gypsies in the trees, remember?"

"Then *you* think of something," Brasley flared.

"Why don't you give your mouth a rest?" Alem shot back.

Rina squeezed her eyes shut tight. "*Both* of you shut up!"

Alem shut up, and surprisingly, so did Brasley.

Rina blew out a sigh, eased her eyes open. "Listen to me. The plan is this. We wait to see what happens. The girl, Mauridan—"

"Maurizan," Alem corrected.

Rina glared at him, and Alem went pink.

"*Maurizan* is going to speak up for us," Rina said. "I infer her mother is of some importance. The gypsies are upset that we're here since they like to keep their camp a secret, but I don't think they're so upset that they'll murder us for it."

"I hope you're right," Brasley said. "I'm hardly an expert on gypsies, but I've always heard they're very secretive and closed to outsiders."

"Then this will be our opportunity to make friends," Rina said. "Right now, we can use all we can get."

"They're coming." Alem nodded his head toward the group of gypsies coming up the trail.

Rina noticed Maurizan was not among them.

Gino stopped three feet from her. The snarl of contempt hadn't left his face. "Come. You shall eat with us. You will be treated as honored guests." His face remained tight.

He calls us honored guests, but he's obviously not feeling it.

"Thank you for your hospitality," Rina said.

Gino nodded curtly. "First, you'll want to refresh yourselves, I'm sure. You shall be escorted to the bath houses."

CHAPTER TWENTY-SEVEN

The bath houses were low log lodges sealed with mud and halfway buried into the side of a small hill. Smoke billowed from a squat stone chimney.

The sun was just dipping below the horizon, and Alem and Brasley shivered, naked, as they handed their clothing to a pair of male gypsies.

Alem made a special effort *not* to look down. Eyes straight ahead.

"I don't see why we have to do this," Alem whispered to Brasley. "I don't need a bath."

"Yes you do," Brasley whispered back. "You stink."

Alem glared at him.

"Oh, don't be so thin skinned," Brasley said. "We *both* stink. We've been out in the wilds, and we smell like campfire and horse and armpit. Be glad for an opportunity to wash it all off."

Alem was more glad about the fact the women's bath house was on the other side of the hill.

"Anyway," Brasley continued, "it's largely a social custom. They'll be offended if we don't join in."

Social. Sure. What's the harm?

They entered the bath house.

Alem was immediately engulfed by steam, which burned his nostrils and lungs. He got used to it after a few moments, blinked at the single oil lamp that strained against the darkness like the distant glow of a lighthouse in the fog.

His eyes adjusted, and he became aware of the men sitting on low benches along the walls, gypsies all sweating naked together in the dark.

I think I might be the anti-social type.

~

Standing barefoot in a patch of old snow reminded Rina of that endless march up the mountain with Kork, the cold and the wet seeping through her slippers and turning her feet into slabs of ice.

Her attention snapped back to the here and now when the gypsy girl asked for her thin blouse. She unlaced it, slipped it off and handed it over.

The gypsy girl gasped.

Damn. Of course, Rina's tattoos. There were parts of Helva where tattoos were not uncommon, but even in those regions, few had such elaborate ink. The designs and magical runes trailed all the way from the base of her neck down her spine to the small of her back. There were more lines across her shoulders. The bull symbol tattoo imbued with magical strength. Rina blushed suddenly, self-conscious. The tattoos would only cause more whispers among the gypsies.

She ducked into the steamy darkness of the bath house, hoping to hide herself. She sat on a wooden bench, her back to the wall. The chatter of the gypsy women hushed immediately. In the darkness and the steam, it was impossible to gauge facial expressions.

Rina cleared her throat. She'd dealt with awkward social situations at court. How hard could this be? "I want to thank you for taking us in. You're very generous."

That set off a whispered exchange among the gypsy women. The whispers died away again almost immediately.

"You are welcome here, Rina Veraiin," came a clear voice through the steam.

Rina tensed. "You know me?" She'd been careful not to offer her last name to anyone these past weeks.

"Gypsy eyes and ears have their secret ways to see and hear." One of the women rose from the benches across the lodge, came toward her through the steam and sat on the bench next to Rina.

She was naked, as they all were, with broad back and hips, full breasts hanging low with middle age, but not *so* low. A handsome woman but somewhat worn. She smiled at Rina, and it seemed sincere although Rina couldn't quite see her eyes.

"I'm Klarissa," she said. "I'm Maurizan's mother."

Rina relaxed a little. If anyone among the gypsies was going to be friendly toward Rina, it would be the mother of the girl she'd saved.

"Thank you," Klarissa said. "For my daughter's life."

"The ones trying to hurt Maurizan were really after me," Rina said. "It would have been wrong not to help."

"She is a curious child and likes to roam too far from our camp. Perhaps this incident scared some sense into her. But ... well, her soul is too adventurous, I think, and our camp seems smaller to her every day. She will run to meet the world too soon."

Rina realized the rest of the women in the steam lodge were listening intently to their conversation.

"Maybe she acts without thinking sometimes, but I thank her for it," Rina said. "Otherwise she might not have brought us to your camp. Although I sense this has made some of your people unhappy."

"Yes." Klarissa nodded. "We were discussing that before you arrived. It's a problem we've already solved."

Rina glanced at the shapes of the women in the steam. *Without the men?*

Klarissa chuckled quietly as if she'd read Rina's mind. "We claim modesty as the reason for separate bath houses, but in fact it's good to have some time away from the men, so we can decide things quietly and calmly."

Rina reached back for a distant memory, something she'd heard about gypsies. The men held all the titles, but the women decided matters behind the scenes. Maybe Rina had come to the right place. Maybe these people could help her.

Still, she didn't want to be in the bad graces of the gypsy men.

"The men seemed pretty upset to have strangers in camp," Rina said. "How'd you win them over?"

"Men." Klarissa rolled her eyes. "Their ruffled feathers are easily smoothed."

The gypsy passed the ceramic jug to Alem. The fumes came through the steam and almost knocked him off the bench.

"Drink, my friend," urged the gypsy next to him. "Drink deep."

Alem remembered what Brasley had said about this being a social occasion and not wanting to give offense. He tilted the jug back and gulped.

It was as if someone had poured flaming lamp oil down his throat. He went dizzy, face hot, felt the jug being pulled from his hands.

Brasley took the jug, didn't hesitate, drank deep. He smacked his lips and passed the jug down the line. "Good stuff. I was worried at first we would not be afforded the famed hospitality of the gypsies. I'm happy to be wrong."

Horseshit. All Brasley had done since entering the gypsy camp was warn that these people were pickpockets and carnival tricksters. He hadn't offered a single kind word. Still, Alem had to admit Brasley could turn on the charm when he wanted. What amazed Alem was how *sincere* Brasley could seem. It was like Brasley's own peculiar brand of magic.

Alem took comfort in the fact that Rina seemed immune to Brasley's charm. *I mean, come on. She's way too smart to fall for his act.*

Right?

The jug came to Alem again, and he drank. Not so harsh this time. The periodic hissing sound came again, somebody pouring water for fresh steam.

"Well, we could tell you weren't a bad sort of folk straight off." Gino's voice was slurred with drink, floated through the steam from a bench opposite them. "But the women get nervous. It's our job to protect the camp. We have to be serious about it."

"Completely understandable," Brasley said. "You have a position of great responsibility. One wrong decision could jeopardize everything, yes?"

Grunts of approval rumbled among the men. This evidently had been the right thing to say. Simple really. Most people wanted approval and understanding, didn't they?

Somehow the jug was in Alem's hands again. He drank.

"This woman with you. Rina. She is … in charge?"

Was that disapproval in Gino's voice or simply curiosity?

Brasley laughed. "Well, don't all women think they're in charge, really?"

More murmurs of approval among the men. Brasley was hitting all the right notes. And he did it without really admitting anything. Again, Alem grudgingly acknowledged Brasley was a clever fellow. What irked Alem was the fact that on some level, Brasley was actually *likable*.

Alem did not *want* to like Brasley.

"She seems a strong woman," Gino said. "And ... attractive."

"Yes," Alem said. "Beautiful." Alem looked up suddenly, realizing he'd said it out loud.

Nobody noticed. The gypsy men seemed to accept that Brasley was the one doing the talking.

"Very attractive indeed," Brasley said. "But, alas, a rose with thorns."

Alem was trying to follow the subtleties of the conversation. What exactly was Gino trying to find out? And was Brasley being insulting to Rina or slyly doing her a favor by scaring Gino away? In the stables, people either kept their thoughts to themselves or said things flat out.

Every time Alem tried to figure it out, he found the ceramic jug in his hands, until the evening dissolved into nothing more than shadowed shapes in the steam.

CHAPTER TWENTY-EIGHT

Rina and Klarissa moved from the steam room to a quiet bath area, both sharing a large tub of hot water. It soothed her aching muscles. Day after day in the saddle had toughened her, but she was sore too. The wooden tub was big enough to fit another five women without crowding but she and the gypsy woman were the only ones. The others had drifted away.

Rina assumed that was by design. A private conversation.

Klarissa told Rina of her people. A people without a homeland.

The camp they were in was as close to a permanent settlement as existed among the gypsies. Technically the camp was located in the southernmost holdings of Baron Kern, but it was deep in the forest, hidden. With an hour's notice, the gypsies could pull up stakes, hitch horse to wagon and vanish. From Klarissa's words, Rina inferred there were many such camps spread throughout Helva. How many and how large they were, well, that was different. Klarissa was sharing information with an outsider. She remained guarded. For a displaced people without a home, secrecy was second nature.

But now Klarissa sensed an opportunity. At least, that was Rina's intuition. The woman thought Rina could help her somehow.

"We have similar problems," Klarissa said. "My people … and you."

Rina sank low into the warm water, up to her chin. "How so?"

"We're homeless, aren't we … Duchess?"

Duchess. No doubt left, is there? She knows who you are. Never mind how. Okay, let's try the direct approach.

"What do you want?"

If she was offended by Rina's frankness, she didn't show it. "How honest shall we be with each other?"

"You seem to know who I am," Rina said. "In which case you probably also know I have little to lose."

"And everything to gain," Klarissa said.

Rina nodded slowly. "I can only promise to listen and to keep an open mind."

Klarissa's smile warmed, her eyes softening. "Well said."

A long pause.

"Klaar is a remote duchy," Klarissa said. "You could describe its relationship with the rest of Helva as distant, yes?"

"We are a loyal part of Helva," Rina said. "We serve at the king's pleasure. But custom in recent years has been that we ask little of his majesty, and his majesty takes little notice of us."

"But now you need him."

Rina thought about it a moment. "Let's say we need help from *somewhere*. Whether it's from the King of Helva or from some … other friend."

"I'd like us to be friends, Rina."

"I'd like that too." Rina even meant it. She had a good feeling about the woman.

"I know something of Klaar." Klarissa said it lightly as if changing the subject. "There is an area where the boundaries of three baronies meet. Sparsely populated except for a small village along Lake Hammish."

"I know the place," Rina said. If she tapped into the spirit, she could easily visualize one of her father's maps, see every river, every valley and forest and ridge. She didn't bother.

"Good land. Good timber," Klarissa said. "Good hunting. A shame more people don't live there. The Perranese have it now, I guess. A shame."

She's shrewd. A land grant for her people. As duchess, I could make it happen. It would be law. I could take a small part of each barony and tell Hammish and the others it's a war tithe. They'd have to sit still for it. So she helps me get Klaar back from the Perranese somehow, and in return, her people get a little chunk to call home.

But how? Was there a gypsy army? Rina estimated only a few hundred people in the camp and many were children or elderly.

When in doubt, resort to honesty. "I haven't been duchess long. I'm not sure what is possible or how to go about it or anything. But I think...I think I understand what you're asking for."

"Please," Klarissa said. "I ask for nothing. We are a poor people with many needs, but we're also a proud people. It has long been our tradition to ask for nothing, but to accept gifts from friends with gratitude and loyalty."

Klarissa moved across the tub and stopped in front of Rina. Another inch closer and their chests would press together.

"Allow me to show you what I mean," she said. "I want to offer you a gift. Something special. Naturally, you may refuse, but I don't think you will."

That depends on what you have in mind, doesn't it? The woman had moved a little too close for Rina's comfort.

"Look at my face," Klarissa said.

Rina looked.

"Look at my eyes."

Like some of the other gypsy women, Klarissa had dark eyeliner around her eyes. Many of the women had gone a little strong with the lip rouge also and used brightly colored eye shadow. Rina found it a bit garish. In the dim light of the bath house, Rina had assumed Klarissa's makeup was the same as that of the other women.

Now upon closer examination, the makeup smudges at the corners of her eyes weren't smudges at all. They were small, finely drawn feathers like little teardrops. The dark liner under each eye was in fact, tightly packed runes, written with a steady hand.

Rina blinked.

Not makeup. A tattoo.

CHAPTER TWENTY-NINE

"Now, when I thrust at you, you slap the blade aside," Tosh said. "But let's try it slow at first a few times, okay? We don't want any accidents."

"Right," Tenni said.

They'd been practicing every day since that horrible night when Tenni had hacked the Perranese corporal to death. It had been ugly and messy, and even though Tosh had been reluctant to teach basic swordsmanship to her, he had to admit it was better she know how to handle herself.

And anyway, Tenni was pretty, so it was a good excuse to spend time with her.

Tosh stabbed the sword at her a couple of times at half-speed, and she batted his blade away easily. She was a fast learner. They both used Perranese swords, which had proved to be fairly easy to come by. Drunken warriors left them all the time at the brothel, and some were too embarrassed to come back and ask for them.

"We've been working mostly on defense," Tosh said. "Want to try some attacks today?"

"Finally."

Tosh frowned. "Don't be so eager. Unless there's a battle tomorrow, there's no hurry."

"There's always a battle. It never stops," Tenni said. "Every minute these foreigners infest our home, the battle goes on in our hearts. I'd kill every one of them if I could."

Oh, Tenni, please don't think that. You're too young and pretty to be filled with hate. "Well, until the battle moves from your heart to the streets of Backgate, let's take it slow."

Tenni frowned, but took up the basic defensive posture.

"Now, for a simple thrust, you'll want your feet to be—"

Tosh froze at the sound of the hatchway above creaking open and slamming shut again. After agreeing to teach Tenni, he'd decided the cave below the brothel where he'd hidden from the Perranese was the best place for the lessons. He didn't want anyone else to see. More to the point, he didn't want word of it getting back to Mother. Maybe she wouldn't care that he was teaching one of her girls swordplay.

Or maybe she would.

Tosh tensed and waited, heard soft footsteps coming around the bend in the tunnel.

The two girls stepped tentatively around the corner. Darshia's hair was pulled back into a tight ponytail. With her was the hawkish brunette who'd lost a brother when Klaar had fallen. Prinn was her name. Both wore loose clothing and carried Perranese-style long swords.

"We're not late, are we?" Darshia asked.

Tosh frowned. "Late for what?"

Darshia held up the sword. "Well … uh …"

Tosh glared at Tenni. "Tenni!"

"What?" Eyes wide and innocent. "Oh, them? I just thought, well, you know. The more the merrier."

"Have you told *anyone* else?"

The girls all shook their heads quickly.

"No one else," Tenni said. "We promise."

Tosh blew out a sigh of relief. "Okay. Fine. But nobody else knows. Tenni, this is your big idea so you're now deputy sword tutor. Start showing Prinn and Darshia the basic defensive stances, and then later—"

More footfalls came around the bend. Tosh turned his head, saw the girl with the chubby face and sandy, frizzy hair called Freen. She was holding a sword. There were two more girls behind her.

"Is this where we do the sword fighting?" Freen asked.

Damn it!

~

General Chen ate at the former Duke's desk in the castle study. Chicken breast and field greens and something called a baked ... what was it? Ah, yes. A potato.

Potatoes were brilliant things. He'd also had them mashed with a heavy dose of butter and fried with salt. Sixty bushels of seed potato were already on a ship back to the emperor. He would not be surprised if such a thing changed the Imperial economy. Or maybe not. In the meantime, Chen had enjoyed potatoes with nearly every meal. Often double helpings.

Chen felt his belly. A very thin layer of softness had formed over the middle. Had his men been indulging in the local cuisine as much as he had? Perhaps too much butter on the potatoes.

Giffen chose that moment to enter. He nodded a slight bow to the General, and Chen gestured him to sit.

"You're finding the Duke's apartments comfortable?" Giffen asked.

Chen smiled tightly. Giffen had assumed he would be moving into the Duke's rooms when he began his puppet rule of Klaar, but as they were the best rooms in the castle, naturally Chen had taken them for himself.

He changed the subject.

"I have not received any word from Captain Tchi's expedition," Chen said. "Should I be concerned?"

Giffen shrugged. "I can't imagine why. Look, she's hiding someplace, probably trying not to soil her pants. Her family is dead. She has nothing. All your man Tchi needs to do is find her and shut her up before she talks to somebody."

Chen grunted. "Perhaps."

Still, if Chen did not hear from Tchi in a few more days he would have to send riders, and really, he couldn't spare any more horses. He hated this place. And the food was making him *fat*. He looked at the plate in front of him. Half a potato remained.

Chen pushed it away.

"I am thinking of moving the garrison outside of the walls," Chen said. "City life is making them soft. Taking Klaar was only the first step. There will be many battles ahead of us."

Giffen shook his head. "Really, I can't advise that, General. The blizzards will start in a month. I don't question the hardiness of your men, but I don't fancy their chances in those flimsy tents."

"There is good timber here," Chen said. "I will start the men building barracks. We'll rotate a company at a time into the city to keep the peace. The population is reasonably docile, yes?"

"Yes," Giffen said carefully. "Klaarians are slowly accepting Perranese rule. For the most part."

"For the most part?"

"The people do not like to see the labor gangs, the former soldiers," Giffen said. "The men are in leg irons, and it's a vivid reminder that they are a conquered people."

"Discontent will pass eventually." Chen drummed his fingers on the desk. "It is decided. I will have the men begin work on the barracks immediately. It will keep them busy and keep them sharp. I don't care for idlers in my army."

"And what about our missing Captain Tchi?"

Chen sighed. *What indeed?*

~

Tchi looked up from his place by the fire where he sat sharpening his sword. One of his men came through the trees toward him.

"Did you find them?" Tchi asked.

In answer, the warrior stepped aside and gestured to the horse he led by the reins. The bodies of five warriors were draped over the saddle.

Tchi stood, went to the slain men, examined them, lips pursed as he thought. He'd explicitly told them to scout ahead. Nothing else. There must have been a reason for them to engage in battle. Perhaps they'd been surprised.

It didn't matter. They were dead. Five of the elite guard.

"Did they encounter a superior force?" Tchi asked.

"There's no way to know for certain," the warrior said. "But I examined the scene of the melee. I think it was only two, maybe three people. But the only bodies were our own men."

That was not encouraging news. Tchi admitted to himself he wasn't sure what to do. He would *not* admit the same to the men.

"Gather a detail of men and bury the bodies," Tchi ordered.

"Yes, sir."

"And bring me our fastest horse and best rider."

CHAPTER THIRTY

As soon as Rina and Klarissa stepped out of the tubs, attendants appeared with soft warm towels. Young gypsy girls scurried around them, patting them dry. Rina recognized one of the faces.

"Maurizan?"

The girl smiled at her. "Hello, milady. I hope you are refreshed."

"Call me Rina. *Milady* doesn't sound right. I'm not duchess of anything. Not really."

"You are to *us*," Maurizan said.

Maurizan sounded so utterly sincere, Rina couldn't stop herself from smiling. And the girl showed no surprise at the elaborate tattoos on her back and shoulders. *Because she knows. She understands what I am.*

"I also wanted to come see you personally," Maurizan said. "To tell you that your friends are well. They're at the feast and enjoying themselves."

"That's good," Rina said. "You have my thanks for making them feel welcome."

Maurizan tossed the towel aside and held up a robe made of some kind of soft animal fur, lined with deep green silk. It was an extravagant garment. Rina noticed another young servant girl helping Klarissa into a similar robe. *I understand. They are a poor people, but Klarissa is an important person. These small luxuries show privilege. Speaking to her like this means something.*

Message received.

"Brasley is very clever and witty," Maurizan continued. "He's entertaining everyone with his stories."

Rina rolled her eyes. "I'll bet."

Maurizan helped Rina slip her arms into the sleeves. Rina pulled the robe around her, cinched it tight with a thick, braided cord. It was warm and soft and quite possibly the most comfortable thing she'd ever worn. Maurizan set a pair of ankle-high leather slippers in front of her. Rina stepped into them. Fur lined.

Could this be what walking on clouds felt like?

"Your clothes are being washed and will be returned to you," Maurizan said.

"Thank you."

"Uh..." Maurizan hesitated. "Alem is also doing well."

"That's good."

"Is he... what I mean to ask is if anyone and Alem... or are you...?"

Rina turned her gaze on the girl. She hadn't meant to glare. It just happened.

Maurizan backed away a half step. "Not that it's any of my... I mean..."

"Maurizan." Klarissa's voice was crisp.

The girl's head snapped around to look at Klarissa. "Mother?"

"Thank you," Klarissa said. "You may go now."

"Of course." Maurizan bowed her head quickly, then turned and scurried away.

Klarissa took Rina by the arm, led her out of the bath house. "Come. Let me show you what my gift for you entails."

The night was clear and cold, but Rina pulled the fur robe close, watched her breath twist away on an easy breeze. Their footfalls crunched in the snow. The bright stars overhead seemed close enough to touch.

Klarissa stepped away and held out one arm.

Something dove at them from the sky, a white flapping, and Rina stepped back, threw up an arm to fend off—

An owl.

It landed on Klarissa's outstretched arm. A small owl with wide, golden eyes, feathers bright white and soft.

"His name is Pontis," Klarissa said. "He's my familiar. There are other familiars, of course, but in my family we've always used birds. The tattoos bond us to them. I can see through his eyes. Sense what he senses."

Rina considered. "If I get the familiar tattoo, will I be bound to an owl?"

Klarissa shrugged. "It depends. Our hunters went out late this afternoon." She motioned for Rina to walk with her. "This way. I want you to meet someone."

Rina followed her down a narrow path that twisted into the trees. The limbs closed over them, creating a tunnel in the forest and blotting out the starry sky.

The flames of a campfire flickered ahead, and when they rounded a bend the trees parted into a small clearing. A gypsy wagon with faded paint sat between two large trees. The wheels were broken, and thick vines crept up the side. The wagon hadn't moved in a long time.

The silhouette of a hunched figure moved around the fire, poking it with a crooked stick. As Rina approached, she saw it was an old woman with a dowager's hump wearing the bright skirt and blouse of the gypsies. She had a bright red cloth with a tight blue floral pattern wrapped around her head and tied under her chin.

The old woman looked up as the two women approached. "This is her?"

"Yes, Mother," Klarissa said. "Duchess Rina Veraiin of Klaar."

Rina had the sudden feeling she should bow or curtsy. She settled for a respectful nod.

"I'm Milda. Turn around, child," the old woman said. "Drop your robe."

Rina hesitated, glanced at Klarissa, who nodded for her to go ahead.

Rina turned, opened the robe and lowered it past the small of her back. The cold air hit her skin, breaking her out in goose flesh.

Milda traced boney fingers down Rina's spine. "Oh, yes. This is Weylan's work, all right."

Rina looked over her shoulder at the old woman. "You know him?"

Milda gestured to Klarissa. "Show her, Daughter."

Klarissa turned, lowered her robe just as Rina had a moment earlier.

Of course. She couldn't have the bird familiar tattoo if she didn't already have the spine tattoo first. Rina hadn't seen it in the steam, and in the tub Klarissa hadn't turned her back toward her. The ink had faded with the years, but the distinct lines and runes were clear. No wonder Klarissa seemed to know so much about Klaar. She'd been there and had known the old wizard.

"The one down the back is called the Prime. Mother has the same ink," Klarissa said.

"You'll have to take my word for it. I'll spare you the sight." The old woman cackled.

Rina and Klarissa pulled up their robes and fastened them. Milda hobbled around the back of the wagon and returned a moment later carrying a wicker cage. Something fluttered within, snatching at Rina's attention.

The old woman beckoned. "Come and see."

Rina stepped forward, bent to look at the bird fluttering on its perch within the cage. It was maybe ten inches long, a bird of prey with a hooked beak, green plumage on top and white underneath. "What is it?"

"A Forest Falcon," she said. "It would have been nice to bring you one of the great mountain eagles, but we had little time. I think they did quite well considering the short notice."

"He's magnificent," Rina said.

"He is young and strong," Milda said. "If you allow me to ink the familiar tattoo on you, then you will bond with him."

Rina searched the old woman's face. "What does that mean exactly? Klarissa says I will see through his eyes."

"Yes. But there's more. You'll share a kinship. When he dies, you will feel it. You will lose a part of yourself. My familiar was a large and crafty raven. He served me a long time, but when he passed, it took me months to recover fully. In everything there is sacrifice."

"There is always a price," Rina said. "Weylan told me that." It was a relief finally to know the old mage's name.

"Is he tutoring you?" Milda asked.

"No," Rina said. "He's dead. The wasting sickness. It took all of his power to hold it at bay, but he used that power to help me instead, and he died." As it came out of her mouth, it sounded to Rina like a confession. How ungrateful would she be if she didn't live up to the gift on which Weylan had spent his life?

"I'm thankful for what you're offering me," Rina said solemnly. "And I accept."

CHAPTER THIRTY-ONE

Rina sat perfectly still on a small wooden stool as the old gypsy woman went about the delicate task of inking the tattoo across her face. A false move and Milda might stab her in the eye, although she seemed to have steady hands for a woman of her advanced years. Klarissa stood close, holding a candle to light her face. They sat under the stars, away from the fire so Rina wouldn't sweat.

Milda had already stenciled the feathers at the corners of Rina's eyes and now worked to neatly print the lines of magical runes. She used one of the falcon's tail feathers, shaved to needle sharpness, to work the ink into Rina's flesh. The ink itself had been mixed with a few drops of the falcon's blood. Milda had stirred it slowly in a ceramic bowl as she whispered ancient spells.

In a moment of vanity, Rina wondered how the tattoo would look on her.

Alem will think I've gone native.

And why Alem's opinion should matter, Rina couldn't guess. But, well, it *did* for some reason. Brasley would of course poke fun at her, but that was to be expected. His attempts at wit hardly affected her anymore.

The old woman sat back, tilted her head as she squinted at Rina. At last she nodded her satisfaction. "It is finished."

Klarissa set the candle aside and began fastening something to Rina's left forearm. She looked down, saw it was a leather bracer, lined on the inside with lamb's wool. Klarissa cinched the leather straps tight and buckled them.

Milda had already trudged back to the wicker cage. She bent with a muted grunt and opened the cage door.

"Try it," Klarissa said.

Rina tapped into the spirit and immediately felt the presence of the falcon. The bird sprang from the cage, flapped its wings three times rapidly for loft and then glided smoothly to Rina's outstretched arm, tucking in its broad wings at the last second as it pulled up and gripped the leather bracer.

There was no language spoken between her and the familiar. The bond didn't work that way. Rather, the bird somehow sensed what Rina wanted, and she could sense the mood of the falcon, knew even now that it was getting used to her, was curious about her.

But she knew also, even in this early stage of their bonding, that the falcon would obey.

"How many in your tribe have the bird familiar tattoo?" Rina asked.

"I do and my mother," Klarissa said. "No others."

"Nobody else? Really?"

"It won't work without the Prime," Klarissa explained. "And there are precious few wizards who know the spells. With Weylan's passing, maybe nobody does."

A shame so few wizards know the secret. An army of ink mages could come in handy. Or maybe that's the point. To prevent such a thing.

Rina closed her eyes, and the falcon instinctively flew into the air, gaining altitude quickly.

As Klarissa had warned, her own senses were completely cut off. She now saw through the eyes of the falcon.

Stars filled her vision, wheeled and blurred as the falcon spun, the ground coming into view. Rina's stomach fluttered as the bird dropped and angled away across the forest. She was flying. The wind washed over her. The world spread out below. She *knew* both of her feet were on the ground, but the illusion was so complete it thrilled her.

She soared.

The falcon's eyes were keen, even at night. But of course they would be. The bird was a predator.

She commanded the bird to turn north without really even knowing how she did it. The falcon simply understood her wishes and obeyed. It traced the path back the way they'd come earlier when Maurizan had led them to the hidden valley.

An orange glow in the distance. A campfire, Rina realized abruptly. She'd never seen one from this height before. The falcon dove for it, landed in a high tree branch.

Perranese warriors and their horses. She counted at least a dozen, but there were likely more. Sentries out beyond the firelight at the very least. They were close. No more than five miles by falcon flight.

Rina's eyes popped open, and she turned to Klarissa. "My friends and I need to leave before first light," she said. "I've seen the Perranese camp. They're bedding down for the night, but they'll come first thing in the morning."

"I'll tell my people to prepare your horses and fill the saddlebags with provisions."

"More gifts," Rina said. "You and your people have been very kind."

Klarissa smiled warmly. "When the time is right, I'm sure you will remember us."

CHAPTER THIRTY-TWO

Tosh descended the ladder into the cave below the brothel and heard the voices by the time he reached the bottom, including the high squeal of Tenni's daughter Emmon.

He rounded the bend and saw Emmon jumping up and down on the bed.

He blinked. *Why is there a bed down here?*

Tenni stood with Darshia, watching and clapping as Emmon jumped. The little girl suddenly saw Tosh and pointed. "There he is!"

"Does it take so much out of you when we train that you need a bed down here?" Tosh said.

"It's for you."

"What?"

Tosh approached the bed and Emmon launched herself at him. He had barely enough time to drop the wooden practice swords and catch her in both arms. She hugged him tight, and then he set her down.

Emmon beamed at him. "It's your place to sleep now."

Tosh pushed down on the mattress with one hand. Soft. "I don't understand."

"Are you saying you want to stay in the pantry?" Darshia asked.

When Tosh had agreed to stay on as cook, they told him they would figure out a room for him eventually. So after the kitchen was cleaned every night, he'd spread a bedroll on the pantry floor. He was generally so tired at the end of the day he could have slept on a pile of rocks. Somehow nobody had ever got around to finding him his own quarters, and all the rooms were used by the girls anyway. Tosh was so happy to have a safe, warm place that he never brought it up.

Evidently the girls had taken the matter into their own hands.

"Bune and Lubin brought it down for us," Tenni said.

Tosh realized he was grinning like an idiot. Something as simple as the fact that he was going to sleep in a real bed again was about to make him mist up. "Thanks. It means—" He cleared his throat. "It means a lot."

"You're spending so much of your free time teaching us swordplay," Darshia said. "It's the least we can do."

"Speaking of which ..." He looked around. "Where *is* everyone?"

"The place is almost deserted," Tenni said, meaning *upstairs in the brothel*.

Tosh nodded, scratching his chin. Two weeks ago, General Chen had completed the Perranese barracks outside of the city walls, and the result was that business at the Wounded Bird had slowed to a trickle.

Darshia said, "Frankly, I'm glad for the rest. Freen has squirreled away a jug of the good stuff, so we're giving ourselves a girls' night. And *this* little girl needs a bath before bed." She tousled Emmon's hair.

"I took a bath two days ago," she whined. "I'm still clean."

Darshia took Emmon by the hand. "Say goodbye to Uncle Tosh."

She waved. "Bye, Toshi-tosh!"

"Bye, sweetie."

He turned back to the bed, pushed down on it again. *Very* soft. Girls' night. Good idea. Tosh welcomed a night without sword practice. The girls were getting better, and those damn practice swords left *bruises*.

Tosh sensed somebody behind him and turned. Tenni still stood there, hands clasped behind her back.

"No girls' night for you?"

She shook her head, reached for the laces of her blouse and tugged them loose. She lifted the blouse over her head, dropped it on the floor.

Tosh froze. "You don't ... I mean, I don't want you to feel you have to—"

"It's not like that." Tenni hooked her thumbs into her skirt, pushed it down over her hips and let that drop to the floor too. "I want to. I want *you*."

She was slender and delicate and Tosh ached for her.

She walked lightly to the oil lamp hanging on the wall, blew it out.

A second later he felt her press against him in the pitch darkness. His hands went instinctively to her bare backside. He grew hard immediately, and she felt him pressing against her belly.

They kissed.

He felt her hot breath on his ear as she whispered, "I love you."

"I love you too."

Her arms went around his neck, pulled him down. They kissed again, tongues finding each other.

"And anyway," she said. "You didn't think I'd give you a bed and then not test it, did you?"

～

Hours later he awoke, felt for her in the bed, but she wasn't there. Perhaps Tenni had gone for girls' night after all. More likely she needed to check on Emmon.

Tosh smiled, thinking of her. How had his life gotten so good in just a few short months? He'd fallen in love with Tenni, never thinking she might feel the same way. He reminded himself sternly that Tenni was one of the working girls upstairs. It would be difficult thinking of her with other men while they—

No. He'd allow himself at least one night to enjoy it. Damn the complications until later.

His internal clock told him it was almost time to go upstairs and fire the kitchen stove anyway. *All those damn years in the army, getting up early and keeping schedules.*

He dressed and went upstairs.

In the kitchen, he fed logs into the belly of the stove and lit the fire. Then he began taking inventory. It had been hard to get a handle on breakfast recently. Some clients stayed with their girl overnight and wanted to eat in the morning. But business had been so slow recently, Tosh couldn't say whether or not there was even a single client in residence. The girls would need to be fed, of course, but they were generally not early risers.

He decided to dice just enough potatoes for the girls. He could whip up some more or fudge on the servings if it turned out they had a few surprise clients.

Tosh daydreamed as he diced, finding a rhythm with the big kitchen knife. He was a good cook and felt he could run a kitchen now. What if he and Tenni and Emmon went away, opened a little tavern somewhere? The Perranese wouldn't miss a cook and a prostitute. Why would they? Eventually the roads would open again. Things would get back to normal and—

A commotion in the common room startled him—the sound of a door slamming open, furniture being overturned.

Tosh grabbed the biggest meat cleaver from the rack and rushed from the kitchen and into the common room, bracing himself for intruders.

Four of them stood in the open doorway of the brothel, their dark travel cloaks flapping in the cold wind gusting from outside. One held an unsheathed sword, blood dripping from the blade. Their hoods were up, and at first Tosh couldn't see who they were in the dim light of the common room's single oil lamp. He gripped the cleaver tightly, readied himself.

Two of them carried a third between them. She sagged in their arms, head lolling and limp.

She?

The one with the sword pushed hard to close the door against the wind. When it was shut, she turned back to Tosh, pulled back the cloak's hood. Tenni looked at him with large, panicked eyes.

Oh no.

"Get her on the table," Darshia said. "Hurry."

Darshia and Prinn carried Freen to the closest table, swept aside the iron candle holders which clattered loudly on the floor. They spread Freen out on the table, pulled back her hood. Darshia dabbed at sweat on the girl's chubby face with a rag. Freen was ashen, weeping softly between groans.

Tosh shifted his gaze to Freen's belly. Blood gushed. Freen tried to hold it in with both hands, fingers sticky with blood.

Freen's body writhed with a sudden stab of pain, a spasm, her back arching and legs kicking as she cried out. Darshia and Prinn rushed to hold her down.

Tenni looked at Tosh with desperate, frightened eyes, silently pleading for him to do something.

"Dumo, save us," Tosh whispered. "What have you stupid whores done?"

CHAPTER THIRTY-THREE

Tosh's hands were slick and hot with blood. He held them against Freen's belly. She writhed and bucked beneath him, pain lancing through her guts. Darshia held her shoulders to the table and Prinn her legs, but Freen was dying and knew it and was going out kicking and moaning through clenched teeth.

"Give me your cloak," he told Tenni.

She did.

The material was light for a winter cloak, and with some effort Tosh ripped a wide strip from it. He lifted Freen's hips, and she howled. Tosh slipped the ripped length of cloak under her then tied it tight across the gaping rent in her belly.

This time, Freen's screams brought the other girls out of their rooms, all wearing loose shifts or nightgowns. They stood in the hall, craning their necks and gaping, not daring to step into the common room.

"Get back to your rooms!" Tosh bellowed.

They turned as one, scampered away. There was the sound of doors slamming shut.

Tosh had never spoken to any of them like that before and would feel bad about it later. At the moment, all he could think was that he needed to stop the bleeding. Freen was already ghostly pale, her lips blue.

Tosh grabbed Tenni's slender hands, placed them on Freen's bloody belly. "Press down. Hard."

Immediately, blood oozed between Tenni's fingers.

Tosh ripped the rest of the cloak into strips. He wadded one of the strips, pushed Tenni's hands out of the way and pressed the material hard against the wound. It was sopping with blood in seconds.

"We've got to stop this bleeding or—"

At the edge of his vision, he sensed the girls backing away. There was only the sound of his own heartbeat hammering wildly in his ears and Prinn's soft weeping. No screams, not anymore. He looked at each of them. They returned blank stares. He looked at Freen.

She didn't seem real, skin and bone white and waxen, blood bright on her lips. Her glassy eyes stared up and far away, looking at something in another realm.

Tosh stood back from the table, wiped his bloody hands on his breeches. He looked at each of them again, but none dared speak. He turned his back and walked, slow and leaden, into the kitchen.

The soapy water in the wash tub was still warm. He took out the cups he'd been soaking and plunged his hands into the water. He scrubbed them with a brush, took them out again for examination. Blood under his nails, caked in the creases around his knuckles. He plunged them back in the water, scrubbed slowly.

He felt somebody come up behind him but didn't turn. The feel of soft, tentative fingertips on his back told him it was Tenni.

"What happened?" Tosh asked.

"I'm sorry," Tenni said. "We never thought that—"

"Please." His voice was quiet but with an edge. "Just tell me how it happened. The basics. No need to make it a fireside story."

"Prinn is friends with a woman in Market Town. Her husband is a baker. This big Perranese sergeant comes around once a week and makes them pay. He asks for more each time. Last time they didn't have enough and he hurt her. I thought Darshia, Prinn, Freen, and I could ... take care of it."

"You mean kill him."

Tenni cleared her throat. "Yes."

"Go on."

"We waited for him," Tenni said. "We thought with just him against the four of us—"

"They're trained soldiers," Tosh said flatly, like he was correcting a small child. "And anyone with sergeant's rank would be a blooded veteran."

"He had another soldier with him," Tenni said.

Tosh sighed.

"You taught us well," Tenni insisted. "We surprised them and our swordplay was good. If Freen hadn't ... If we hadn't been crowded in the alley—"

"If!" Tosh slammed his fist on the counter, shattered a ceramic mug and cut his hand. Tenni flinched.

"It's *always* IF," he shouted. "Every battle, every skirmish, every ugly knife fight in a dank alley. Always the *ifs* are waiting around the corner to fuck you up. The most seasoned veteran can still slip in dog shit and fall on a sword."

"I'm sorry," she said, voice barely above a whisper.

He grabbed her roughly by the shoulders. "What if it'd been you instead of Freen? You think I want to see your belly spilling out on the table? Do you think I could stand that? I can't lose you just when we've found each other!"

She cried instantly, great racking sobs as she gulped for breath, eyes streaming, snot running from her nose. She'd been holding it back, but now the emotion all heaved out of her at once. She tried to talk, mouth working, eyes pleading, but could only cry and sniff.

He pulled her in tight, wrapped her up in his arms. She trembled against him, still sobbing. "Shhh. Never mind," he said. "I'm sorry."

They held each other for long seconds. Finally, Tosh heard somebody shuffling across the room, a throat clearing.

He looked up, saw Darshia, hesitant in the kitchen doorway.

"Forgive me. I didn't want to interrupt," she said. "But Mother wants to see you, Tosh."

~

Mother stood with her back to Tosh, looking out the frosted window at the snow-crusted roofs of Backgate. Winter's gray light made her face look troubled, the lines on her face deeper. She fidgeted with something in her hands, but from Tosh's vantage point, standing just inside the door of her private office, he couldn't see it.

Tosh shifted his weight from foot to foot as he told her what had happened to Freen, starting with Tenni's ill-advised attempt to take on the Perranese extortionist and ending with Freen's bloody death in the common room downstairs. He related the facts without emotion as if he were reporting to one of his old army captains, but his guts churned and he felt cold sweat on the back of his neck.

She's going to throw me out. I was supposed to cook, not give fencing lessons. Women like her don't put up with trouble like this.

"Were any of the other girls hurt?" Mother asked.

"No, ma'am."

A pause.

"Are they any good?"

Tosh blinked. "Ma'am?"

"The girls," Mother said. "With the weapons."

Tosh hadn't been expecting the question, hadn't even thought about the girls' swordsmanship in those terms. It had become an activity to pass the time, exercise, nothing more. He had to think about it for an extra moment.

"They're not bad, I suppose," Tosh said. "Not like regular soldiers, mind you, but they're coming along faster than I'd expected."

"Why is that, do you think?"

Tosh wiped the sweat from the back of his neck. More dampened his armpits. "They're better listeners, for one thing. Also, a lot of the men who join the army have already handled a weapon a little bit maybe, but they've learned wrong and picked up bad habits. So they need to be cured of that before they can learn the right way ... which is to say the army way."

"The girls are blank slates."

"Yes, ma'am. That's a good way to put it."

"And you've taught just those four?"

"Mostly them, but a couple of others too. But I *don't* encourage it," he added hastily. "Most of the girls don't even know."

She turned back to him, and Tosh saw that she fidgeted with a gold ring. It was thick and set with the seal of Klaar. A man's ring. Mother rubbed it idly between a thumb and forefinger like some good luck charm.

Mother's brow was knit, her face pulled down by a frown. "So they can be taught? They can get better?"

Tosh hesitated. "I ... suppose. It's not traditional in Klaar, but I've heard of plenty of places where women fight."

Mother nodded, thoughts flickering behind her eyes. "Good."

"Uh, ma'am?"

"What is it, Tosh?"

"Are you, uh, are you saying you want me to keep on teaching Tenni, Prinn and Darshia? After what happened to Freen, they might not be up for it anymore."

"What I'm saying is that I want you to teach them *all*," Mother said. "Every girl at the Wounded Bird. I want you to put swords in their hands and make them killers."

CHAPTER THIRTY-FOUR

Dawn bloomed on the horizon, washing the wide-open grasslands in pale orange light. Lonely and crooked trees a mile apart dotted the landscape like bent old men, their shadows stretching away from them in the burgeoning sun.

It was their third sunrise together since leaving the hidden gypsy valley. They were headed west and had camped the previous night in the waning tree line of the forest where it turned the landscape over to the rolling prairie ahead.

Alem squinted at the dawn as he looked back east. He stood with hands on hips, frowning back into the dark forest.

"Stop that." Brasley slung his saddle onto his horse's back, cinched it tight. "She says they aren't following."

Alem grunted, didn't turn around.

"Tell him, Rina," Brasley said.

Rina paused at her own horse where she'd been checking her saddlebags. She closed her eyes.

Alem turned his head slightly to look at her. He always watched her when she did the trick with the falcon, her face blank like she'd somehow frozen herself in time, existing apart from the rest of the world.

When Alem had first seen the tattoos around Rina's eyes, he'd been mesmerized, had barely even heard Brasley's jokes about Rina going native. He recalled the vision of her in the barn in Hammish, the tight lines of runes down her lithe back. Thinking about her this way made him light-headed. It was already too much and too ridiculous to find himself in love with a duchess. That she was also ... what? A sorceress? It made the notion that she might ever return his feelings that much more farfetched.

Thicko. Idiot. Fool. Put it out of your mind. It'll never happen.

And yet, she didn't treat him like a servant. It was clear she appreciated him, and more important, she trusted him. Two nights ago, when Brasley had gone to fetch water from the stream, she'd sat close to him by the fire, tilted her head toward his to speak in hushed tones.

"You saw the tattoo on my back," she'd whispered. "In the barn back in Hammish. Didn't you?"

He'd only nodded, afraid to speak, afraid that he'd seen something he shouldn't have, that he possessed knowledge of which he wasn't worthy. He felt oddly that he was being accused of something, but the feeling passed and was replaced with the peculiar honor one feels when trusted with a secret. Strange how honors and burdens are so often confused.

"The tattoos are magic," she'd said simply. "Tell no one."

"I won't," he'd said.

"That's why I need to go to the Nomad Lands," she'd explained. "To see a wizard."

She'd paused, fixed him with eyes so sincere and needful that he'd thought he might weep. "Will you come with me?"

Alem had nodded. "Yes."

And then their conversation had been cut short upon Brasley's return.

Alem had not broached the subject again. But every time she closed her eyes to commune with the falcon, as she did now, Alem watched from the edge of his vision, hoping to glimpse a miracle, wanting to see what magic looked like.

Her eyes popped open, and she sucked in a deep breath of cold air the way she always did when coming back, like her body was starting up again.

"Klarissa's people are still drawing them off to the south," Rina said. "Even if they turned around right now and rode without stopping, it would take them three days to reach us."

"See?" Brasley said. "Stop worrying like an old hen. Every time you look over your shoulder, you make me nervous."

"Not nervous enough." But Alem shrugged, tore his gaze away from the forest and mounted his own horse.

They rode at a slow gallop, a steady pace but nothing that would tire the horses too quickly. The land unfolded before them, rolling gently, hills not very high and valleys not too deep. The trees remained infrequent and far from one another as if each of the gnarled, rough-barked things had staked out its own territory. The sun rose, the sky stretching cloudless and startlingly blue in every direction.

They'd periodically slow the horses to a walk to let them rest, and it was during one of these periods that Alem reined in his mount suddenly and stopped. The others stopped too and looked back at him.

"She said they've been drawn off to the south by the gypsies," Brasley reminded him. "I thought we'd put this particular worry to rest."

"Just wait a minute, okay?"

Brasley looked to Rina, who shrugged. He sighed and slouched in his saddle.

They were in a wide, low area between two hills, the slopes very gradual. The three of them watched the prairie behind them for long minutes, and Alem was about to call it quits when a figure crested the hill in the distance, a lone rider on a large white horse.

Alem shot a glance back at Brasley. "See? I knew we were being followed."

"Yes, your powers of clairvoyance are truly astounding. But that isn't a Perranese column. It could be anyone. Or are we supposed to piss ourselves every time we see a lone rider in the distance?"

But there was little heat in Brasley's sarcasm. The three of them continued to watch the rider with mild trepidation. He'd reined in his horse and sat atop the squat hill looking down at them. He was cloaked completely in black, hood pulled forward to obscure his face. His appearance seemed ominous for no other reason than his sudden materialization out in the middle of the wilderness, and after so many days of pursuit by the Perranese, nerves were on edge. The rider watched them for another brief moment, then wheeled his mount around, heading back the way he'd come and disappearing down the other side of the hill.

"Where's he going?" Alem asked.

"Three of us and only one of him," Brasley said. "Maybe we made him nervous."

"We made *him* nervous?"

"There's always the chance he's just another traveler."

"I'd feel better if we knew for sure," Rina said.

"The falcon?" Alem suggested.

"He's south, watching the Perranese," Rina said. "I'll call him back, but it will take time. I'm not sure I want to wait. That rider knows we've seen him now."

"Then what do we do?" Brasley asked.

She turned her mount, kicked it lightly in the flanks and clicked her tongue, spurring the horse to a gallop. "We ride on."

~

The sun sank, and the velvet night sky spread itself endlessly over the prairie, stars glittering bright, a tapestry cold and beautiful. In a dell near one of the gnarled trees, a small campfire glowed. Twenty yards away, another of the crooked trees grew uncharacteristically near the first.

The dark-cloaked rider on the white steed paused to watch the flickering scene. The semicircle of horses blocked most of the rider's view of the small camp, but a single silhouette could be seen moving in front of the fire, and likely the other two were close. It was a cold night.

The rider dismounted and left the horse behind. It was well-trained and wouldn't wander. Sound traveled easily in the open grassland, and from beneath the dark overhanging limbs of the second tree it might be possible to overhear the conversation of the three travelers. This was the rider's aim.

Approaching the camp called for stealth, and the rider didn't hurry. Careful steps. Not a sound.

Once the rider was beneath the tree's low limbs, Alem dropped from his hiding place, landing hard on the rider. He sensed Rina dropping from her spot a few feet away and Brasley running toward them from the campfire with a torch in his hand.

"I've got him," Alem shouted.

He wrapped his arms around the rider, wrestling to get on top of him. He was slighter than he appeared within the billowing cloak, a small man. Alem climbed on top, and the figure beneath him uttered a high-pitched yelp.

That didn't sound right.

Alem threw back the rider's hood just as Brasley arrived with the torch, illuminating the scene.

The rider was red haired, a light smattering of freckles across her nose, bright white skin and piercing green eyes.

"Maurizan!"

CHAPTER THIRTY-FIVE

Maurizan sat hunched at the small fire, cupping a mug of weak herbal tea in both hands, cherishing the warmth.

She confessed she'd been following them since their hasty departure from the gypsy camp, shivering under a thin blanket every night because she'd worried a fire would give her away. Long days in the saddle. She admitted she hadn't expected them to cover so many miles each day. When the gypsies traveled it was by slow-moving wagon caravan. Her meals had been cold jerky and hard biscuits.

"Following somebody without letting them see you is more difficult than I thought," she said.

"Better we discovered you now than in a month when we're halfway across Helva," Brasley said. "It's only three days back to your mother. You can start at first light."

Alem frowned at Brasley but said nothing.

"I don't want to go back," Maurizan said.

Brasley shrugged. "Too bad."

Maurizan's fierce eyes stabbed at Brasley. "If you send me away, I'll just come back. I'll follow you to the other side of the world. You'll have to kill me to stop me."

Silence stretched into a long, awkward moment.

"Why?" Alem asked quietly.

"Because there's nothing to go back to. My birthright was stolen." Maurizan jerked her chin at Rina. "*She* knows what I'm talking about."

All eyes went to Rina.

Rina's head spun, eyes meeting Maurizan's.

Maurizan didn't flinch from Rina's stare. "My grandmother was given the Prime. As was my mother. I was meant to have it as well. And now I can't. It was meant for me, and now I'll *never* have it. I'll never be anything but a little, stupid gypsy girl."

Alem and Brasley looked at one another, the question plain on their faces. The prime what?

Rina turned away. So that was it. It was completely wrong and unfair. The idea that Rina had deprived Maurizan of anything was ludicrous. And yet ...

The wizard Weylan had died in the act of inking the Prime tattoo on Rina's back. It would be easy for a young girl's mind to twist this into an act of theft. If Maurizan had been set to receive the gift of the Prime from Weylan, and if Rina had suddenly appeared out of nowhere to snatch this gift out from under her ... yes. It hadn't been intentional; Rina hadn't known ... but she could understand how Maurizan might feel fate had betrayed her.

"What do you want?" Rina asked. "You know what's happened can't be undone."

"I want to come with you." There was something bold in Maurizan's voice. "Change is coming to Helva. My mother says we stand on the edge of great events. I want to be part of them. I want to be important. I was *meant* to *do* something important. You took that away from me. Mostly. But I can at least be near what is happening, witness it. I can't be as important as I'd hoped, but I can do ... something."

Rina looked away, crossed her arms.

"Nonsense," Brasley said. "Rina only just laid eyes on you a few days ago. She's stolen nothing. You're a delusional, spoiled little girl and—"

"Brasley." Alem's voice was low but tight.

Brasley held up his hands and backed away. "Fine. No harsh words. No hurt feelings. But she goes. We have enough to worry about. She goes in the morning."

"It's not your decision," Alem said.

"It's not yours either!" shouted Brasley.

"It's mine," Rina said. "So everybody else shut up."

Alem turned back to the campfire, absently poked at the embers with a stick. Brasley threw up his hands and turned away. Only Maurizan held firm, her eyes never leaving Rina's.

Rina held Maurizan's gaze for a long moment. The campfire cracked and popped. Stars twinkled overhead.

"She stays," Rina said. "As long as she wants. It's her choice."

Brasley sighed extravagantly. "Fantastic. How could this trip get worse?"

CHAPTER THIRTY-SIX

The cold rain had been steady all day, and after they passed the inn, Brasley brought his horse alongside Rina's and asked, "Is there any good reason we're passing up a perfectly good, warm, dry place to sleep?"

Rina glanced back at the inn. She thought about telling Brasley they were low on funds, but that wasn't true. They were by no means wealthy, but they could certainly afford a couple of rooms. It was a small, shabby village and a small, shabby inn, so it wouldn't be expensive. Unfortunately, it likely also wouldn't be all that comfortable, although it certainly would be warm and dry.

"We still have four hours of daylight." She glanced at the sky; the rain clouds were so thick and dark that calling it daylight was being generous. Still, she'd felt driven ever since leaving the gypsy camp. She had to make it to the Nomad Lands, had to find Talbun. Every minute seemed a delay that put Klaar farther and farther out of her reach. The Perranese would dig in, and they would own the duchy, and they'd have a foothold in Helva.

Then it will be the king's problem, won't it? That thought had a fleeting appeal. That she could go off, start a new life without looking back. Let somebody else handle the Perranese.

But no. Like the people of Klaar, Rina was independent minded, but she was still a loyal subject.

They'd crossed the grasslands in ten days, keeping west but also veering south, where they'd picked up a narrow road that made traveling a bit easier. The same gnarled trees dotted the landscape, but in clumps of twos and threes or even a dozen, and small farming villages had sprung up about a day from one another, the wide fields around each one barren for the winter, but she seemed to recall the locals grew some variety of grain. At least that's what she remembered her father saying, and as always she felt something go tight in her chest when she thought of him.

The rain had come before dawn's light and hadn't eased.

A wave of fatigue rolled over her suddenly and she had the sharp feeling she should turn the horse back toward the inn. Just to be warm for a few hours. Just to sleep on something softer than the ground.

No. They rode on, the village dwindling behind them, Brasley grumbling in the saddle.

Rina glanced back, saw that Maurizan was riding close beside Alem; their heads leaned together in conversation. That had been the norm the past week, and Rina wondered if Alem was the real reason Maurizan had followed them. Her childish infatuation with the boy was obvious to everyone but Alem, a situation that irritated Rina for no good reason.

That night a campfire proved impossible. Everything was soaked. Brasley kicked the small pile of wet kindling, scattering sticks and cursing under his breath. "So is everyone enjoying their riding holiday to the ass end of nowhere?"

"Give it a rest, Brasley." Rina kept her voice flat.

Anger flashed briefly in Brasley's eyes before he turned away.

They all curled under wet blankets beneath a cluster of the gnarled trees about a hundred yards off the road where the land rose just enough to keep the rainwater from puddling around them. They awoke the next morning sore and cold and none of them in any better mood than Brasley. They climbed groaning into their saddles and headed off southwest again, the horses' hooves splashing the mud of the wagon-rutted road.

If they passed through a village big enough to have an inn, they'd stop, Rina decided. Everyone's morale needed a boost. She regretted not stopping before. The wet, cold misery had sapped them all. Even a farmer's barn would be welcome. Sleeping in the hay and the stink of horseshit, they would at least be dry.

But as the day waned, there was still no sign of civilization. They resigned themselves to another night under wet blankets.

In the failing light, Brasley's horse stepped into a hole. It had been filled with water and he hadn't seen it. The horse pitched forward, going down in front, and Brasley flew out of the saddle, landing with a cold splash in the mud. His horse sprang up again, trotting a few yards away, spooked but unhurt.

"Damn it!" Brasley sat up and slapped the puddle next to him with open palm, splashing more muddy water. "This is ridiculous. We've been traveling in the cold and the wet and getting saddle sore, and for what?"

Alem dismounted, offered Brasley a hand. "Come on, man. Get up. You're just out of sorts."

Brasley slapped his hand away. "Out of sorts! Really. I can't imagine why." He stabbed a finger at Rina. "You *know* this is wrong. The king should have been told about the Perranese *immediately*. You've let your private obsession cloud your judgment, and you're dragging us all along for the ride."

Rina sat in the saddle, shoulders slumped. She looked down at Brasley in the mud, her face blank. The only sound was the patter of rain. Brasley was right about one thing at least. They couldn't go on like this.

She dismounted and drew her rapier, the blade coming out of the scabbard with a metallic hiss loud enough to make Maurizan gasp behind her.

"On one knee, Brasley."

He blinked up at her, suddenly less confident. "What—?"

"Do it."

Brasley knelt in the mud, looking up at her, a mix of worry and curiosity on his face.

"You're an untitled, lesser son of a minor nobleman," Rina said. "We have to do better than that if you're going to be my envoy to the King of Helva." She tapped his shoulder with the tip of her sword, tried to remember the words her father had used on such occasions. "Under the holy eyes of Dumo, as Duchess of Klaar and before these witnesses here present, I hereby name you Sir Brasley Hammish, bound now by oaths to protect and serve me and the Duchy of Klaar until such time as you are released from my service or death takes you." She tapped the other shoulder. Okay, she'd paraphrased slightly, but the words were close enough. "Rise, Sir Brasley."

Brasley didn't rise. He stared up at her. "Can you do that?"

She shrugged. "I'm either a duchess or I'm not."

He rose slowly, one of his knees popping. The rain fell. "I ... I don't know what to say."

"You were right," Rina said. "The crown needs to be told about the Perranese. Likely they won't be able to do anything until the spring thaw, but they still need to know. And somebody needs to speak up for Klaar at court. You're a silver-tongued devil, so I guess that's as close as we have to a diplomat." Rina allowed a slight smile to twitch at the corner of her mouth. "And anyway, you're a huge pain in the ass. The sooner we get you back to clean sheets and fine living, the sooner you'll stop bellyaching. I think life at court will agree with you better than life on the road."

He grinned. Sheepish. "Still, I'd feel better if I had a signed letter proclaiming my knighthood. Something with your signature and the Duke's seal in wax."

Rina shrugged again. "I don't have my father's signet ring. Sorry. But a letter at least can be arranged."

"It'll have to do."

"This is the court of the King of Helva. And you're now a knight and the official representative of the Duchy of Klaar. You've got to strut in there as arrogant as a peacock and make them listen to you." She smiled more warmly now. "I feel you're the *perfect* man for the job."

CHAPTER THIRTY-SEVEN

Tosh put the girls through their paces, or rather Tenni did while he watched. She, Prinn, and Darshia were nearly as good as Tosh now, which is to say far from master swordsmen, but good enough to keep alive on a battlefield until it was time to run away.

They had to bring the girls down in shifts since there was only room in the cave for about a dozen of them to pair off and have room to spare. Tenni was putting them through some basic stances. When the next shift came down, Darshia would take charge.

When it had been put to the girls that they would now learn swordsmanship, their reply had been surprisingly enthusiastic. Only two women had packed their things in the night and slipped away. Tosh had been surprised more hadn't left. Perhaps the girls simply didn't know what they were in for.

Neither did Tosh, not really. Mother hadn't deigned to say what her plan might be, only that it *behooved oneself to be prepared*. Tosh had reported frequently on the girls' progress, and Mother had nodded quietly every time, tensely quiet, as if some secret scheme were coming to fruition.

The cave below the Wounded Bird was thick with girl sweat. Tosh didn't mind.

The first shift ended, and the women went upstairs to bathe and then pleasure the slow trickle of Perranese warriors who patronized the brothel. Nobody in Klaar could quite understand why the bulk of the foreign garrison had been moved outside the walls when a perfectly good city was available to shelter them through the brutal winter. There had been three harsh blizzards since the arrival of the Perranese, but Klaar was still waiting for *the big one*, the storm that inevitably arrived each winter to punish anyone foolish enough to dwell in such climes.

When the others had gone, Tenni went to Tosh and planted a soft but lingering kiss on his lips.

"You're enjoying this too much," Tosh said.

Tenni kissed him again on the cheek. "Not *enjoying*, but I think it's a good idea."

"Why?"

"No woman starts out to be a whore," she said. "I hope you think I'm worth more than that."

Tosh sighed. "Of course. I didn't mean—"

"I want to do something else, to rise above where I am. *What* I am. And I want to fight against those who've invaded my home. This way I can do both."

Tosh nodded, kept his face serious. He didn't want Tenni to think he wasn't listening, wasn't taking her seriously. "I know. Honestly, I do. But the thought of you ending up like Freen..."

She moved in quickly, her arms going around behind him to pull him close. Her face against his chest. She heard his heart beat. "I know. But this is the time. Don't you feel it? History is thrusting us into the path of... something. I don't know. Really, I'm not sure how to explain, but can't you sense it? The world is being tossed into chaos, and there are just us select few who see it, who can do something, and if we don't... well, I'm not sure the gods will forgive us. That we would be offered this chance and then cower. I can't believe it. I won't. We *must* rise to the occasion."

Tosh struggled to understand. As a soldier you kept your head low and waited for storms to pass. Tenni seemed always to be looking into the distance, seeing something greater, maybe something that wasn't even real. She seemed to perceive a world that was beyond his ken. Tosh didn't have the heart to disagree. "I understand. Of course."

She smiled and pulled him close again. "You don't really, do you?"

No. Instead he said, "I know I love you."

"Good enough." She cupped his groin, and he gasped, eyes wide.

He said, "We don't have time to—"

"Ten minutes until the next shift comes down," Tenni said. "Show me what you can do."

Tenni was more than satisfied with Tosh's ability to rise to the occasion.

∿

Two weeks later, Mother called Tosh to her private office. He wasn't as nervous this time. The Wounded Bird had been quietly going about its business, servicing the rotating battalions of Perranese soldiers. And with Klaar now growing accustomed to the Perranese occupation, most of the local clientele had returned as well. Tosh cooked meals and trained the girls after hours. He made love to Tenni and played with Emmon. It would be a simple thing to think of life as just about perfect.

Except he would then see Freen's lifeless, glassy eyes and remember the blood on his hands. Tosh reminded himself that the ground underneath your feet could open up at any time without warning. In his entire life, he'd never had so much to lose. That was life, wasn't it? You spend so much of it trying to find happiness, and then when you get some, you worry every day something is going to take it away.

"Tosh."

He looked up, saw Mother staring at him. "Sorry. Just thinking. You wanted to see me."

"Are the girls progressing?" she asked.

He scratched his chin. "I'm not sure how to answer that. Compared to what? I don't know what the expectation is."

She refilled the glass on her desk with red wine from a decanter that was mostly empty. For the first time, Tosh noticed Mother's cheeks were flushed; a few disheveled strands of hair had pulled loose from her tight bun. "Just … give me your best guess. Do you want some wine?"

"Yes, please."

She gestured impatiently at the chair across from her, and Tosh sat. She filled another glass from the decanter and slid it across her desk toward him. "Can they fight or not?"

He grabbed the glass quickly, sipped slowly, giving himself a moment to think. "A half dozen of them are pretty handy."

"And the rest?"

"They've only just learned how to stand and hold their weapons without hurting themselves," Tosh told her. "Getting used to the weights of their blades."

She rubbed her eyes. "When can all of them be ready?"

Tosh didn't want to ask but did anyway. "Ready for what?"

Mother rubbed her eyes, sighed, refilled her glass and tossed half of it down with one gulp. She reached across the desk to touch something. It was the ring she'd been fiddling with last time. "You know Lord Giffen?"

"Personally?"

"No. I mean you know who he is, yes?"

Tosh nodded. Of course. If it wasn't for Lord Giffen, Klaar would be under direct control of the Perranese. According to hushed tavern gossip, Giffen was doing everything possible to keep the occupying regime from being too heavy-handed with the local populace. The occupation would have been much worse if not for Giffen.

"I've heard things, Tosh. I have eyes and ears everywhere. You might not think a woman who runs a brothel would have a far reach, but I do. Someone like me has friends in both high places and low. Important men have counted on my discretion for years."

Tosh didn't know how to respond to this, so he sipped wine.

"We'll need to wait until the time is right." Mother closed her fist tightly over the ring. "If we handle it poorly it will make the situation worse instead of better. So there's time. Keep training the girls. They'll be ready by the time we do it."

"I'm sorry, Mother," Tosh said. "But do what?"

"Don't you know?" she said. "We're going to kill Lord Giffen, of course."

And that's when the ground opened up beneath Tosh's feet.

CHAPTER THIRTY-EIGHT

The harsh winter wind rattled the shutters, and the dwindling fire in the hearth flickered. Giffen curled into a ball beneath the double layer of furs. He *almost* regretted telling the servants not to disturb him during the night. Normally they would slip in during the wee hours to stoke the fire and then silently slip out again.

But Giffen had company and didn't want to be disturbed. He'd made it clear to the servants. Stay away. Giffen is busy with a lady.

Well, perhaps *lady* was being generous, but never mind. He felt her shift under the furs next to him, and a smile spread across his face. He pictured her, curvaceous and dark-haired, eyes as blue as ice. Full lips and high cheekbones. Fingernails and toenails painted a bright red. Giffen suspected she spent the bulk of her day grooming herself just to be ready for him, which was just fine with Giffen.

He'd spent most of his life serving others; let the peasants fall over themselves pleasing *him* for a change. It's what he'd always wanted. No more groveling and simpering for Lord Giffen. The Klaarian rabble could damn well dance to his tune from now on. All of his scheming had finally paid off. From now on, Giffen would have exactly what he wanted and woe unto anyone who stood in his way.

Giffen turned over and spooned with the whore. What was her name again? Ah, yes. Sarin. That squalid little place over in Backgate had sent her as some sort of tribute. He inferred some sort of arrangement. The brothel would keep him happy in bed, and in return, Giffen would not find a reason to close the place down. A fine arrangement. If Sarin continued to approach her duties with the same level of enthusiasm as she had the night before, Giffen didn't foresee a problem.

He cupped one of her ample breasts, and she sighed contentment, squirming back against him. He pinched a thick nipple between thumb and forefinger. Yes, he was plenty warm enough without the fire. He was satisfied with just about everything. Life was good. Except...

It still rankled him to be at the beck and call of the Perranese, specifically General Chen, but the invaders were a necessary evil. Giffen reminded himself that Klaar was merely a stepping stone to the conquest of Helva itself. Soon the foreigners would move on to bigger and better things, and they would reward Giffen by leaving him to his own devices as lord of Klaar. A carefully orchestrated deceit was making it appear that Giffen was Klaar's savior. He'd always despised the accident of birth that made him a commoner. Yes, he'd been a man of some power in service of the Duke. But that wasn't good enough—an oversight that was currently being corrected.

And then Giffen would be the *new* duke with all the privileges that entailed.

Sarin ground her soft backside against Giffen's growing erection.

He kissed her ear, and she purred. Giffen hadn't planned a session of pre-breakfast copulation, but if Sarin were eager, then who was Giffen to refuse? He positioned himself to enter her. She gasped, twisting to kiss him, her mouth wet and inviting.

A knock at his chamber door.

You have got to be fucking kidding me.

"Go away!" Giffen barked. He pawed at Sarin's tits, trying to maintain his erection.

The door cracked open, and a wide-eyed, nervous servant stuck his head around it. It was the scrawny lad who had been assigned as his valet. "Beg pardon, your lordship, but General Chen wants to see you. Uh ... immediately."

Giffen mumbled a curse. The only man who could take him away from a warm bed and a soft woman was the Perranese general. He pulled the furs over his head and groaned.

The valet cleared his throat. "Sir?"

"What?"

"Shall I tell General Chen you're on your way?"

"Tell him I'm busy plowing this comely whore up her luxurious backside."

The valet blinked. "Really?"

"Of course not, idiot!" Giffen threw back the furs and swung his legs over the side of the bed. "Now fetch my robes before I have you skinned."

Chen had begun taking his meals in the small dining room just off the castle kitchens. Heating the formal dining hall this far into winter consumed too much fuel. So Chen sat at a small table only big enough for a few people, sipping tea and picking from a plate of steamed cabbage and fish. The soft layer around his middle had begun to diminish after he'd started eschewing the butter and potatoes.

His plan to move the bulk of the garrison outside the city had been successful so far. There had been grumbling at first—a sign in and of itself that the change had been necessary—but once full discipline had been reinstated, the men's fighting edge had again been honed razor sharp. He kept them rotating. A battalion inside the city walls to keep the peace. Another battalion at Harran's Bay to rebuild the deep-water docks. A company to erect a rough palisade around the barracks. Another company to cut timber for both the dock and palisade projects.

Chen had assigned a third company to scour the outer and lower villages for livestock, but these settlements had been picked clean weeks ago, and with snow clogging most of the passes, it had been more efficient to reduce the force to a mounted detail to patrol for enemy spies.

So far, the bulk of Helva remained blissfully unaware of the Perranese presence on its soil—a fact that seemed about to change if Chen understood the situation correctly.

He refilled his teacup from a delicate porcelain pot just as Giffen entered the room.

"You wanted to see me, General Chen?" Giffen moved to the room's small fireplace, warmed his hands.

"Yes." Chen gestured to the seat across from him. "Sit if you like."

Giffen hesitated only a moment as if reluctant to leave the fire, then sat. Chen filled Giffen's cup from the teapot.

Giffen nodded his head. "Thank you."

"You'll be happy to know the men are doing well in the barracks," Chen said. "Two iron stoves in each barracks suffice. What are they called again?"

"Pot-belly stoves."

"Yes, exactly." Obviously named for men who'd stuffed themselves with buttered potatoes. "It is still very cold,but the men are hardy."

Giffen sipped his tea and shrugged. "It hasn't gotten *really* cold. Not yet. The big blizzards are still to come."

Chen tried to cover his surprise by jamming a wad of cabbage into his mouth. He chewed, thinking. He swallowed, then said, "We will reinforce the barracks' insulation and lay in triple the fuel for the stoves, both peat and wood." He hated that he might be wrong about moving the men outside the city. Irrational. Giffen was from Klaar. He'd know the local weather better than Chen. It would be foolish not to listen even if he did consider himself the man's better. "Still. We will make preparations to move the men back inside the city walls if need be."

Chen thought he saw Giffen hide a smug smile behind his teacup and had to stifle a sudden swell of fury. Letting an inferior goad you was a sign of weakness. Chen wouldn't allow that. He mastered himself. Pride must be eliminated from the equation. Only problems and their solutions mattered.

"A wise precaution, General," Giffen said.

And yet Chen could not resist an opportunity to put a dent in Giffen's smug facade. "Captain Tchi sent a rider. He arrived in the wee hours this morning with the news that he and his men lost Rina Veraiin in the forest south of Kern." He cut a chunk of fish, brought it up to his mouth. "She could be almost anywhere by now."

Giffen frowned. "This is bad news."

Chen chewed the fish, swallowed. "Yes."

"Well, what do you plan to do about it?"

Chen speared another chunk of fish with his fork, shrugged with deliberate nonchalance. Let Giffen squirm. "What is there to do?"

Giffen fidgeted in his chair. "If your presence here is known, then the king could send troops before your Emperor sends his fleet."

Chen ate a bite of cabbage and nodded.

"The point was to hold Klaar *secretly* until the spring thaw," Giffen said.

"Why are you telling me the plan?" Chen said calmly. "I know the plan. It's my plan."

"If the Veraiin brat has raised the alarm, the king's army could be on its way *now*."

Chen sipped tea, wiped the corner of his mouth with a napkin. "Yes."

"Forgive me, general, but you do not seem concerned."

"What should my concern look like to you, Giffen? Shall I wave my arms in the air and run around in circles? Calm yourself. We always knew it was a possibility word would leak. Frankly, I'm surprised we've kept ourselves hidden this long. Our best hope is that the heavy snows come and block the passes. Then the king could send every soldier in Helva and it wouldn't matter. One way or another, war must wait until spring."

Giffen pushed his teacup away, sat back in his chair, shaking his head. "Wait, this isn't right."

"What isn't?"

"You said they lost her south of Kern? Did she go into Kern itself?"

"Yes," Chen said. "Tchi and his men were forced to wait outside of town to avoid being discovered. They've killed more than a dozen of the locals who spotted them and hid the bodies. But they picked up her trail again to the south of the town."

"Have any of your patrols apprehended scouts on the border?" Giffen asked.

"No."

Giffen snapped his fingers. "The brat hasn't told anyone. They don't know."

"How do you arrive at this conclusion?"

"Arlus was reasonably close with the Baron of Kern," Giffen said. "Rina could have sought asylum there easily. Kern would have sent scouts to verify her story."

"You're guessing," Chen said.

"But they're *good* guesses, General. Kern would have found the situation irresistible. He's been angling to marry off one of his idiot sons to Rina, and if he can wrangle to make her his ward with Arlus dead then he can add Klaar's lands to his own." He shook his head again but with confidence this time. "No, no, no. We are missing a piece of the puzzle. Rina Veraiin had ample opportunity to raise the alarm but didn't. The passes to Klaar are quiet when they should be alive with scouts in Kern livery."

Chen considered. As with the weather, Giffen would have a better grip of regional politics than Chen would. "Educated guesses. But still guesses."

Giffen gestured acquiescence. "Naturally I can't know for certain, sitting here sipping tea. What we really need are spies."

"Ah." Chen smiled. "Funny you should mention spies."

CHAPTER THIRTY-NINE

The wind lashed Harran's Bay, and the commander in charge of rebuilding the docks pulled his men back to the shelters again. This was madness. Two men had drowned already and a third had perished from exposure. Progress on the new docks was costly. Soon even General Chen would have to admit the weather was too bitter to work.

The commander watched the longboats row toward shore. The ship—the last ship to come from Perran until spring—had been spotted on the horizon by rooftop watchmen earlier that morning. They'd expected the ship for a week, and when it finally arrived, the commander dispatched a rider to alert Chen.

The commander feared briefly the foamy waves would swamp the longboats. The sea was rough, deadly, but they both beached themselves at last on the small patch of shore between the rocks. Sailors began to unload the first batch of cargo, although it was not the cargo that was important.

Three men—two from the first boat and one from the second—tromped toward him. These men were why the commander waited out in the cold instead of going into one of the shelters to warm himself. He'd been ordered to offer them every respect and service.

The first two hunched against the cold, leaning into the wind as they walked. They wore thick layers of heavy furs with the hems of bright silk robes hanging below. It wouldn't matter how they dressed or how many more furs they piled on, the commander knew. All of the Perranese had the same reaction at first. This desolate place seemed impossibly frozen. They'd been told time and time again to ready themselves for the hostile climate, but nothing really could have prepared them. The commander's bones had not stopped aching since he'd arrived.

The third man was something else. He was a head taller than the others, a wide-shouldered, powerfully built hulk under a heavy cloak whose hood was pulled forward, hiding his face within deep shadow. He walked with his back straight as if the wind couldn't touch him. He was the only man at Harran's Bay not cowering from the harsh weather.

The other two stopped in front of them, the hulk halting a few steps behind. One was older, with long, braided white moustaches. Bony and thin. The other was younger by two decades, with a round face and a closely trimmed black beard.

"I'm Prullap," said the round faced one. "Are y-you the m-man in ch-charge?" He was trying not to shiver and was failing.

"Yes, sir." The commander bowed. "I've been holding horses for you and your comrades. General Chen has asked you to proceed on to Klaar immediately."

"N-now?" Prullap glanced at one of the nearby shelters then back at the commander. "*Right* now?"

The commander shrugged an apology. "I'm afraid so, sir."

A detail of Perranese warriors escorted the three newcomers to Klaar. They crossed the Long Bridge well after dark, the gates clunking closed behind them as they were waved through to the keep.

Grooms appeared to take their horses to the stable, and they were ushered inside the castle and immediately taken to an ornate reception room. A fire roared in the hearth, and Prullap and his bony compatriot immediately rushed to warm themselves. Prullap had to make a physical effort to keep from weeping as the feeling seeped back into his feet and hands, hot needles as the circulation returned.

"We're being punished," Prullap said through chattering teeth. "It's the only explanation."

"No," said the older one with the braided white moustaches. His name was Jariko. He was stoic and just as cold as Prullap but was better at hiding it. "It is an opportunity."

Prullap laughed without mirth. "An opportunity for what? To lose our jewels to frostbite?"

"Those who come after us will have to answer to us," Jariko said. "We'll be the experts. We'll be experienced."

Prullap rolled his eyes. "If we live."

"There is that, I suppose." Jariko glanced sideways at the younger man, pitched his voice lower. "Shall we be frank with each other?"

A pause. "What do you mean?"

"How many spells can you hold?" Jariko asked. "And how many in your spell book?"

Jariko sensed Prullap go rigid next to him. Among wizards, such a question was like asking a man the length of his member.

Prullap asked, "You propose some kind of ... alliance?"

"We both serve the Empire," Jariko said. "But I think it would behoove us to also look out for each other. They selected us to accompany the first wave of the invasion for a reason. We're powerful enough to be of some use but also commonplace enough among our brethren to be expendable. Surviving until spring means we grow stronger. The Mages' Council will be forced to let us select from the Imperial spell book. There will be land grants and titles."

Jariko allowed that to sink in a moment before adding, "But only, as you say, if we live."

Prullap said, "I watch your back and you watch mine, eh?"

Easier said than done, Jariko realized. Spell casters were generally envious and distrusting of one another. Spells and magical secrets were jealously guarded.

A long moment stretched, the fire snapping and crackling.

"I can hold three spells," Prullap said in a whisper. "Sixteen in my book."

Jariko smiled to himself. "I can hold five. Twenty-two in my book." He could actually hold six and assumed Prullap was hedging as well. It was only natural.

Prullap nodded back over his shoulder at the dark figure in the corner. "What about him?"

Jariko turned slightly and looked. The hulk sat cross-legged on a bench, back straight, his hood still covering his face. The brooding figure seemed to draw all the light and energy in the room to be devoured in his dark corner although Jariko understood this was an illusion. The mysterious man had kept to himself for most of the voyage across the sea and had answered questions with grunts, nods or shrugs. He projected an aura that made it clear he wanted to be left alone, and the ship's crew and other passengers were only too happy to oblige.

Jariko turned back to the other mage. "We know what *he* is. There's no help for us there."

"Agreed," Prullap said.

They lapsed into silence, and minutes later one of the locals entered the chamber, a pallid, greasy man in fine robes. His smile was filled with lies, and Jariko instantly disliked him. Evidently, smarmy bureaucrats were cut from the same cloth in all lands.

"I'm Lord Giffen," he announced. "You've arrived just in time. General Chen has an urgent task for you."

So soon? Jariko was still half frozen. They'd not even been offered a hot meal and already there was work for the wizards. Probably something that would get them killed. Maybe Prullap was right. Maybe they *were* being punished.

Typical.

CHAPTER FORTY

B rasley had to find just the right sort of pub, which meant he first had to find a town big enough to have one.

In the week since leaving Rina and the others and traveling north, he'd passed through a dozen villages and farming communities, none suitable for his purpose.

Rina had charged him with a simple mission: travel to Merridan and report through proper channels to the king that the Perranese had invaded Helva and taken Klaar. Simple enough.

But no, it isn't simple at all, thought Brasley. One does not simply show up to the capital in travel-stained clothes and demand an audience with his majesty to report an invasion from across the sea. Brasley was only a few years older than Rina, but he'd seen much more of the world than she had, including Merridan, the capital of Helva. Rina was strong willed and would make a good duchess. But not yet. She still didn't know how the world worked.

What Rina didn't realize was that simply delivering a message to the king wasn't good enough. The message, once delivered, would be out of his control, merely information working its way up the hierarchy to the throne. Brasley—*Sir* Brasley now—meant to control the message, shape it. And that meant whispering it into the right ears before it reached the king.

And that took money.

Rina had given him a small purse of copper and a few silvers, enough to feed him and put a roof over his head on the way to Merridan. Under no circumstances would that be enough for Brasley to make the impression he needed to make upon arriving in Helva's capital. And there was only one way he knew of to turn the small purse of coins into a big one.

Brasley placed a card next to the others in the common hand in the center of the table. "The Mermaid Queen."

The cards were triple layers of squared parchment sealed in clear wax. Each player was dealt nine cards. There was a discard pile on the table from which players might choose to take another player's unwanted cards, and next to that a shared hand with cards all players could use. The game was called Kingdom Cards and represented various battles and political maneuvers. Bets were placed on each event and the winner took the pot. It was a complex game Brasley had been playing since he was nine years old, taught by his aunt who not only knew all of the game's nuances but who was also an expert at cheating.

However, this wasn't a crudely made deck like the ones Brasley had used before in low-class pubs in bad neighborhoods. The depictions on each card had been expertly illustrated by a top artisan. The mermaid queen's breasts were especially exquisite.

The brewer to his left frowned a moment before adding his own card to the common hand. "The Bailiff." He glowered at Brasley as if daring him to find fault with his choice. The brewer was a large, barrel-chested man whose puffy face had continued to grow redder the last three hours after each loss.

Brasley examined the card, nibbling his bottom lip. By tossing down the Bailiff, the brewer was trying to turn the event into a political maneuver. That gave Brasley a good guess at the nature of his remaining cards. Brasley glanced down again at the cards in his hand. No, a battle would definitely be better for him. He might need to fold the hand if it went in that direction, but that depended on the next card.

Brasley looked across the table at the tailor. He was a gaunt man with timid eyes. He pulled a card, licked his lips as he thought about it then pulled another instead. He dropped the card into the shared hand.

Brasley squinted at it. The Archer. A weak card but it would definitely be a battle.

The brewer muttered something disagreeable and folded. The tailor looked unhappy, as though he already regretted his play.

Yes, finding the right kind of pub in the right town had been key, Brasley mused. It was a river town called Klent about a day's ride south of Merridan. The merchant-class tavern was called the Pickled Pixie, a lively place but not the sort of establishment in which a fellow would expect to get knifed, and the stakes would be high enough to do the trick. Most of the lower-class pubs preferred dice games anyway. He'd be able to take these men for some good coin and then quickly leave town.

Brasley glanced at the growing pot on the table. It would be more than enough. A new jerkin and doublet, hose and cloak. Something with a lot of gaudy gold embroidery. For some reason the upper class of Merridan *loved* gaudy gold embroidery. And new boots. Brasley was a firm believer in the old saying *The clothes make the man,* and nowhere was that more true than in Merridan. And there would be some coin left over too, enough to spread around, to tip a servant, to buy wine for a lord or lady and to generally ingratiate himself in the proper circles.

Brasley realized he was actually looking forward to it. *No more riding in the rain. No more cold nights camping under a tree. Warm inns and civilization!*

They all waited for the fourth man at the table to play his card. Like the brewer, the fourth man was big, with broad shoulders, a thick-featured rocky face and jug ears. His round belly didn't look like it would slow him down much if he wanted to go after somebody. The fourth man had confused Brasley at first. He wore a tattered and stained tunic, hair greasy and disheveled, boots muddy. He seemed out of place in the tavern with the merchants and guildsmen. Brasley had later found out the man was the town's jailer, which explained his fat coin purse. Jailers were well known for relieving prisoners of their coins and other possessions.

The jailer threw down his card and snarled, "Ogre General."

Brasley raised an eyebrow and frowned as if he were worried. In fact, he was pleased. Ogre General was a strong card, which indicated the jailer would stay in for another round.

There was a pause while everyone sipped from pewter tankards of strong ale.

There was a round of betting, and Brasley was pleased to see that the tailor had stayed in the game as well. The pile of coins in the center of the table grew. They each discarded, and Brasley selected a "Stronghold with Moat" card from the discard pile to give the illusion he was still strengthening his hand.

Another pause for ale, then another round of betting. The pile of coins had grown well beyond Brasley's expectations. A suite at Merridan's best inn and a private bath would suit him just fine.

And someone soft and pretty to bring him wine and wash his back in the tub.

The size of the pot clearly made the tailor nervous. He licked his lips, eyes darting from face to face before throwing down his final card. "Cavalry Charge."

Not bad, Brasley thought. The tailor'd had a better hand than Brasley had suspected, but still not good enough. Even the jailer would have a better card. Brasley had tried to keep track ... which was almost impossible. Used cards were shifted to the bottom of the deck and the deck shuffled every dozen hands, so keeping track of which cards had been played already could be tricky. But Brasley's best guess was that the jailer would play either Storm Giant or Silver Dragon.

The jailer threw down his final card. "Storm Giant."

"Blast." The tailor threw in his remaining cards.

Brasley made a face as if the jailer's play had wounded him.

The jailer cracked a smile for the first time. A front tooth was missing. He reached for the pile of coins, mostly copper but quite a good bit of silver too.

Brasley threw down his card. "The Titan."

The jailer jerked his hands back as if he'd been bitten. "Fuck me."

Brasley *tsked* as he reached for the coins. "Language, sir. There are ladies present."

The jailer glanced sideways at the two prostitutes working the bar, then frowned back at Brasley. "You cheated."

The tailor gasped. That's why Brasley liked working these merchant-class pubs; they were generally a polite crowd. The jailer had the money to be here but wasn't really in the same social class.

And that meant he wasn't too worried about being polite.

Brasley said, "Sir, as I am a gentleman, I'll forget you said that." He began scooping the coins toward him.

The jailer reached out and latched onto one of Brasley's wrists with a meaty hand. Brasley imagined that this was what it felt like to be grabbed by a troll.

The tailor scooted his chair back and left the table.

"The Titan was already played," the jailer said.

"You're mistaken, sir," Brasley said. "We've shuffled since the Titan was played." They'd been there six hours. He was counting on nobody remembering that far back.

"My ass," the jailer said. "The Titan was played the first hand after the shuffle."

"It was the last hand *before* the shuffle." Brasley spoke slowly as if tolerating someone with a mental deficiency.

In fact, the oafish jailer was right. It was a trick that had always worked until now. A second deck of Kingdom Cards was in his horse's saddle bags—*minus* The Titan. The second deck was made by the same artisan and nearly identical. If they checked his saddlebags and found the other deck, or went through the cards on the table and discovered the second Titan card …

Brasley looked up and caught the barkeep's attention with his eyes. "Is this how you let good customers be treated in your establishment? Manhandled by thugs?" Brasley was minor nobility and the jailer was a common lowlife. Hopefully the barkeep would recognize that and act appropriately.

"These men are my regulars." The barkeep stabbed a finger at Brasley. "*You* I don't know."

Okay, that backfired.

Brasley let one hand drop to his side. "Gentleman, this is ridiculous." A small gentleman's knife slid out of his sleeve and into his hand. He flicked it open, keeping it out of sight below the table. "Now, come on. Nobody likes a sore loser."

"I say we look at the cards," the brewer said. "And if he is a cheat, I'll help you take him out back and paste him."

Brasley tensed. *Shit.*

Brasley said, "Gentleman, before you do anything rash I must point out that—"

He stood abruptly, sweeping the small blade of the gentleman's knife across the jailer's knuckles.

The jailer screeched, high-pitched and alarmed, letting go of Brasley's wrist.

"Bastard!" The brewer reached for him, murder in his eyes.

Brasley upended the table at the brewer, coins and cards and tankards flying, ale splashing and patrons at nearby tables backing away from the altercation. He didn't wait to see the result; he turned and ran for the front door.

They shouted after him.

"Grab him!"

"Get the son of a bitch!"

"Call for the watch!"

Brasley burst out of the pub. He'd had the foresight to tie up his horse just outside. He mounted just as a number of angry patrons burst from the pub, some waving cudgels.

"Thief!"

"Cheat!"

The brewer grabbed for him, trying to pull him out of the saddle, but Brasley kicked him in the face, spinning him away spitting blood. He spurred his horse away from the crowd. He heard somebody call again for the watch and glanced over his shoulders.

Four men in bowl helms and the livery of the town ran after him. Brasley thanked Dumo they weren't mounted, but two of them lifted crossbows.

Shit shit shit.

He ducked low in the saddle, urging his steed faster. A crossbow bolt whizzed by overhead. Crossbows reloaded slowly. If he could just avoid the second crossbowman's shot, he should be free and clear to—

A hot, fierce pain bloomed in his side, almost knocking him out of the saddle.

Oh no. No no no.

Brasley spurred the horse faster, each bump in the saddle sending shocks of pain through his body. If he could get well away, he'd stop and examine the wound. He crossed a stone bridge over a wide stream, marking the edge of town. He glanced again over his shoulder. No pursuit.

But he couldn't stop yet. Just a little further and he could turn off into the woods.

He felt warm blood trickle down his side. His head went dizzy. As blackness crowded the edge of his vision, all he could think was that he was now penniless, his winnings scattered in puddles of ale across the floor of the pub behind him.

CHAPTER FORTY-ONE

Brasley crossed into one of Merridan's poor southern neighborhoods at dawn, walking his horse and limping, the pain in his side flaring and throbbing with every step. The good news was that the crossbow bolt that had pierced his side hadn't hit any vital organs; moreover, the wound would likely not fester although it had cost him the last of the good brandy in his flask to clean the new hole between his ribs. He'd ripped his last spare shirt into strips for a makeshift bandage. It was already scabbing and would heal properly.

After being struck by the crossbow bolt, Brasley had swooned in the saddle. He'd woken a few moments later, shoulders slumped, head down, his horse nibbling grass on the side of the road. He'd found a stand of trees with low hanging branches and hidden himself while he tended his wound. He hadn't really lost too much blood, but the bolt must have been a shock to the system because he'd slept the rest of the day away. It occurred to him, not for the first time, that if he ever made a name for himself, it would *not* be as a great warrior.

Brasley had felt some vague mix of relief and apprehension when the great mass of Merridan had risen up ahead of him. A permanent brown haze hovered over the city, the result of tens of thousands of cook fires constantly pouring smoke into the sky. Some claimed a million souls dwelt within the city walls and outlying suburbs. Brasley couldn't quite believe that. On the other hand, why not? Merridan was the capital city of a vast, sprawling kingdom, the center of religion, culture, and power for a continent.

This part of the city reeked of livestock. It was a place where all the outlying districts brought animals and produce to market. Farmers, not nobility, came through the drab southern gate but Brasley was too weary to circle the enormous city to the grander eastern or western gates.

Brasley remembered the brass-hinged eastern gate with the three-story fluted columns on either side from his visits to the city with his father and uncle—General Aujusto's Gate they called it, named for one of the many heroes of the ancient Mage Wars. To the right of the gate a twenty-foot bronze sculpture depicted the general on a throne atop a pile of skulls. The statue was a brief history lesson, the skulls representing Aujusto's vanquished foes and the throne a gesture to the general's ambition for the crown, an ambition that would eventually bring about his assassination. Brasley's family had brought him to Merridan as a teen to gawk at the grandeur of Helva's capital. And gawk he had. The city could swallow Klaar ten times over.

But there was nothing grand about the squalid square he found himself in now, a wide expanse of gray stones covered with the shit of goats and cattle and horse and sheep. The wide-mouthed stone well in the center of the square explained everything. Sellers brought their animals here to be watered before the auctions began. Cattle and swine sold in mass for meat were penned in the large corrals outside the city gates. The animals being watered in the square were prize breeders and show animals, but there were still so many that their stench was nearly overwhelming.

And if Brasley hadn't lost all of his money on a stupid card cheating scheme, he would have been able to find a clean inn and take a hot bath. He liked the aroma of roast pork much more than the stench of the live pigs scrambling past him now. He sat on a stone bench at the edge of the square, enduring the stink, trying to ignore the squealing din of the livestock so that he could figure just what in blazes he would do next. He was penniless, and that limited his options down to almost nothing. *I'm a tired, dirty, wounded failure, and I have no idea how to turn things around.* He chuckled mirthlessly at his own dilemma.

Perhaps a solution will fall out of the sky.

"You, sir! You there on the bench."

Brasley didn't look up at first.

"My good man, your attention please."

Brasley frowned and turned.

Two men occupied a carriage at the mouth of the square. One was old, bright white hair pulled back into a tight ponytail. The other stood up in the open carriage, waving for Brasley's attention with a walking stick. Both men were well appointed, long velvet coats and silk shirts fastened at the throat with colorful bows. The standing man looked young, probably only just of age, a spoiled lordling out with his father, perhaps. He had the pale, soft look of a man who had been waited on hand and foot all of his life.

Brasley would have *loved* the chance to cultivate a similar look.

"Is that your horse?" the lordling asked.

Brasley looked back at his horse, then back to the noble. "Yes."

The lordling waved him over with the walking stick. "Let's have a look, then."

Have a look…?

Of course!

Brasley had taken his saddle off the horse to give the animal a rest, and he realized how it must seem. He looked like the rest of the men in the square who'd brought their animals to auction. They thought his horse was for sale.

Brasley leapt to his feet immediately, smiled. "Of course, sir. Only happy to oblige."

He led his horse toward the two nobles, realizing why they were reluctant to step down from the carriage. He looked at his boots. They were splattered halfway up the shins with animal shit.

Brasley tried to recall what he knew of the horse. He'd borrowed it from his father's stables six months ago, so it wasn't technically his. He wasn't much for animal husbandry, but he knew enough to understand it was a good animal, strong and young, a tall stallion the deep color of midnight. The sort of animal a young knight might take to war or that a spoiled noble could take on a hunt.

He brought the horse close enough to the carriage for the lordling to reach out and stroke its nose.

"What's his name?"

Brasley had no idea. He knew men who'd loved their horses, but to Brasley the beast was simply transportation.

"Titan," he said, remembering the game of Kingdom Cards.

"A magnificent name."

"For a magnificent steed," Brasley said. "Bred from the finest stock."

"He's just what I'm looking for." The lordling turned to the old man. "Father, what do you think?"

The old man sat forward, looked the animal up and down with a squint. "Let's see the teeth."

Brasley pried the horse's lips apart, gestured to the teeth with a flourish.

"A decent animal," the old man admitted reluctantly.

"I want him," the lordling said. "He's big and black just like I imagined. I'll look fearsome astride Titan, won't I, father?"

The old man frowned, waved the boy to silence and turned back to Brasley. "We'd like to purchase him."

"Excellent." Brasley's smile oozed sincerity. "I wish you luck at the auction."

That got the old man's attention. "Don't be ridiculous. The horse auction is last after the pigs and goats and chickens. I'm not waiting around in this shithole until then."

The lordling looked stricken. "But father, you said if we came down *before* the auctions started, we could make a better bargain."

"No," the old man corrected. "I said I would send one of my *huntsmen* down to pick one out for you."

The lordling stomped his foot. "But I want to pick out my *own* horse."

He stomped his foot. The spoiled bastard actually stomped his foot.

"Mylkin, will you please *shut up*."

The old man composed himself and turned a haughty eye on Brasley. "Thirty silver. That's fair. It's a good animal, but you might wait all day for the horse auction and still not get that."

"Perhaps," Brasley said. "But as you observe, I've resigned myself to being here all day." He gestured at his own disheveled appearance and shitty boots. "Your lordship must determine exactly what it's worth to you to speed your person back to a more hospitable environment."

As if to punctuate Brasley's assertion, a bull in a passing cart pissed a hot yellow stream which splattered on the paving stones.

The old man sighed.

Brasley left ten minutes later with a hundred and fifty silver coins and his saddle thrown over his shoulder.

CHAPTER FORTY-TWO

Rina had turned south after parting with Brasley, heading overland, villages and other settlements, even the odd farmhouse, growing scarce and finally vanishing altogether. The wilderness had swallowed them utterly. Over the course of a week, the green lands had turned brown and dry, and then the earth had grown cracked and hard. Nights were still cold, but they now shed their cloaks in the daylight as it was warm enough for shirtsleeves, even hot enough to be uncomfortable in the midday sun.

Two months behind them, Klaar was just now being chewed by the teeth of winter. Two weeks ago, Brasley had headed north to Merridan where the ladies at court would still be wearing winter fashions and yet already eyeing fabrics and patterns for their spring wardrobes.

All Rina could think as she sat astride her horse on the crest of the low ridge was how many layers of clothes she could shed and still remain decent when the southern heat really began in the coming months. Already the hottest part of the day made her tug at her clothing, wishing for a cool breeze, and technically it was still winter. She was a woman of the north and her blood wasn't made for this.

She puffed the stub of a chuma stick, inhaling the smoke, which eased the tension in her shoulders and neck. It seemed like she'd been riding all her life.

Heat and discomfort vanished when she tapped into the spirit.

As always, her environment became something of an abstract concept as she closed her eyes, opening herself to a view of the world through the senses of the falcon. It took off from its perch on her outstretched arm and flapped for altitude before gliding gently toward the village below them.

They'd reached the edge of the Nomad Lands, the vast desert which stretched south and west until it became the land of Fyria, Kork's homeland. One day, out of respect for her former body-guard and mentor, she hoped to visit the place, but for now, her destination was at hand.

The village in front of them was a drab, brown, ramshackle affair, a dirty, dusty smudge on a wide, bland, baked landscape. *Bigger than Hammish*, Rina thought, *but smaller than the village of Crossroads back home*. Not that the sad village was really enough to hold anyone's attention, with the great mountain of orange stone rising beyond it. Two thousand feet high, it rose inexplicably from the flat land all around it. They'd been walking toward it for two days before reaching the top of the ridge and spotting the village.

And the village, at the moment, was everything.

Rina, Alem, and Maurizan were down to half a skin of water and food for one more meal. If they couldn't get what they needed from the village, they would die.

The falcon came in low over the village. Through the bird, Rina smelled the cook fires, a heady mix of sharp, exotic spices and smoky meat. There was a well of fresh water in the center of the village. The falcon circled lower and screeched, drawing the attention of one of the villagers who looked up suddenly. He was dark eyed, and olive skinned, and looked up with a frightened scowl, part apprehension and part defiance.

The falcon perched on the roof peak of a shabby hut and scanned the main street of the village. Men and women scurried from building to building like they were afraid to be caught in the open. All had the same loose-fitting, draped robes and olive complexions. They seemed strange and foreign. *Because they are. You're a long way from home, Duchess.* Rina had sent the falcon to see if it was safe, to find out if strangers might be welcome to come down into the village and haggle for food and water.

But the faces were all mysterious and unreadable, some hidden behind veils.

If she hadn't been tapped into the spirit, she would have been struck sharply with a feeling of homesickness and discouragement. She wasn't prepared for the world beyond Klaar, filled with its perilous oddities, its unfamiliar people and places. She might have been nervous under other circumstances, but her predicament was simply information to be analyzed and categorized and either put to use or discarded.

Even as Rina observed the village through the eyes of the falcon, she was aware of Alem and Maurizan on their horses next to her. They'd been good traveling companions and had grown close to each other. It was only now, looking inward and tapped into the spirit, that Rina could examine her feelings.

She vividly recalled a night around the campfire when Alem had made some joke and Maurizan had laughed, touching Alem lightly on the arm. When Rina had felt irritation, she'd told herself that it was because she'd been tired and in no mood for frivolity. She now understood it was because she hadn't wanted Alem to enjoy Maurizan's attentions.

Looking inward while tapped into the spirit was dangerous, Rina realized. She saw herself with the same clarity she saw the rest of the world. The many intersecting lines of emotion that connected to even the most trivial events in her life were dizzying in their complexity. If she wasn't careful, she could fall into the depths of herself and never come out again as she picked apart every relationship with everyone she'd ever known.

If she'd been able to feel shame, she would have for the way she resented the young gypsy. But why? What claim did Rina have on Alem? Some instinct told her to release her hold on the spirit, and she did.

The vague sense of fatigue washed over her immediately, not too severe but palpable. Even when the exertions were minor she could still feel it. There was also the knot in her stomach from her unexpected and unwanted look inward. She felt some ownership of Alem that wasn't justifiable, and Maurizan's obvious youthful infatuation with the boy continued to grate on her nerves. It was foolish and unreasonable, but there it was.

Because he's the only one you have. You sent Brasley away, and the girl doesn't like you.

The thought of being utterly alone in the world twisted something in her stomach.

"What did you see?" Maurizan asked. "Is it safe?"

Rina sighed. "I don't know."

"That's not helpful," the gypsy said. "We need to know."

"If you don't like how I do things, you can go your own way," Rina said crisply. "Nobody invited you."

She spurred her horse and trotted downhill toward the village. It wasn't something she'd planned, but sitting there helpless and irritated had suddenly become unappealing. She heard the hoof beats of the others following. So this was it. They'd go into the foreign village and see what happened. Rina frowned. Not her father's idea of reasoned leadership. Full speed ahead and damn the consequences.

I'm no leader. I'm not anything. I'm no duchess, that's for sure.

She puffed the chuma stick in the corner of her mouth. The smoke hung in the air. There was no breeze.

The three of them trotted down the main street of the village, the horse's hooves kicking up dust as they entered the main square. Women in loose robes, faces covered with veils and hoods, scattered from the well, splashing water from earthen vessels as they scurried, eyes cast down and away from the strangers.

Okay, not a good sign.

Alem pulled his horse alongside Rina's. "Maybe this is a bad idea."

"There might be a reason the village is so remote," Maurizan said behind them. "My people know a little something about not wanting to be found."

"We're not leaving without food and water," Rina said. "And information."

Alem gestured to a hut across the small square. There was a wooden stand in front of the hut, a dismal display of pale melons, some long yellow fruit that came in bunches and what looked like apples but with fuzzy rinds. Flies buzzed around the stand.

"I could try over there," he suggested. "A flash of silver might bring them out."

"Let's give them a chance to come out on their own." Rina nodded at the well. "In the meantime, let's get the water."

Maurizan and Rina tossed Alem a half dozen empty water skins, and he began filling them at the well. This was at least one of their problems solved. Alem drank deeply, splashed his face with a handful of the cool water.

"Here they come," Rina said behind him.

He turned to see the five men striding across the square toward them.

Rina puffed the chuma stick, flicked her reins, maneuvering her horse between Alem and the approaching men.

"You want some help with them?" Alem asked.

She frowned down at him, raised an eyebrow. *Are you kidding?*

Alem shrugged. "It's only polite to ask."

She dismounted and handed the reins to Alem. "Load the water skins onto the horses. We might have to leave in a hurry."

She turned toward the approaching men, hands spread, palms up. *See, no weapons. We don't want trouble.* "Hello."

"That's our well," said one of the men, voice gruff and heavy with an unfamiliar accent.

"We've traveled a long way across barren lands," Rina said. "We're thirsty."

"You're thieves." The man's hand fell to the hilt of a curved sword Kork had called a scimitar. She'd trained occasionally with the blades to get the feel but still preferred her rapier.

Rina tapped into the spirit and appraised the men.

They wore blousy, overlapping robes like the rest of the villagers, but with the loose fabric bound by strips of cloth at the ankles and wrists to keep the billowing material from getting in the way during combat. She took in the way they stood and moved. Legs just a little too far apart, stances just a bit off balance. These were men educated in the blade but out of practice. They would be slow to start and best finished quickly.

"We aren't thieves," she said. "We can pay."

The man's dark face spilt in a wide, white grin. He was missing an incisor on one side. "You'll pay with your lives."

He drew the scimitar as he rushed forward.

He probably thought he had an extra second to make his strike, the time it would take for Rina to draw her sword. He was wrong. She sprang forward as he swung, ducking below his blade and ramming an elbow into his gut. Rina heard the air *whuff* out of him. She grabbed a fistful of the man's robe, turned her body and pulled in one of the simple throws Kork had shown her. With the strength from the bull tattoo it was easy. He went up and over, landed hard on his back, dust kicking up from the rough stone. That took the remainder of his breath, and he sprawled there, mouth working to suck for air.

Already the other four were in motion, blades drawn and screaming some kind of blood-curdling war cry.

She went low and twirled a leg back, catching one man's ankles and upending him. She drew her blade, popped up and parried a sweeping strike so hard the scimitar flew out of the man's hands. When he shifted his gaze upward to watch his lost weapon fly into the air, Rina kicked him in the chest. He flew back twenty feet, landed hard, and curled into a ball.

The final two came in slowly, spreading apart in an attempt to get on both sides of her. They were wary now. Rina hadn't been the easy prey they'd expected.

She braced herself, watching both of them in her peripheral vision.

"Enough," came a new voice from behind her.

She didn't turn, keeping the two men with scimitars in front of her. She judged the new voice as too far away for a sword swing. If he attacked, she'd be able to turn in time.

The two men lowered their swords.

"Pick up your brothers and go."

The two men picked up their fallen comrades and dragged them away.

Rina sheathed her rapier and turned to face the newcomer. She spared a glance for her friends. Alem stood behind her horse. He'd cocked his crossbow and had loaded it with a bolt. Likely he'd thought to assist her, but she was glad he hadn't fired into the melee. He wasn't that good a shot and would just as likely have hit her as one of her opponents. Still, it was the thought that counted, she supposed.

Maurizan leaned forward in the saddle, her hand cupped at her side in a way that Rina now recognized to mean she was holding the hilt of the dagger stashed up her sleeve. With a flick of her wrist she could send it flying or slip it in between a pair of ribs. Rina hadn't seen her do it, but she'd watched the girl move and handle the blade and knew the gypsy girl had it in her, had maybe even used the dagger before to some bloody end. Whatever Rina's opinion of Maurizan, she had to give her credit. She'd been ready to fight.

The voice of the newcomer didn't match his looks. His commands to the men had been confident and strong. But his face was lined and old like some ancient brown tree, his hair and beard long and white. He wore the same folded, draped robes as the others in the village, but instead of a vague brown or beige color, his clothes were a glossy deep green. A silver pendant of a snake wrapped around an eye hung on a chain around his neck.

"Who are you?" he asked.

"Rina Veraiin," she said. "We're travelers. Your men wanted that fight, not me."

The old man nodded. "I think you must not be familiar with the etiquette of the Nomad Lands. Water is life. This is our well. Steal horses or gold and you would not take as much from us."

"I told them I'd pay."

"You cannot drink gold," he said.

"I'm sorry. We didn't know."

The old man nodded slightly. "I accept your apology. Go in peace, and we will think no more of it."

"We don't want to stay where we aren't welcome," she said. "We'll go on."

The old man shook his head sadly. "No. You cannot. I am a priest of the Kashar. The people in this village serve the mountain. It is a forbidden place for outsiders. You can turn and go back the way you came, but you cannot go on."

CHAPTER FORTY-THREE

Tosh looked up to see Mother enter the common room. It wasn't an unprecedented sight, but it was unusual. There were no clients at this late hour. As she strode toward Tosh, Mother raised an eyebrow at a pair of the girls, who stood immediately and left.

She stopped in front of Tosh. "A word, if you please."

Tosh nodded. "Of course."

"Who's the best?" she asked.

Tosh understood what she was asking. The obvious answer was Tenni. She had trained with the sword the longest and had a natural aptitude. Most of all, she was driven. She *wanted* to learn. It would not be much of a lie to tell Mother that Darshia was best, or even Prinn. Both girls had come a long way. Tosh would be proud to stand next to either of them on the battlefield, and whatever Mother had in mind, Tosh wished more than anything to keep Tenni as far away from it as possible.

Except Tenni wouldn't tolerate that.

And it wasn't in Tosh to lie to Mother.

"Tenni."

Mother nodded as if she'd already known the answer. "Bring her. And a pot of tea."

Tosh went to the kitchen. A girl named Urma was there, sixteen, too young to be working at the Wounded Bird, but that wasn't true really. There were girls on the street who'd started younger. Urma had rich, brown hair, freckles and a sweet face. Tosh also noticed she had white, straight teeth, a feature most of the brothel's clients overlooked when they came in wanting big tits and a round ass. Tosh couldn't stomach rotten teeth in a woman, but who was he to say what primed another man's pump?

When Tosh stepped into the kitchen, Urma abruptly moved away from the jar that held the sweetbreads, eyes going wide and innocent, hands clasped behind her back.

Tosh didn't really care if the girl filched a snack. "Where's Tenni?"

A shrug.

"Get her," he snapped.

She bolted from the kitchen.

Over the weeks, Tosh had become something of an authority at the brothel. The younger girls hopped when he gave a command. Even veterans like Darshia and Prinn usually honored his requests without question. It wasn't a responsibility he'd asked for or wanted. It had just happened. Even the bruisers Lubin and Bune followed his lead.

Tosh ripped the strong, black tea leaves into shreds and dropped them into one of the good ceramic pots, poured kettle water in on top and covered it with the lid. He put the pot and cups on a tray and carried the lot back into the common room where Tenni sat across from Mother at the center table. He poured each of them a cup and sat.

Mother sipped, squinted at Tosh. "Have you told anyone what we discussed?"

"No."

Tosh glanced at Tenni. He knew her well enough to read her face. She was curious but also slightly annoyed that he knew something she didn't.

"I'm glad you know how to keep a secret," Mother said.

He hadn't told anyone because he didn't *want* it to be true. Maybe Mother would come to her senses and they could all forget about her reckless plan. He should have known better. Mother didn't forget, didn't forgive and didn't yield.

"Since Lord Giffen began his puppet rule, the Perranese have relieved him of his duties as steward," Mother said. "Chen has filled all vacant administrative positions with his own bureaucrats. A self-important stick insect of a man named Dra'Kreeto has been appointed Chamberlain for Castle and Keep and performs all of Giffen's old duties as steward ... just at a slightly different rank."

They sipped tea.

Mother's eyes flicked up to Tenni and Tosh over her teacup. "Do either of you know the man?"

Both shook their heads no.

"No matter," Mother said. "Urma knows what he looks like and will show you tomorrow. I want both of you to recognize the man on sight."

Tosh frowned. "He's one of Urma's clients?"

"No," Mother said. "But Urma's mother is a barmaid at a tavern near the castle, a place called the Bawdy Baron. Have you been there?"

"Too classy for a simple soldier," Tosh said.

"Dra'Kreeto is a frequent patron," Mother said. "After Urma shows you what he looks like, watch him a few days. See when he comes and goes to and from the tavern. It's my understanding he has armed men with him at all times. Find out how many and how well armed."

"What's this man to us?" Tosh asked.

"Isn't it obvious?" Mother said. "After you observe him a few days and discover when he might be vulnerable, I want you to murder him."

Silence stretched, only for a moment, but Tosh suddenly felt heavy. The room seemed to darken.

Tosh spread his hands. "But *why*?"

"I'll do it," Tenni said.

Mother ignored the girl and narrowed her eyes at Tosh. "In a very short time, you've made yourself a valuable addition to our family here at the Wounded Bird, Tosh. But I'm the boss, the captain, the queen, however you want to put it. When I need to explain something, I will. Right now I don't. You don't have to like it. You also don't have to stay. Are we clear?"

Tosh swallowed hard. "We're clear." The idea of being turned out in the thick of winter didn't appeal. The thought of being separated from Tenni was worse.

Mother's eyes shifted to Tenni. "You'll do what you're told and when."

Tenni averted her gaze. "Yes, Mother."

Mother patted her hair, exhaled slowly, composing herself. "See what you've done? You made me lose my temper."

"Sorry, Mother," Tosh said.

"It's not your fault." Mother sighed. "So much to do and so little time. It wears on the nerves, doesn't it?"

Yeah, and scheming to murder a Perranese official is as soothing as warm milk.

"Oh, I almost forgot to mention," Mother said. "Naturally, it has to look like an accident."

~

"I *demand* to see General Chen at once!" Giffen's face was red, a light sheen of sweat from running up the stairs to the general's—formerly the Duke's—private office.

The prim functionary sitting at the table and frowning didn't impress Giffen in the least. Giffen had spent his share of time as a prim functionary himself. He could muster just as much self-importance and bluster as the general's private secretary.

However, the two guards who stepped up to bar his way couldn't be ignored. No amount of bluster would get him past their blades.

"I told you, *Lord* Giffen,"—he said *Lord* as if they all knew the title to be a fiction—"that the General is in conference with his officers at the moment and not to be disturbed. If you'd care to wait—"

Giffen had just drawn breath to harangue the petty functionary with fresh obscenities when the heavy wooden door of Chen's office swung open. A dozen Perranese officers flowed out, talking among themselves in their own tongue, walking past Giffen and shouldering him out of the way as if he were a surplus article of furniture.

When the officers had passed into the corridor, Chen stepped out, frowned. "Giffen. I've been expecting you."

Giffen said, "General, did you really send an expeditionary force into the lowlands?"

"No."

Giffen blew out a sigh of relief.

"It was an *attack* force," Chen said.

Giffen's face turned a new and interesting shade of crimson. "But why? This is reckless! All of our secrecy has been undermined! You can't possibly think—"

Chen calmly held up a finger, and Giffen clapped his mouth shut.

"Before you say something regrettable," said the general, "come into my office. I'll explain."

Giffen sneered past the secretary and into the office. Chen shut the door behind them.

Giffen opened his mouth, but a sharp glance from Chen shut it again.

"Do you think me a fool?" Chen asked.

Is this a trick question?

"It's just..." Giffen cleared his throat. "On the surface, it would *seem* that sending a large force out of Klaar would be ... rash. Our plan has been to keep your presence on Helvan soil a secret until reinforcements can arrive in the spring."

"The secret is out," Chen said. "Plans change."

Giffen's eyes widened. "What do you mean the secret is out?"

"It was a hopeless ambition in the first place, if you ask me," Chen said. "The idea that we could land an invasion force on the continent and not be discovered is ludicrous. I told them so at the war council."

Giffen paced. "The king will send troops. We're undone."

"Calm yourself." Chen's patience was strained. "Word has reached Merridan of our arrival, but this contingency has been foreseen."

"Foreseen?" Giffen clenched his fists. "Damn it, what do you mean?"

Chen spun and advanced upon Giffen, jaw set and eyes sharp. "I'm in no mood, Giffen. I'll explain, but if you don't like it, it's not my concern. You understand?"

Giffen fought down his scorn. "Explain then."

"It was always known the gamble could fail," Chen said. "In fact, it has mostly succeeded and only failed at the very end."

Giffen rolled his eyes. He should have known he couldn't count on these foreigners. In Giffen's eyes, the plan was simple.

They would use Klaar as a foothold and then move on with the spring thaw. Giffen would be left to rule the duchy without interference. But if Helva knew of the invaders, then an army might be marching to repel them even now.

"What do you intend?" Giffen asked.

Chen said, "The only thing that matters is that I follow orders. It is by a happy circumstance that my orders coincide with my preference. I'm a battle general. Garrison duty doesn't suit me. I'm glad for a chance to press forward."

"And for what?" asked Giffen. "You can't conquer Helva with the men you have now."

Chen smiled patiently. "Of course not. That was never the plan." He gestured to a table on which there was a map of the kingdom spread wide. Both men leaned over the map and peered intently.

"My orders are specific." With a forefinger, Chen traced a trail from Klaar down into the lowlands of Helva. "These lands are sparsely populated with scattered villages. I've promoted Tchi to Commander and sent him with eight hundred men to seize the region. There are no major townships or cities, so the force should be sufficient."

"It doesn't matter if there aren't major cities," Giffen said. "The king will still see it as an incursion."

"Of course," Chen said. "We're counting on it."

"I'm afraid I don't understand."

"Our spies at court in Merridan tell us the king now knows we occupy Klaar," Chen said. "What our spies do *not* tell us is what the king might do about it. Seizing a chunk of the lowlands gives us a bargaining chip. Our diplomats can allow the king a minor political victory by demanding we withdraw, which we will do happily. We won't leave Helva, obviously, but we'll retreat back to Klaar, which will be enough for the king to save face. He'll tell his courtiers the Perranese are *contained* in some unfashionable, backwater duchy that nobody wants to visit anyway."

Giffen considered. It wasn't a terrible plan, but there were too many variables, one of which was trying to predict the king's mood. "It won't end there. However unpopular Klaar is at court, the duchy is still Helvan soil. The king will be obligated to take action."

"Yes, but later," Chen said. "Diplomatic envoys will be sent with demands. Responses will be carefully composed and sent back. More envoys will be sent for clarification. Negotiations will stretch into weeks and months. Helva has known peace for years. Its people have grown soft. War is an uncomfortable business and nobody except a few saber-rattling hawks will be eager for conflict. They don't know what we know. The Perranese Emperor is committed to conquest. The diplomats will talk and talk, but the ships will arrive and the armies will march."

Chen smiled thinly. "We will have our war, and nothing can stop it."

∼

They barely made it down to the lowlands before the snows closed the pass behind them. Returning to Klaar—to the city itself—would not be possible until spring. If the column of soldiers had delayed even a few hours, departure would not have been possible.

The first few hours of marching had been bitter and dreadful, the snow flying on a harsh, stinging wind. The weather had eased once they'd come down from the mountains.

Tchi rode his horse up and down the column, inspecting the men. At first, Tchi had inwardly questioned General Chen's decision to build barracks and house the men outside the city walls.

But the men were the better for it—sharp, disciplined and in shape. Tchi had seen garrison troops go soft, but the general had avoided that problem admirably.

To Tchi, eight hundred men was an awkward fighting force. Not large enough for great conquests, but still too large to move and strike quickly. But Chen had explained his mission, and Tchi had to admit it was the right force for the job.

The first village they reached beyond Klaar's border had taken a look at eight hundred armed and fully armored men and had capitulated immediately. As had the four villages after that. The routine was the same every time. They would identify the mayor or village elder or whomever passed for an authority figure and have him declare in front of the assembled villagers that they were all now loyal subjects of the Perranese. Tchi's men would then confiscate half of the village's livestock, grain and potatoes in support of the troops.

They'd kept killing to a minimum. Tchi wasn't keen to leave an enraged population behind them.

Tchi reined in the horse, pausing at the enclosed box wagon, a sort of miniature moveable fort on four wheels which rattled and shimmied along the muddy road. He resented the wagon for stealing away two of his precious horses. He'd only been allowed twenty, and they were needed for the advance scouts.

He leaned toward the wagon, knocked on the door.

The door opened and Prullap's round face appeared. He and Jariko had been wrapped in furs since the trek began, huddling out of the icy wind in the wagon. The wizards were not soldiers and not expected to march. So far they had also not been very useful.

Prullap grimaced as the cold air hit him. "What is it?"

"We're coming to a town," Tchi told him. "It's bigger than the previous villages."

"I'm sure your men are more than capable," Prullap said. "You have our full confidence."

"I was hoping for a bit more," Tchi said. "Scouts report a sturdy palisade around the town and a barred gate. If you could conjure something especially destructive, it would help. I'm not keen to storm the walls, and it would take time."

Prullap frowned. "Let me consult with Jariko. Perhaps we can come up with something." He slammed the door shut.

Tchi spurred his horse to a gallop and wondered just exactly when the wizards would prove their worth. Frankly, he still thought he could make better use of the horses.

CHAPTER FORTY-FOUR

"I am called Brint," the priest of Kashar said. "We tend the temple on the mountain. I'm sorry, but my duty requires me to bar your passage. I intend no personal animosity."

Rina's gaze flitted to the mountain and back to the priest. "If you're guarding them, shouldn't you be up there?"

The priest shook his head, smiled in an attempt to be pleasant. "No, you misunderstand. We are not guards. The guards dwell in the tower at the base of the mountain with the wizard."

Rina's ears twitched at the word *wizard*.

"We are caretakers." Brint gestured to a box wagon across the square. As the name indicated, the wagon was a sturdy wooden box on four wheels. There were generally two uses for this kind of wagon, the first being to cart around spoiled nobles who wanted protection from bandits or inclement weather. The other purpose, as was the case here, was to transport goods that needed to be locked up. A group of men loaded foodstuffs into the back of the cart, various fruits and dried meats, sacks of grain and flour and jugs of wine. "We take the necessities to those in the tower. Soon we will do the same again for the priests on the mountain. We are all servants here and wait for them to awake."

Rina cocked her head to one side. "They sleep? I don't understand."

"It is the Long Dream," Brint told her. "They commune with Kashar. It is a most holy time. For a generation we have waited for the high priests to awaken. The servants of Kashar are ever watchful and ever patient."

Rina said, "I don't like being told where I can and can't go."

A sheepish shrug, a look on Brint's face like an apology. "All in the village serve Kashar. Every hand will rise against you. They will not relent until I call them off, and I won't. There is no joy in this, but I will do what I must."

No, I don't think I'd enjoy that either. Could she do it? Slay an entire village simply because they stood in her way? If she tapped into the spirit, yes. Instinctively, she thought it quite possible. And it was horrifying that she'd contemplate it. Weylan had warned her. Embracing power was easy. Letting it go again was something else.

She squinted at the sky. "The afternoon is getting away from us. If you're sending us away, I'd rather wait until first light."

Brint considered, tugging at his long beard. "Very well." He gestured at a nearby hut. "That dwelling is empty. Take it for the evening. We will provide you with what food we can spare to take with you. I hope this small hospitality makes you think better of us."

"Thank you." Rina motioned to Alem and Maurizan to unsaddle the horses. "We'll be gone before first light and won't trouble you anymore."

As Alem and Maurizan carried saddles and packs into the drab hut, Brint approached Rina, pitched his voice low so that only she could hear. "We will post no guards on you. Leave in the morning with the blessing of Kashar."

Rina raised an eyebrow. "You trust us?"

Brint smiled. "For the sake of courtesy, I would like to say yes. But really, my trust is irrelevant. If you attempt to approach the mountain, I believe you'll find the wizard's hospitality much less agreeable than mine."

~

The squat hut was cramped within, blankets thrown over pallets of straw only a little more comfortable than camping on the cold ground. The three of them lay in a tight circle around an iron stove; a small fire crackled within, the smoke venting through a hole in the low ceiling the circumference of a soup bowl.

"Now?" Alem whispered in the darkness.

"Not yet," Rina whispered back.

"This is a terrible idea," Maurizan whispered.

Rina frowned. "I didn't come all this way *not* to see the wizard."

"You don't even know it's the same wizard."

"How many could there be on the edge of the Nomad Lands?" Alem said. "It has to be the same wizard."

No, it doesn't, thought Rina. There were other wizards in the world. "Even if it's not, maybe this wizard can give me directions. I'm sure all these mages run in the same social circles."

A pause.

Maurizan said, "Is that a joke?"

Another pause.

"I don't know," Rina said.

"They might have a guild," Alem suggested. "You know, like glass blowers or cobblers."

"Or assassins," Maurizan said.

"Assassins have a guild?" Alem asked.

"Mother says so. Do stable boys have a guild? You know, to address pressing concerns about hay and oats."

"I was *head* stable boy," Alem said.

Rina heard them attempt to suppress their laughter in the darkness.

"Okay, enough," she said. "I'm tired of waiting."

She heard them shuffling around, pulling on boots.

"I still say this is a terrible idea," Maurizan said.

Rina sighed. "Fine. If we're all killed, I promise not to blame *you*."

They went to the hut's entrance. There was no door, just a canvas flap which Rina swept aside. The moon had already crossed the sky and vanished, but starlight blazed brilliantly overhead. She paused in the doorway a moment and tapped into the spirit. Her eyes made use of the starlight more efficiently this way, soaked it in, and she could easily see the empty square, the other darkened huts.

She strained to listen. Nothing.

She closed her eyes. The falcon made a wide circle above the village. Nothing stirred.

Rina couldn't quite trust that the old priest hadn't set a pair of eyes to keep watch on them, but apparently he was as good as his word. *More likely he just doesn't care. He did his duty and warned us off, didn't he? If we want to risk the wizard, then that's our stupid necks on the line, not his.*

She reached back and tugged on Alem's sleeve; he, in turn, did the same for Maurizan, the signal they were heading out. They'd agreed beforehand there would be no talking. They padded single file across the square. The crisp night air felt good after the stifling hut.

They reached the back of the box wagon without incident. The wagon's thick double doors were secured with a bulky iron padlock. Rina took Maurizan by the hands and guided her to the padlock. The gypsy girl ran deft fingers over it, taking extra care to trace the edges of the keyhole. She reached back to the pouch on her belt, opened it, and fished out two lengths of metal, shorter and thinner than knitting needles. She inserted them into the keyhole and began to work the lock. Rina recalled Brasley's warning to watch their coin purses upon entering the gypsy camp. They had a reputation as thieves. Maybe there was something to the stories after all.

The lock popped open. Rina remembered the girl was working with almost no light. She couldn't see nearly as well as Rina. Her respect for the gypsy's skills ticked up a notch, and she realized she really knew nothing of this young girl, skilled with a dagger, able to pick a lock. What other secrets hid behind that bright, youthful face?

Youthful? She's two years younger than I am. Who am I kidding, acting like some gritty veteran?

And yet Rina had come through so much in such a short time. If she didn't think about it too much, the death of her parents was like some distant ache.

And she never let herself think about it.

They pulled the wagon doors open, freezing momentarily as the hinges creaked.

Nothing happened.

Rina patted each of them on the shoulder. A farewell. Just a temporary one, she hoped.

She crawled into the back of the wagon and heard the doors close behind her, the click of the padlock being set back into place. She hid as best she could between two barrels, pulling a sack of flour in front of her.

If the plan went as hoped, Alem and Maurizan would take the horses and circle around to meet her beyond sight of the village. Although exactly when they would meet again was still a question.

As for Rina, the servants of Kashar would unwittingly take her with the provisions to the tower of the mountain's guardians. And into the clutches of the wizard.

CHAPTER FORTY-FIVE

The gardens and courtyards of the king's palace had long been the meeting place of Merridan's nobility. Ostensibly the center of social activity, it was also a place where deals were struck and fortunes were made. Intrigues abounded. Gossip proliferated. Alliances were forged or betrayed, and dalliances initiated in shadowed alcoves or remote groves.

Brasley arrived mid-afternoon swathed in deep purple.

He'd stretched his money from the sale of his horse magnificently. He'd purchased a variety of fabric from a reputable cloth merchant but had taken it to a tailor in an unfashionable part of the city. He'd hovered over the poor man as the tailor had made Brasley half a dozen outfits in the current style. It had been half the cost of a tailor frequented by the popular lords and ladies at court.

He'd taken a room at an inn on the border of the Palace and Merchant districts. The location wasn't quite good enough to elevate his standing, but neither was it poor enough to detract. He'd bathed and shaved. He was a new man.

The stone archway along the south end of the king's palace stretched the entire length of the structure. Brasley walked slowly, chin up, eyelids heavy as if slightly bored. His confidence stemmed, in part, from knowing he looked right. The outfit wasn't formal enough for evening, but for an afternoon, the leather pants and high boots and dark purple doublet were perfect. The cloak, of a lighter, contrasting shade affixed with a silver chain, added a bit of dash.

He looked good, and that was important since he thought his best chance was through one of the young ladies. He'd spent an hour smiling and nodding at various beauties before spotting a familiar face, the very pretty young thing he'd been searching for.

Elise Quence was a stunning young brunette Brasley had met two summers ago at a coming out ball in Sherrik on the southern coast. The Marquis of Sherrik's seaside palace was an open, sprawling affair, and Elise had cornered Brasley on a secluded veranda at sunset. At the time, it hadn't mattered to him that she was the daughter of a prominent baron popular at court in Merridan. Brasley's only concern had been how she'd shoved him into a corner, hidden behind two potted plants, mashing her mouth against his, her tongue snaking inside. When he'd put a hand down the front of her blouse, she hadn't objected.

I just hope she remembers me.

She stood with two other gentleman and another lady all about Brasley's age, laughing at some private joke. Brasley noticed the men wore clothing just a half cut better than his, but likely he was just being self-conscious. He hovered some distance away, waiting to catch her eye.

Elise's gaze finally drifted to his. A moment of surprise and then the hint of a smile. A slight nod before she returned to her conversation.

It was accomplished. Brasley removed himself, sauntering past a fountain to a secluded spot surrounded by high hedges where he sat himself on a stone bench. He sat quietly, listening to the trickle of water in the fountain.

He let his thoughts drift south to Rina and the others.

Brasley hoped they were faring well and felt a brief pang of guilt for leaving them. The thing was, Brasley simply *despised* being dirty. The stable boy Alem was used to living in filth, and as for Maurizan, well, who could say what gypsies were accustomed to? But they were wanderers, so she was probably comfortable with life on the road. It had been Rina who'd surprised him. She was high nobility and had always enjoyed every comfort. Brasley figured a week sleeping outdoors with campfire smoke in her hair would send her scampering to the nearest friendly baron for sanctuary.

It hadn't quite happened that way. The girl had proved to be made of sterner stuff.

Woman, Brasley thought. *She's no longer a girl, not really.*

And the woman was driven by something. Revenge? Certainly, but something more, something Brasley might never understand. But he could still help. He was doing it now. Brasley Hammish might be a less-than-perfect companion in the wilderness, but among the nobility, it was he who was best equipped to negotiate the intrigues and subtleties at court. The first thing he needed to do was penetrate as deeply as possible into one of the most prestigious inner circles he could manage.

That's where Elise came in.

Except she hadn't come to meet him quite as quickly as he'd hoped. Maybe she wasn't coming at all. Had Brasley lost his charm? The notion washed over him like a sudden splash of ice water, but he warmed again when he saw her come around the hedge, an impish smile playing across her face.

Elise was every bit as attractive as he remembered. The bust line of her deep burgundy dress flirted with impropriety, her bodice pushing up the shocking white globes of her breasts to the point where they nearly escaped. Her dark hair flowed down over white shoulders. She wore a cloak that should have been fastened in front against the winter chill, but at court, fashion generally triumphed over comfort.

"Brasley Hammish," she said. "Where *have* you been keeping yourself, young man?"

He rose from the bench, not too quickly, smiling and taking the offered hand, kissing her lightly on the knuckles.

"If I regaled you with tales of all my recent adventures, we'd surely fritter away the rest of the day," he said. "So instead, I'll simply declare that you look as lovely as ever."

She stepped closer, her thigh touching his. Nobody could see them in the enclave of hedges. "And you're as bold as ever. Imagine coming all this way to see me after hearing I'd been married." She pressed closer, her breasts mashing against him. "So impetuous."

Brasley had heard no such thing, but it made his task easier to pretend he had. "It's only knowing you're married that's restraining me. I respect your recent nuptials too much to attempt anything you might consider … compromising."

Her hand moved up his inner thigh, and Brasley felt himself go stiff.

"Restraint is *so* overrated." She beamed a predatory grin at him. "Don't you think?"

Focus, man. Don't let her distract you.

But he couldn't stop looking straight down at her cleavage.

Brasley cleared his throat. "You still keep in contact with your cousin Fregga, don't you?"

Elisa's grin dropped, and her hand halted its progress up his leg. "What?"

"I was hoping you could arrange an introduction," Brasley said. "We met briefly a couple of years ago, but I'm afraid I didn't take the time to make the proper impression."

Elise blinked.

Her confusion was understandable. Why would any man alive reject the gorgeous Elise in favor of the horse-faced Fregga?

"Fregga's father Count Becham is still Minister of Trade for his majesty, yes?"

Comprehension dawned slowly in Elise's face, the smile sneaking back to her lips. "Why, Brasley Hammish, you've become an ambitious lad, haven't you? On the hunt for a good match are we? Finally thinking ahead."

This was the exact meaning he'd hoped to imply, a young rake looking to marry into money and power. It was the sort of motivation someone like Elise would understand, even approve of. He shrugged and smiled as if slightly embarrassed, not *quite* an admission.

Let her think what she needs to think.

"I'm throwing a garden tea at my estate tomorrow afternoon to show off my new husband to acquaintances and distant relations who'd been unable to attend the wedding. Fregga is invited." Her hand resumed its exploration of Brasley's thigh. "I could invite you too, I suppose."

"That would be most gracious."

Her hand found what it was looking for and squeezed. "And now what are you going to do for *me*, naughty boy?"

CHAPTER FORTY-SIX

Rina had dozed, woke suddenly as the box wagon swayed and jostled. Dusty sunlight spilled in through the wagon's arrow slits. The wagon hadn't set out as early as she'd predicted and seemed to be taking too long to reach the tower. She shifted, stretched her legs. The cramped space had quickly grown uncomfortable.

She closed her eyes and tapped into the spirit.

The falcon flew high above the wagon. The mountain loomed ahead very close, so they'd made better progress than she'd thought. The wagon appeared to be heading for an ugly, jagged scar at the foot of the mountain which soon revealed itself to be a narrow ravine.

She released the spirit. She didn't want to drain herself. Rina had found that, in some respects, tapping into the spirit was like exercising a muscle. After so many weeks, she could now do more with less, but it was still wise to conserve herself. Even when embracing the spirit only briefly, there was still a letdown once she let it go again.

Some time passed, and she tapped in again, seeing the world through the falcon's eyes.

The ravine opened wider beyond the narrow entrance, rocky slopes rising steeply on both sides, the dusty road twisting around until the tower hove into view. It was wide at the base, narrowing as it went up, maybe sixty feet high, and built of large blocks of the native stone, a faded orange color like the cracked desert. A ten-foot wall with an iron gate spanned the mouth of the ravine in front of the tower, and men in full armor and the livery of Kashar—green with the image of the snake circling the eye—swung the gates inward to allow the wagon to enter.

Before releasing the spirit, she told the falcon, in the vague wordless way they communicated, to circle back and find Alem and Maurizan. She'd want to check in on them later.

Unless she was killed.

A minute later, the wagon rattled to a halt. Voices. The sound of someone unlocking the padlock on the other side of the door. More voices. How many were out there?

Maurizan was right. This is a terrible plan.

The door of the wagon creaked open, flooding the interior with sunlight. She held her breath, shrinking down in between the barrels, willing herself to smallness. Voices and footsteps dwindled. She peeked around one of the barrels. The door of the wagon had been left open, so she crawled to the edge and looked around the corner into the wide courtyard.

Two of the brown-robed villagers carried heavy sacks of grain toward the tower, flanked on either side by guards carrying halberds. Nobody looked in her direction, so she scampered out of the wagon and darted around the other side, blocking the view of her from the tower. Hiding in the wagon had gotten her through the gate. Now she needed to devise a way to get into the tower and force an audience with the wizard.

Maybe if she could sneak around the back and—

A horn blared. The rattle of weapons and clank of armor. A dozen soldiers in Kashar livery came around both sides of the wagon, pinning her in a semicircle, halberds lowered to menace her.

Or I could just get my idiot self captured. That'll get me into the tower too, right?

⁓

There had been the momentary urge to fight them, to draw her rapier and tap into the spirit, to feel the power flow through her. Rina again considered Weylan's warning. Would there come a time when she could no longer resist, when she would give in to every urge to tap into the spirit until she used herself up?

An unnerving thought, but she put it out of her mind. They'd taken her rapier and knife and were escorting her to the wizard.

Which is all Rina had wanted in the first place.

The man walking next to her had taken off his helm; an officer of the guard, she figured. He'd been terse but polite as they climbed the slow winding stairs to the top of the tower. She'd expected to be clapped into irons or hauled away in chains, but that hadn't happened.

"Thank you for taking me to the wizard," Rina said.

"Don't thank me," he said. "Little enough happens around here of interest. The wizard will want to know about an intruder. Disposing of you might provide some amusement."

Great. You came a long way to get killed, Duchess.

"Can you at least tell me if the wizard's name is Talbun?"

His eyes flicked to her face with a hint of surprise, maybe. "The wizard will answer all of your questions." A shrug. "Or not."

The tower's top floor was spacious and open, a circle of arched and columned windows. A cool breeze tickled the flames in a half dozen braziers. The view was magnificent. She took a collection of brown humps on the horizon to be the village back east. The desert hardpan stretched north and south, and of course the mountain filled the view west. She passed divans, walking on lush and colorful rugs. A table to her left was laid out with fresh fruit and a silver pitcher and goblets. She realized she was hungry.

The guard took her to a nest of silken pillows. A woman reclined there. She regarded Rina from beneath heavy, bored eyelids. She was naked from the waist up and barefoot; a loincloth of some shimmering golden material gathered between long legs; breasts large and round and preternaturally buoyant. Her hair was so blonde it was almost white. Gold anklets glinted in the sunshine; her lips were full and red.

She was so breathtakingly beautiful that Rina almost turned away, as if the woman gave off some radiance that threatened to burn. Rina felt another urge to tap into the spirit but resisted.

The woman's eyes slid to the guard. "What have you brought me today, Joff?"

Joff made a perfunctory bow. "She snuck in with the routine supply wagon."

A long, luxuriant sigh. "Strip her and stake her out on the desert along the road. Her bones will warn away others."

"I'm looking for a wizard named Talbun," Rina spoke up quickly. "Weylan sent me."

The woman narrowed her eyes, rose slowly and gracefully like a feather lifting on a warm current.

Again, Rina had the impulse to avert her eyes, but she held the woman's gaze as she approached. She leaned forward, looking at Rina's eyes. "That's not makeup, is it?"

Rina shook her head.

"I'm Esthar Talbun," the woman said. "What do you want?"

"You—?" Rina had expected a grizzled old man like Weylan. Not a beautiful woman barely into her twenties.

A knowing smile spread across Talbun's face. "What is the point of being an all-powerful wizard if I can't look young and beautiful forever? Weylan was never given to such vanity, but I like to indulge myself. You say he sent you?"

"He said you might…" Rina glanced at Joff. Magical secrets were closely guarded. She didn't want to talk openly in front of anyone. "Weylan said you might have something that could help me."

Talbun made an offhand gesture to the guard. "Leave us."

Joff said, "But, for your protection, milady—"

Talbun laughed, traced a delicate finger down Joff's jaw line. "Darling Joff. Do you really think there's anything she can do to *me*?"

Joff bowed again. "Of course. I'll be just one floor down if you need me." He glanced again at Rina before turning to leave.

Talbun fixed her gaze again on Rina. The wizard's eyes turned cold and sharp. "Now. Show me."

Rina unfastened her cloak and let it drop. Her blouse followed. She unbuckled her belt, slid her pants down and let them puddle around her ankles. She stepped away from the pile of clothing, completely naked, the cool air breaking her out in gooseflesh.

Talbun circled, looking Rina up and down. Rina caught scent of the wizard, like cherry blossoms in spring, but not sweet or cloying like perfume. Rather it was like the woman's natural fragrance, something fresh and clean coming from her pores, wafting on the breeze.

Talbun ran a finger down Rina's spine, tracing the lines of the Prime tattoo. "Yes, this is Weylan's work. It's been years, but I'd recognize it anywhere." She ran her fingers over the bull symbol on Rina's shoulder. "This must come in handy. I'd like to see you in action, young lady. I'm sure it would be a treat."

Talbun removed her hand suddenly, and the air seemed to go still. "He's dead, isn't he?"

Rina swallowed hard. "Yes."

"How?"

"The wasting sickness."

"If he were alive, he would have sent word ahead you were coming." The wizard sighed. "A pity. You were his last. Not many wizards can ink the Prime. Perhaps he was the only one left. Maybe there will never be another Ink Mage again. If there is another wizard in the world who knows the secret, I haven't heard of him."

"You can't ink it?"

"No," she said. "Wizards don't like to share their tricks. There was a time, many years ago, when I thought Weylan and I were close enough to—what's this?"

Talbun bent, prodded at the single rune tattooed low on Rina's side, so small it had almost passed notice.

"Weylan said my skin had to be perfect for the tattoos, but I had a wound," Rina told her. "He slathered it with a healing balm, then followed with the tattoo."

A slow intake of breath, a faraway look coming into Talbun's eyes. "Weylan, you clever old devil." She'd turned away from Rina, talking to herself. "Could it really be that simple? Maybe that's why nobody had thought of it before." She turned back to Rina, a sly expression on her face. "But easy enough to test."

Talbun threw up a hand and spat words into the air, arcane syllables that Rina struggled to remember but couldn't.

Across the room, a knife rose from the table and flew end over end toward the wizard, the hilt slapping into her palm.

Rina's eyes widened. "What are you—?"

Talbun stepped forward and thrust the knife into Rina's belly.

The blade sank to the hilt. Blood gushed hot and red from the wound, washing over the knife and Talbun's hand.

Rina went rigid, eyes bulging, mouth working for air, shaking hands pawing at the knife without strength.

"Does that sting, darling?" A look of mock pity on the wizard's face. "There, there. It's almost over. It will all be over and done with very soon. And then no more pain at all."

Talbun jerked the knife and twisted as she removed the blade, slashing the wound wider; more blood sprayed and splashed on the wooden floor.

Rina found her breath and screamed. She clutched at her belly with both hands, blood spilling out impossibly fast, sticky and hot between her fingers and down one thigh. She took a halting step, slipped in her own blood and fell, landing hard on her side, rattling bones and teeth.

Her head spun, vision blurring. She blinked up through the haze at the grinning face of the wizard. It was as if someone had pulled a warm blanket over Rina's face, the world going dark as her life poured out of her and wouldn't stop.

CHAPTER FORTY-SEVEN

She refused to let the darkness take her.

Rina's head hung heavy, but she lifted it to lock eyes with the wizard. It cost her almost everything she had left. The strength in her body leaked away, a bone-chilling cold seeping in to replace the blood that had left her body.

The darkness pulled at her. Part of her wanted to go there, to swim in sweet, silent relief.

No.

She groped for the spirit, but for the first time it was out of her reach. It tickled the tips of her fingers, tantalizingly close, but she couldn't seize it, couldn't hold on. She hadn't the will. She was slipping away. She kept reaching, stretching with her mind.

"Go on." Talbun's voice cut through the shadow. "You can do it."

Rina gritted her teeth. A fresh surge of blood oozed between her fingers with each heartbeat. She lay on the floor in a red pool, body quivering and drenched in sweat.

So cold.

"The question is," Talbun said softly, "Are you worthy of Weylan's gift, or will you waste it?"

Hate rose so suddenly within Rina it almost gagged her. She stretched her mind, twisted and contorted her willpower, strained every part of her—

And tapped into the spirit.

She pushed pain to the horizon of her consciousness, set her hatred aside. There was only cold awareness now, the wound, the wizard, her body, the blood—all merely elements of a scene unfolding around her, information to be weighed.

And there was something else.

A low warmth in her side, building and intensifying. It spread out from the bloody rent in her flesh, along her whole body until it reached the tips of her fingers and toes.

Rina looked at the wound. The gash began to close together, new flesh pink and soft, knitting and joining. Strength seeped back into her body.

She stood. She wiped blood away from the wound, smearing it across her belly. Where there had been a deep, ugly wound only smooth flesh remained.

She looked at Talbun, mouth agape. "How?"

"Think," Talbun said. "You know how."

In her mind, Rina traveled back through the weeks. She perfectly recalled the scene in the mountain cave, Weylan's annoyance at the cut on her side and his application of the healing balm. His words were perfectly clear in her memory. *I'm getting a little inventive. This will either work out very well for you or ruin the entire process. We'll see, I suppose.*

"Weylan somehow joined the healing balm with the Prime."

Talbun nodded. "Weylan took a gamble, thought it might be a simple matter of timing. The healing balm was still working its magic in your flesh when the Prime bonded to you. Like the trace of some other metal introduced at the forging of a new blade. It will either make the weapon stronger or corrupt and ruin it."

Rina traced her fingers through the blood on her side and across her belly. Weylan had risked her life on the experiment, and it had paid off. There'd been an equal chance it wouldn't have. "He could have killed me."

"But he didn't," Talbun said. "I'd release the spirit if I were you. Healing takes a lot of energy."

Rina recognized the wisdom in this immediately and let go of the spirit. A vague fatigue pulled at her, and the raw emotions she'd kept at bay flooded in again. Anger flared in her eyes. "You *stabbed* me."

"It wouldn't have meant as much if I'd simply explained." As Talbun spoke, she moved to a thin rope hanging along the wall and pulled it.

Rina thought she heard the distant tinkle of a bell.

"You can heal yourself," Talbun said. "But it still *hurts*. You can still be killed. You can be damaged beyond the spirit's ability to bring you back. You needed to know this, to *feel* it."

I think I'd still prefer if you'd just told me.

A servant appeared, an old woman in a veil. The wizard spoke to her in a foreign tongue, and the servant scurried away again.

"You'll be my guest," Talbun said to Rina. "We'll discuss what happens next."

"You'll help me?"

"There is something I can do for you, yes," Talbun said. "Whether you consider it *help* will be for you to decide."

The servant returned with a brass basin of warm water. She knelt in front of Rina and began sponging the blood off her stomach and thigh.

"I'll have my people launder your travel garments," Talbun said. "In the meantime, I think I can come up with something civilized for you to wear while we dine."

~

"The wagon is coming back," Alem said.

After leaving Rina, Alem and Maurizan had reached the ravine at the foot of the mountain well ahead of the supply wagon with Rina hiding in the back. They'd found a grouping of large boulders with a hidden area behind it where they'd tethered the horses. They'd watched from their concealment as the wagon had passed through the first time on its way to the tower.

Now it went back the other way.

"What do you think?" Maurizan asked.

Alem looked at the men atop the wagon. "I don't know. The men driving the wagon don't seem alarmed. Like everything is normal. Maybe she got through okay."

"Maybe." Maurizan put her hand on his shoulder. "Maybe not."

"You know what she can do," Alem said. "I can't believe—"

"Against a wizard?" Maurizan made a disgusted sound of disbelief deep in her throat. "Pull the other one."

"You want to abandon her?"

"Of course not," Maurizan said. "But how long do we wait? Anything could have happened."

Alem didn't have an answer. "We wait."

She squeezed the hand on his shoulder. "Come back with me. Our people can take care of us." Something in her voice grew tight. "You and I, together." She frowned, her eyes intense. "Do you think she is for you, Alem?"

"I don't know what you mean." But his voice was so tight not even he would have believed him.

"Rina Veraiin will never know happiness," Maurizan said. "She is consumed by her own potential, by what she thinks fate has destined for her. She wears her destiny around her neck like a lead weight. It will drag down anyone who tries to hold her up."

"She's trying to right what's gone wrong," Alem said.

"Yes," Maurizan agreed.

An awkward silence.

"We'll wait a day," Alem said. "Maybe two."

Rina was cleaner than she'd been in days—body bathed, hair washed and rinsed in scented oils. She wore an ankle-length loincloth of shimmering silver material lighter than anything she'd ever felt. All of the servants in attendance were female, but she couldn't quite bring herself to go topless like her host. She wore a sleeveless shift of the same material which fell to her navel.

She touched her side again where the wound had been. *It's a miracle.*

No, it's magic.

So what's the difference?

"You look quite stunning, Rina Veraiin."

Rina turned to see Talbun approach, walking between two blazing braziers. They'd been stoked as night had fallen.

"Thank you," Rina said.

"Do you have a man?"

The vision of Alem's face came to Rina unbidden. "No."

"Shall I arrange one for the evening?" Talbun asked. "In case you'd like the additional warmth?"

Rina went red. "What? I ... I mean no thank you."

The wizard grinned. "My apologies. I forget how young you are."

Rina smiled awkwardly. "No it's just ... maybe some other time."

"Of course." Talbun motioned to one of the servants. "When you're more in the mood."

The servant handed Rina a silver goblet and filled it with dark red wine.

Talbun saluted Rina with her own goblet. She gestured at the nearby table. "Sit. Be comfortable. The cooks have been hard at it most of the day."

They sat on soft cushions at a low table. Servants filled the plates. Roast goat, glazed and spiced as Rina had never tasted. Something not quite like rice. Rina caught the words *curry* and *couscous* but they were as foreign as Weylan's arcane gibberish. She never seemed to be able to get to the bottom of her goblet. The servants scurried fast to refill it. Dessert was a cinnamon pastry so light it was like chewing a cloud.

A servant refilled the goblets.

Wizard and duchess reclined in their pillows, satiated, sipping wine.

"Why are you here?" Rina asked.

"Here?"

Rina felt warm, light-headed. "In this tower. You serve the Kashar?"

"I'm not a member of the cult, if that's what you mean," Talbun said. "I've exchanged my services for a favor."

Rina drank wine. "Tell me. I'm curious."

"The high priests have gone into the Long Dream," Talbun said. "There they will commune with Kashar, their deity. They wait a century, sleeping, to ask their god the questions of the universe. In exchange for my keeping strangers away from the mountain, they will ask a question on my behalf."

"You've waited a century?"

"Almost," the wizard said. "Two more years."

"So long." Rina shook her head. "How do you stand it?"

"It is but a fraction of my life," Talbun said. "I have walked these lands for ages, since before Weylan was born." She saw Rina's incredulous expression. "It's true, I swear. Remember what I told you. My powers maintain my youth. The world passes under my nose, and I care not. My ambitions are my own, and I have a question for one of the gods."

"And what would someone like you ask a god?" Rina asked.

"Well." The wizard grinned and sipped wine. "It's a long story."

"Who ... I mean what ..." The wine was in her head. Her thoughts swimming. She had trouble wrapping her mouth around the words. "What kind of god is Kashar?"

"The snake and the eye," Talbun said. "Knowledge and the ability to put it to use quickly. To strike at the right time. A god for thieves and gamblers and opportunists."

"What about exiled duchesses?" Rina smiled crookedly, drank wine and spilled some down her chin. She wiped it away with the back of her hand.

"The gods aren't so generous," the wizard said, "but I am."

"Are you?"

Talbun laughed softly. "No. Not really. But I owe Weylan. And I'll honor his memory."

"You have a tattoo for me."

"Yes."

Rina sobered, or tried to. "Tell me."

"I can make you fast," Talbun said. "Faster than a deer escaping a hunter. A tattoo that goes on your ankles. You could outrun an arrow, a flood, an avalanche, and the world would be a blur in your eyes." She shrugged. "But I need the components. Some very rare ingredients. If you want the lightning bolts, you'll have to fetch them."

"Just tell me. I'll get them."

"Will you?" The wizard's face was a mix of amusement and curiosity. "Not the sort of thing you can pick up at the local market."

"Tell me how." Rina felt like she was floating. She sipped wine, felt it burn warm down her throat.

"We need the ash from a holy tree," Talbun said. "There's one at the top of the mountain. An ember from the fire of a lightning strike."

Rina laughed. She understood the wine had taken over but didn't care. "So you're saying I have to wait for a storm. Sit around here until lightning strikes?"

"Don't be ridiculous," Talbun said. "I'll *call* the storm. We'll have lightning by tomorrow afternoon."

CHAPTER FORTY-EIGHT

Brasley thrust himself savagely into the woman on all fours in front of him, shaking the feather bed so hard he thought it might rattle apart. She squealed sharply with each thrust, pushing her soft ass back at him in perfect rhythm, flesh slapping flesh.

To Brasley's pleasant surprise, Elise's cousin Fregga was an absolute animal in bed.

"Take me, Sir Brasley," she grunted breathlessly. "Faster! Harder! Make me your wench!"

Brasley thrust harder.

Fregga had a long, dull face and bland eyes, but underneath her dress she had a curvaceous body with a round, plump ass and large heavy breasts that swung beneath her as Brasley took her from behind. Her body began the slow tremble that signaled her approaching climax.

Fregga had been surprised and grateful when Elise told her that a handsome, young nobleman had wanted to meet her. That gratitude had manifested itself three hours later with Fregga's head between Brasley's legs in the back of a closed carriage, her warm, wet mouth eager to please.

Afterward, she'd been bewildered anew when Brasley had said he simply had to meet her again the next day. She'd smiled so broadly it had almost split her face in two. Had love at last found plain, dull Fregga?

The guest quarters above her father's carriage house provided a much more comfortable and private spot for a rendezvous. It simply wouldn't do for the Minister of Trade's daughter to be seen climbing the stairs to a young nobleman's room in some low-rent inn.

Brasley held her hips, fingers sinking into soft flesh. A glowing sheen of sweat covered both of them. He pulled her back into him as he thrust. He was getting close now too.

Fregga grunted through gritted teeth, guttural. A spasm shook her body and she went rigid. "Yes, oh, yes!"

That sent Brasley over the edge, and he finished inside her. They collapsed together, panting.

She curled next to him, purring. "Tomorrow. We have to do that again tomorrow. That was ... amazing."

"Actually," Brasley said, "I thought I'd quite like to meet your father tomorrow. If it can be arranged, I mean."

Fregga gasped, and Brasley was suddenly concerned he'd overplayed his hand.

She propped herself up on one elbow, looked straight into his face. "You want to meet my father? You're serious?"

"Well ..." Brasley shrugged. A crooked smile. "I mean, if we're going to carry on like this ..." He let the suggestion hang there. It was a way of suggesting something without promising anything, and Brasley felt suddenly like a bit of a bastard.

He shoved the feeling away and kissed her on the forehead.

"Oh, Brasley!" She threw her arms around him and pulled him close, burying her face into his neck. "Oh, my darling Brasley. I love you. I love you so much."

Yes, I was afraid of that. I really am an utter bastard, aren't I?

~

The next morning Brasley put on his best outfit, a black doublet with silver piping and a scarlet cape worn off one shoulder. Black pants tucked into high black boots. He'd polished the boots. He was freshly bathed and shaved. His polished sword and scabbard hung from a braided leather belt.

He presented himself at the front door of Count Becham's mansion. Fregga had alerted the butler that Brasley was coming, so the butler, accustomed to seeing nobility come and go in the manor, regarded Brasley with mild boredom but didn't balk at admitting him and escorting him through the ornate mansion and down a long hall to Becham's private study.

A second before the butler entered the study ahead of him, he glanced back down the hall and spotted Fregga peeking around the corner at him, face nervous.

Brasley summoned a confident smile and winked at her.

He followed the butler into the study.

"Sir Brasley Hammish of Klaar." The butler bowed and then excused himself.

Count Becham rose from a plush, wingback chair, squinted at Brasley.

"Count Becham." Brasley smiled and extended his hand, crossing the room.

As he approached the count to shake hands, he took in his surroundings. Shelves lined with leather-bound books. Expensive. Carved knickknacks of rare polished stone. Thick rugs and heavy velvet drapes on either side of a window that overlooked a well-manicured garden. A large desk carved from rich exotic wood. The room seemed pristine, unlived in, as if the owner thought it useful to display the trappings of wealth with little appreciation for the objects themselves.

Becham himself ran to fat, the result of a soft, privileged life, jowls and muttonchop side whiskers the same white as his hair. He wore a long, black coat and a red vest with a pattern of wavy lines, a ruffled silk shirt and house shoes with large silver buckles.

Becham shook Brasley's hand, at the same time eyeing Brasley like he wasn't sure *why* he was shaking Brasley's hand.

"I know you're a busy man, sir," Brasley said. "I'm most grateful you've made time for me this morning. Very generous."

"Yes... well." Becham cleared his throat, pinned Brasley with an openly curious stare. "Who *are* you?"

Brasley blinked. "Uh... Sir Brasley—"

Becham waved away Brasley's words. "Not your name, boy. I heard my man clearly enough. I mean, why are you here, and what business do we have? I don't even know how you got onto my daily agenda."

Brasley felt sudden respect for Fregga's cunning. Somehow she'd arranged this. Perhaps she had some sway with the count's personal secretary.

"It is about your daughter. If you'll allow me to explain—"

"My daughter?" Becham frowned, took a menacing step forward. "What about my daughter? Has something happened?"

Brasley's hands came up quickly in a placating gesture. "Sir, nothing alarming has happened, I assure you."

"Talk, boy. I'm losing patience."

"I met Fregga recently at her cousin Elise's tea party," Brasley explained. "I've come to ask permission to see her socially."

"You want to see my daughter?"

"Yes."

"My daughter *Fregga*?"

Brasley was given to understand that the count had four daughters, two of whom were younger than Fregga. The other two were already married and had been taken off the count's hands.

"Naturally, I intend to pursue the matter with all proprieties intact and to follow all appropriate social customs." This was as much as Brasley could say without actually declaring his intent to court Fregga for marriage.

And he was not quite willing to go that far.

"Oh." A slow comprehension dawned in Becham's face. "Oh!"

The possibility that Becham might be close to unloading his final daughter changed the tone of the conversation dramatically.

Becham slapped Brasley on the back and grinned. "You've chosen wisely, my good man. Wisely! Fregga is a fine woman."

The count produced a decanter of good brandy and a pair of fat chuma sticks. He filled two crystal goblets and lit the chuma sticks with a candle. They puffed and drank. Small talk. Becham asked about the long trip from Klaar to Merridan. Brasley said it was good to bask in warmer climes.

"What *does* bring you to the capital?" asked the count.

"I've been appointed envoy to speak on behalf of Klaar." The letter from Rina was tucked inside Brasley's doublet in case he needed to produce some proof of this claim.

"Ah, a man of importance," Becham said. "Working our way up in the world, eh? Grooming yourself for his majesty's diplomatic corps, perhaps?"

Let the man think what he wants. "For now it is enough to serve Klaar."

"So what do you have planned for our young Fregga, eh?"

Becham might have been inquiring about Brasley's long-term intentions.

Brasley chose to understand the question a different way. "There is a recital the day after tomorrow on the palace lawn.

Weather permitting. Naturally, I welcome whatever chaperones would satisfy propriety."

"Of course, of course," the count said. "I could tell right away you were a man of good breeding. I'm sure we have an old aunt clanking around the manor somewhere who can accompany you."

"Then with your permission, I'll take your leave, sir. The business of Klaar keeps me constantly busy." This was a lie but a fiction he wanted to establish right away in case he needed to weasel out of dinner invitations or other tedious family gatherings.

"Naturally," said the count. "Don't let me keep you."

Brasley bowed slightly and turned toward the door. *Not too fast. Give the man a chance.*

"Sir Brasley?"

Brasley paused in the door way, turned back to the count. "Sir?"

"I realize you're new to the city," Becham said. "If there is anything I can do to help, I hope you'll ask."

"Thank you, sir, but I don't think ..." Brasley cocked his head as if a thought were just now occurring to him. "Actually, there might be something, but I hate to trouble you."

"Come now. Let's have it."

"I'm off to the Royal Bank later to establish Klaar's line of credit," Brasley said. "Can you recommend the name of a clerk there who might help speed the process?"

Becham's belly laugh filled the room. "Rest at ease, Sir Brasley. You might not realize this, but of all the people in Merridan, you've come to the one man who has the Royal Bank in his back pocket. Don't give it a second thought."

And just like that the final element of Brasley's scheme clicked into place.

CHAPTER FORTY-NINE

Tosh sat at a corner table in the Bawdy Baron. It was an upscale pub, and Mother had provided him with clothes good enough to pass him off as a reasonably well-to-do merchant. The shoes pinched his feet. Tenni sat next to him looking beautiful in a yellow dress fit for a merchant's wife. Mother had given her the longest, bulkiest fur cloak she could find to hide Tenni's sword.

They ate a meal and sipped good wine. Tosh drank the wine too fast. He was nervous. He nodded for one of the barmaids to refill his goblet. Better a little drunk than nervous. Nerves could paralyze a man when he needed to strike.

But too drunk could make him sloppy.

Tosh was there to kill a man, and he wanted it finished.

He pushed the food around in his dish with a spoon. No appetite. He reached for the wine, made himself stop, then reached for it again and drank.

Tenni put her hand on his other arm. "Easy."

He looked at her, offered a crooked smile that failed miserably to convince her he was just fine. "Why aren't you as jittery as I am?"

"I'm having a fine meal with my man, and I'm wearing a pretty dress," Tenni said. "What could be better?"

He brought the goblet to his lips again.

"Slow down," Tenni said.

Tosh frowned but set the goblet back on the table.

His eyes flicked to the bar where Urma helped her mother pour drinks. He caught her eye, and the girl shook her head. No sign of their prey yet.

"Who has Emmon?" Tosh asked.

"Prinn."

Tosh nodded. After Tenni, Prinn and Darshia were the best with a sword, and for that reason, he'd picked them for tonight. But Mother had overruled him. Tosh picked a pair of pretty blondes instead, Anne and Ralline, since they seemed level-headed and hopefully wouldn't panic when blades flashed from scabbards and blood splattered.

When Tosh had asked why he couldn't have Prinn and Darshia, all Mother would say was that she'd explain later.

"I don't like this place," Tenni said.

"I thought you were glad for the chance to wear that pretty dress."

She frowned, her eyes sweeping the room before settling on Tosh. "I like the dress. But this place is too full of people worried how they look in their dresses or their fine doublets. Somehow a dank Backgate tavern seems more honest."

"Yes, honest," Tosh said. "When they stick a knife between your ribs, you never have to wonder why. Sometimes I think—"

All heads turned to look at the newcomers coming through the pub's front door, cold wind blowing in with them. Under the thin man's furs Tosh glimpsed brightly colored silk robes.

A Perranese official of some rank. Three guards with him, furs draped over full armor, swords swinging at their sides. Tosh guessed who it was but glanced at Urma anyway.

Urma nodded.

"That's Dra'Kreeto," Tosh whispered to Tenni.

She narrowed her eyes at him. "When?"

"Let him eat and drink and get sluggish," Tosh said. "Then let the girls go to work."

"Right."

"We've got some time," Tosh told her. "We'll need to be ready to leave when he does, but it has to look natural."

"I know."

"We can't follow too close," Tosh whispered. "We just need to block the way in case Bune and Lubin—"

"I *know.*"

Tosh raised an eyebrow.

"Damn it, now *I'm* nervous." She reached for her own goblet of wine and drained it.

The serving girl returned, and they let her refill the goblets.

"If this goes right, we won't have to lift a finger."

Tenni frowned at him. "You don't think I can do my part?"

"I know you can," Tosh said. "Don't be so eager for blood."

She tilted the goblet back again, not looking at him.

Tosh shifted his eyes to Anne and Ralline across the pub. They were also making a special point of not looking at him. He just hoped they knew what to do and when.

You've got to trust other people, man. You can't do it all yourself.

But he was responsible. These girls were here because he'd taught them the sword. If he hadn't done that, Mother never would have—

No. Focus. You've got bloodshed to do and you don't want to fuck it up.

They sipped wine and waited. The serving wenches cleared the empty plates away from Dra'Kreeto's table. They brought him a thick and expensive snifter of brandy and a fat chuma stick. He smoked slowly, touching his brandy only occasionally.

Tosh watched Anne and Ralline.

Anne and Ralline watched Dra'Kreeto.

Tosh had to give the girls credit. They were patient. Urma had told them to wait until the Perranese official was two-thirds through the brandy. Tosh was sweating behind the ears. He glanced at Dra'Kreeto's guards at another table. They sipped tea, sober and calm and big. They looked like they could kill everyone in the pub without breaking a sweat.

This is stupid. You're going to get killed. Get up and walk out now.

Tosh glanced at Tenni. No. She wouldn't leave, and he wouldn't leave without her.

He drank wine. He sweated under the arms now.

Anne and Ralline rose from their table and moved toward Dra'Kreeto. His glass was nearly empty.

Tosh felt like he might vomit. His eyes shifted to the Perranese soldiers. They took no notice of the girls.

Anne and Ralline paused at Dra'Kreeto's table. Casual. Just a couple of working girls. The Bawdy Baron wasn't like the Wounded Bird, but of course there were working girls. Dressed nicely but showing just enough cleavage to make it clear what sort of wares they peddled. Urma had explained how it worked here. The establishment didn't own the girls, but they got a kickback from any action. It was an arrangement that favored the tavern since they could kick out any of the girls who got too aggressive and disturbed the patrons.

Anne and Ralline weren't aggressive. They almost passed Dra'Kreeto's table without stopping, casting a glance, a quick smile. They were dressed just right, so the Perranese chamberlain would know exactly what they were. Prostitutes. The girls' attire at the Wounded Bird tended toward flimsy shifts and loose robes that fell open at opportune times. Such displays wouldn't do amid the upstanding patrons of the Bawdy Barron.

The girls wore tight dresses which offered more than the average show of cleavage, yet remained within the bounds of propriety. A bright paper flower tucked behind the ear let clients know a girl was open for business. They weren't allowed to approach potential customers, but if a man beckoned them over they could then conduct any business they liked, as long as the pub got its share.

The girls had played it just right, and Dra'Kreeto gestured to the other chairs at his table. Urma had told Tosh earlier the blondes would do the trick. Dra'Kreeto evidently liked yellow hair. Tosh had paid off the pub's usual girls the night before to clear out the competition.

A titter of laughter floated across the pub. Anne leaned in, touched the chamberlain's arm, maintaining eye contact the whole time. *She's good*, Tosh thought. *No wonder she had so many regulars.* As far as Tosh could tell, Dra'Kreeto was completely taken with her.

Tosh watched the conversation. He couldn't hear, but he could guess. It had been prearranged. Dra'Kreeto nodded, maybe agreeing on a price. Anne gestured to Ralline. *Can my friend come too?* Dra'Kreeto intrigued, questions on his face, Anne shaking her head. *No not too much extra, not too expensive for a man of your means.*

Dra'Kreeto said something to Ralline, who smiled and blushed. Some kind of compliment, maybe. The three of them rose from the table, heading for the door together.

The three soldiers rose immediately and followed.

Tenni nudged Tosh. He'd forgotten he was supposed to be leaving too. He rose without seeming to hurry and paid the serving wench.

Outside, the night stung bitterly cold. A narrow path had been shoveled down the center of the usually wide cobblestone road, making a path just wide enough for two people to pass each other. Tenni clung to him, shivering.

The weight of the long dagger at Tosh's back felt cold and awkward.

Dra'Kreeto, the girls and the soldiers paused ahead of them at the mouth of the alley. They'd arrived at the make-or-break part of the plan.

Mother had wanted the chamberlain's death to look like an accident. A runaway cart rolling over him in the street, maybe. But she'd also wanted it done fast. Tosh had explained that a believable accident would take time to arrange, but it turned out there'd been a rash of robberies in the neighborhood recently. Mother had said that was good enough. There would be reprisals if a Perranese official were slain in a robbery, but none of it would be connected to the Wounded Bird.

In theory.

For the plan to work, they needed to turn down the side alley where Bune and Lubin waited. Each of the girls had one of the chamberlain's arms, and Anne gestured down the alley. *My place is down there. We could be out of the cold that much sooner.*

Tosh saw Dra'Kreeto shake his head. If he balked at Anne's suggestion, then matters quickly became complicated. Tosh would be forced to make a quick decision—attack Dra'Kreeto in the open street in front of Dumo knew how many witnesses, or call off the attack altogether. Would Anne and Ralline have to spend the night with the chamberlain to avoid arousing suspicion?

Blast it all, we rushed this plan without thinking it through.

Chamberlain, guards and girls turned down the alley.

Tosh let his breath out, hadn't realized he'd been holding it.

Tenni pulled him along. Their part was to hover near the mouth of the alley, keeping watch, and to make sure nobody followed. If the plan went off as hoped, Bune would emerge from the shadows and demand Dra'Kreeto's purse. Of the three guards, one or two would move forward to fend off the robber. *Divide and conquer. Spread out those Perranese soldiers.*

And surprise was on their side. Tosh tried to take some comfort in that.

Tosh and Tenni stopped when they were in position. From the corner they could follow Dra'Kreeto's progress down the alley as well as watch the road they were on.

Tenni took Tosh's arm and squeezed.

Lubin stepped out of the shadows, cudgel in hand. He raised his voice for the benefit of those he knew to be listening. He wanted to make sure everyone knew the stage play had started. "Hand over your coin purse or I'll knock your fucking teeth right out of your head."

The soldiers didn't hesitate, swords flashing from scabbards. Two rushed toward Lubin, spreading apart to come at him from two angles. The third soldier put himself between his master and the ensuing fray. Anne and Ralline clung to the Chamberlain. They would act afraid, and he would comfort them and so the surprise would be all the more.

Tenni pulled on his arm. "Tosh."

Bune stepped out of the shadows next to Lubin, and the two Perranese soldiers stopped short, suddenly less sure of themselves.

With all eyes on the two bruisers, nobody noticed Anne hiking up her skirts, reaching for the dagger strapped to her thigh.

Tenni pulled on his arm more urgently. "Tosh!"

He turned his head, looked where Tenni pointed.

Urma had come halfway down the lane after them. She must have been in a hurry because she'd forgotten her cloak. She gestured frantically at something behind her.

Tosh looked beyond her.

A half dozen Perranese soldiers marched up the road.

Oh, fuck me fuck me fuck me.

A crunch and a clang drew Tosh's attention back to the alley. Lubin and Bune bashed helmets and skulls. One of the soldiers staggered back. The other was on his knees in front of Lubin. The big man brought his cudgel down with both hands. The cudgel stove in the helmet, smashing the skull underneath. The soldier jerked once and fell over.

Anne was already in motion against the soldier who'd stayed back to guard Dra'Kreeto. She thrust the dagger into his armpit where there was a gap in the armor, just like Tosh had shown her. Blood gushed over her hand. She twisted and withdrew the blade, the soldier falling forward into the red-splattered snow.

If Ralline hadn't hesitated, the plan might still have had a chance.

Maybe it was the thought of blood that made her balk. She brought her dagger around too slowly to take advantage of the surprise. Dra'Kreeto grabbed her arm and screamed something in Perranese.

Anne moved in to help, stabbed Dra'Kreeto low in the side. Not a killing blow. Dra'Kreeto screamed again.

The six Perranese soldiers back down the road broke into a run.

Urma jumped in from of them, waving her arms.

Tosh's eyes went wide. *What are you doing?*

She was trying to stop them or distract them or maybe—

The lead soldier backhanded her, and her head spun around, drops of blood flying.

The next soldier slammed the butt of his spear into the back of her head. There was a sickening crack, and Urma flopped limply, face down into the snow.

No!

The soldiers shouted for Tenni and Tosh to stand back as they turned into the alley. They saw Anne and Ralline on top of Dra'Kreeto, their daggers rising and falling to finish him.

When the last soldier passed, Tosh drew his dagger. He thrust under the back of the soldier's wide helm, slamming the blade home at the base of his skull. Tosh rode the soldier down into the snow, the dagger still jammed into his brain. He yanked the blade free and rolled off the dead man just in time to see another soldier bearing down on him with a spear.

Tosh caught a glint of steel in his peripheral vision.

Tenni leapt forward, sword sweeping, and parried the spear thrust. The soldier spun the spear in the other direction and caught Tenni hard on the shoulder with the butt. Tenni hissed in pain.

From the ground, Tosh lurched at the soldier, jabbed the dagger through his knee. The soldier screamed, tilted to one side. Tenni swung her sword at an angle, planting it in his neck, armor, flesh and bone all giving way.

Tosh staggered to his feet, looked at Tenni.

She nodded.

Down the alley, the other Perranese soldiers were dead. Lubin and Bune loomed over them, gore dripping from their cudgels. Anne stood on wobbly legs, her bloody dagger loose in her grip. Bune supported her under one arm. A nasty wound in her shoulder pumped blood. It dripped down her other arm.

Ralline lay face down in the snow, her yellow hair spread out around her.

Tosh turned back to the road. "Urma!"

He ran back to the place where she'd fallen in the snow. He turned her over gently, looked at her face. Spatters of blood mixed in with the freckles. Her face was strangely calm. It was impossible he'd seen such casual violence done to her scant moments ago.

He sensed somebody behind him. "Tosh." Tenni's voice. "Tosh, we have to go."

Tosh brushed Urma's hair out of her face, tucked the stray strands behind a petite pink ear. "Just... give me a second."

"Lubin and Bune are taking Anne back," Tenni said. "And Ralline."

Tosh lifted Urma. The girl's weight shifted in his arms, lifeless and rubbery, and a sob wracked Tosh's body, his eyes going hot and blurry with tears. She weighed next to nothing, but Tosh staggered, knees suddenly weak.

Tenni grabbed him with both hands, turned him the right way. "Come on. I've got you."

Tosh opened his mouth to say something, but couldn't think of anything that mattered. He tried not to cry, but the ache behind his eyes overpowered him. He let it go and cried with abandon, his animal keening echoing along the deserted, snow-crusted streets of Klaar.

CHAPTER FIFTY

Rina stood at one of the casements atop the wizard's tower. She'd been watching the dark clouds gather all morning, blotting out the sun. The landscape below was nearly as dark as night. Thunder rumbled in the distance, moving closer.

She glanced back at the wizard.

Talbun sat cross-legged on the floor, eyes closed, a constant muttering of arcane syllables tumbling from her lips. She sat within a circle of runes. The ancient markings scorched the wooden floor, and an acrid fume rose up around her. To the wizard's left, a spell book open to the appropriate page. To the right, a stencil in brass. Runes and a lightning bolt and an inkwell and needle. Her tattoo awaited.

But only if she were successful.

Rina closed her eyes and tapped into the spirit again. Immediately, she saw the world wheel and blur through the eyes of the falcon as it dove toward the boulder where Alem and Maurizan hid. She'd been searching for them on and off the last few hours. Alem stood suddenly, recognizing the falcon. He waved, his big grin splitting his face.

That's right. I'm still alive. I'm not wizard fodder yet.

The falcon circled three times and then flew away.

When she released the spirit, she saw that Talbun's eyes were open, watching her.

"It's done," the wizard said. "The storm will peak soon. The tree is the tallest point at the top of the mountain. When lightning strikes it, you must fetch an ember. It must still be burning. You have the bowl, yes?"

Rina touched the small bowl hanging around her neck. "Yes."

It was a heavily lacquered earthen pot with holes around the rim for air and a lid that fit tightly. It hung in a sling of netting, a leather strap around her neck. This would be the vessel for transporting the ember. If she let it go out, then the trip would be for nothing.

"I have a question," Rina said.

Talbun nodded. "Go on."

"You're sure lightning will strike the tree? You have that much control?"

"I can't aim lightning bolts like I'm firing a crossbow if that's what you mean," Talbun said. "But I will rain lightning down upon the mountain, and the tree is the highest point. It will be a miracle if at least one strike doesn't hit the mark."

"Yes, about that." Rina cleared her throat. "Doesn't that mean lightning will hit *me*?"

That half smile again from the wizard. "Almost certainly."

Ah.

"One more thing, Duchess." The wizard's face went hard and serious. "I've never been to the top of the mountain. I've never seen the temple. I don't know what's up there waiting for you. But I know the cult likes its privacy."

"Aren't you supposed to be guarding them?"

"You're not going up there to harm them," the wizard said. "I don't feel I've betrayed my duty." A shrug. "And anyway, I owe Weylan. In this way, I honor his memory."

"If I return alive," Rina said, "I'll be in your debt."

The enigmatic half smile returned to the wizard's face. "Maybe. See that box?"

Rina looked to the large table in the center of the room. A small wooden box with a latch, like something for keepsakes or love letters. A deep red, polished wood.

"Take it," Talbun said. "A parting gift. If what's inside happens to prove useful ... well, then I suppose I'll allow you to return the favor some time."

~

Joff and a brace of guards escorted her to the front gate. He carried a torch even though it was midday. It was that dark. Flashes of lightning lit the sky intermittently with jagged blue lines. A cold wind tugged at her cloak. The mountain loomed above them.

"A path twists back and forth up the mountain," Joff said. "You'll come to a landing and stairs that lead the rest of the way up to the temple. That's where we leave supplies for the monks. I've never been up the stairs, so I can't tell you anything more. Good luck to you."

The gate clanked shut behind her.

Lightning crackled across the sky.

In the flash, she saw two figures standing a hundred feet ahead of her. Alem holding the horses. Maurizan standing next to him.

Rina smiled, jogged toward them. In just the short time inside the wizard's tower, Rina had missed the familiar faces.

Alem waved, walking the horses to meet her. The lightning spooked the animals, but Alem had them under control. It was his one real talent. Horses. And he was becoming a good shot with the crossbow too.

As she approached, Maurizan moved closer to Alem, put one of her hands on his arm. A bit too possessively, Rina thought.

Something pinched in her gut. She frowned and slowed to a walk.

"I was relieved to see the falcon," Alem said.

"I've sent him away for now," Rina said. "The storm."

"We'd almost given up on you," Maurizan said.

Rina offered the gypsy girl a tight smile. "I'm sure."

"Did you get what you came for?" Alem asked.

"Not quite yet." Rina's eyes shifted to the top of the mountain. "One more little side trip."

Alem followed her gaze up the mountain. "Aw, come on!"

The rain came cold and stinging.

CHAPTER FIFTY-ONE

Tenni pushed open the front door of the Wounded Bird and entered quickly, a freezing wind at her back. Patrons looked up and grumbled briefly as she shut the door again behind her. She leaned against it, panting, and threw her hood back. Her eyes adjusted to the lamplight and she scanned the common room.

For the first time in weeks, all the customers were local. Not a Perranese soldier in sight.

Prinn sat at a table in the corner, chatting up a bald bearded man built like a blacksmith. She saw Tenni, whispered something into the man's ear and then immediately came to her.

"Well?" Prinn asked.

"They're going through the neighborhood around the Bawdy Baron like a fire," Tenni whispered. "They're searching houses, and they're questioning people in the streets. Not gently."

The bodies of the chamberlain and his guards had been found. Word was that General Chen had been livid. He'd summoned another company of soldiers from the barracks outside the city.

"I saw one man dead in the snow, blood all around him. The soldiers dragged his wife from their home. I think it was because the bodies were found under the snow in the alley behind their house. A butcher's shop with rooms above."

"Have they connected it with us?" Prinn asked.

"Because of us people are dying," Tenni said.

"And I don't want to be one of them. Do they know?"

Tenni shook her head. "I didn't hear anything. The soldiers asked questions, and when people couldn't answer, they were beaten. I think the Perranese were glad when they couldn't answer. I think they mostly want to send a message. I don't know. I didn't stick around."

Prinn put a hand on Tenni's shoulder. "Good thing. Getting killed now won't help anyone."

Tenni rubbed her eyes. So tired. So bone weary these last days, weeks. She cleared her throat. "Where is he?"

"The kitchen." Prinn hesitated. "You might want to give him some space."

Tenni frowned. "I'll decide that."

She pushed past Prinn and headed for the kitchen.

Tosh held a chipped vase, tilted it back, gulping that foul brew Bune and Lubin had introduced him to. He wiped his mouth with the back of his hand, tried to focus on Tenni with bloodshot eyes. "You were there?"

She nodded.

"And?"

She shook her head.

"Bad as we thought, eh? Of course." He took another swig from the vase. "You didn't think they'd be satisfied cracking one little girl in the back of the skull, did you?"

Tosh cracked five eggs, began throwing them into a skillet, shells and all. He splashed in too much oil and way too much salt.

"Tosh, what are you doing?"

"I'm the fucking cook, aren't I? I do what cooks do. Teach whores to kill with a sword in between meals. Except sometimes the whores die, don't they? When they teach you to fight with a blade, they don't teach you how to die on one because that just comes natural, doesn't it?"

"Tosh."

"When the Perranese killed the rest of the army in the street, I hid here with the whores. And now the whores do my dying for me. And then I can just train more and then they'll die and old Tosh will still be here. There will always be more whores. The world will never run out." He drank again.

"Tosh, please."

He threw bacon in another pan; the grease splattered. It dripped into the fire and flared.

Tosh turned back to Tenni, mouth twisted in a snarl. "Next it'll be you." He tilted the vase back, overflow dribbling from the corners of his mouth, gulping. "And then when Emmon's old enough it'll be her turn."

Tenni punched Tosh in the nose.

A crunch of cartilage, and Tosh staggered back against the grill, arms flapping out to grab anything to break his fall. He upended the two frying pans and went down hard. Half-cooked eggs and bacon grease splattered him.

He screamed.

Tenni gasped. "Tosh! I'm so sorry."

He wiped at his nose and it came away red. "Blood. I'm bleeding blood."

She held out a hand but backed away again. Unsure. "Oh, Tosh."

"Fucking shit."

Tosh tried to stand, slipped in grease and fell again.

Someone cleared her throat. Tenni turned. Mother stood in the doorway, hands clasped primly in front of her.

"Go sleep it off, Tosh," Mother said.

Tosh's head turned slowly side to side, eyes blinking like he was trying to blink the world back into focus. "I'm ... fine."

"If you can't make it to your bed on your own, I'll have Bune and Lubin help you," Mother said. "Come see me in the morning. We need to settle some things."

CHAPTER FIFTY-TWO

They climbed the mountain, bent into the wind, rain flying in sideways to lash their faces, the sky lit up with a fantastic display of lightning which would have sent sane people running for cover. Thunder cracked so loudly, it shook the mountain under their feet.

Rina looked back. Alem and Maurizan struggled to haul the terrified horses up the narrow trail by the reins. Below, she could just make out the wizard's tower in a lightning flash. The Kashar village beyond was lost in rain and darkness.

They were soaked. Rina shivered. She could tap into the spirit and cut herself off from the cold, but she suspected she'd need all of her strength for what was to come.

They reached the landing, panting and miserable. The stone steps ahead of her led up into the darkness.

She went back to Alem, her mouth close to his ear so she could be heard over the rain and thunder. "I go alone from here."

"We can help," Alem insisted.

"You know what I can do," Rina said. "But I can't watch out for you and accomplish what I need to do at the same time."

Alem bit his lip, thinking. The look on his face made it obvious he didn't like it, but he nodded.

Rina pointed to a dark opening in the wall of the mountain. It could barely be called a cave, but it was better than nothing. "That's where they drop supplies for the monks. Wait there."

Alem nodded.

Rina drew the enormous two-handed sword from the saddle sheath. She rested the blade on her shoulder. She wouldn't be able to wield it until she tapped into the spirit.

She squeezed Alem's shoulder, smiled at him as the rain ran down her face. No words came to her.

"We'll be here," he said.

She nodded, turned and climbed.

The stairs rose steeply and curved gently to the left. Her legs ached by the time she reached the top, her chest heaving for breath.

Lighting stabbed the ground fifty feet away, thunder clapping so close over her head she thought the mountain would tumble down upon her. She went to one knee, a reflex, closing her eyes tightly, her whole body tense.

The sky is trying to kill me.

She lifted her head slowly. The next flash of lighting revealed an expansive courtyard of large, square paving stones. Across the courtyard, a tall archway.

She stood, tapped into the spirit and lifted the sword.

She stole across the courtyard, seeing more clearly now through the darkness, sword up and ready. She touched the bowl hanging at her chest to make sure she hadn't lost it. Her hand drifted down to the leather satchel slung over her shoulder and the leather box within that Talbun had given her. She hoped she wouldn't need it.

She approached the archway and saw it was the shape of a giant eye. A huge stone snake had been carved twisting around the arch from one end to another, the head of the snake the size of a fat sheep.

Rina watched it warily as she passed beneath the arch.

She was in a flat area at the top of the mountain, completely ringed by giant boulders. The path led one way across the clearing to a wide, squat stone building, wide steps leading up between fluted columns. A peaked roof, another stone rendering of the snake encircling the eye just below the peak.

The temple of Kashar.

But Rina's path lay in the other direction, to the huge oak sprouting inexplicably from the baked earth and stretching more than a hundred feet into the air, growing in a place where no other green thing existed. It was older than the temple itself, indeed was why—in part—the cult had selected this site for their temple. An omen of life where life was impossible.

Lightning danced around the top of the tree.

A sound reached her above the relentless downpour. Since she was tapped into the spirit, she could separate one sound from another—the thunder, the rain, her own footfalls in the mud and … something else.

The sound of stone scraping on stone, slow at first then faster and then gone and replaced by something scraping along the mud.

She turned suddenly, sword in front of her.

Two eyes burned red in the darkness and rose to loom over her. She saw what it was immediately, but in the next flash of lightning the creature was revealed in all of its terrible glory.

The serpent rose twenty feet over her, coiled on top of itself, readying for a strike. It moved with the liquid flexibility of flesh, but its scales were the flat, pocked gray of old stone. Rina recognized the snake immediately. The stone carving that had been twisted around the archway at the entrance. It had come alive upon her intrusion. Its mouth gaped, fangs like daggers.

Rina discovered a vast store of terror within her, a staggering capacity for fear which would have paralyzed her if she'd allowed herself to feel it. She opened a dark closet within herself and shoved the fear inside, locking the door behind it.

The serpent struck, its massive maw intending to clamp down and rip into her with its fangs.

She dodged aside and swung the sword, using all the strength of the bull tattoo. The blade clanged off the snake's jaw in a shower of sparks, knocking the head aside. Rina felt the vibration all the way up through her shoulders. She might as well have been banging her sword against the side of a castle.

The serpent's hiss filled her ears as it rose again for another strike. She brought the sword up and braced herself, jaw set, eyes hard.

She saw the creature's tail swing in from her right but not in time to do anything.

It struck her in the side like the snapping end of a bull whip and knocked her twenty feet back into the thick trunk of the mighty oak. She felt ribs break, the breath knocked out of her. She grunted, blinked rain from her eyes.

And saw the open mouth flying toward her again.

She rolled to the side, her ribs screaming, and the giant snake head slammed into the tree trunk where she'd been a split second before.

Rina sprang up in a fighting crouch. Already a warmth spread through her side, mending ribs, Weylan's healing rune pulsing in her skin. She'd lost the two-handed sword when the serpent's tail had slammed her, and she reached for the rapier at her side.

But the serpent didn't strike again. Its stone fangs had sunk deep into the trunk of the giant oak. The great snake thrashed and writhed, trying to dislodge itself.

Rina sensed the tail sooner this time and jumped straight into the air. It passed beneath her, and she leaped out of the way to avoid the backswing.

Lightning. The splintering sound of wood.

Her head jerked up to see the limb plunging down toward her head. She dodged, and it landed next to her, a branch as big around as her thigh. She knelt quickly at the end that had been struck by lightning, but it was already wet.

No, it wouldn't be that easy, would it?

Another jagged lightning strike lit the top of the tree. The higher branches glowed with flame. Rina didn't know how long it would last in this downpour. She went to the trunk, ran her hands over the rough bark. The tree was old and warped, knots and fissures covering its surface. Hand and toe holds wouldn't be a problem.

She climbed.

Each flash of lightning illuminated the raindrops falling toward her face like a barrage of crystal sling stones hailed down upon her from the heavens. Like stars rushing down toward her from the fires of the sky.

She climbed faster. The top of the tree blazed, but the rain came so hard it would douse the fire soon.

Rina reached the lowest branches and the climbing went easier. She looked down.

The serpent had freed itself and had coiled around the trunk, spiraling slowly upward. The glowing red eyes advanced toward Rina, the menacing hiss a deadly promise.

The part of her that was the young girl Rina Veraiin strung together a collage of curses so inventive that Kork would have been proud even as he scolded her.

But it was the Ink Mage that controlled her actions. She calculated the serpent's speed, looked up again at an appropriate limb.

She could make it.

She redoubled her speed, fingers digging into the bark, searching for a hold. She ripped a nail, ignored the pain. The sky blazed blue white as another bolt struck the tree above her. Thunder shook the world.

Rina pulled herself up to the limb she'd picked from below, threw a leg over and heaved herself into a sitting position. She checked the progress of the serpent. Thirty feet and still coming.

Another part of Rina's mind noted her ribs had completely healed. It was added to the rushing river of information flowing through her consciousness. The rain, the lightning, the serpent.

Twenty feet and closing.

She pulled the leather satchel into her lap and withdrew the small wooden box Talbun had given her. She opened it, the red-hot glow from within washing over her. Inside, three glass balls each the size of a hen's egg but perfectly round. Within each, fire swirled, like a volcano trapped behind glass.

In half a heartbeat, Rina replayed her conversation with the wizard.

"Throw them hard at the enemy," Talbun had instructed her. "And stand back."

"What if I fall and knock one by accident?" Rina had asked.

"The magic knows friend from foe," Talbun had assured her.

Rina plucked the three glass spheres from the box, discarded it, dropped two of the balls back into the satchel, hoping the wizard was right about the magic not turning on her. She already had lightning and a serpent to deal with. She didn't need rogue magic trying to kill her too.

Fifteen feet.

She held the ball like a throwing stone, cocked it back to her ear, arm muscles tight and ready to release.

Ten feet.

She threw, hand and eye perfectly coordinated. The ball struck the serpent below the right eye, shattered and—

—the shock from the explosion lifted her off the tree limb. She flinched away, fire scorching her face, bits of stone embedding in one side of her face and ripping away a chunk of her earlobe.

The world tumbled—rain, lightning, fire.

Rina flailed out with her arms, hit the limb hard in the chest and wrapped her arms around it. Blood dripped down one side of her face, mixed with the rain.

She looked down.

No sign of the stone serpent.

She pulled herself back onto the limb, paused to pick the gravel out of her face. Already the healing magic worked to close the wounds.

Rina climbed toward the fire at the top of the tree.

She reached the lowest burning limb, made sure she had good footing, and then drew her dagger. She pried a glowing chunk of wood into the lid of the earthen bowl, scraping in some ash as well. She dumped it into the bowl, secured the lid.

Rina looked down. It would be a long, slippery climb, but she had to hurry, had to return with her prize before it went cold.

Something slammed hot into her back. Rina's entire body vibrated and she fell, cracking small branches on the way down until she smacked hard into a thick, forked limb. She sucked hard for breath, her mind telling her what had happened. *You've been struck by lightning.*

It could have been worse. She could have fallen all the way to the ground. Would her healing power be enough to survive a fall like that? Rina didn't want to find out. Yes, it could have been *much* worse.

A sudden motion below caught her attention. She looked down.

The stone serpent slithered up the tree again, one eye burning red as blood and fire.

CHAPTER FIFTY-THREE

The horses were so restless that Alem finally had to do something. He cut strips from a blanket and tied them around the horses' eyes. They calmed but still flinched with every crack of thunder.

Calling the shallow gouge in the side of the mountain a cave was being generous. Alem and Maurizan had tied the horses all the way at the back, which left Alem and Maurizan hunched at the mouth of the cave, rain blowing in on them when the wind shifted.

Alem took the remains of the blanket and dropped them around Maurizan's shoulders before sitting next to her.

She leaned toward him, had to shout over the downpour. "I've never seen a storm this bad."

"Neither have I," he shouted back.

She scooted closer to him, shivering.

Alem tried not to think about her, how close she was, and how nice her wet red hair looked tucked behind her ear. He may have been a world-class thicko, but it was obvious she had feelings for him although why he couldn't guess. Maybe that was the most intoxicating thing about her, that she so openly wanted him. How could a man stand fast against a tide of such raw and honest emotion?

And why would he want to?

Because that means you've given up. It means you're admitting what will never happen.

His eyes drifted to the steep set of stone steps that led up to the temple.

Alem thought about Brasley instead. He hoped the jackass was okay wherever he was. Maybe he'd had the right idea after all. Alem wouldn't have minded a warm bed in a comfortable inn. And a hot meal.

A stab of lightning hit so close it blinded him. Earth-shattering thunder followed immediately, and Maurizan gasped and grabbed his arm.

Alem blinked the spots from his eyes.

Maurizan looked up at him, embarrassed, but she kept her hand on Alem's arm, almost like she was staking a claim. She squeezed softly, and the embarrassment in her face melted into a tentative smile. She scooted closer still, her leg pressed to his.

Maurizan opened her mouth to speak, closed it again, piercing him with her gaze, the plea in her eyes so plain it was painful to see.

Alem put an arm around her shoulder. "You're shivering." There was suddenly something nervous bouncing around in his stomach. He felt hot and cold at the same time.

Her eyes were enormous and deep, and to Alem they seemed almost like they cast some spell. Maybe they did. The same sort of magic all women have.

"Alem." Her voice was barely a whisper, yet it pierced the rain and thunder.

He wasn't sure he could breathe, his heart hammering against his chest.

She tilted her face up to him, mouth falling slightly open. "Please."

He felt dizzy.

Maurizan's other hand slipped in behind him, held his neck, pulled him forward, down to her, insistent, pleading.

Alem's lips pressed hard against hers; their tongues found one another, an explosion of textures and desires.

It felt like something he'd been waiting for all his years, like he hadn't lived until now. It was warm and wet and frightening and wonderful. Thunder boomed. Rain lashed the earth. It seemed her lips wanted to devour him. It felt like triumph.

And it felt like giving up.

CHAPTER FIFTY-FOUR

One glowing red eye came up after her. She'd put out the other one with Talbun's magical explosive. She thought she'd finished with the beast.

Rina had been mistaken.

There was a crater below the right eye of the great snake where the stone had been blown away, as if rogue masons had set to it with hammers. She'd put a dent in the serpent, that was for sure, but it was far from vanquished.

And now it was coming back for her.

She sucked in a lungful of breath and climbed.

A glance over her shoulder and she knew she wasn't fast enough. The serpent would overtake her. She paused on the next thick limb, hand dipping into her satchel. She came out with another of the explosive glass balls. It wouldn't kill the thing, but maybe she could slow it down again.

She reached for the next branch above her, and turned to sling the glass ball with the other hand.

And the serpent was upon her.

The gaping mouth and stone fangs filled her vision, but its wide body lodged fast in the fork of two thick limbs, its huge jaws snapping shut an inch from Rina's nose. It struggled violently to free itself, thrashing and hissing. It opened its mouth wide once again to bare its fangs.

And Rina tossed the glass ball down its throat.

She leapt onto the snake's head, arms encircling it, and used the bull strength to clamp the beast's mouth shut. The ball in the snake's throat exploded just behind its head, and Rina was flying. Head and Ink Mage tumbled down through branches and leaves.

Rina flailed out again with her arms, but couldn't grab hold this time. She fell through some branches and bounced off others. The hard ground arrived to slam into her. She heard and felt things crack and crunch along her body. Her sight dimmed. She struggled to stay conscious and cling to the spirit.

She felt the healing rune flare in her side. *Come on. Faster.* Rina knew the pain was there waiting for her if she released the spirit.

Bones mended. Ankle, knee, rib, shoulder.

You're using too much. You'll use yourself up.

How long did she lie there? It felt like hours, but it was only minutes. She pushed herself up, touched the bowl hanging from her neck by the leather strap. It was still intact. A minor miracle.

She heaved herself to one knee. Stood. She needed to heal more, but she was draining spirit rapidly. *Just a little more.*

She looked about her. The snake head lay three feet from her, the body beyond that. The serpent appeared to be no more than a broken statue now. Whatever had animated the creature had been blown away by Talbun's magic. She retrieved Kork's sword.

Rina couldn't stall any longer. She was draining herself. She had to release the spirit. Now.

But she didn't.

Weylan warned you, didn't he? Will you be able to step away, Duchess?

She released her hold on the spirit.

Pain flooded her. Her legs went watery, and her eyes rolled back in her head. She wilted into the mud, the cold rain pelting her slack face.

CHAPTER FIFTY-FIVE

He sat cross-legged on the floor in one of the tower rooms. General Chen had been happy to let him have the space. Few were keen to climb so many stairs on a daily basis.

Ankar didn't mind, didn't leave the room very often anyway, choosing to meditate long hours instead. The room was well away from the other residents of Castle Klaar, and he liked to stare at the view of the town spread out below him.

And he liked the privacy. The close quarters aboard ship on the trek over had been almost intolerable, and the other two wizards—what were their names again? Ah, yes, Prullap and Jariko—had chattered like old hens the first week, trying to pry his secrets from him. He'd glowered at them once and hadn't been pestered the rest of the voyage, choosing mostly to meditate on deck in the chill of the sea air.

Ankar always felt just a little too hot.

He stood, threw back his hood, tugged loose the bow at his throat and let the cloak fall. He wore only a thin loincloth underneath and soft, ankle-high leather boots.

Ankar was bald and covered from head to foot with tattoos. Not much of him was left open for more. He had been warned by the wizards who inked the tattoos that too many could overload him. Those wizards were dead now. Ankar had killed each one of them after letting them first ink the new magic into his skin. None would come after Ankar to get the same power. He alone possessed so much ink magic. He had tattoos to give him strength and speed. Sewn into his skin was magic that let his eyes see clearly to the horizon, that would let him hear a gnat fart at a thousand yards. The tattoo on his throat made his voice so sweet that he could beguile the weak-minded. The tattoo on his skull was a shield to prevent supernatural forces from invading his mind. Other tattoos gave him more powers still, some minor, some great.

Ankar was a one-man fortress, a conqueror, a nation unto himself. Ostensibly, he'd come to Helva at the behest of the Emperor. Technically, he was to offer his services to General Chen.

But Ankar's ambitions were his own. He went to the window and threw open the shutters. A bitter wind bathed him in winter. His skin was so hot, always. The magic writhed just under his skin like something alive, pulsing in his veins even when he wasn't tapped into the spirit. Perhaps the wizards had been right. Maybe Ankar was overloading himself. He was a big man, muscled, broad back and shoulders. That was a lot of skin. A lot of ink. He would control the magic with the very force of his will.

Ankar would be master of ink mages.

In the past twenty years, Ankar had met only three other ink mages. Like Ankar, they'd sought out wizards with tattoos to offer, so it was only natural that Ankar and these other mages should cross paths. There had been no question they would battle. Ink mages guarded their power as jealously as other wizards. He'd slain all three.

Ankar breathed in through the nose, held the breath a moment before releasing it slowly through the mouth. He stood straight, eyes closed, and let the cold air wash over him. He stood that way a moment and was tempted to tap into the spirit. He resisted. For all his power, he suffered the same weakness as all ink mages. If not careful, he could use so much magic that he might drain himself. In his duel with the third ink mage, he'd come perilously close to doing just that.

He opened his eyes, turned his hands over and looked down at his empty palms. His musing had reminded him why he'd come to Helva—not to serve the Emperor, although he would do that also—but rather to chase the rumor of a final tattoo. The palms of Ankar's hands. The only unmarked skin on his body. No ink.

Somewhere in Helva there was a priest. Ankar would find him.

And the final tattoo would make him the most powerful ink mage in history.

CHAPTER FIFTY-SIX

The first two things she realized after her eyes flickered open were that she was lying flat on a hard table and that she was naked. She tried to lift her head, couldn't, like it was a boulder attached to her neck.

Rina realized she should have felt bruised and battered after her battle with the great stone serpent. She didn't. The tiny healing rune on her side had worked its magic. She felt only a deep fatigue.

And ... something more.

A slight sting on her ankles, a fly bite.

A pinprick.

"It's finished." Talbun's voice. Soft hands on Rina's feet. "I figured as long as you were asleep I might as well use the time to ink the tattoos. With the stencils it didn't take long."

Rina managed to turn her head. Talbun was there at her side. She wore a loose red robe.

"Your friends brought you here, unconscious and tossed across a saddle," Talbun said. "They're downstairs. My people are feeding them, allowing them a bath and rest. By the look of them, they've been on the road a good long time."

Rina managed a slight nod.

"You didn't look so great yourself." That quick, mocking smile. Rina didn't mind. She was alive.

She felt dry, rough hands on her back and shoulders, lifting her suddenly into a sitting position. Two old women, Talbun's servants.

A third woman held a steaming cup to Rina's lips; an acrid smell hit her nose. The cup tilted back; the hot liquid flooded Rina's mouth, spilling down her throat. Warmth spread through her, into her muscles and bones. The fatigue eased. Her eyes slid sideways to the wizard.

"Nothing magical," Talbun said. "A century of herb lore has proven to be a useful hobby."

Rina sipped again, swung her legs over the table, bare feet cold on the floor. She glanced around. She was back at the top of the wizard's tower. "My clothes."

"I threw them out," Talbun said. "They were a bit tattered."

Tattered was an understatement. Rina's brutal encounter with the great stone serpent had been rough on her wardrobe. She finished the tea, looked up to see the wizard staring at her, curiosity plain in her eyes.

Of course. She doesn't know. The monks never told her what kind of guardian might be up there.

"A statue of the Kashar snake over the entrance arch," Rina explained. "It came alive when I passed below it. It was *big*." She described how the thing had tried to kill her.

"Powerful magic to animate something like that," Talbun said. "You're fortunate it was only your clothes that were ruffled."

"I got ruffled plenty," Rina said. "Your little magic fireballs saved me. And Weylan's healing rune."

"I'm surprised no one tried such a thing before Weylan," the wizard said. "I've heard there are thousands of tattoos in the world, endless possibilities. Many have probably been lost, died along with the wizards who guarded the secrets. And I've also heard rumors too absurd to be true."

"Like what?"

A half shrug, a sly smile. "Tattoos that go directly on the eyeball. A dragon tattoo on a tongue that lets the ink mage breathe dragon fire. I'm not sure how you'd tattoo a tongue."

Rina laughed. She looked down at her feet. The golden tattoo of a small lightning bolt decorated each ankle. She was tempted to tap into the spirit and see what happened.

Not yet.

"I still need something to wear."

Talbun snapped her fingers and one of the old women scurried forward. She carried an armful of black clothing. Two more women behind her held black armor.

"A very silly young girl used to wear this," Talbun said. "Back when she thought armor could protect her."

"Yours?"

"Yes." The wizard took the black clothing from the servant and handed it to Rina.

The material was light and fit close against Rina's skin. She pulled the shirt over her head. Long sleeves. The pants were sturdier. She stepped into them, buttoned them up. Wool socks and high leather boots. The other women brought forward the black armor.

It was not a complete set, not the heavy cumbersome plate that knights wore into the field. They lowered the armor onto her shoulders, fastened it in the back. The breastplate was clearly made for a woman. Tightly knit black chainmail hung at the sides and in the armpits. It would not protect quite as well as plate, but would allow better maneuverability. Thigh and shin guards. Bracers. The metal was surprisingly light but strong.

"I never wore a helm," Talbun said. "I always fancied the way my hair looked. I suppose I should have gotten my head caved in for vanity, but it never happened."

Rina tried to imagine the wizard in armor, holding a sword, but couldn't quite picture it.

The servant brought her a long mirror, and Rina took stock of herself.

She thought she might appear clumsy and bulky, but she didn't. The armor was sleek and fit tightly up against her body, almost as if it had been fashioned to her specific measurements.

In the mirror, she saw Talbun come up behind her.

"You wear the armor well, Rina Veraiin, beautiful and lethal like the spirit of death itself."

I suppose that works out to a compliment. Maybe?

The wizard's face grew serious. "Go easy at first with your new power, Rina. With the lightning bolt tattoos you are now as fleet as the big cats who hunt the southern plains. Trust me, you *don't* want to run into a tree or something at that speed."

Rina pictured herself running face first into an oak tree and burst into uncontrollable laughter.

CHAPTER FIFTY-SEVEN

Tosh's hangover was trying to kill him. Gnomes with iron mallets hammered the back of his eyes. He was sweaty, and clammy and miserable, and he'd still be in bed if Mother hadn't been expecting him.

He climbed the stairs to her top floor office, wincing with each step. He knocked.

"Come in," from the other side of the door.

Tosh entered, closed the door behind him.

Mother rose from behind her desk, hands clasped in front of her, prim and stern. Chin lifted. She glared at him. "You seemed happy here at the Wounded Bird, Tosh. What's changed?"

Tosh decided to be blunt. "I don't know why you're looking for trouble. You're just getting girls killed. Maybe you'll get me killed."

A pause. Mother's jaw was tight, a vein working in her throat. "I see."

The collar of Tosh's shirt was damp from hangover sweat. "I . . . I just don't understand why you want us to do the things you're asking us to do."

"The Perranese are foreigners, invaders," Mother said. "You don't want them out?"

Tosh shuffled his feet. "Of course. But ... I mean it's not like the king has an army at the gates to rescue us. People conquer other people all the time. The Perranese keep the peace. They leave us alone, don't they? I mean, sure, if I had my way, they'd be gone. Things would go back to normal. But it's not for people like us to start some kind of revolution. That's for more important types."

"Really?" Mother raised an eyebrow. "How important do you have to be to want your homeland back, Tosh? Who exactly among us is qualified to start a revolution and who isn't?"

"I don't know. Not me."

Mother drew in a deep breath, let it out slowly. For the first time, Tosh noticed a weariness in her eyes, a grayness in her slack face.

"I can see how you want to protect what you have," she said. "Your life here. Tenni. It's understandable."

Tosh wanted to object, but couldn't. She was right. "I just don't see why we're looking for trouble."

"I could tell you there are bigger things at stake here than the little private life you're protecting," Mother said. "But that would be hypocritical. I have my personal reasons too."

She opened a small wooden box on her desk, plucked out a ring. Tosh had seen her fiddle with it before and figured it for some kind of keepsake. Maybe a family heirloom.

"This was Duke Arlus Veraiin's signet ring," Mother said.

That caught Tosh's attention. "Why?"

A long sigh originating in the depths of memory. She looked down at the ring as she spoke, turning it over in her hands. "Arlus's wife had always been so sickly. Especially after Rina was born. It was a difficult birth, nurses attending to her all the time, and Arlus always there by her side, trying to run a duchy and care for a sick wife at the same time. He was a great man, but there are limits to endurance and patience and strength."

Tosh didn't hear this, didn't want to know whatever it was Mother was going to say. It felt too much like she was putting some kind of responsibility on his shoulders, a weight he didn't want. It was unfair. It wasn't Tosh's problem.

But she'd taken him in. He owed her ... something.

Didn't he?

"A man like Arlus needed somebody to lean on," Mother continued. "Somebody who could comfort him and never expect anything back."

Please don't tell me what you're going to tell me.

"We were lovers for almost twenty years," Mother said.

Tosh winced.

"I never told anyone," she said. "Would never have done anything to embarrass or compromise him."

Shut up. Please shut up.

"He loved his wife," she said. "But he needed me."

A long silent moment. Tosh's head pounded, stomach churned. He could think of nothing to say, wanted nothing more than to slink away and hide.

"We killed the chamberlain because one of my girls has her hooks into the new chamberlain," Mother said. "I've placed another girl in Lord Giffen's bed."

Please ...

"When the time is right I will strike. While there is breath in my body I will not suffer Arlus's betrayer to live, won't tolerate his murderer on the throne of Klaar. And now you know, Tosh. It's all on you, isn't it? You can decide to help. Or not. You could even turn me in, couldn't you? Might even collect a nice reward. Is that what you intend, Tosh?"

He shook his head slowly. A bead of cold sweat rolled down his spine.

"You need to decide then," she told him. "I'm trusting you. You need to think about it and decide what you will do."

Tosh had already decided. He'd need to pack some things soon and get as far away from Klaar as possible.

CHAPTER FIFTY-EIGHT

Rina's hair trailed behind her in the wind, the grin wild on her face. When tapped into the spirit she could keep her emotions at bay if needed, but this time she wanted to feel the joy, the pure rush of speed.

She glanced at Alem grinning back at her. He ducked low in the saddle, leaning forward, spurring his gelding at full speed next to her on a long straight section of the dirt road. Alem was a good rider, and Rina had told him not to go easy. He was riding for all he was worth.

Rina pumped her legs harder and pulled away from him. Her jubilant laughter flew away on the wind.

When she was a hundred yards ahead of him, she carefully slowed and stopped, remembering Talbun's warning. Rina wasn't used to running so fast. She could step in a hole and snap an ankle, and while the healing rune would eventually mend any broken bones, it would still *hurt*.

Alem had slowed to a trot, reined his horse in next to her. "Okay. *That* was impressive."

Rina released the spirit as she stepped close to Alem's gelding and took the reins. She could feel it in her legs. Her muscles hummed. The lightning bolt tattoos might give her speed, but that didn't mean her legs were conditioned for it. Might take time to build up those muscles.

Still...

She grinned up at Alem. "I'm not going to lie. That was *amazing.*"

He grinned back down at her, the warmth spreading to his eyes, and Rina felt something flutter in her stomach.

Their heads turned at the sound of Maurizan's horse trotting to catch up, and the light fluttering in Rina's belly turned into a cold stone.

"Okay, I admit it," Maurizan said, bringing her horse alongside Alem's. "That was pretty fast."

"Pretty fast." Alem snorted. "She outran my horse."

Alem's comment teased the grin back to Rina's face, but her eyes slid to Maurizan's and the grin dropped again. She sighed. "I've got to go on ahead of you."

Alem frowned. "Without us?"

"You saw. I can get there faster if I run ahead."

"We'll follow as soon as we can," Alem said.

"No. I want you to meet me. Here, I'll show you." Rina tapped into the spirit and dropped to one knee, searching her memory for one of father's maps. She'd seen it with her own eyes. It was just a matter of searching her mind for it, and when she found it she began to sketch in the dirt, drawing a line in the dirt road that ran along the river north to Merridan and then Tul-Agnon beyond. Halfway to Merridan a bridge crossed the river and another road led east and north back toward Klaar.

Rina drew an X in the sand. "There's a village at the crossroads here. There's an inn, or there used to be, at least. I don't know how long I'll be in Merridan. I don't know what's going to happen. Take the rest of the money and wait as long as you can."

Maurizan's eyes shifted from Rina to Alem. "And if we *can't* wait?"

"We'll wait," Alem said firmly.

"Well, then. No time like the present." Rina's smile was wan and reluctant. She nodded at each of them once, then turned.

And ran.

~

The world blurred.

Her arms and legs pumped like a machine, and at times it felt like her feet barely touched the ground. She passed through tiny villages, past the alarmed, disbelieving faces of farmers not sure what they'd seen—maybe the apparition of some long-dead sorcerer riding the wind, a ghost, a trick of the light.

She would push herself until she knew she needed rest, sleep off the road under a tree and start again as soon as she was ready. It became harder each time to rip herself away from the embrace of the spirit. Weylan's ghostly warning rang in her head, but she ran on. She ran by starlight. She ran on through the day.

A man could ride his horse into the ground and make it to Merridan in a little over a week.

Rina reached the outskirts of the city in three days.

CHAPTER FIFTY-NINE

Merridan's Central Postal Exchange was in the posh part of the city only a few blocks from the palace. Rina was acutely aware of how she looked—road weary, muddy, hair matted. Likely, she smelled too. Her appearance earned her a few suspicious glances, but maybe it was the black armor and the rapier hanging at her side that kept anyone from commenting or getting in her way.

Walking beneath the vaulted arch of the Central Postal Exchange was like entering the frenzied palace of a foreign monarch. A long line led up to a podium on a raised dais. Runners in the livery of the Postal Exchange scurried in every direction.

The line moved slowly. Rina looked around for another option. There was none. If she wanted to talk to an official representative of the Postal Exchange, she needed to wait in line, and seeing the looks on the faces of people on the way out, she suddenly didn't feel very optimistic. But this is where Brasley had told her to come. It was a big city. Brasley hadn't known exactly where he'd end up, and the Central Postal exchange was an easily identifiable landmark and a natural place to leave a message.

Rina finally reached the head of the line, and the stuffy dignitary stared down at her over his podium. He had a long, curled moustache and wore a uniform as ostentatious as a general's— gold piping and buttons, a brass badge of office with the king's crest.

"What is your business with the Central Postal Exchange?" he demanded.

Rina lifted her chin. "I am Duchess Rina Veraiin of Klaar." It was worth a try. Maybe a title would impress him. Maybe not. This wasn't a backwater like Klaar. It was the capital of the kingdom, and likely one couldn't swing a cat without hitting a duchess or an earl or a count. "I was told to come here in case I had any messages."

One of the functionary's eyebrows ticked up half a notch and Rina thought he was deciding if he believed her. She certainly didn't *look* like a duchess.

He held up a finger. "A moment."

He opened a large book, ran a finger down one page, chewed his lip, flipped to another page. His face brightened "Ah."

From beneath the podium he brought out a bell and began ringing it. The sound was so loud and piercing that Rina flinched.

The response to the bell was immediate. A pair of tall double doors flew open across the chamber and a pair of runners in postal livery sprinted toward the podium.

Rina worried she'd inadvertently set off some kind of chain reaction. "Uh, maybe I—"

"Special instructions have been left for you, Duchess Veraiin. Where is your retinue?"

"I have no retinue."

"I see. And where is your luggage?"

"I have no luggage."

He frowned, his moustache twitching with annoyance. Evidently, not having luggage and an entourage didn't match his idea of a duchess. He turned to the two runners who turned out to be pimply-faced youths maybe fourteen years old. "Bring around one of the postal carriages immediately."

They bowed tersely and ran away at full speed.

Everything happened rapidly after that.

Rina was hustled out of the post office to where an enclosed carriage drawn by four horses waited in the street. A driver nodded to her respectfully. One of the pimply youths held the carriage door open for her, and the other clung to the rear of the carriage in the footman's position. She climbed in, not even having the time to form one of the dozen questions that swirled in her mind.

Ten seconds later they were clattering down one of the city's cobblestone streets, citizens leaping out of the way as they flew past. They turned into an extravagantly wealthy neighborhood; various flags and coats of arms were displayed on the gates of each manor. Abruptly the carriage turned and passed through a gate. The two-story manor house ahead of her was enormous, with fluted columns on each side of the grand entranceway.

Two lines of servants stood in rows on either side of the steps leading up to the front door like some kind of welcoming committee. *Did they know? Did somebody run ahead to tell them she was coming?*

The carriage stopped and the footman was there in a flash, opening the door and offering a hand to help her down.

She looked up as she exited the carriage, saw a man slowly descending the stairs toward her. He wore long, plush robes, some kind of official gold chain around his neck, a soft, floppy hat with a garish red plume from what enormous bird Rina couldn't guess.

With a lurch in her gut Rina thought she understood what was happening. Somebody very important had discovered what was happening in Klaar. Now Rina was being called to task.

Somebody important—maybe the king himself!—wanted to know why there had been a delay in warning the rest of Helva that the Perranese had invaded.

She looked at the man again, trying to guess who could possibly—

Oh, shit. It's Brasley.

~

The servants had escorted her to a second-floor, corner room with wide windows that offered a good view of the extravagant neighborhood. Not that Rina saw it. She'd flopped into bed, had slept the rest of the day and through the night into mid-morning.

They brought her breakfast as she soaked in a large tub of hot water. Maids circulated steadily through the room to add warm water to the tub.

Rina plucked a pastry from the silver tray next to the tub, bit into it. Light. Some kind of berry filling. It was perfect.

"This isn't really necessary," Brasley said from the other side of the tri-section, silk screen. "I would gladly have waited for you to finish your bath."

"Then you would have been waiting a long time because I'm not getting out of this tub any time soon," Rina said. "Maybe not ever."

"It's awkward to talk like this when I can't see your face."

"Just stay on your side of the screen. You know what my face looks like."

A sigh came from the other side of the screen. "I suppose you have questions."

"A manor house? Servants? New robes? Yeah, you could say I have a few questions."

"Please. Not *just* a manor house," Brasley said. "This is the Consulate of Klaar, the official presence of the duchy in Merridan. The flags haven't been delivered yet."

"How can you *afford* this?"

"As the official representative of Klaar, I was able to establish a line of credit at the Royal Bank."

"*What?*"

"I had to prepare for your arrival, didn't I? You're a duchess, after all. You have a reputation to maintain."

"I haven't been duchess long enough to establish any kind of reputation," Rina said.

"I've been taking care of that," Brasley said. "I've been whispering in various ears what an important person you are. Into the ear of the secretary of the Royal Bank, for one."

"So really *I'm* paying for all this."

Brasley laughed. "Unless we can't get rid of the Perranese. In which case nobody is paying for it."

Rina laughed too.

"There's lots to do," Brasley said. "You do need to get out of that tub."

"No."

"I'm serious. There are people coming to take your measurements. Better if you're not wet."

"Measurements for what?"

"Clothes," Brasley said. "You can't meet the king in that grim armor you arrived in."

Rina's heartbeat ticked up. "You were able to arrange an audience?"

"Audiences are booked full for the next two months. It's impossible. And the wrong way to go about it anyway. The last thing you want is an official audience with the king."

"Then what are the clothes for?"

"A ball."

"A what?"

"A formal ball at the palace. Everyone important will be there," Brasley said. "And don't worry. I'll be your escort. It will look good for you if you're there with somebody handsome."

CHAPTER SIXTY

Six days' hard riding, up at dawn and riding into the darkness each day. Always keeping the river to their right. They were lucky Alem knew how to take good care of the horses.

They paused when they finally reached the bridge. Alem's gaze drifted up the road north to Merridan and Rina. He was strongly tempted to keep following the road north. No matter how powerful the tattoos made her, she was still alone in a big city. Brasley might not even be there. Frankly, Alem didn't completely trust the man.

But Alem had never been to Merridan, and his understanding was that it was huge beyond all comprehension. He could wander for weeks and never lay eyes on Rina. The only reasonable thing to do was to follow Rina's instructions.

He turned his horse east and galloped across the bridge, Maurizan riding close after him.

Three hours later she shouted for him to stop, and he did.

He looked back at her. "What's wrong?"

Maurizan slid from her horse, walked stiffly to the side of the road, rubbing her backside. "My ass! My ass is what's wrong."

Alem fought to keep the grin off his face. "Looks fine to me."

If she was amused, she was doing a great job of keeping it hidden. "Why are we riding so hard? I've been in the saddle more than I've been on the ground these last few days. I'm raw in places a lady should not be."

He dismounted and followed her into the tall grass along the side of the road, letting the horses graze. "What if something's gone wrong? She might have to leave Merridan as soon as she gets there. I don't want her looking for us and we're not there waiting for her."

Maurizan turned abruptly, grabbed a fistful of his shirt and pulled him close. "I'm getting a little sick of hearing about *her*."

She pulled his face down to hers, mashed her lips hard against his. His arms went around her. Maurizan's tongue snaked into his mouth. Her other hand roamed down the front of his pants, and Alem went light-headed as her fingertips brushed against his growing length. Her fingers tightened around him as her kisses became more insistent.

He pulled away, panting. She smiled up at him, threw her cloak off, pulled loose the laces at the top of her blouse. It fell open to the top of her cleavage; goose flesh rose in the cool air.

Alem looked around frantically. "Here?"

"I think you know I've been waiting," Maurizan said. "I'm sick of waiting. We haven't passed a village in an hour."

Alem looked around again. They were in the middle of nowhere. Trees. Tall grass. "I ... uh ..."

She pulled him close again, kissing him. She stepped between his legs, her thigh rubbing him.

He pulled away.

Don't! Thicko! What are you doing?

Maurizan blinked at him.

"We should ... we should get going."

Fool!

She blinked at him again.

"There's not much daylight left, and we really should get as far as—"

The loud smack of flesh on flesh. His head spinning around. Bright stars exploding in front of his eyes. He staggered back. Hot pinpricks spread across one side of his face. He lightly touched the cheek where she'd smacked him.

She's fast.

When Alem finally blinked his eyes clear again, he saw her riding away east down the road. He ran for his own horse to catch up.

CHAPTER SIXTY-ONE

They rode in the open carriage down Temple Street, passing all the places of worship, the temples bigger or smaller according to the popularity of the deity. The Temple of Dumo was the biggest, naturally, and unpopular sects like the Cult of Mordis didn't have temples within the city limits, finding it more practical to set up shop at some secluded spot in the wilds.

Nobody knew where the outlaw cults called home, but they hadn't troubled anyone in years.

Rina pulled her cloak tightly around her. The night was cold, and the material of the custom-made ball gown was fashionable but thin.

"I wish you could cover that with some makeup or something." Brasley sat in the carriage next to her.

Rina frowned. Brasley was concerned what people would think of the tattoos around her eyes. Evidently fashion and favor could shift on a whim at court. Rina didn't care. The tattoos were part of her now. People could accept them or not.

"There's no point in worrying," Rina said. "And if you mention it again, I'll punch you in the throat. I'm already nervous enough."

Brasley threw up his hands. "Fine. Fine. At least the others are covered."

The blue silk ball gown had long sleeves that concealed the tattoos on her upper arms and a high stiff collar in the back that covered the tattoo on her neck. The collar fastened in the front with a glittering sapphire brooch. At Brasley's insistence, the front opened to reveal a bit more cleavage than Rina would have wanted, but Brasley had told her it was the current style and he didn't want the other snooty women at court turning up their noses at her.

The carriage turned onto King's Boulevard and immediately hit a traffic jam. Hundreds of other carriages were trying to pull up to the palace to disgorge passengers, the entire aristocracy of Merridan all attempting to arrive fashionably late at the same time.

Brasley stood in the carriage to get a look. "This will take forever."

"We should get out and walk," Rina suggested. "It'll be faster."

"Faster but not appropriate," Brasley said. "My duchess may be from a backwater region, but by damn she's going to get the same fanfare as anybody else."

He grinned and urged the driver to speed up into the line, cutting off the carriage of another noble who shouted obscenities.

What would have been a five-minute stroll turned into thirty minutes of waiting in the carriage line, but at last Rina and Brasley arrived at the front entrance. An attendant in the garish livery of the king climbed out first, followed by Brasley, who deftly slipped a coin into the attendant's hand and briefly whispered into his ear. The attendant nodded and offered his hand to help Rina down from the carriage.

The attendant drew a deep breath and then bellowed, "The Duchess Rina Veraiin of Klaar and Sir Brasley Hammish of Klaar."

Heads turned to look while simultaneously pretending not to care. A mutter ran through the crowd.

Brasley offered his arm. Rina took it, and they entered the grand arched entrance hall.

"Was that really necessary?" she whispered from the side of her mouth.

"One's name should always arrive slightly ahead of one's person," Brasley whispered back.

As they passed through the hall, pages scurried up to relieve them of their cloaks. They paused at the top of a high stairway, and a herald shouted their names again, but this time nobody paid attention. Rina paused to gawk at the sea of people in the ballroom below.

A swirl of colors, all the exotic birds showing off their best plumage. And so *many* of them. Rina would never have thought Merridan teemed with so many earls and barons and counts.

And duchesses.

Rina's father had always referred to the Merridan aristocracy as *way too many idle mouths to feed*. Now she had a hint of what he'd meant.

Brasley nudged her gently, and they slowly descended the wide stairway into the social snake pit that passed for the upper crust of Helva's capitol.

At first, there were a number of awkward moments in which they ran a whirlwind gauntlet of introductions to minor nobility. Rina marveled at Brasley's ability to match names and faces without fail, and at how he seemed to know the family history of each person they talked to. Rina did her best to smile and nod and mumble something polite. A few of the ladies gave her odd looks, and Rina realized it must be the strange sight of her tattoo.

Just as her head began to spin, she felt an arm go around her, and one of her hands in Brasley's. They spun a slow circle around the dance floor amid the festive throng. Brasley was light on his feet, and Rina was surprised to find the experience enjoyable.

"What are you smiling at?" he asked.

"You're a good dancer."

"Of course," he said. "How else do you think I charmed half the women you just met? I've been sweating on Klaar's behalf at some of the fanciest parties of the season."

Rina grinned. "Your sacrifices have been noted, Sir Brasley. What happens now?"

"We wait."

Not a very satisfactory answer, but Rina found herself swept along by the music, and she had to admit again that Brasley was rather charming in his own way. Her thoughts drifted to Alem. And to Maurizan. She hoped they were safe out there on the road and felt a pang of guilt that she was wearing a new dress at a royal ball while they were probably holed up somewhere cold and wet.

Rina's thoughts were interrupted by a face scowling at her from the crowd. Rina blinked, looked again as Brasley spun her around. No doubt about it, a plain woman with a wide, curvy figure in a deep green dress was staring daggers at her.

"What's wrong?" Brasley asked.

"Why should anything be wrong?"

"I've held enough women in my arms to sense a mood shift."

I'll bet you have. Her eyes shifted to the woman in the crowd. "Her."

Brasley followed Rina's gaze and winced. "Ah. Yes. Please don't worry about Fregga."

"You know her?"

"Fregga and I have been keeping company." Brasley cleared his throat. "Her father was instrumental in setting up accounts for Klaar at the Royal Bank."

Was Brasley actually going a little red?

"I should meet her," Rina said. "Assure her she has no reason to be jealous."

"That *won't* be necessary."

He was about to say something else when the music stopped. The mass of people all turned in the same direction toward a bright throne high on a raised dais.

A herald lifted his voice to carry across the hall. "His Royal Highness Edmund Pemrod II!"

A cheer went up, and Rina felt Brasley take her hand and pull her through the crowd.

"Where are we going?"

"It's been prearranged," Brasley said. "Come on."

"But the king."

She caught a few of the king's perfunctory pleasantries as he addressed the crowd, and Brasley led her down a side hall. The king's muffled voice died away as he led her farther down the deserted hall, their heels clacking on the tile and echoing.

Brasley stopped abruptly, knocked on the door. It creaked open a moment later and he hurried Rina inside; the door shut again behind them. They were in a spacious lounge, with cushioned chairs, thick rugs, colorful tapestries depicting bland landscapes.

An old man stood before them in a heavy black robe. He wore a black velvet skull cap that fit close to his bald head. He was dour, face gray, a sparse white beard. Stooped and frowning.

Brasley gestured to the old man. "This is Kent, the Lord Chamberlain of Helva. Lord Chamberlain, I'd like to present Duchess Rina Veraiin."

The nod of Kent's head was almost a bow. "My pleasure, madam."

Rina curtsied deeply. "Lord Chamberlain."

"Please make yourselves comfortable," he said. "It shouldn't be long."

The chamberlain left the room.

Rina's head spun to Brasley. "*What* is going on?"

"I told you," Brasley said. "Arranging an official audience takes forever. So I just had to arrange something *unofficial*, didn't I?"

"And what exactly does that mean?"

"To be honest, I'm not sure myself." Brasley went to a sideboard laid out with goblets and a crystal decanter of wine. He filled one of the goblets for himself. "But the Lord Chamberlain did say to make ourselves comfortable." He tossed back the wine, filled the goblet again. "Want one?"

"I'm too nervous to put anything in my stomach."

Brasley shrugged and sipped.

Rina started as the door flew open again and a dozen armored men in royal livery poured into the lounge. They spaced themselves around the room, standing at attention, backs against the walls. The Lord Chamberlain followed them, and the next man who walked in was—

Rina curtsied as low as she could without falling over. "Your Majesty."

"Never mind all that." The king gestured for Rina to get up. He lifted his chin at Brasley. "You there. Pour me one of those."

"With pleasure, Your Majesty." Brasley grabbed a clean goblet and filled it.

King Pemrod's crown was a simple gold circlet. He took it off his head and tossed it onto one of the nearby chairs. He was old, even older than the Lord Chamberlain, a man well into his nineties, but still stood straight and had a spark in his eye.

A mane of thick white hair. He unbuttoned his purple cape and let it fall.

He took the goblet of wine from Brasley and drank deeply. "Ah. That's what I need. Damned formal balls. For some reason these aristocratic freeloaders like to get together once or twice a year to hear their king tell them how wonderful everything is. Fine. Why not?"

He held the goblet out for a refill, and Brasley obliged.

The king looked Rina up and down. "You're Klaar's new duchess." Not a question.

"It's kind of Your Majesty to make time for me this way," Rina said. "In such an informal setting."

"Oh, it's not so kind, really," the king told her. "It's rather convenient for me too. Don't misunderstand, I don't see just anyone like this, but if I grant somebody a formal audience then it's official. It's on the record. You understand? But if I see you like this and you say something I don't like, I can decide I didn't hear it. As far as the world is concerned, we've never met. I don't know you." He sipped more wine, smacked his lips. "If you tell me a Perranese army has landed on Helvan soil I don't have to do a damn thing about it because it never happened."

Rina swallowed hard. "You already know."

"The capital is lousy with Perranese spies," the king said. "And our spies spy on their spies. If you're duchess then Arlus must be dead."

Rina bit her lip and nodded.

"My condolences," Pemrod said. "I met him once. I won't say we hit it off, but it was obvious he was made of stern stuff."

She opened her mouth to say something but suddenly felt a lump in her throat.

"What's all that business?" He gestured at her eyes with a backhanded wave.

"Tattoos, Majesty."

"Is that what all the young people are doing now? Can't say as I care for it. Never mind. You took your sweet time getting here."

"Majesty?"

"To Merridan," he said. "With invaders at the door I thought maybe you'd have gotten here a little sooner to ask for my help. That is what you wanted, isn't it? For the king to send along his soldiers and chase the savages back into the sea?"

"Yes, Majesty, something like that." It made her suddenly feel like a beggar. Is that what the king wanted? To make her understand she'd come begging, that his aid could be given or withheld on a whim?

Rina's eyes flicked to Brasley's. The frown on his face was a clear *I told you so.*

"Well, they are on Helvan soil, so as king, it's my business, I suppose. Especially now that they've come down from Klaar to make incursions into the lowlands. Oh, didn't you know that?"

She hadn't known. She didn't know anything. She was a stupid girl with tattoos on her face.

There was a moment of silence where he seemed to take her measure.

"You're of marrying age, aren't you, Duchess?"

She blinked. The question had caught her by surprise. "Very soon, Your Majesty."

"I have a grand-nephew," The king said. "So young to be a duchess. Klaar would benefit from a bit of experience. Somebody solid. Wouldn't do to send my armies up there to shoo the Perranese away just to have them come back next season, now, would it?"

Uh...

"That's a most generous thought," Rina said. "Perhaps I could meet your grand-nephew... *after* the current crisis in Klaar has been resolved."

Pemrod pursed his lips, nodding slowly. The silence that stretched this time was twice as uncomfortable as before.

He turned to his Lord Chamberlain. "Kent, I suppose we must *officially* address this matter. What's the wait for an audience now? Three months?"

"Four, Your Majesty."

"Four is it? My goodness, this is a busy time of year. The wheels of government turn slowly, don't they?"

There was not an ounce of warmth in the smile he offered. "The crown will be only too happy to grant you an audience to discuss your problem, Duchess. In four months."

∼

"Four months! That oily son of a—"

"Will you keep your voice *down*, please," Brasley whispered.

They were in the hall just outside the lounge and walking away quickly, the angry clack of Rina's shoes on the tile like reproachful *tsks*.

She fumed. Imagine suggesting the only way Klaar might get timely aid from the crown was if she married the king's fat, ugly grand-nephew. She actually had no idea what the man looked like, but with her luck...

"You could have at least *met* his grand-nephew," Brasley said.

"Shut up."

"We'll have to pack quickly when we get back to the manor," Brasley said. "I wouldn't be surprised if Klaar's line of credit at the Royal Bank suddenly dries up."

"Damn, I didn't even think of that," Rina admitted. "Would he really—"

"Duchess Veraiin," a voice called after her.

She turned to see Kent approaching. She composed herself and lifted her chin. "Lord Chamberlain."

"Might I have a word?" Kent turned and looked pointedly at Brasley.

Brasley bowed to Rina. "If you'll excuse me. I'll arrange for our driver to bring the carriage around front." And he left.

"If you're leaving town and on your way back to Klaar, there is a certain temple not far out of the way," Kent said. "The Temple of Mordis. I think you and the high priest there might find it interesting to meet one another. I can give you directions."

"I'm not very religious, Lord Chamberlain. And in any case, I was raised in the Temple of Dumo, like most people."

"It's just that I happened to take an interest in your tattoo." Kent pitched his voice lower. "And I assume you have the Prime inked down your back."

Rina's eyes slowly widened. "On second thought, Lord Chamberlain, yes, I think I would like directions to this temple."

CHAPTER SIXTY-TWO

The fist came up so fast, Alem almost didn't see it. The flesh on flesh *smack* spun his head around, knocking him across the table, scattering beer mugs and patrons. And then he was on the floor. Lots of arms grabbing him, pulling him to his feet again. Hoots and jeers. What was happening?

Oh, yeah. I'm in a fight.

The arms that had lifted him pushed him back toward the big man who'd hit him, which was actually the last thing Alem wanted.

The man was barrel chested, with a red, sweaty face and sparse black hair slicked back on a melon head. Five days of stubble on his face and teeth like little yellow pebbles.

Alem threw a watery punch. The man batted it aside, and stars exploded again in front of Alem's eyes as he was struck again. The next thing to hit Alem's face was the floor. Bells rang. How had this started again? Oh, yes. They'd come to the inn to get out of the rain, for food, a room for the night. The drunk had gotten too aggressive with Maurizan, hands going everywhere, not taking no for an answer. Alem had leapt in to defend Maurizan's honor.

And how's that working out for you, thicko?

Alem tasted blood, spit a red glob onto the floor. He shook his head and looked up.

Maurizan leapt on the man's back, and everyone in the common room laughed. Maurizan and the big bruiser twirled a little circle as she pounded on his shoulders with her little fists. The man's friends called out insults—some to her, some to him.

Maurizan reached down, nails digging in, and scratched three deep rents across his face. Blood. He screamed.

The laughter stopped.

The man roared, reached back and grabbed two handfuls of Maurizan's red hair. He dragged her off of him and slammed her against the floor, knocking the wind out of her. She writhed there, mouth working, trying to get a lungful of air.

"Leave her alone." Alem's voice sounded weak in his own ears.

The bruiser loomed over Alem, reached down and grabbed his tunic. Alem flopped, his limbs like lead.

"First, I'm going to cave your head in, lad," he said. "Then I'll show your girl a fine time. After you, she's probably yearning for a real man who's got more than peach fuzz on his nuggets."

More laughter.

Alem pawed at the man's fist, tried to get loose.

A slim hand appeared on the man's shoulder.

He started to turn to see who was behind him, but then he was off his feet, flying through the air, tumbling and rolling and smashing through a wooden chair, his comrades scrambling out of the way.

Alem looked, blinked his eyes back into focus.

She stood there like a stab of darkness, back straight, eyes flashing, black armor dripping, hair wet and matted. The eye tattoos added to her sinister appearance. One hand rested on the hilt of her rapier.

Brasley came in behind her, quickly surveyed the situation. "Typical."

The bruiser stumbled to his feet, shaking his head. He focused on Brasley.

"No, no, not me." Brasley pointed at Rina. "She's your problem. Good luck."

The man growled, charged forward and swung at her, his fist coming around so hard and fast he might have been trying to knock her head clean off of her body.

Rina's hand flashed up, and she caught his fist.

The room went stone quiet.

The two of them stood frozen like that a moment. The man stared wide-eyed at her little hand holding his meaty fist. He licked his lips nervously, obviously wondering where things went from here.

Rina squeezed.

The *crack pop crunch* of the man's fingers and knuckles made Alem wince.

The lummox screamed and went down, rolling into a fetal position. He cradled his hand as tears welled in his eyes.

"If any of you people are friends with this man, you might want to get him out of here," Rina said. "Now."

A trio of drinkers came forward to scoop up the man and made a hasty exit, dragging him out.

Rina walked slowly to Alem, bent, offered a hand to help him up. "Miss me?"

The innkeeper fell over himself getting them rooms, but even though they were all exhausted, they were also restless and so found themselves around a table near the common room's big stone hearth. The fire was low but warm, and they exchanged stories. Maurizan seemed glum for whatever reason but came out of her sulk to listen intently when Rina described her blue ball gown. Alem tried his best—but failed—to hide his pessimism upon hearing the king would do little to aid Klaar.

Brasley sucked the last bit of meat from a chicken leg, tossed the bone onto his plate and stood. "I'm going to chase down the barkeep for more wine. Anyone need anything?"

Rina hunched over a parchment, scribbling with a quill, the chewed stub of a chuma stick smoldering in the corner of her mouth. She held out her mug without looking up. "Beer."

"Brave girl." Brasley took the mug and set out to find the barkeep.

"What are you writing?" Alem asked Rina.

"The backup plan," she said.

"Care to share it with me?"

Rina smiled around the chuma stick. "Too risky. You'd talk under torture."

"The stink of that chuma stick is torture."

Rina took the stub from her mouth and blew a cloud of smoke into his face. She laughed.

He coughed, waved the smoke away. "You're hilarious."

Brasley returned, set the beer mug next to Rina's elbow and sat. He drank deeply from his own goblet. "I really love this inn. The beer is warm, and the mead is too sweet. But at least the wine is terrible."

"Poor Brasley misses his manor house and his servants." Rina dipped the quill into the inkwell and continued scribbling. Some chuma ash fell onto the parchment. "Damn it."

"We could be there *now* if you just agreed to be nice to the king's lousy grand-nephew." He tilted the goblet back for another big swallow.

Alem looked up. "Who?"

"And you could be in Fregga's loving arms right now, too," Rina said.

Brasley choked, some wine dribbling down his chin. "Let's change the subject. Have you told these two that you're dragging us off to some death temple?"

Alem blinked. "What temple?"

Rina still didn't look up. She still filled the parchment, coming to the end of her letter. "They're not coming."

"I'm not?" Alem said. "Where am I not coming?"

"Wonderful," Brasley said. "So you're just dragging *me* along?"

Alem frowned. "You guys can hear me, right?"

Rina sat straight, lifted the parchment and blew on it to dry the ink. She gulped down a third of her beer, wiped her mouth with the back of her hand. She turned to Maurizan, face growing serious. "I need your help."

Maurizan looked up, startled to be addressed directly. She'd been quietly pushing the food around on her plate with a spoon. "Me?"

Rina folded the parchment, leaned across the table to hand it to the gypsy.

A moment's hesitation, then Maurizan took the letter, unfolded it. She nibbled her bottom lip while she read.

"I don't suppose I get to read it next," Alem said.

Maurizan looked up, met Rina's eyes.

"You understand what I need," Rina asked.

Maurizan nodded.

"You'll do it?"

Maurizan nodded again, more slowly this time. "I'll do it."

The gypsy looked around the table at everyone. "Well. It looks like I'm in for an early start tomorrow." She stood. "I'd better pack. I hope the rain stops by morning."

They watched her climb the stairs, faces long.

Brasley pushed away from the table too. "I'm for bed. See you in the morning."

Alem turned to Rina. "You have some horrible errand for me, don't you?"

She smiled. Alem was smart. She liked him so much, she didn't have the heart to tell him about the horrible errand. Not yet. "I'm working up the courage. Give me a minute."

"Okay. The horses are still tied up outside. I'll move them to the stable."

Rina puffed the chuma stick and watched him go. Whatever she asked Alem to do, he would do it, and for some reason that made her all the more reluctant. The four of them had only been reunited for a single night, and now they'd have to scatter again.

She downed her beer, rose from the table, and followed Alem outside.

The rain came unrelenting and cold. The inn's front porch had a wide overhang, so the horses tied to the hitching post wouldn't get drenched. Maurizan's and Brasley's horses stood together, ears twitching. Her horse was missing and so was Alem's gelding. He'd already taken them to the stables. She thought about waiting there for him to come back for the other two horses.

But instead she found herself marching through the rain and mud toward the stables. The stub of the chuma stick had wilted. She plucked it from her mouth and flicked it away.

She stepped in a deep puddle and went down in a splash. Her left boot filled with water. "Shit!"

She got back to her feet and entered the stable.

It was dim inside, lit by a single oil lamp. Alem had already taken the saddles off the horses. He saw her and laughed. "Have a nice swim?"

She glared at him, overturned a feed bucket and sat on it. She tried to pull the boot off, grunting and heaving.

"Let me help you." He knelt, grabbed the boot and started to pull.

Rina suddenly flashed on a memory. In her room. The boy who had come in for the laundry. She'd made him help with her boots to tease him. She gasped.

"What's wrong?" Alem asked as the boot came off.

"It was you. With the laundry basket. That day in my room." The last day she'd been just a girl, just her father's daughter. The same day everything had changed forever.

He laughed again, shaking his head. "I thought you'd never remember." He pulled off the other boot. "Usually, the castle people don't even look at the servants. You probably didn't mean anything, but it really got under my skin when you mocked me. I sort of thought maybe—"

She leaned forward and kissed him.

He pulled away slowly, shocked. "I ... what—"

Rina grabbed the back of his head, pulled him forward and kissed him again, hard. His arms went around her, pulled her hard against him as their tongues met.

Rina liked him, but it was more than that. She wanted to be that girl again, teasing the boy who'd come for the laundry. Alem had sparked a memory, of a life she used to have. She wanted to freeze the memory in time, climb inside it. Part of her understood there was no going back. A more urgent part of her didn't care, wanted this moment and this moment alone.

She tugged at his clothing. He lifted her black shirt over her head, ran his fingers over the tattoos on her arm. Her heart beat so fast. She was dizzy and breathless. He bent, cupped one of her breasts, took a nipple in his mouth. He bit down a little too hard and she gasped.

Her hands went for his belt, unbuckling. There was no stopping this now. She didn't want to, didn't care.

Alem lifted her in his arms and dumped her into the pile of hay in one of the empty horse stalls. She lifted her butt and let him pull down her pants. She kicked them away, and then his were off too and he was crawling between her legs.

She reached down to guide him, a moment of pressure then he eased in. He found a steady rhythm, covered her mouth with his to muffle her moans. Rina wrapped her legs around him, crossing her ankles at the small of his back.

She held onto him so hard and so tight that she thought they might never come apart again, even as she knew that in the morning she would have to send him away.

~

Maurizan paused at the stable door when she heard the moan. It wasn't the moan of somebody ill or in pain, and her heart skipped a beat. She eased the door open a crack, just enough to see inside.

And she saw.

She stepped back from the stable door, feeling leaden and sick. She turned abruptly, splashed back through the rain to her horse. She took the letter Rina had written out of her pack, held it in front of her, poised to rip it into little pieces.

She paused. She could always rip it up later if she decided to. She stashed it again in the pack, and mounted her horse and spurred the animal into the downpour, following the muddy road east, the cold rain stinging her face and washing away the tears.

CHAPTER SIXTY-THREE

The sun rose, bathed the muddy world in dirty orange.

Rina sat in the saddle, puffing a fresh chuma stick. She wore the black armor, Kork's cloak over it, but enough cold still seeped into her bones. She missed Alem's warmth next to her. She missed his touch.

She missed Alem. One night together and now he was gone again.

Alem had been truly angry for the first time. He was the most long-suffering person she knew, but when she'd said what she'd needed him to do, he hadn't been happy. At all. Finally they were together.

And apart again.

Brasley stumbled out of the inn, rubbing his eyes, his pack tossed over one shoulder. He squinted up at Rina. "You send the stable boy on his way?"

"Head stable boy," Rina said. "About an hour ago."

"You'll probably never see him again, you know," Brasley said.

"Your unwavering optimism is an inspiration to us all," Rina said.

"And the gypsy girl?"

Rina was worried about Maurizan. Not about her safety but about what she might do. When Rina and Alem had finished in the stable, the gypsy girl was nowhere to be found. If Maurizan had seen, if she knew…

A jealous girl could ruin everything.

"She's gone too," Rina said.

Brasley climbed into his saddle with a grunt, turned a weary eye on Rina. "Death Temple?"

"Death Temple."

At least it had stopped raining.

~

The Temple of Mordis was four days out of the way. The ride was long and uneventful. *Tedious* was the word Brasley favored. They'd lucked into a shabby inn at a small village one evening, but the rest of the nights were spent huddled around a usually inadequate campfire.

Most of Rina's thoughts turned to Alem. She sent the falcon searching for him often, but found him only once, riding hard.

Back to Klaar.

She'd sent the bird in search of Maurizan also, but there was no sight of the girl.

Rina followed the Lord Chamberlain's directions faithfully. A path broke off from the main road and twisted through a dim wood. On the other side, they saw the temple in a wide meadow. The single building was squat and bunker like, topped by a black dome of some dark, glistening stone. The building was surrounded on all sides by a twelve-foot wall. The entire compound was maybe a hundred yards across.

They rode up to iron gates at a walk. As they drew near, the gates slowly swung open.

A single man emerged and strode toward them. He wore black armor not unlike Rina's but bulkier. A dark, open-faced helm with a black, glossy horse tail sprouting from the top. "Are you Duchess Veraiin?"

Rina reined in her horse twenty feet from the man. "I am."

"Come inside," he said. "You're expected."

CHAPTER SIXTY-FOUR

Tchi understood immediately that his strategy had been a mistake.

The small town had fortified itself behind a rickety palisade. Tchi had bypassed it with the thought of isolating it. To make it an island alone, forlorn and forsaken in a place where other places about it had been conquered. Indeed, that's what Tchi and his men had done. Conquered. They'd gone from village to village and had subjugated each population, put them under the thumb of Perranese rule.

He'd hoped to cow the town. Cut off. Alone. They would see it was hopeless. Wouldn't they?

But no. Instead, the town had offered a false hope. Tchi would vanquish a village, and most would submit, but there would always be a stubborn few, a couple of defiant ones who would escape and flee to the fortified town, find refuge behind the palisade. And finally the town swelled with the foolish hopeful. They were given spears, and they stood behind the walls and they waited, anger growing, revenge like a fruit ripening on the vine and ready to be plucked.

And so Tchi's men surrounded the town and suffered the taunts from the foolhardy brave within who didn't know they simply waited to be killed.

But there would be a cost. If Tchi and his troops stormed the palisade, the cost would be high. Too high.

And that's where the wizards came in.

"Bring them," Tchi told his sergeant. "It's time they earned their keep."

A few minutes later, a brace of soldiers escorted the wizards Prullap and Jariko to Tchi's position before the city gates.

"I don't want to spend lives on these palisades," Tchi told the wizards. "Do you have spells for the job?"

Jariko smiled, something smug in his demeanor. "Please. You talk to one of the great wizards of the modern age. You have only to ask, and we shall deliver the city to you."

"I do ask it," Tchi said impatiently. He gestured to the gates. "Gentlemen, the gates are yours."

Prullap and Jariko bowed, turned and walked toward the gates.

Jariko leaned his head toward Prullap and whispered, "Can you keep them off me while I work the spell?"

"Of course," Prullap said.

They stopped in front of the gates, and Jariko began the spell, tossing a pinch of brimstone into the air and muttering the words. He spread his hands, a fiery glow building between his fingers.

Men appeared at the top of the palisade with long bows and loosed a ragged volley of arrows.

Prullap barked arcane words, and the arrows went limp in mid-air and fell to the ground. It was all Jariko needed to finish.

Jariko brought his hands together, molded a seething ball of fire from nothing. He flung his hands forward, and the ball of flame spun and grew and shot towards the gates.

The flames struck with a deafening explosion; the wooden gates shattered, singed splinters flying in every direction. The smoke cleared, revealing that the gates had been destroyed.

Perranese soldiers poured into the breach. Tchi could already glimpse the defenders throwing down weapons and begging for mercy. The battle was over mere seconds after it had begun.

Tchi watched his men take the town. Already he was calculating the change in his plans. He would need to leave men to garrison the place. What could he accomplish with his depleted force? All choices seemed bad ones.

A rider approached. One of the advance scouts.

"Report," Tchi commanded.

"Our spies in a village to the west have reported sighting a person matching the description of the Veraiin woman."

"Tell me everything," Tchi demanded.

The scout told him the exiled duchess rode swiftly toward a remote temple in the vicinity. The Perranese had thought her beyond their reach, hidden somewhere. Now it turned out she was nearby.

Tchi considered only a moment. "I'll need all the available horses. And a hundred men."

CHAPTER SIXTY-FIVE

The Cult of Mordis worshipped Death.

But to Rina, the grim men inside the temple walls just seemed tired. Scattered soldiers in dark armor leaned on spears as Rina walked past on the way to the temple. There were bedraggled civilians inside the walls too, a few women and children. Apparently the place was not just a temple but also a very small village.

"The faithful are few these days," said the soldier leading them. "But this temple is home to one of the Elders. He is wise. He knew you were coming. High Priest Krell has the sight."

"The sight?" Rina asked.

"He sees things. Whatever the gods choose to reveal through the mists. Predictions and foretelling." The soldier shrugged. "I'm just a guardsman. I only know what I hear."

They arrived at the arched doorway in front of the temple. The guard gestured to the entrance. "From here you go on alone, Duchess Veraiin."

Rina's eyes went to Brasley.

Brasley said, "You *know* how much I've been wanting to tour the Death Temple, but you heard the man."

"Thanks." She turned and entered the building.

The dim, stone hallway was lit every twenty feet by a candle in an iron sconce. Wax drippings piled knee-high under each stone, marking years or maybe decades. There was something cold about the place, and Rina pulled her cloak tightly about her.

She arrived at a stairway of black stone and climbed.

The top of the stairs opened into a wide room with a high ceiling. She realized she stood underneath the black dome they'd seen as they rode in.

Her eyes were drawn to the shriveled man seated on the stone chair directly below the center of the dome. Frail in a black robe, bare feet, skin chalky and thinly stretched over old bones. He looked like a stiff breeze would scatter him.

"Welcome, Rina Veraiin." His voice was dry and unpleasant. "I'd hoped you'd be the first one here and not the other one. Mordis has been merciful in this."

Rina walked slowly toward him, eyes darting into the shadowed corners. She didn't feel threatened, but she didn't like the temple. It was dark, and the priest had an unnerving way about him. "Did someone send word I was coming?"

The priest rose from the chair. He was stooped, a slight tremble in his limbs. "I have foreseen."

"The sight?"

The priest waved a hand at the dark dome above him.

Rina looked. The inside of the dome was filled with glittering stars, exactly like the night sky although not a sky she'd ever seen before. A ringed planet drifted lazily across the nightscape. A streaking meteorite flashed by before winking out of existence.

"I sit here as the immensity of the universe moves around me," the priest said. "I am allowed glimpses."

"You knew I was coming, but do you know why?"

"Your tattoos make you powerful, Duchess," the priest said. "But they weaken you, drain you."

"That's in their nature," Rina said.

"What if you could replenish yourself?" asked the old priest. "I can give you a tattoo that does that."

She raised an eyebrow. "Oh?"

"It's called The Hand of Death," he told her.

"That sounds a bit ominous."

A dismissive gesture from the old man. "The cult has dealt with such misconceptions since its founding. In almost every act of life there is a little death. Every time you eat fish or fowl or even a vegetable, something gives its life to sustain another. My cult represents the more thankless side of the eternal circle."

"And what do you want in return?"

He smiled thinly. "Not me. I am but a servant."

"Then what does the Cult of Mordis want in return?"

"An errand," the priest said. "A favor to be collected at a later time."

"I'm not selling my soul for a tattoo," Rina said.

"Nobody wants your soul, Duchess. But debts must be paid."

"Can you be a little more specific?"

He laughed, a reedy, sick sound.

"You said there was another," Rina reminded him.

"Another who wants the tattoo, yes. I will trade it to you or to him. Not both."

Another Ink Mage? "Why?"

"You and he are a fork in the road," the priest said. "I cannot see all ends. But only one of you gets The Hand of Death. This much is clear."

She thought about it, remembered her battle with the stone serpent, how it had almost completely drained her of spirit. To be able to replenish ...

But she'd have to make a bargain not knowing what the payment would be, and that was too much of a risk. She refused to commit to some unknown errand in some vague future. Rina shook her head. "Sorry. I'm not the one."

The priest shrugged. "We shall see."

"I mean it," Rina said. "If I had it my way, I wouldn't even have these tattoos. I just need them to fight the Perranese."

"If you want to fight the Perranese, you needn't wait," he said. "They are at our front gates even now."

"What?"

He waved offhandedly at the stars overhead as he lowered himself back into the stone chair. "I have seen it."

She turned abruptly and raced down the stairs two at a time and into the courtyard beyond.

The little village churned with frantic activity, armored men racing for the front gates which shook with a thunderous boom.

Brasley was suddenly next to her. "They've got some kind of makeshift battering ram."

She didn't pause to talk to him, raced for the front gates where men were trying to brace it with rough-hewn logs. It thundered again as the ram struck. The sound of splintering wood.

She spotted a ladder and climbed to the top of the wall. The soldier who'd escorted her into the temple was there.

"How many?"

"I count about a hundred," he said.

"How many do you have?"

"Fighting men? Twenty, including me."

She watched as the ram pounded the gate again. The Perranese soldiers had cut down a thick evergreen and were using the trunk.

"Can the gate take it?" she asked.

"Not much longer."

"You have a plan?"

"Fight the best we can once they're though the gate," he said. "I'm open to suggestions."

Damn it.

She looked back at the village, women and children scurrying into shabby huts. She looked back out at the Perranese army and the woods beyond. It would be easy. Jump down, and with the lightning bolt tattoos on her ankles she could get away.

But she'd have to leave Brasley and the people of the village, who might or might not find mercy at the hands of the Perranese. She could fight them. She would kill many before she was drained. But not enough.

"Damn it!"

Rina slid down the ladder and ran back to the temple at full speed.

She entered the dome chamber. "Krell!"

"I'm here, duchess."

"I accept your bargain."

"Come forward," said the priest.

She approached. Stood directly in front of him.

"Your sword hand is your right?" he asked.

"Yes."

He reached out and grabbed her left wrist. He was surprisingly strong. Krell turned her palm upward.

"You enter into this covenant freely?" The priest asked. "You will honor your debt?"

"Just do it before I change my mind."

She saw now that the nail of his right index finger was sharp and hooked. He pierced the skin of her palm with it.

She winced, but the old priest held her hand steady.

He dragged the nail across her palm, and blood welled hotly.

Except it wasn't blood. Instead, white hot light poured from the wounds. He continued sketching her flesh until her hand was burning agony. Rina refused to cry out, refused to look away.

At last he sat back, nodded his satisfaction.

Rina examined her palm. The glowing outline of a skeletal hand, finger and thumb bones.

"Behold The Hand of Death," the priest said proudly. "May you wear it well."

CHAPTER SIXTY-SIX

The gates shattered inward just as Rina emerged from the temple.

She tapped into the spirit and ran.

The first wave of Perranese pushed into the compound. A few died on the spears of a line of temple guards, but they went down quickly as more soldiers pushed through.

Rina swept past her horse and drew the two-handed sword without pausing.

She'd killed five before they even saw her.

The two-handed blade severed a head from a neck. Sliced a gaping rent into a Perranese belly on the backswing, hot intestines spilling to the ground. They crowded to get at her. A slice on her arm. One along her ribs. She ignored the pain, the wounds healing almost immediately.

She swung the sword and advanced, driving the Perranese troops back beyond the gate. Everywhere she swung the huge blade became a panicked, writhing scene of blood and screams and severed limbs.

She was aware of the frenetic activity behind her, ox carts and other random debris being pulled into the gap as a makeshift barricade. She risked a quick glance and saw Brasley fighting with the temple guards.

The Perranese regrouped and charged. They seemed perplexed and infuriated that a lone woman stood in their way. Several came in for a direct attack as others surged around to get on all sides of her.

Rina spun, swinging the two-handed sword twice in a complete circle, the blade biting deeply. The blood of her foes dripped from her face. Her hands were slick with it.

She had to give them credit. They were game for it, kept pressing in close, swords raised, even as their comrades died screaming around them. Kork would not have been impressed with her defense. Some blades she batted aside, parried or blocked. Others she ignored, taking the wound and letting the healing rune do its work. Rina's only desire was to attack and to kill.

She stood in a circle of bodies, ankle deep in blood and gore and the filth of bowels loosened in the throes of death.

And still they came.

Rina felt the strain, the tattoos reaching the bottom of her spirit well. She was running out. Using it so fast—the bull tattoo for strength, the healing rune. It was time to test the new tattoo. Now or never.

When the next soldier thrust at her, she blocked the blade and stepped in to grab the man's face. He went rigid, eyes bulging, mouth working in a wordless scream. She felt his spirit flow into her, both thrilling and appalling her.

She cut down three more men then grabbed the fourth, draining him as well. He went gray in front of her, his body becoming a lifeless husk. She released him and spun, slicing another attacker almost in half.

She drained three more men, leaving the dried corpses in her wake.

And now the Perranese turned and fled.

Some from her flashing blade. Others from The Hand of Death.

They threw down weapons and jumped on horses, fleeing as fast as their mounts would carry them. Rina gave chase, running them down like lightning and hacking them from the saddle. Bodies littered the countryside, horses galloping away in random directions without riders.

She returned to the ruined gates and climbed over the barricade. The temple guards backed away from her. She held the head of a Perranese soldier by the hair.

Rina turned to Brasley. The look on his face was so terrified that Rina looked behind her quickly, expecting to see more charging soldiers.

No. It's me. He's afraid of me.

She was covered head to foot in blood. The blood of a hundred men who'd never had a chance.

Rina Veraiin had become a monster.

CHAPTER SIXTY-SEVEN

Dawn was still a few hours off and the night was bitterly cold. Tosh stole toward the back wall. He looked huge and misshapen in the moonlight, wearing multiple layers of travel furs. They made him sweat, but in an hour when the cold seeped in, he'd be glad for them. Still, there was no guarantee. Plenty had died out in the wilderness in the deep winter temperatures despite being similarly clad.

It didn't matter. Tosh had decided to leave. He was all done second-guessing himself.

Or was he? Even now he paused. Could he really leave Tenni like this? He told himself he'd come back for her. He'd get set up somewhere safe and come get her then. And anyway, if he remained to participate in Mother's madness he'd certainly get himself killed.

He found himself in the same spot where he'd killed the Perranese soldier so many weeks ago. He'd checked to confirm that the Backgate garrison had moved their latrine, but the leftover tang of urine still hit his nose hard.

He looked up at the wall, planned how he'd do it, came up with the same ideas he'd had the first time: crawl up the side of one of the abandoned buildings. He could reach the top of the wall from there. He hoisted his pack over his shoulder and made a start.

Climbing proved awkward in the thick furs but he finally made it to the roof of the first ruined building. The stonework of the adjacent building provided good finger- and toe-holds, and in a minute he was on the roof of that building, too, five feet below the top of the city wall.

So, could he climb? The city walls were smoother than the stonework he'd climbed earlier. Maybe he could jump, and grab the edge then pull himself—

A lumpy animal appeared on top of the wall, and Tosh's eyes went big.

No. Not an animal. A leg.

Somebody was coming over the wall, and he was wearing the same heavy travel furs as Tosh.

The man heaved himself completely to the top of the wall, grunted then fell—

—onto Tosh.

They went down hard and rolled off the roof to the next roof below, slid and hit the ground hard. Tosh suspected he would have broken bones if he and the mysterious stranger hadn't both been wrapped in so many furs.

Tosh got to one knee, back and ribs aching. "Son of a bitch."

The other man lay on his back, pawing at the air, trying to get his breath back.

Tosh crawled to him, pushed back the hood of his travel furs. When he saw the man's face he gasped. "I know you."

"P-please," Alem said weakly. "Please help me."

She told Brasley to follow as fast as he could, but she couldn't wait. She needed to leave without him. He nodded, still shocked and numb from the massacre at the temple gates. He waved her goodbye.

And Rina ran, the power of the spirit humming through every limb. She carried the two-handed sword, sheathed, under one arm.

She sent the falcon out over and over again to find Alem. Nothing. So Rina ran on faith, hoping that Alem had made it safely back to Klaar, that he would carry out her instructions.

If not, all of this would be for nothing.

The world became a blur of white winter. The weather turned colder, the snow deeper with every step she took toward Klaar. She stopped only long enough to rest and replenish her spirit.

She felt no emotion when she crossed the border into Klaar, her homeland. No stir of patriotism. The snow was knee deep. Rina ran and ran and finally arrived at the place where, so long ago, she and Kork had emerged from the dank tunnels beneath the city.

She stood, searching with her eyes, a stiff cold wind lifting her hair and the edge of her cloak. If they weren't here ... if they'd failed to come or if Maurizan hadn't delivered the message ...

A mound of snow ten feet to her left shifted and startled her. The man in the travel furs stood, snow falling off his back. "Hello again, Duchess Veraiin. We saw you coming in the distance and hid ourselves until we could make sure who it was." He turned, put his fingers in his mouth and whistled high and shrill.

More mounds of snow all around her shifted as men stood up from their hiding places.

"I almost didn't recognize you, Gino," Rina said. The thick brown furs were a far cry from the garish outfits the gypsies generally wore, but she did spot the end of a bright purple scarf peeking out from a fold in the furs.

"Klarissa sends her warmest regards," Gino said.

"I hope I can thank her in person some day," Rina said. "And Maurizan, for delivering the message."

Maurizan stepped out from behind Gino and pushed her hood back. Her eyes were as cold as the wind that tugged at Rina's hair. "Don't thank me. I'm not here for you. I'm here to fight alongside my brothers."

Rina met the gypsy girl's gaze and nodded once. *Okay. Have it your way.*

"How many?" she asked Gino.

"Forty," he said. "That's all that could come on short notice."

Forty men. It wasn't enough. "That's fine. Follow me. You won't find the tunnels so pleasant, I'm afraid. It's where the castle sewers drain."

Gino grinned. "I don't care about the smell. I just hope it's *warmer.*"

～

Tosh entered Mother's office.

She looked up. "How's our guest?"

"Tenni's getting some broth into him," Tosh said. "We thought he might have some frostbite, but he's okay."

"Uh-huh." She shuffled papers on her desk—monthly bills, invoices, the ongoing banalities of running a brothel.

"Mother?"

"What is it, Tosh?"

"Remember, how you said you were waiting? For an opportunity?"

"An opportunity?" She looked up, taking a moment to understand his meaning. "Oh. For revenge, you mean."

Tosh nodded. "I think the opportunity has arrived."

CHAPTER SIXTY-EIGHT

Alem knew the back door to the kitchens as well as anyone. He and Tosh pressed their backs against the stone wall, peeking around the corner and watching Prinn approach the door. Alem looked at the half-dozen women with them from the Wounded Bird. They hid swords under their cloaks.

"And you assassinated the Perranese chamberlain *why* again?" Alem whispered to Tosh.

"Because one of Prinn's customers is the chamberlain's replacement," Tosh replied. "She has a password to get in whenever she wants. Once the door is open, we rush inside."

"And then what?"

Tosh shrugged. "Get killed, probably."

I was afraid he'd say that. "I wish we could have brought more of your girls with us."

"Darshia is leading the rest of them in a raid across town," Tosh said. "If they can free the soldiers on the labor gangs, they've got a cache of swords hidden away. If those men have any fight left in them, it might make all the difference."

"What about those two big fellows? They'd be good in a fight."

"I sent Bune and Lubin with Darshia," Tosh said.

Alem was starting to wish *he'd* gone with Darshia.

He was about to say something else, when the kitchen door creaked open.

"Now!" ordered Tosh.

They rushed the door, pushing it open and rushing inside past Prinn, swords drawn, ready for whatever might be within.

A matronly woman in an apron saw them, opened her mouth and drew breath to scream.

Alem clapped a hand over her mouth. "Bruny, it's me!"

Slow recognition in her eyes. Alem took his hand away.

"Alem?"

She looked thinner and more haggard than he remembered her. He took her by the shoulders. "Bruny, there's going to be fighting. Get to your room. Don't come out until it's over."

"But . . ." She looked at the women with their swords. "Okay." She hurried away.

"Where now?" Tosh asked.

"Down." Rina's directions had been explicit. "To the dungeons."

The door to the kitchen swung open, and all heads turned.

A Perranese soldier stood there, munching a carrot. He looked at everyone in the kitchen, his mind slow to process what he was seeing. Abruptly, his eyes went wide. He dropped the carrot and went for his sword.

Alem fumbled for his own sword, one they'd given him at the Wounded Bird.

Prinn and one of the other women—Tosh called her Tenni, Alem remembered—surged past him, one going high, the other low. Prinn thrust, catching the soldier under the arm. Tenni going for the groin. The soldier grunted and stepped back, blood splashing down his side. The women pressed the attack, riding him down, slashing again with the swords.

Prinn cut his throat.

"Hide that body," Tosh commanded.

Prinn dragged the dead soldier into the pantry.

"Listen to me," Tosh told the women. "There aren't enough of us to fight the whole castle. We kill anyone who sees us, but other than that keep it tight and keep it quiet. Am I clear?"

Each woman nodded, grim-faced and resolute.

Alem had not realized prostitutes were so dangerous.

∾

They waited in the darkness.

"How much longer?" Gino asked.

"I don't know," Rina said. *And stop asking me, damn you.*

Forty of them plus Rina. All fidgeting nervously in the dark and smelling like sewage. She had to remind herself they hadn't been waiting that long. It always seemed longer when sitting idle and anxious.

Her fear was that at some point she'd have to call it off, turn and tell these people they'd made the trip for nothing. If Alem had been captured or killed—

The grinding sound of stone on stone was followed by a flood of dim torchlight as the small door slid to the side. A silhouette appeared. "Sorry I'm late." Alem's voice.

"Alem!"

"Yeah, sorry. I hope you haven't been waiting too long. I had a devil of a time getting over the wall and—"

Rina rushed in, mashed her lips against his, a slim hand going behind his head to pull him against her. She finally pulled back and said, "Okay, now get out of the way. I've got gypsies with me."

They poured into the little jailer's room and spilled out into the corridor where Rina found a dead Perranese soldier lying in a pool of his own blood.

Rina turned to look at them all, and they fell silent, expectant.

She closed her eyes, tapped into the spirit and saw through the eyes of the falcon. The bird glided low over the city's front gates. Everything seemed calm, and as far as she could tell no alarm had been raised. That wouldn't last long.

She told the falcon to fly out over the Long Bridge, confirming the presence of the barracks that the Perranese had erected for reasons she couldn't guess. The bulk of the army was still being housed outside of the city. It was a baffling blunder that Rina planned to take advantage of.

If she lived.

She released the spirit and looked up. Every eye was on her. She looked at them. The gypsy men—and Maurizan—favored the two-handed dagger fighting style, quick stinging strikes. The women who'd come with Alem carried the curved, single-edged swords they'd obviously stolen from the Perranese. A strange blend of peoples, and not much of an army. But each of them looked ready to spit death in the eye.

She cleared her throat. "We have to get out of the castle as fast as we can. We have to run for the city gates and close them. If we don't, if we allow the army camped outside back into the city, we don't have a chance. Do you understand?"

The crowd murmured that they did.

Rina drew the two-handed sword, tossed the sheath aside. "Then follow me."

CHAPTER SIXTY-NINE

G iffen gulped the remainder of his wine and then set aside the goblet, unlacing his robe as he approached his bed.

Sarin lay back in the pillows, grinning at him. The thin, silken shift hid none of her fabulous attributes. Giffen climbed onto the bed, crawled toward her, purring like a cat. She giggled. He reached for a breast, cupped it, and she cooed.

A scream.

Giffen paused. He shook his head, deciding to ignore it. He pulled down the top of her shift, and one of Sarin's heavy breasts popped out. He ran a thumb over the nipple, licked his lips, anticipating all the various things he would do to her.

Another scream, muffled and distant but clear. The clashing sound of metal on metal.

He sat up and turned toward the door. Possibly this was something he should look into.

Giffen turned back to Sarin. "Did you just hear—"

Sarin came at him, thrusting the little knife, the grin on her face twisted to an expression of animal rage.

The knife would have pierced his heart if he hadn't turned at the last second. Instead, the knife plunged into his side, and Giffen went rigid, mouth dropping open, eyes popping. She pulled the blade out of him, blood splattering across her shift and face, and lifted the knife to strike again.

He caught her wrist and they tumbled over together, tangled in the sheets and rolling off the bed. He landed on top of her. She tried to bring the knife up, but Giffen banged her hand hard against the floor until her hand opened and the blade clattered away.

She brought her knee up into his balls.

He grunted, going red. His hands went around her throat.

At first Sarin tried to pry his fingers away. Then she went red too, thrashed and bucked beneath him, pounded his shoulders with her fists. He squeezed harder.

Then she went stiff. Then she went slack.

He rolled off her, panting and dizzy, looked down, saw the life leaking red out of him.

Giffen tried to stand; his legs went weak and he flopped down again. He closed his eyes. He felt cold.

At the first sound of trouble, Chen drew his sword and rushed into the hall, cocked an ear and tried to determine from which direction the disturbance came. He thought about returning to his room and donning his armor, but whatever the disturbance might be, it could be over by the time he strapped on a chest plate and shin guards.

A panicked shout drew his attention and he ran toward it. He rounded the corner, saw one of his officers on the floor in a bloody heap, three women with swords standing over him.

The one closest to him charged, a thin girl with mousy brown hair, her sword up, thrusting confidently but slowly. Chen blocked it past him and sliced her throat open on a sweeping backswing.

She dropped the sword and spun away, blood spraying through her fingers as she uselessly tried to staunch the flow.

Chen brought his sword up in a ready stance.

The other two came more slowly, spreading apart a few feet to give each other room to move. A short, graceful blonde and a fierce-looking brunette with a hawkish face. A brief hesitation and then they came, one high and one low—not a bad maneuver, one he guessed they'd practiced.

Chen swung fast, one blade to another, batting both of their swords aside. He kicked the brunette in the knee and she stumbled back, cursing. He brought his blade back just in time to parry another thrust from the blonde, and Chen immediately stepped in and thrust the sword through her belly. He turned to face the other girl, but couldn't move his sword. He looked down at the blonde.

Instead of wilting and sliding off his blade to the floor, the blonde had reached up to grab his wrist, holding the sword fast inside her.

"Prinn!" When the blonde shouted, flecks of blood dotted her bottom lip. "Prinn!"

The brunette limped forward, bringing the sword to bear. Chen realized too late he'd have to let go of his sword to defend himself.

Before he could do that, she thrust upward, underneath his ribs. It was a good strike, slicing through a number of vital organs, and Chen knew he was finished before he hit the floor.

This was madness. And Tosh was lost. He'd never been inside the castle before.

Halfway up from the dungeons they'd encountered the changing of the guard, a half-dozen Perranese soldiers, easily dispatched, but not before they could raise the alarm. They were almost out of the castle when three squads of Perranese soldiers hit them from two directions.

The fighting had been confused, loud and bloody. They'd been fractured into a few different groups, forced down different hallways. He thought he saw Duchess Veraiin and a group of the gypsies heading for the way out, but he couldn't be sure.

He turned down another hall, hoping to find any of his girls.

There!

Prinn knelt in the middle of the hallway near two dead Perranese soldiers. The fighting had apparently spread throughout the entire castle. He wondered if they were winning or losing.

Prinn turned to look at him, her face smeared with tears and blood. It looked like something was in her lap. Tosh took a step toward her—

Tosh dropped his sword.

Tenni was so white, waxen and unreal. Prinn stroked her hair, sobbing quietly.

No, that's not right. That's not her because… because, see if… because…

The hallway tilted, and Tosh threw out his arms to balance himself and suddenly he was on the floor. He rolled over, got to his hands and knees.

And then he was heaving his guts out.

∾

The Ink Mage sat cross-legged in front of the open window, letting the cool air wash over him. It did little good. His skin was slick with sweat. The power was burning him up from the inside. He boiled with a destruction eager to be unleashed.

Ankar tapped into the spirit.

His every sense was alive, and Ankar sensed … something. Like he could feel it in the floor, vibrating up through his body.

He reached out with his hearing, his sense of smell. A battle.

Ankar grinned. *It's started.*

He stood and stretched, muscles bunching.

Ankar chose no weapon.

He donned no armor.

He left his room and descended the stairs into the chaos below.

CHAPTER SEVENTY

The streets in front of the castle were utter chaos. The dead lay everywhere. She'd made it out of the castle with about twenty of the gypsies, including Gino and Maurizan.

A disheveled, unkempt man in rags stopped suddenly in front of her, a sword in his dirty hand. "Who are you?"

I'm your duchess. "I'm on your side. What's going on here?"

"There's a bunch of us. We were with the labor gangs, but they busted us out and gave us swords," the man said. "We've been killing Perranese wherever we can find them."

"The front gates," Rina said. "They've got to be closed or we're all dead."

"To the gates!" he screamed like a madman. "To the gates for Klaar!"

The man and two dozen of his ragged comrades ran toward the gates, waving blades and shouting hoarse war cries.

Rina turned to Gino and Maurizan. "Follow as fast as you can."

She didn't wait for an answer, tapped into the spirit and ran. Her feet barely touched the cobblestones as she flew down the street, past the ragged warriors and toward the gates.

The square in front of the gates was a flurry of activity. It was like watching the battle at the temple gate all over again, but the sides had changed. The huge bars had already been slid back from the gates, and soldiers pulled on the chains to swing them open.

Rina could see through the open gates, down the Long Bridge to the other side where Perranese troops were already forming up to make the crossing.

She'd killed three of the men at the gate before they realized she was among them. They charged and fell, Rina's two-handed sword rising and falling, a trail of gore following the blade wherever she swung.

She gave two men The Hand of Death and drained their spirit, then waded back into them, leaving writhing bodies in her wake, the limbs of her foes bleeding and scattered.

And then the others were there, ragged warriors and gypsies, crashing into the Perranese.

Rina grabbed Gino by the shoulder. "Get these gates closed."

"Where are you going?"

She pointed down the long bridge at the advancing army. "There."

Rina ran through the gates, fifty yards down the bridge, stopped and planted herself. She stood with the two-handed sword point down, leaning on the hilt. She waited.

I don't have to kill a whole army. I just have to keep them back until the gates are closed.

The sounds of battle rose and fell behind her, and then stopped. She glanced back at the sounds of the gate clanking shut and the bars sliding back into place.

She grinned at the approaching army. *You're too late.*

The army stopped suddenly, stood there looking down the length of the bridge at her.

Obviously, I'm so intimidating, they don't dare—

A huge shadow passed over her, jerking her attention upward.

The hulking man landed hard twenty yards in front of her, cracking the stones beneath his feet and shaking the entire bridge.

Rina stepped back, bringing the sword up. She looked behind her at the gate, back at the enormous man in front of her. *Did he jump from the city wall?* He wore only a loincloth and ankle boots. Steam rose from his skin.

And he was covered head to foot in tattoos.

Oh ... shit.

He advanced. "Well. So you're the other one."

Rina remembered what Krell had told her back at the Temple of Mordis. Two champions.

"Show us what you've got, then."

He leapt at her, almost like he was flying, and she barely had time to drop to the ground and roll out of the way. Both of his feet came down hard where she'd been a moment before, cracking stone again.

Rina bounced up, swung the sword, thrust, swung again. He was never where she aimed her strike, always seeming to melt away like a ghost.

"How many do you have?" He asked. "Speak up. How many?"

She shook her head. "Not as many as you."

Rina ran in quickly, feeling the lightning bolts on her ankles hum with energy, and was in front of him within an eye blink. He still managed to evade the one-handed sword thrust, but she put all of the bull strength into her other fist and caught him with an uppercut just under his chin. His head snapped back and he grunted in pain and surprise.

And then he backhanded her across the face, and she flew twenty yards, landing roughly on the stone. Something had cracked in her jaw. Already she felt the healing begin.

Rina stood, panting, and brought the sword up.

"You get up?" he said. "The little girl is made of stern stuff. Good, I like a challenge."

She worked the jaw. It was already better.

"I am Ankar," he said. "Some want to know the name of their demise when they meet it."

"I'm not telling you my name," she said. "So you can die curious."

Ankar laughed. He held his right hand up and flexed it. It turned gray and rough.

Rina launched, swung the two-handed blade. He caught it with the gray hand and the blade *clanked* in his palm.

Stone! He's turned his arm to stone.

Ankar squeezed, and the blade shattered. He swiveled and kicked her in the ribs, and she stumbled back, wincing in pain. At least two of her ribs were cracked. She backed away slowly to give the ribs time to heal. Her sword was gone. She considered the rapier at her side.

No. A sword won't do it. Not with this one.

She looked down at the palm of her hand, the outline of the skeletal fingers. The Hand of Death. Krell had told her only one of them could have it. Only one.

And Rina Veraiin was that one.

She ran at Ankar as fast as the lightning bolts would let her.

Halfway to him, the Ink Mage grinned, and everything slowed down.

It's him. He's slowing down time.

She strained to go faster, drawing nearer, reaching out. If she could just lay her hand on the man ... if she could just reach ...

Ankar opened his mouth. His long, wet tongue flopped out.

There was a tattoo on it.

Of a dragon.

Rina's eyes went wide.

Oh no.

Fire roared from Ankar's gaping maw, and the wave of flames swatted Rina out of the air, engulfed her. The inferno reduced her world to an ongoing, searing pain, hair and clothing singeing, skin going crisp and black.

She faded, maybe just for a second, and when she came to again, she lay face down in the middle of the stone bridge. Her entire body was cracked and black; the flesh beneath the outer crust of baked skin oozed like molten liquid. The skin of her face had melted over one eye. With the other eye she saw Ankar laughing and walking slowly toward her.

A tattoo on a tongue. A dragon. Talbun would be amused.

"You should see yourself," taunted Ankar. "Just a disgusting scorched blob. After I finish you, I'll knock down those gates, and we'll be back where we started."

He walked toward her as he boasted. Rina's hand trembled badly, but she was still able to reach into the singed satchel at her side. Her hand closed around something, came out with it.

She tried to fling it at Ankar, but her hand barely flopped forward, the little glass ball rolling and bumping along the bridge and finally coming to a stop ten yards away in a crack between the bridge stones.

Ankar didn't even see it. He was full of his own voice. "It's a shame, really."

He kept striding forward...

"I was especially curious about the ones around your eyes. Gave you an interesting tribal look, too."

...and stepped on the last of the three glass fire balls that Talbun had given to Rina.

The explosion lifted Ankar twenty feet into the air. His right foot separated from his right leg which had been blown from his body, leg and foot flying in two different directions in a spray of blood and smoke and dust. He came down again and kept right on falling into the deep chasm along with the rocky debris of the bridge.

When the dust cleared, Rina saw there was now a two-hundred-foot gap in the bridge. The Perranese army had bunched up on the other side, looking across the empty space at her with disbelief. She lay with one arm dangling over the edge.

With the last of her strength she rolled over, facing back toward the gates. They were open now, and a small group of people ran toward her.

Alem was in the lead.

He knelt next to her, saying something, but Rina's hearing had given over to a fierce ringing. Alem's strained smile was so obviously meant to comfort her that she wanted to cry.

But instead she let the darkness take her, and that was some comfort too.

EPILOGUE

The tiniest pinprick of light in a vast implacable darkness. She swam toward it for a long time, but it never got closer, or at least it didn't seem to. She became more aware of things. Realized she was hanging on to the thinnest most fragile thread of the spirit possible. She pulled herself along by it, pulled herself toward the light. But she had to be patient. Pull too hard or too fast and it would snap.

But eventually the light grew brighter, and she reached for it, grabbing the edges like some hole in the night. She pulled herself up ... and through.

Rina's eyes flickered open. She looked up at Brasley's smirking face.

"I like your new hairstyle," he said.

Her hand went to her head. A thin layer of fuzz. She remembered. She was burned all over and—

"I need a mirror."

Brasley laughed and brought her a small hand mirror. She sat up in bed, anxiously examined her reflection. Her skin was perfectly smooth and healthy. Her hair, on the other hand, was only an inch of fresh growth. She was hideous.

"You look very nice," Brasley said. "And anyway, it'll grow back."

She looked around. She was in her father's old bedroom. The bedroom of a duke.

Of a duchess.

"Have you been here the whole time?" she asked.

"Me? No. I only arrived two days ago."

"Two days? How long…?"

"You were out for nine days," Brasley said. "At first there was a lot of talk of burials and somber ceremonies, but evidently duchesses don't die like they're supposed to when massively burned over their entire body."

Her head drooped and she rubbed her eyes. She felt whole but fatigued. For nine days Rina had clung to a thread of the spirit while the healing rune had done its job.

"Anyway," Brasley said. "It's Alem who's been by your bedside almost every hour."

Rina looked up. "Where is he?"

Brasley smiled. "Let me step out a moment while you get dressed. Then I think I might know where he is."

She wore a simple dress and shoes. Someone had laundered Kork's cloak. She wrapped it around herself. She wore thin gloves. Rina thought about the skeletal tattoo on her palm and thought she might always wear gloves from now on.

Brasley was patient enough to answer her questions on the carriage ride to the front gates.

Giffen was nowhere to be found, but they'd discovered a dead woman in his room and a vast quantity of blood on the floor and bedding.

The Perranese had retreated to the coast, where they were presumably waiting for their fleet to pick them up, at which time they would flee back across the sea to lick their wounds.

The gypsies had left and had carried their dead away with them.

They arrived at the front gates, which had been left open. Brasley and Rina passed through them and walked to the edge of the ruined bridge where a man sat with his legs dangling over the side, drinking from a fat, earthen jug.

As they approached, Rina saw it wasn't Alem but one of the men who'd been with him in the dungeon.

He turned and saw her and made as if to rise. "Duchess."

"Please don't," she said. "I'm not in the mood to be duchess just yet. Let me join you."

She sat and let her legs dangle next to his.

Brasley sighed. "I'm sure it would be terribly comic to somebody somewhere for the three of us to come through so many adventures only to be blown into a chasm by a stiff gust of wind. Well, why not?" He sat alongside the other two.

"I'm sorry," Rina said. "I don't know your name."

"Tosh."

"Thank you, Tosh. For all you did."

"How's the little girl?" Brasley asked. "Emmon, is it?"

"She's with her Auntie Prinn. She's ..." Tosh sniffed, wiped his nose with the back of his hand. "She's made of stern stuff. She'll be fine."

Rina wanted to ask but didn't know how.

"Well, it looks like the gang is back together again," came a voice behind them.

Rina turned, her face breaking into a huge smile at the sight of Alem walking toward them. Inexplicably, he carried a lit oil lantern in the broad daylight. She didn't care.

"It's good to see you awake," he said.

"Don't look at me." She ran a hand over her head.

"It'll probably start a whole new fashion." Alem sat next to her.

The four of them kicked their legs. The wind blew cold. Tosh passed the jug to Rina, who drank and passed it down the line.

"Gentlemen, I'm going to have to be a duchess soon, and I don't know how."

"I'll help if I'm able, milady," Tosh said.

"You're a duchess in your own duchy," Brasley said. "Whatever you say or do is by definition the correct thing."

"Here," Alem said. "Maybe this will help. I brought you a present." He handed her a chuma stick.

Rina laughed and took it. Stuck it in her mouth. She understood why he had the lantern now. She leaned in to light it, puffed the stick to life. Her eyes went up to his face. She didn't know what would happen between them. Rina was a duchess, and Alem was a stable boy—*head* stable boy—and she couldn't imagine what anyone might think about such a pairing. Maybe nobody would care at all.

One thing she knew for sure was that she wouldn't worry about it today. Or tomorrow. Not until she had to.

Brasley drank from the jug and looked at the other side of the broken bridge. "I can't imagine how we're going to fix that thing."

Rina smiled, remembered what Kork had always said when it came to the Long Bridge. "Magic."

They sat like that for a long time, passing the jug, Rina puffing on the chuma stick, legs dangling free over the edge of the world.

ACKNOWLEDGMENT

I'd like to thank my agent David Hale Smith for all he's done. Another big thanks to Alex Carr and the entire 47North team and Amazon. Much appreciation for my patient wife Jackie and son Emery.

And thank you, readers. Let's all meet back here as soon as possible for the next one.

ABOUT THE AUTHOR

Victor Gischler was born in Sanford, Florida. He is a world traveler and earned his Ph.D. in English from the University of Southern Mississippi. He received Italy's Corsair Award for adventure literature and was nominated for both an Anthony Award and an Edgar Award for his mystery writing.

He currently lives in Baton Rouge, Louisiana, and would grill every meal if his wife would let him.

Please join Victor on Twitter for hijinks and nonsense @VictorGischler.

Kindle Serials

This book was originally released in Episodes as a Kindle Serial. Kindle Serials launched in 2012 as a new way to experience serialized books. Kindle Serials allow readers to enjoy the story as the author creates it, purchasing once and receiving all existing Episodes immediately, followed by future Episodes as they are published. To find out more about Kindle Serials and to see the current selection of Serials titles, visit www.amazon.com/kindleserials.

Printed in Great Britain
by Amazon